# HOT WINGS

## THE HOT CANNOLIS, BOOK TWO

**ELI EASTON**

**TARA LAIN**

*To Robert, ever my sounding board and favorite cheerleader!*
*-Eli Easton*

*To Todd, my honey, who takes such good care of me and lets me take care of him. Thank you for all the extra support. I love you so much!*
*-Tara Lain*

# NOTE TO READERS

Thank you so much for reading HOT WINGS! This book has been an amazing adventure for us since there's a whole world of fire aviation we needed to explore and master in order to create our hero, Dell. But wow, do we love him! We think you will too. And then we were faced with redeeming a complex and troublesome character, Donny Canali, in order to make him the guy we (and Dell) love. Our early readers seem to feel that after a good start at the end of HOT SEAT, that Donny has shown himself to be a true hero.

Now for some news! As some of you know, Eli and Tara have planned four books in this series to start. Unfortunately, during the writing of HOT WINGS, Tara discovered she had to have some surgery. While not life threatening or anything, it requires enough recovery and rehabilitation that it will interfere with the intensive writing schedule that Eli and Tara maintain to create these stories. Soooo, happy news, the books will be written, but not as a team. Eli will write book 3, HOT PURSUIT, and, when she's back in the thick of it, Tara will write book 4, HOT LIPS. Tentatively, look for at least one of the books in June, 2022.

Meanwhile, we're thrilled to present HOT WINGS, which

can be read stand alone, or you can plunge into the world of the Canalis in HOT SEAT. Also be sure to grab Eli's novella, FIREMAN'S CARRY, which introduces two of the heroes, Mike and Shane. The story is FREE throughout 2022. Enjoy!!

Get HOT SEAT on Amazon
Get FIREMAN'S CARRY on Prolific Works
bit.ly / YBBBGroupGiveaway

# PROLOGUE
## MARCH

"Team six, get back! Pull out now!"

The barking voice was my father's, and it came over the speaker in my SCBA helmet as I hacked at the foundation of a dead bush with an axe. I straightened up, sweat dripping down my face and blurring the lenses of my goggles. It was freakishly hot today—in the high 80s in fucking March thanks to another heat inversion, or heat bomb, or whatever the talking heads were calling it these days.

I motioned to Brian, Liam, and Jordy. "C'mon! Leave it."

We abandoned the work we'd been doing to establish a fire line to the west of the outermost houses of Sierra City and headed back up the steep hill where we'd come down.

"Did it jump?" Brian asked through our headsets.

"Must of," Jordy replied.

I didn't try to talk. Walking up a steep hill with all my gear, axe, and pack would have been a good workout if I wasn't already trashed from busting ass on the fire line for the past two hours. Not to mention dying in the heat. I scanned the area. The grass was brown thanks to a dry California spring. Not unusual, sadly. Tall pine trees towered on both sides of the power-line break we followed. The haze of smoke that'd been there when we'd come down was now thick and the dark tan color of burning wood.

"It's definitely closer," I said.

"Who's pulling us out? Was that your dad, Donny?" asked Jordy.

His voice was all neutral, but I heard the implication. It wasn't often our Gridley fire station worked a blaze alongside Pa's station, which was in Oroville. And when it happened, I always got razzed about it. Well, me and my brother Mike got razzed, but he was still on leave after that scary, near-suicidal accident he'd had at a warehouse fire in December. When Pa was around, the guys acted like we were favored or protected or some such shit. I didn't mind the razzing so much, 'cause it was normally just shit talking. But the idea that Pa would pull us out of necessary work because of overprotective paranoia was just dumb.

"That's *Chief Canali* to you, asswipe, and he knows what he's doin'." I panted loudly into the mic, then shut up so I could make it up that fucking hill.

At the top, I stopped to catch a breath, hands on my knees. I was in damn good shape, but Ma's excellent Italian cooking gave me a few extra pounds to drag around.

"Join the firefighters, they said. You'll get to hike while you work, they said." This was Jordy, who panted and groaned. I chuckled and wiped a sleeve over my nose and chin to catch the sweat.

"What doesn't kill you makes you stronger. Except in your case, Jordy. It just makes you crankier," I teased, giving Jordy a grin.

"Holy mother of God." Liam's words, and the fear in his voice, had me standing tall and looking around.

We'd walked the power-line break to get into the area since there wasn't a trail or road nearby. In front of us, the hill fell away more gradually, the power-line break a narrow brown avenue that shot straight through the trees. Down below, that break was now on fire. Brown billows rose thick and toxic, hiding our path out. The fire was maybe a quarter mile away, flames feasting greedily.

"Shit," breathed Brian. "What the fuck do we do now?"

I switched my headset to the command frequency. "Base, this is Team six. We need a new exit route. The power-line break is compromised. We're at the top of the hill, about a mile from Calvade Road staging area. Over."

Pa answered immediately. "There's not enough clearance in the break for you to push through? You need to try. Double-time. Over."

If the grass under the power lines had been green, like it should be this time of year, and if the power-line break wasn't overgrown and poorly maintained, filled with windfall branches and dead scrub, there'd be a way through. But it wasn't. I looked at the fire below, where the grass and brush under the power-line towers was clearly on fire, and then around at the faces of my team. Jordy was shaking his head adamantly and Brian's eyes were bleak.

"We can go down and take a closer look, Chief," I radioed in. "But from up here, it sure as shit doesn't look like it. Over."

"Getting closer isn't gonna do jack," Jordy protested. "We can't get through that. There's gotta be another exit. Tell 'em, Donny."

My instinct was to tell Jordy to shut it and do what Pa wanted, get closer and see if we could find a break. But that was the cowboy in me—ramrod your way through anything. Kowabunga! And I'd do it just because Pa asked. I'd jump a building if he told me to. But caution and levelheaded thinking had been drilled into me at school and in training. I was responsible for other guys, not just myself. Liam, who was fairly new, was pale as a ghost with fear. Brian had a five-year-old and new baby at home. Jesus, if he got hurt, his wife Katie would kill me.

Reluctantly, I spoke back into the radio. "It looks pretty solid and thick down there, Chief. Could we head toward Sierra City? Over."

It took a while for Pa to respond. Probably he was looking at maps and talking to the others at command. He came back on. "It's hot to your north and south. There's a clear route along the river, but it'd be eight, nine miles on foot if you have to go that way. We're gonna try air support. Hang tight."

But I already heard it—the sound of a plane.

"They can't land here," said Liam. "Not with these power lines."

I scanned the skies and spotted it, coming in from the north. Hell, you couldn't miss it. The plane was screaming yellow and red. It looked kind of like a fire tanker, but not one I'd seen before.

"Look!" Brian pointed at it.

"Good eyes, Brian. We saw it ten minutes ago," snarked Jordy.

"What is that?" asked Liam. "It doesn't look big enough to hold us all."

"It ain't a ride, newb," said Jordy happily. "Watch and learn."

The plane banked hard toward us, flying sideways, and then it dropped like a stone. I gaped as it levelled out, still descending, aiming right for us. It roared over our heads, a few feet above the power lines. Something hit my face as it buzzed us, and I reached up to wipe it off—water. The under-carriage of the plane was dripping water.

And then that bright bird of a plane flew right over the power-line break fire. Low, so fucking low! I saw its belly doors open and water gush out before it vanished into the smoke.

"Holy shit! Who the hell is flying that thing?" I murmured. I'd never seen any Cal Fire pilot fly like that.

"Oh God. Did he crash?" Liam's voice, scared.

"Are you kidding? Not that motherfucker!" Jordy flashed a huge grin.

And then the bright yellow-and-red plane shot heavenward from out of the smoke, banking hard. It flew back over our heads, still climbing, heading to whatever water source it was using, probably a nearby lake.

Pa came on. "Donny? Er—Team six? Did you see the drop? The pilot's gonna keep laying down water to get you out. Over."

"Hell yeah, we saw it!" I radioed back. "Smooth moves. We'll be tiptoeing through the tulips all the way home. Thank the pilot for us. Team six out."

When we walked out of the woods at the staging area, I ripped off my helmet and dropped my gear, thankful to get some air. It was smoky here, of course, but I was used to that. At least it wasn't as bad as what we'd just walked through, the soggy ground still steaming and choking smoke from the fire on either side.

"I have to tell ya, I saw my life flash before my eyes for a moment back there," said Brian. The guy still looked spooked.

"No shit," agreed Liam. "I was thinking I should have kept my ass back in New Jersey."

"Hey, Cal Fire's the real deal," I told him. "I've been in plenty of hairy situations, but we've always gotten out."

"Yeah, this org's what you call pre-fessional," said Jordy.

"Damn straight."

Pa walked up, looking all manly in his black-and-yellow fire gear, his expression hard and businesslike, the way a chief should be. "Team six. Glad to see you. Good work out there." Then he looked at me, and his eyes softened and shone with pride. "Good job, Donny."

A lump appeared in my throat the size of a fucking basketball. Pa's approval was everything and filled me with too many feels to bear. I might have gone for a back-slapping hug

—we were Italian, so it was allowed—but we were on duty. "It got a bit dicey," I admitted. "Good to have you on the horn." And then I had to change the subject before the other guys saw me getting sappy. "Hey, who was that pilot? Never seen anybody fly like that."

"Shit yeah!" said Jordy. "Guy dropped so fast, I thought he was gonna crash on our heads."

Pa grinned. "That's Dell Murphy, the new guy who transferred here from Oregon. He did good, right? Did you see it?"

"Good?" I scoffed. "Fucking aero-batic show, man. I felt like we should have bought tickets. I need to shake that guy's hand."

"That was the new pilot from Oregon?" Jordy said in a bewildered tone. "But I thought I heard he was a queer."

Silence dropped like a rock and the guys stared at Jordy. I dared a glance at Pa. He was staring at Jordy, too, his smile frozen so hard it looked like a death rictus. His skin had gone tight and his eyes pained.

Just four months ago my baby bro, Mike, the latest and last of Pa's firefighting *Hot Cannolis,* had come out as gay. To say it had been a blow to Pa would be the understatement of the fucking year. In our profession, being macho was everything, and we Canalis took pride in being the most macho of all. Pa still didn't seem to know exactly how to deal with it—with the other guys, crew, maybe his fellow brass, for all I knew. I don't know who all gave him shit about it, but Jordy sure wasn't going to be one of them. Not while I was standing there.

"What's his being gay got to do with anything?" I took a threatening step toward Jordy. "That supposed to mean he shouldn't be able to fly or something? He was an army pilot, right, Pa? I mean, Chief?"

Pa straightened his spine, his chief mask back on. "Pilot Dell Murphy flew combat missions in Afghanistan while you were playing Nintendo in junior high. And he saved your ass today. So show some respect!"

Jordy grimaced guiltily. "Sorry, Chief."

"All right. You guys get some water and take a breather. I'll give you a sitrep shortly." Pa stalked off, already talking again on the radio.

"Sorry," Jordy said again to me. He stepped closer and lowered his voice. "But you were the one talking shit about gays right up until Mike came out. Now, suddenly, we all gotta be PC."

I opened my mouth to deny it, but he was right. I used to talk shit as much as anyone. But when Mike had nearly died in that warehouse fire, and it became clear that hiding being gay was the thing that was fucking with his head so badly, everything had changed. Talk about a wake-up call. And I'd gotten to know his boyfriend, Shane, and discovered he was actually a pretty cool dude.

"Well, I was wrong to do it. I didn't know what the fuck I was talking about back then. End of story."

"Okay! Just sayin'. It's not like the whole world can turn on a dime just 'cause you did. I wasn't even talking about Mike."

"Fine. It's over. So shut up about it."

"Fine. I'm gonna go get some water." Jordy stalked off.

Brian clapped me on the back. "Anyway. Glad to still be breathin' with you, dude. And thank God for your dad and that pilot." He walked off too.

Yeah, Cal Fire wasn't gonna be waving rainbow flags anytime soon. But that was okay. Because I was there and I'd protect Mike, along with my brother Tony, and Pa, and any other Canalis, from the resident bozos. And I'd do it for as long as it took.

No one was gonna hurt Pa or make fun of our family. Over my flaming freaking corpse.

# ONE
## MAY

## DONNY

"Are you seriously telling me I have the house to myself tonight?" Mike looked at me like I'd offered him a platter of BBQ ribs sitting on top of a naked woman. Or, in his case, a naked guy.

"Yeah. But if you have Shane over, keep it in your bedroom," I ordered. "Or at least use Lysol after and never, ever tell me about it. I wanna still be able to enjoy a beer on the couch."

Mike muttered something about where else I could enjoy my beer and walked off, phone in hand, no doubt ready to call Shane with the good news. But not even the thought of what my baby brother might get up to while I was gone could dampen my mood as I hefted a duffel bag over my shoulder and went out to my truck. It was a two-hour drive to the Cal Fire Training Camp at Ione, and I was anxious to get on the road.

Man, this was gonna be awesome. Going to a training intensive was always fun. It was a nice break from the day-today at the fire station, and I liked learning new stuff, being the best firefighter I could be. But I'd fought especially hard to get assigned to this class. I'd had to compete with two other firefighters at my station who wanted it, but Chief Reiger picked me. Which made me hot shit, I guess. Or a Canali. And if some of the others grumbled that I'd gotten it because of my name, so what? Let's see their family sacrifice as much for Cal Fire as the Canalis had, and then we'd talk.

This intensive on fire aviation would teach us the latest in gear and protocols. After this, I'd be the aviation liaison for my fire station, which was enough to make me drool. I'd always admired fire pilots, but since Dell Murphy saved our bacon in that Sierra City fire, I'd been obsessed.

I never did get a chance to shake his hand, but I would today because this intensive was being taught by Murphy himself. I was stoked to meet him but also, honestly, nervous as fuck. My heart was pounding as I drove down the mountain from Resolute and skirted the traffic at Sacramento. By the time I maneuvered the long road to the remote Ione Training Center, I was jumping out of my skin.

I'd been to Ione lots—took my basic fire training there and been to a dozen events or classes since, including Mike's graduation when he completed training. The campus wasn't much to look at—scrubby brown hills, some green trees, metal and cement buildings. But I guess it didn't look too bad for a place where things were set on fire pretty much on a daily basis.

I pulled up at the barracks dormitory and glanced at my watch. Two minutes to ten. Shit! No time to put my stuff in the dorm. I was gonna be late.

I charged out of the car and ran down the path to the main building. I didn't want Dell Murphy thinking I was a loser before I even met him. I should have left home earlier. Or driven faster. My head had been in the fucking clouds all morning long.

I yanked open one of the glass doors at the side of the building, dashed inside—and smacked into a solid body coming from the restrooms.

I spun back, thudding against the glass door. "Shit. Sorry. I—"

The words froze in my mouth as the guy, who'd been brushing off his long, starched uniform sleeves, looked up and glared at me. He was tall and built, with dark blond hair, intense hazel green eyes, and an annoyed expression that crackled with command. He was also wearing a navy Cal Fire dress uniform and had his firefighter stripes on his sleeves like mine, but he sported a red stripe on his left as well in honor of military service. Military. Damn. My stomach did a one-eighty, like a trick pilot in a flying demonstration. Oh fuck. My gaze dropped to his nametag and my worst suspicions were confirmed.

*Pilot Dell Murphy.*

I swear, my fucking heart stopped. Jesus, he was imposing. As tall and big as me, maybe bigger. And intense. Like, his *aura,* as Aunt Carlotta would say. He was military all right, and he was looking at me like a drill sergeant at a slacker recruit.

While my tongue was hiding in my mouth, Dell's expression went from annoyed to curious as he studied me. His eyes warmed and one side of his lips tilted up. What? Did he think this was funny?

A hot rush of shame washed through me, and that finally jolted me out of my frozen state. I wasn't gonna be laughed at by this guy, hero or not. I gave him my most charming smile. "Oh, hey. Pilot Murphy, right? I was trying to get to your class on time." I held out a hand. "Donny Canali. I'm stoked about taking this intensive. And I've been wanting to thank you for the work you did at that power line near Sierra City in March. I was one of the guys stuck out there."

Dell Murphy ignored my hand for a moment, still staring

at my face. But just when I was about to feel stupid for having my hand waving in the breeze, he shook it. "Glad I could help. And call me Dell. You said Canali?"

"Yep. Firefighter Donny Canali. Gridley station."

He smiled a confused little smile, which still had the wattage of an exploding transformer. Shit, this guy.

He said something, then looked at me, waiting.

"Huh?"

"I asked where Gridley is. I'm pretty new to Cal Fire."

He was still shaking my hand with his strong grip, which made all those nerves spark up again in my belly. I tugged it free. "Oh, right. Yeah, I knew that. That you're new, I mean. The Gridley station's northwest of Sac. Er—that's Sacramento. Not too far from Oroville."

"Ah." Dell glanced at his watch. "And now we're both late. Let's rock and roll, boyo."

Boyo? That was cute. He turned and walked down the hall. I watched him go for a moment—damn, a lot of guys would kill for a physique like that—before hurrying to catch up. At least I wouldn't have to try to find the classroom.

The training room had maybe thirty chairs and they were almost all taken, so I had to sit in one of the two empties in the front row. I slumped down in my seat and went to get something to write with only to realize the notebook I'd brought was in my duffel bag—in my car. *Excellent, Canali.* I had a notepad app on my phone, but my fingers were too big for that stupid little keypad. Still, I had to at least look like I was taking notes, so I got it out and remembered to set it to silent.

Murphy turned to the group. At the flash of his eyes there was instant quiet.

"Good morning. I'm Dell Murphy, and I'm a fire bomber pilot with Cal Fire. I'll be your instructor. In this intensive, we'll cover the newest in fire aviation tech and best practices along with some specific protocol I developed with my copilot while working wildfires in Oregon, techniques we found speed up coordination and response." He waggled a finger at a guy farther down in the front row and this cool-looking dude stood up. He was tall and thin with short curly black hair. He looked part Asian and part black maybe, but his eyes were blue. Dell said, "This is my copilot, Tyrone Chan, better known as Ty. You'll get to know him over the next few days."

Ty gave a little salute and sat down. Dell tapped a laptop on the podium and a picture of a hot yellow-and-red plane appeared on the big screen at the front of the room.

"This is the Viking CL-515, also called the First Responder. She's the newest and best water bomber in the world, and she rings in at a price tag of thirty-mil."

There were a few sharp breaths from the students.

"I don't have to tell the people in this room about the growing threat of wildfires as our forests dry out and are attacked by invasive beetles and plant parasites. There's only one force that can stop the loss of millions of acres of this natural, and finite resource, and that's you guys. You men and women sitting in this room."

His words, and his intense expression as he looked us over, gave me chills.

"But air support helps make your job possible. With it, we have a fighting chance to keep this state from becoming a dead zone. That's why Cal Fire continues to invest in better gear, better personnel, better tech. And this class is going to take our capacity to the next level. It's my job to get you there."

Wow. This guy could lead a charge to Hell, and I'd be right behind him screaming like a Berserker all the way. Fuck yeah. It was all up to us to save California, the most beautiful place on Earth. I suddenly felt like I was in a scene from *Independence Day* or something, where a small badass crew had to save the world.

As the class went on, it was just as rapid fire as Dell had been flying that plane, and I had to concentrate hard to keep up. It was good info, but my brain was being squirrely. I kept picturing the way Dell had buzzed us that day, swooping in as easily as a freaking hawk on that fire. Only now that I'd met him, I could picture Dell in the cockpit, all intense and heroic. And then I imagined him in Afghanistan, flying through smoke and enemy flack like Tom Cruise in *Top Gun.*

Shit. I thought of myself as a badass, but what was I by comparison? I'd gotten a degree in fire science at Butte just after high school, then joined Cal Fire. I'd fought wildfires during California's fire season for three years now. But compared to Dell Murphy, I hadn't done shit.

No wonder he was so confident and cocky. No wonder he had that aura like he was a goddamn Avenger or something —the guy all the women swoon over and all the men wanna be. Still, I wished my stomach and blood pressure or what-ever would calm down. There was no reason to freak out like some fanboy. Probably, once you got to know him, Dell Murphy was just a regular guy with regular guy faults.

Of course, that would never happen. Dell probably hung out with the big brass, not regular firefighters like me.

Three hours of charts and graphs later, we finally broke for lunch. I wasn't used to sitting so long, so it felt great to stand up and stretch my legs. Sandwiches and chips and drinks had been set up in the hall, and we all trooped out there. It was a perfect day. It seemed like we had hot spells earlier and earlier, but this May day was warm, sunny, and around 75 degrees. I took my sandwich, chips, and Mountain Dew outside.

A bunch of the students from class were sitting down at picnic tables under an overhang at the side of the building. But I wanted sun, so I said *hey* to a bunch of people as I passed—firefighters I'd trained with or worked wildfires with —shook hands with a few guys and ignored the interested looks from Janine, a firefighter from Tahoe. She was cute, and she'd always made it clear she was open to getting to know me a whole lot better, but nice girls like Janine were not my type.

Across the parking lot, one guy was sitting on a low stone wall in the sun, so I walked over there.

"Hey. This looks like the place to get some rays." I sat down. "You're from Riverside, right?"

The guy nodded, chewing. "Sam. And you're a Canali."

"Sure am. I'm Donny." I ripped open the white wrapper on the ham sandwich I'd picked up. I'd wanted to grab two, 'cause I ate a lot, but I knew from past experience at Ione that they provided one big sandwich per student. Cheapskates.

I'd just taken my first huge bite when I saw Dell Murphy walking toward us carrying his lunch. Shit. Shit.

I choked on the bite, coughed like a mo-fo, and had just cleared my throat with a sip of Mountain Dew when Dell sat down on the wall a few feet from me. He gave me an amused glance. "You okay there, Canali? Don't let that sandwich get the better of you."

I felt my cheeks burn. Fucker. But I was used to getting shit from my brothers, so I smiled. "I was surprised to see you, is all. I figured you'd entertain us during our midday break by flying figure eights or something."

Dell chuckled. "Nah. I charge for that shit." He looked up at the sky, took out a pair of retro mirrored sunglasses from a pocket, and slipped them on. "Gotta love that sunshine. I just moved here from Oregon. I'll take every second of Vitamin D I can get."

"Got that right," said Sam.

Trying to act cool, I ripped open a bag of chips. Fortunately, I managed to do it without spilling chips all over the ground.

*He's just a regular guy. Chill.*

I tried to convince myself, but visions of Dell looking

rakish in those sunglasses while flying into danger as a military pilot refused to leave my head. Truth? He intimidated the fuck out of me.

"You like it so far? California, I mean." I asked casually.

"What's not to like?" He gave me a warm smile.

*See? He doesn't think you're a loser. So relax.*

"That's what I always say. Who'd wanna live anywhere else? My cousin, Tito, came out here from New York, just for a short stay. That was over a year ago. You won't wanna leave either. Guaranteed."

Dell unwrapped his sandwich. "Oh? Is this Tito a firefighter too? You have a lot of family in Cal Fire, right? The Canalis."

I was flattered he'd heard of us. "Abso-fucking-lutely. Not Tito, no, but there are a lot of us in Cal Fire."

Dell gave me a once-over. "That's what I heard. I also heard they call you The Hot Cannolis." His smile was teasing.

Sam snorted a laugh. "Do they? That's good."

I groaned. "Fuck me. You did not hear that nickname already."

"Sure did." Dell leaned forward and bit into his sandwich, his gaze fixed on the group over by the picnic tables. "I have to say, I thought it sounded ridiculous. Then I met you."

I blinked and took a big bite of my sandwich. What did he mean by that? His tone was neutral. Did he mean I looked Italian? Or that he'd thought we sounded like a big joke but realized now we weren't? Or maybe he did think we were a joke. No, that was being paranoid.

I decided to laugh it off. "You got a nickname? You must, right? All guys in the military have nicknames."

"Did you serve?"

"Nah. I always wanted to be a firefighter, so I went that direction right after high school."

He nodded and looked away again. "You're still young."

"I'm twenty-five. How old are you? I mean—" My face went hot. That was a weird thing to ask.

He chuckled. "Thirty-one. Not an old man yet."

"You've done a shit ton for only being thirty-one."

He gave me another momentary glance. "What, did they pass out my resume at the Gridley station or something?"

Now he thought I was stalking him. Great. "Er… my dad's chief at the Oroville station. He was spouting off your background before you ever came onboard." I shrugged. "Guess Cal Fire was happy to get a guy like you."

He nodded without looking at me. "So what is there to do around here?"

The change in topic had my head spinning for a second. "Uh… there's trails through the woods. If you like to run. Or hike."

Sam spoke up. "There's no drinking on campus, so the firefighters hang at a place called Tilly's Club in Ione. It's a dive, but good for a drink or a game of pool. Darts."

Right. That's what Dell meant. Duh.

He nodded. "I've driven past it. Never been in."

I finished my sandwich and chips, trying to enjoy the sun, but still tied in knots sitting next to Dell Murphy no matter how much I told myself he was just an ordinary guy.

Yeah. No. Ordinary guys weren't fucking military pilots and fire bombers. They didn't look or sound like Captain America. They weren't Dell Murphy.

Who, it turned out, had reddish hair in the sun. I'd thought it was blond, but there was definitely red in it in direct sunlight. He had good, thick hair. Like the Canalis.

I wondered how much he could bench press with shoulders and arms like that.

"There's a gym," I blurted, as he wadded up the paper from his finished sandwich. "On this campus, I mean. If you like to work out."

"Yeah, I saw that earlier." Dell stood up. "Think I'll go to

Tilly's Place tonight. Maybe I'll see you guys there." He looked right at me when he said it.

I opened my mouth. Closed it. "Yeah, sure. Maybe we can get a group from class to go."

"Later then." Dell Murphy took off his shades, slipped them in a pocket, and walked away.

# TWO

## DELL

*Whew. What a ride.*

I walked away from Canali and had to fight the urge to turn around and look again. Beautiful. He strained even my capacity for hyperbole. Eyes so dark it was like looking at a starless night. Cheekbones that'd make a Renaissance sculptor weep, and lips? Shit. Made for kissing.

Was he the one I'd heard about? Had to be. Only an unfair universe would make that man straight.

Dayum. Tonight could be very interesting.

I keyed my way into my room in the barracks they'd set aside for the instructors to use during the course and stopped at the sight of my friend and copilot, Ty, stretched out in all his feline glory on my single bed, sound asleep. They'd bunked him in the communal barracks and he hated it. Obviously, he'd decided sleep was more important than lunch.

I made a fast trip out to the head, washed the food smell off my hands, and strode back to my room.

Ty was sitting up and rubbing his eyes as I walked in. "Hey, man, thanks for the Zs."

"You want more? I can do the afternoon session solo."

He slapped a hand to his mouth in mock horror. "What? You don't need me to be your human pointer? The Vanna White of aerial firefighting?" White teeth flashed in his wide grin.

"Awww. You're much prettier than any TV hostess."

"Only in your weird-ass eyes, my favorite homo."

"Ah, you overwhelm me with endearments, my friend." I pressed a hand to my chest. But oh, he was so wrong. Anyone, male or female would find my n'er-do-well friend pretty as sin. Ty was a classic example of the universe playing tricks on the unwary, because he was straight as a plumbline, but at the same time was a colorful and fabulous creature, the product of a Chinese father and a half-African and half-European mother.

He'd sported platinum blond hair when I met him after he'd joined the fire aviation contractor I worked for in Oregon. Of course, at the time, I'd grown my hair to my shoulders and adopted a full beard as a rebound from my military 'do, so informality reigned. When we both decided to join Cal Fire, we'd cleaned up a bit, and Ty had let his natural hair grow back.

He stretched and yawned. "Speaking of pretty, holy crap, who was that you were pretending not to talk to at lunch? And fast work, by the way. You zeroed right in on the hottest firefighter in California."

I chuckled. "That, my friend, is Donny Canali, one of the legendary Canali clan."

His eyebrows shot up. "The gay one?" The tale of the Canali brother who'd come out had spread like its own brand of wildfire through Cal Fire shortly after we'd joined.

I pressed my palms together in supplication. "I have no idea, but I will be lighting a candle tonight."

"I bet you will," he barked. "That dude is calendar worthy." For a straight man, Ty did have good taste in men.

Joking aside, I was pretty sure the studly Canali in my class *was* the gay one. He was too nervous and awed in my presence for it not to be attraction, those big brown eyes practically adoring. I oh so very much hoped.

I glanced at my watch. "Speaking of tonight, I'm going over to Tilly's at seven with the chance of meeting up with some of our students. Want to come?"

"Sure. Will the Hot Cannoli be one of them?"

"Could happen. So why don't you stay here and say a novena for me in your sleep and we'll meet at quarter of seven"

"You sure you don't need me?" He waved his arms like he was pointing to things on a screen.

"I'm sure half the men and all the women in the class will die of disappointment, but sleep's an important commodity if you're going to survive flying with me."

He lay back on the bed, his boots hanging off the edge and his arms crossed on his chest. "Don't I know it, man. Don't I know it."

———

I steered my Jeep into the parking lot at Tilly's with Ty staring at his phone beside me. Since I didn't drink, I was always designated driver, but we did alternate vehicles. As I turned off the ignition, my phone rang and I frowned when I saw it was my mam. I answered. "Hey, love, what's up?"

"Are you coming over tonight, Rivendell?"

I gave a very soft sigh. "No, Mam. I'm teaching that special course in Ione. Remember I told you?"

"You did? Oh well, you know my mind sometimes. The elves steal all my thoughts."

Yeah, the elves were responsible for a lot of things in our family. Along with the trolls and orcs. My mam had been obsessed with the Lord of the Rings since before I was born and I'd lived with its inhabitants on a daily basis. "How's Gala? Did she go to the library?" I held my breath.

"No. She wasn't feeling too well, so I told her it was better to stay home and rest."

This time my sigh wasn't so soft. "Mam, she'll never feel better if she doesn't get some sun and exercise. They were really looking forward to seeing her at the library. They're looking for volunteers and Gala can walk there from our house." I'd specifically searched for something Gala could do close to home. I loved my mam, but she could piss me off.

"She's just not ready, Rivendell." Mam's voice had that sulky, stubborn sound she got when she wouldn't budge.

"Okay, fine. I'll speak to her when I get home."

"What time will that be? I saved dinner for you."

I wiped a hand across my face. "I won't be home tonight. I'll see you in a couple days. I'll text Gala the details." I hung up and Ty put a hand on my arm.

"Let it go. You know she just doesn't like to hear anything that doesn't suit her."

I gave him a smile and took a deep breath. "You do know my mam."

We both jumped out of the Jeep, and he walked over, slid an arm around my shoulders, and gave a squeeze. My mam could get to me like no other, and Ty knew it from close experience. I gave him a smile of appreciation. "Thanks."

"Uh-oh."

I looked up and followed his gaze—to where the gorgeous Donny Canali stood at the door of Tilly's staring right at us with wide eyes.

When his gaze met mine, he seemed to try to smile, but then gave up, turned and rushed into the bar.

Ty raised his dark brows. "That's one dude with some seriously wrong ideas."

"Um hm. And no easy way to change them."

"Yeah. You can't start coming on to one of your students in the middle of Tilly's."

"The curse of responsibility." I grinned. "Let's go face the music."

Tilly's was already in full swing thanks to nearly my entire class having showed up. I didn't go to bars as a rule, and never with students. I preferred my companions to say *Yes, sir* for far more enjoyable reasons. But tonight? Oh yes. My wandering gaze locked on that face that launched a thousand fables. Donny sat at a table in the middle of the group. One of the other female firefighters, Audrey, had moved in close to him.

The firefighter from Tahoe, Janine, stood up and waved. "Pilot Murphy. Over here." A couple of the guys joined in the wave.

I moved over to the big group of students, carefully not looking at Donny. I didn't want him to feel singled out. I took one of the empty chairs Janine pointed to and Ty slid into the other. "What can we get you guys?" Janine asked.

"Beer." Ty smiled.

I held up a finger. "Cranberry juice and seltzer."

Janine flashed dimples. "Aw, come on. You can trust us."

"Designated driver." I gave her a wink. It was an easier explanation than the whole heredity discussion. My dad's side of the family had serious issues with alcoholism. Having grown up with it, I'd cut that sword of Damocles out of my life at an early age.

Janine and a guy named Rick went over to the bar to get our drinks and some of the peripheral conversations started up again. The students near us looked a little uncomfortable —what do you say to the teacher?—but George, one of the older men asked, "How long have you two been flying together?"

Ty looked at me. "Uh, two years. We met when we both flew fires up in Oregon and it just clicked."

Somebody else asked, "Were you in the military, too, Ty?"

"Nope. I was a crop duster down in central California for a while before I decided to go battle the flames."

George said, "How about you, Sir? How long have you been a fire pilot?"

I sipped the drink Janine had handed me and glanced at Donny. Those dark eyes riveted on me as if they'd been glued, which made my heart do a jig. Smiling, I replied, "First, you don't have to call me sir. I'm just a regular firefighter with a lot less experience than some of you. In answer to your question, I was in the military for ten years and became a pilot there, then started flying for a fire aviation contractor in Oregon when I got out. That was three years ago. But every fire pilot knows that the pinnacle of greatness is Cal Fire. The best of the best."

Yes, I was laying it on with a trowel, but they loved it and the whole group cheered and gave high fives.

"Damned straight!" That came from Donny and our eyes met and we both smiled. Actually, make that three smiles. Him, me, and my cock.

Janine came back from the bar with more drinks and planted herself between me and Ty. She started asking questions, and we all shot the shit. Pretty soon Audrey had squeezed herself so close to Canali that she was practically sitting on his lap. But whenever I glanced at him, I found his eyes on me. She might be crowding his body, but I had all his sweet, sweet attention.

About forty minutes later, a few people finished their drinks and started their goodbyes. Audrey was still stuck like a barnacle to Donny. Either I was wrong about him, or she was clueless. I figured I might as well give it one more chance.

I got up and looked around for the head. One of the firefighters said, "Pilot. Back there." He pointed to a hall in the back of the pub.

"Thanks." I cut through the group and walked to the Men's. It was nearly empty, and I went straight to the urinal. I had my mickey in my hands when the louder crowd noise signaled the door opening behind me, and then, oh yes, Donny Canali stepped up two urinals down. He'd passed the test. Casually, he whipped it out.

*Control the eyes. Control the eyes.* I had to force myself not to grin. Men pretended they never stared at other men's junk in the restroom, but damn if every man, straight or gay, didn't do it. Comparison? Window shopping?

He said, "Hey, sir."

"Hey. It's Dell, especially in the lav."

He chuckled, sounding a little nervous. "Good to get out of the noise for a minute."

"Yup."

He shook it and I couldn't resist. I snuck a glance. Oh fuck and I meant that literally. He was a big guy all over. Drool pooled in my mouth.

He zipped and stepped back to the sinks and I did the same. We were both doing a pretty thorough job of hand washing. Time for another test. "Looks like you found your-self an admirer there, boyo."

"What? Who?" He shook his head. "Audrey? Yeah. No. She's not my type."

"Too strong? Afraid she'll whup your ass?"

He gave a snarky grin. "No, too nice." We both laughed in that guy way. He said, "Actually, I'm looking for a comfort-able way out. I don't want to hurt her feelings, but I drove with some guys and she's already asked for a ride home with them."

"Easy. Ride back with Ty and me."

His face lit up and my Irish soul wanted to compose sonnets to its beauty. "Could I? That'd be great."

I pointed to the door. "You go on out. I'll text Ty and let him know the score."

He frowned suddenly. "Uh, hey, I don't want to be a third wheel and cut in on your plans for tonight."

I stared at him intently. "The only thing two-wheeled about Ty and me is the nose gear on the plane we fly. In fact, he'll be grateful to be spared my conversation."

"Okay, if you're sure." He looked pleased and hurried out the door.

I pulled out my phone and grinned as I texted.

Ten minutes later, we'd said our goodbyes and Ty, Donny, and I headed to the door with poor Audrey looking like somebody killed her hobbit.

When we got to my Jeep, Ty stopped. "Hey, I think I'll go spend a little time with Janine." He pointed across the parking lot to a red mustang where Janine was leaning, waggling her fingers at us. If Ty had lettered a sign that said, *I'm not with Dell; I'm straight,* it wouldn't have been more obvious. Good man. He grinned at Donny. "Don't worry. He's way more sober than I am." With that, he strolled in his feline gait toward Janine.

I grinned and shrugged, then crawled into the driver's seat. Donny hurried around to the passenger side and hopped in.

As I maneuvered out of the lot, Donny cleared his throat. "I was uh, surprised about Ty. I guess I thought—"

"That Ty was gay? Nope. Just my best mate."

I glanced over in time to see him nod with a little smile. Either he looked relieved or I was seeing what I wanted to see.

I cleared my throat. "It's still kind of early. I know we start at stupid hours in the morning, but if you'd like to get a drink someplace quieter, we can stop."

"That'd be great. I've got about a million questions."

I chuckled and navigated my way through town to a place I liked that sat off the main drag. I pulled in.

Donny looked around. "Where are we?"

"The Waystation. They've got good grub and beer and wine, if you want. I found it shortly after I started teaching here." They were also a lot more open-minded, a funky little place with some LGBTQ waitstaff. But I didn't mention that.

We got out of the car and, as we walked in, Donny said, "I'll bet it gets tiring being with your students all the time. All us fan boys." His laugh sounded a little embarrassed.

"I like being an instructor. It allows me to get to know personnel I wouldn't normally meet while flying a plane."

That made him smile again as if maybe he thought I might be talking about him. Good guess, boyo.

Inside the Waystation, country western music played softly in the background and the room was dimly-lit with candles on the tables. The customers were divided between a few single men at the bar, several male and female couples and a group of teens in a booth. I led Donny to a booth and slid in one side. A waiter hurried over. "Hey, Dell. Nice to see you again. What can I get you guys?"

"A coffee for me, Matt."

Donny asked for beer and cute Matt with his blue highlights had to work at peeling his eyes off of that face. Oh my, smart man. I share your taste.

To drag my mind into more neutral territory, I said, "So tell me about the famous Canalis."

He didn't even pretend to not understand and grinned affectionately. "There's a passel of us and most are firefighters. My dad's the chief at Oroville and one of my brothers, Tony, is there too. My other brother, Mike, is at Gridley station with me. My uncle's a fire chief farther south and two cousins are in Cal Fire." He shrugged. "And the ones who aren't firefighters tend to be cops."

"Ah, do you bottle the testosterone and offer it for sale on Amazon?"

For a second, a crease flashed between his brows, but then

he laughed and his face relaxed. "You're not the first to say it."

"So that's your family. What about a girlfriend? Someone serious?" I spoke as lightly as I could, but there was no way to disguise the question.

Donny shook his head. "Nah. I don't do *girlfriends.*"

Oh baby. Fuck yeah. I couldn't hide my grin, but fortunately, Donny's attention was on Matt delivering our drinks.

After Matt left, we clinked glasses. I said, "To fighting fires, wherever they are." If my tone had a touch of innuendo, he could interpret it as he wished.

"Well, except maybe in a fireplace on a winter's night." His eyes were warm, and the words sparked heat in my belly. But then he seemed surprised to have said that. He took a big mouthful of beer. "So, uh, were you like, born in Ireland? Your accent's American, but you use words that sound Irish sometimes."

I shook my head. "No, I was born in California, but my da was as Irish as Paddy's pig, as they say, born in the tougher parts of Dublin, he fought his way out and came to New York. But like most sun-starved Irishmen, he craved good weather and moved to California where he swept my mother off her feet." I took a drink of my coffee. "He never gave up his Irish brogue, his love for fables and fairies, or his undying thirst. He could tell a better story and drink more whiskey than any man I ever knew." I held up my glass in a mock toast. "My mam left him when I was ten, but he stayed in my life until he died of kidney disease when I was twenty." And that was about as much as I'd say about my family to any man I didn't know, no matter how pretty his face.

"Damn. That's tough. I'm sorry. Is that why you don't drink?"

"It was a long time ago, and yes. My da was enough to make any man a teetotaler for life." The dark wave of memories washed over me, and I thrashed to the surface, forcing a pleasant smile. "So. How'd you qualify for the course? I understand each station only chose their top candidates to be ground liaison, so it must be a big fucking deal."

He actually blushed, and I'd happily have kissed the roses from those cheeks. "Yeah, my pa was pretty damned happy when Chief Reiger gave me the nod."

We sipped and shared a basket of fries for another hour while I mostly watched the sparkle in his eyes. Obviously, Donny Canali loved his family and his father most of all. The man's good opinion clearly mattered a lot to him. I understood that. My da might have been a drunk, but I'd still idolized him.

I'd happily have sat there spinning my own daydreams about dark eyes and broad shoulders for the rest of the night, but the brass didn't love the students being out too late and I didn't want black marks on Canali's final report. I glanced at my watch. "I better get you back before pumpkin time."

"Well damn." He smiled. "I still have so many questions."

I pulled the phone from my jeans' pocket and said, "Maybe we can get together after class tomorrow?"

He looked torn. "I need to get back to Resolute after class. Ma—my mother—she's planning on me being there for dinner. It's a family thing. Any interest in running in the morning? There's a nice trail that starts from the training center."

Getting hot and sweaty with this guy didn't sound like a hardship. But I said, "You sure you can handle that, Canali? I'm pretty fast."

He gave me a smile so charged it made my toes clench in my shoes. "I think I can take you."

"Yeah?"

"Yeah."

I had to look away and down a mouthful of coffee before I did something stupid. "Then I'll meet you outside the dorms at six."

"Awesome. Jesus, I might have to write all my questions down. I really appreciate your talking to me on your time off."

I hoped the boy was playing coy.

It took too few minutes to drive back to the training center. I parked in my spot outside my quarters.

Donny looked over at me. "Night, Dell. It was fun."

I wanted to kiss him, but I shrugged as casually as I could. "Don't keep me waiting in the morning, Canali."

"No way." His Adam's apple bobbed. "See you tomorrow. Uh, morning I mean. To run."

As Donny walked to his barracks, I let myself into my room. Shit, my fucking palms were sweating and my dick was hard. Donny Canali was the most intriguing thing to happen to me since I'd left the army. I'd never found a way to comfortably ask if he was the gay brother, but I thought I had my answer. That spark between us could burn half of California.

# THREE

## DONNY

"Eat dust, Canali!"

Dell took off like a shot as I gaped. "No fair!" I raced after him.

Jesus, he was fast and just as fucking fit as I'd imagined. Maybe more so. Damn, those thighs looked like rocks. We ran up a baked brown hill, Dell hardly slowing at all. I grinned. Fucker. I had home turf advantage since I knew this trail and he didn't.

He was too far ahead for my liking as we crested the incline, so I watched him power down the other side while I ditched to the right. The main trail circled some woods down below, but I knew the short cut. I got to the bottom and saw him coming on my left. I turned right.

"Now who's cheating!" Dell hollered. I just grinned and kept running.

When I reached the stream, Dell was hard on my tail. I turned and shoved him backward, and he shoved me, nearly sending me into the water as I laughed. I started over the stepping stones, as fast as I could go on the slippery rocks.

Halfway across, Dell yanked on my shirt and I turned and pushed at his arms, both of us trying to get each other to step off the rock into calf-deep water, roughhousing like he was one of my brothers.

"Oh, shit!" he laughed.

"Whoa! You're goin' down, Murphy!"

"Not yet, Canali!"

He leaped onto a rock to one side and was around me, quicksilver fast. Damned jackrabbit. I wasn't gonna be outrun by a thirty-plus-year-old. I chased after him. There was no way he was getting back to the training camp first. I had my reputation to consider.

The path narrowed as it went through woods, becoming more of a hiking trail, twisty and with roots. One of his sleeves caught on a branch. It only took a few seconds for him to free himself, but I caught up to him and threw a light elbow as I went past. "Too slow, old man!"

I powered on up the trail, hearing Dell's panting right behind me, practically feeling his breath on my neck.

So much for asking questions during a nice, leisurely run. But this was way more fun anyway. Shit, it was the most fun I'd had in ages. It felt good to run full tilt after sitting on my ass the day before.

He reached out and got a handful of my T-shirt, yanking me back and then passing me with a shit-eating grin. "All's fair in love and racing!"

"Ooh, now you're askin' for it!"

When the trail broke into the open and widened, we raced hard—neck and neck at first, but he gradually pulled ahead. There was a long, open descent down a track that could get muddy, only it was dry now. Then I remembered there was also a section of loose scree.

"Hey! Watch out!" I shouted at Dell, who was now a good hundred yards ahead of me.

But I was too late. Dell was going fast, too fast, and he lost his footing as the scree rolled underfoot. He waved his arms, trying to slow down, trying to catch himself, but it didn't work. In half a second, he was down, landing hard on his ass and right side.

Oh, fuck. That had to hurt.

I slowed down and jogged up to him, chagrined. "Sorry, man. I forgot about the scree. You okay?"

Dell took off his sunglasses and glowered up at me. "Ow." But he sounded more teasing than in genuine pain.

"Seriously, you okay? You get road rash?" His right leg was bent forty-five degrees, shoe on the ground. We both wore shorts and short-sleeved T-shirts thanks to the warmer morning air. That garb didn't offer much protection in a fall like this. I put my hand on his thigh and ducked my head to look under. Yeah, there was a nasty-looking red rash on the back of his quad. Only a few spots were deep enough to bleed. Still. Looked painful. I squeezed his thigh. "Ouch. Hey, maybe you can pick up some hazard pay for that, huh? Wounded while on duty."

We were close. I didn't realize how close until I looked up at his face. His eyes had gone half-lidded, and the way he was looking at me caused a slow turning in my gut.

"Maybe you can kiss it and make it better."

Before that could register in my frozen brain, Dell slipped one hand behind my neck and pulled me down. And then he kissed me.

*Dell Murphy was kissing me.*

He was so strong about it, like it was just happening and that was it. His palm gripped my nape firmly as he passionately attacked my mouth. His tongue moved in to set up shop. I was so shocked I couldn't even move. My body washed hot, then cold, then hot again with surprise, outrage, and something like an electric charge. Pure muscle memory had me kissing back. Sort of. And then a wave of fear and shame crept over me.

I didn't know how long it went on. No time at all. Ages. I got ahold of myself enough to push him back, hard. He landed on his elbows, looking up at me with a smug smile. And then he must have seen something on my face, because his smile dropped like a stone. "Donny?"

"I'm not fucking gay!" I shouted. We weren't too close to the center, and probably no one was around to hear me, but I still shouldn't have shouted it. Only I couldn't help it.

Dell's face went a horrified shade of bright red. "Really? Shit. Shit, I'm sorry."

"Jesus Christ!" I stood up, my knees wobbling. I ran a shaking hand through my hair. Fuck, my whole body was shaking.

"Donny, I'm sorry!" Dell looked panicked now. "I thought… the way you looked at me. And I'd heard a Canali firefighter was gay, and you said girlfriends weren't your thing."

"I mean getting *serious* with a girl, Dell! Fuck." I backed up, mind spinning.

He stood, favoring that skinned leg. "Donny, I swear, I'd never knowingly come on to a straight guy. I really am sorry."

A nasty voice in my head said Dell was right to look so worried. If I made a stink, it wouldn't go well for him. And I had the family connections to make a deal of it. Pa would be livid if I told him.

But… no, I wouldn't do that. For one thing, I'd never want anyone to know he'd kissed me. But also, it would be a ratfink thing to do.

"Forget it." I shook my head hard. "I owe you one for that Sierra City rescue. So don't sweat it."

"Donny—"

I turned and ran—I ran as hard and as fast as I could.

———

I would have skipped class and driven right the fuck home if I could have. Only I wanted this damned credit, and there'd be a lot of questions if I bailed. So I showered, stripped my bed in the dorm like you're supposed to, and tossed my duffel bag in my truck. I barked and glared at anyone who tried to talk to me, and hunkered down in a seat at the very back of the classroom. Plopping my notebook in front of me, I stared into it, doodling random shit. Audrey stopped by, but when she got a whiff of my mood, she moved on.

The class quieted when Dell entered. I didn't look up. He sounded sure and confident as he began to lecture, as if nothing had happened. I tried to focus and take in the material, but it was impossible. Just the sound of his voice was like nails down raw flesh inside me.

*The way you looked at me.*

*I'd never come on to a straight guy.*

Dell had totally thought I was gay. Me, Donny Canali. He really had!

*The way you looked at me.*

I hadn't fucking looked at him! I'd been in awe, yeah. And maybe I'd fanboyed some. But I hadn't been *looking* at Dell in a gay way. Had I?

Shit, no.

Had I?

*Maybe. And maybe you fucking knew it too.*

Okay, maybe it had occurred to me, in a fleeting thought, that Dell was a gay guy and he might be talking to me, running with me, because he was interested. After all, he'd invited me out for a second drink at the Waystation last night, just me. And maybe I'd been okay with that if it meant getting to be around Dell, getting to hear his stories, getting to maybe be friends with someone like him. Humans used their looks to their advantage in all sorts of situations. I wasn't above using mine.

*Sure. It's all fun and games till someone's tongue is in your mouth. Now you know what it feels like to lead someone on.*

Lead him on? I hadn't flirted with Dell, not intentionally. And I wasn't fucking gay! That was the main thing. I wasn't! And Dell had been all over me.

The longer I sat there in class, the more the memory of that moment upset me. The kiss had been such a shock, I hadn't even fully taken it in at the time. Remembering it, the feelings came back even stronger—hot and cold flashes, nausea, fear, excitement, and even a little turned on because, like, I was a guy. The way he'd sort of… taken over me was…. Shit, anyone would respond to that! Thinking about it made my heart hammer and sent prickling heat burning along my spine like a fever.

I knew I should be able to laugh it off, forget it like it was no big deal. That'd be the right thing to do. After all, Mike was gay, and I was cool with him and Shane. But this…. This was not cool. It was a million miles from cool. I was totally losing my shit.

I somehow survived the morning, alternating between forcing myself to concentrate on the material for minutes at a time before returning to internal stewing. Good thing there were lots of handouts. Hopefully, I'd still be able to do the job I was supposed to do after taking this class.

At the lunch break, Audrey wandered over to my chair, so I suggested she grab some sandwiches for us and meet me in front of the dorms. She was thrilled to do it, and I felt guilty for using her, but it let me avoid facing Dell or anyone else in class. The afternoon session went much the same as the morning one had. Eight hours later, I was still as pissed about what had happened as I'd been at the time. Even more.

As soon as Dell dismissed the class, I was ready to get the hell out of there and drive back home to Resolute.

I made it out of the classroom without glancing at Dell and had just reached my truck when I heard my name.

"Donny Canali!"

I stopped, keys in my hand. I turned slowly to face him. At the sight of Dell walking determinedly toward me, emotion slammed through me again. I wanted to punch his handsome face. And, weirdly, I also still admired the guy, was kind of desperate for him to like me. Wanted to *be* him.

He stopped a few feet from me and glanced around. And yeah, there were other students wandering by. Probably watching us.

"Look." He sighed. "I wanted to apologize again for misreading things so badly. That's never happened to me before."

"Well, you really fucked up this time. Because I'm not gay," I hissed, low.

He nodded, jaw going hard. "I got that, yes. Duly noted."

Part of me wanted to plead with him, say, *but we can be friends.* Part of me hated the idea of him being this great pilot out there on the team that only had this last, ugly memory of me. But I was too raw to do the smart thing. So what came out was: "Just stay the fuck away from me, Murphy."

"Roger that," Dell said flatly. He turned and left me standing there in the parking lot with no idea what to do with what I felt.

# FOUR

## DELL

I dragged myself down the stairs from my apartment over the garage and trained my brain on my mam's kitchen where I was sure to find coffee. Focusing on bean juice kept me from giving myself one more mental kick in the ass for being so fucking stupid, the activity I'd been engaged in most of the night. I hadn't made a mistake that bad, gaydarwise, since I was a kid. But dayum, Donny Canali had given off *I'm crushing on you* vibes strong enough to cloud any man's early warning system. Unless I was just so attracted to him myself, I'd seen what I wanted to see. Shit!

I opened the back door into the kitchen of the small, pleasant California ranch house I'd bought for Mam and Gala in a little town called Florinda. It had nice sidewalks for strolls and friendly neighbors and was a half hour from the McClellan base where I worked. The housing prices were more affordable than most places in California, so I'd been able to buy it on my military pension and Cal Fire salary together. I'd given Ma and my sister Gala the main house while I took the apartment.

Gala sat at the table, her head buried in a book with her dark curly hair poufing around her face. Her love of reading, along with mine, had been instilled by my mam, who lived with her head in stories and tales.

As my nose led me to the coffee maker, Gala looked up from her story with a snarky smile. "Oh dear, you look like a few miles of unpaved road."

I snorted at her, poured my coffee, black, into a cup from the cabinet, and plopped my butt into the chair opposite her. "I think I mentally walked those unpaved roads when I was supposed to be sleeping." I shook my head and took a big mouthful of coffee. "Where's Mam?"

"Dying her hair, I think." She grinned and sipped the weird green mixture of spinach, kale, and the good lord knew what else that she chugged every morning as part of her after-cancer care regimen. The sight of it gave me a little pang—the one I always got when reminded of her bout with cancer. I studied her face, but her coloring looked good today, a healthy mocha and not the sickly green latte she'd had for a year or so. Gala was fine.

"Is she keeping her hair purple?" I asked, forcing a smile.

"I guess we'll know when we see it." She looked up. "Are you going back to Ione today?"

"No. The ground liaison course is over."

I must have frowned, because she asked "Uh-oh. What happened? Did the training go badly?"

"What? Oh no, the class went fine."

She cocked her head. "So what's the trouble, boyo?"

I gave a soft laugh. I loved when Gala used my Irish expressions. Of course, in my case, they came from my da, but Gala had a different father, though no one knew who he was. After Mam left my da, she'd had what she called her "wild period"— Gala was the result, dark to my fair, delicate to my big and sturdy. She was eleven years younger than me, and I'd been her father in many ways.

I ran a hand through my hair. "The trouble is I made a mistake, and I feel bad about it. But it's no big thing."

A crease popped between her arched brows, and I squeezed her arm in reassurance.

"That's not like you. You're a *let it go* guy. If this mistake kept you awake last night, it must be serious." I shrugged, but her frown deepened. "A guy?"

I nodded. "I made a play for a guy I thought was gay and found out he was straight."

"Define play."

I sighed. "I kissed the dude."

"And I'm guessing it wasn't a gentle peck either. You don't do anything halfway, Dell."

I groaned guiltily.

"Well damn."

"And on top of that, he was one of my students at the training."

"Double damn!" She sat back, surveying me. "That doesn't sound like you. If anything, you're too cautious and don't approach guys who are practically waving flags to get your attention."

I raised a brow. "How do you know that, squirt?"

She had dimples you could lose a pencil in, and she flashed them. "From Ty, of course."

"He's a blabbermouth."

"So you must have really liked this guy if you macked on him that hard."

"Yeah, well, maybe so, but too bad for me. Now go get your jacket, we'll see your doc, and then I need to get to work."

"Okay, I guess." She got up grudgingly, set her book aside, and carried her grungy, green-slimed glass to the sink. Way too many doctors in her life made her edgy and tentative about a lot of things. Finding out the results of her latest CAT scan was at the top of the list of scary.

"Should I go check on Mam?" I asked.

"No. I will. I'm pretty sure when I get home, I'll be cleaning purple and green dye out of the bathroom for the rest of the day."

An hour later, after a clean checkup reviewing her latest scan that had us both smiling, I dropped her off at the house again. Gala got out of the Jeep and turned to me. "Why did you think that dude was gay? He must have done something to give you that impression, right?"

Visions of those dark eyes gazing at me to the exclusion of everyone else in the room flashed in my mind, but I said, "No. I just got all hot and bothered over him and lost my judgment. He had a touch of hero worship, I guess, and I misread it."

She leaned over and kissed my cheek. "He couldn't have picked a better hero. See you tonight for dinner. I'm making healthy lasagna, but don't worry. You won't taste a single vegetable."

The glow I got from Gala almost pushed the recriminations out of my mind as I drove to McClellan, my fire bomber base. Since I had heavy family responsibilities, I'd joined Cal Fire with the stipulation that I be stationed somewhere I could settle with my family and buy a house. McClellan fit the bill and worked perfectly since the CL-515 was hangared there. I was also good at program planning, field operations, and pilot training from my years in the military, so I did some of the work of an Aviation Officer while technically being a Fire Pilot. Win/win all around.

I parked and swung into my office, a well-appointed cubicle in the Aviation Operations building. After checking my emails, I pulled on coveralls and strode out to the maintenance hangar to check on some tweaks we were making to a couple of the older CL aircraft.

"Hey, Murphy." Jed Johnson, the most senior of the maintenance engineers, hailed me from where he and a couple other guys, Phil Burns and KC somebody, were looking at plans. "How'd the training go? Did you get those guys whipped into shape?"

"Bet your ass." I grinned as if I hadn't a care in the world.

We poured over the plans for several minutes and then KC, a cute guy in his twenties with a roving eye that didn't seem to discriminate gender, said, "Who'd you get for ground liaison? Any good ones?" His mischievous grin suggested the good part of his question might have more to do with chest size than firefighting skill.

"All the stations sent their best people," I said neutrally.

"Any feeeemale firefighters?"

I had to chuckle. "We had three. Audrey somebody, Janine Smith, and Marjorie Reynolds. Marjorie struck me as super smart and focused."

He snorted. "Yes and she could bench press me."

"That's because you're such a lightweight." I gave him a snarky smile. "Anyway, all firefighters are strong. It's hauling all that equipment."

"Yeah, well I like my equipment haulers to have a little more equipment." He laughed again.

"I've met Janine Smith. Tahoe station. Nice work if you can get it," said Phil dryly.

"Oh yeah, Janine is hot," laughed KC, mind right back in the gutter.

I plastered on my most casual expression. "Among the men, we had one of the Canalis."

"No shit. Did you get the gay one?" A lot of guys would have asked that question derisively, but not KC. He really wanted to know.

No, I really really hadn't. I shook my head. "Donny Canali was in the class."

"Dayum, he's hard-core. And stupid handsome like all the Canalis. Good firefighter but a touchy bastard."

I looked at the plans. "So who is the gay one?"

"That'd be Mike," said Phil. "The youngest. He'd only been with Cal Fire for a few weeks before saving a bunch of civies in the Crest Lake fire. Got a Medal of Valor for that." His tone was admiring, and I appreciated his words, like he was not-so subtly informing us that Mike was more than just *the gay one.*

"Sounds like one badass firefighter." I gave Phil a look of thanks.

But KC was still musing. "You know, before Mike came out, I'd have said Donny probably rolled gays in the alley, but he's loosened up since then, I hear. Real defensive of his brother. Still, I wouldn't want to piss him off."

*No shit, Sherlock.*

*Way to pick 'em, Murphy.*

————

I needed a shower to clean out my brain, but all I managed was my body. Towel in hand, I stepped out of a quick wash down in the men's barracks and hurried to get into my uniform. We had brass to entertain.

It had been a fucking week since the training session ended, since I'd managed to piss off the highly pissoffable Donny Canali, and I still couldn't get the SOB out of my head. Why? Jesus, he was straight for starters, and, in the immortal words of KC, a touchy bastard. It was fucking clear that I'd misread his admiration as more and—

Fuck! I threw the boot I'd been pulling on against the wall. I wasn't that stupid. I hadn't misread it. I just plain fucking hadn't. I knew sexual attraction when I saw it, and it had been crawling out of Donny Canali's eyes and landing on me.

I took a deep breath and retrieved the boot. Okay, so he was in denial. Denial? Jesus. He'd been claimed by the goddamned fucking ring of Mordor.

I sighed as I stood. Yeah and I wasn't joining the Fellowship of the Ring any time soon.

If Donny Canali was gay and that deep in denial, the best thing I could do for myself was to stay far, far away.

As I walked out onto the tarmac, Ty fell in beside me.

I pulled my head out of my ass and said, "Hey, boyo, what up?"

"I've been reviewing the ground support instruction manual with some of the visiting teams from the fire stations." He shook his head. "Good we're doing this. That thing is way out of date." He nodded toward the collection of people standing in front of the CL-515 hangar. "This should be fun. Get to talk about our baby."

I nodded and forced more enthusiasm into my smile.

A big group of brass and personnel from the various Northern California fire stations stood outside the hangar as Ty and I walked to the front of the group and joined Chief Montgomery, our CO on the tanker base. He gave us a nod and started introductions, talking about me, Ty, and the aircraft. Ty took over and explained the basic characteristics of the plane, and then it was my turn.

I led the visitors up onto scaffolding we'd constructed just so they could get a good view inside the CL-515. As they filed by, I explained the features of the cockpit.

One of the chiefs, from Tahoe I thought, asked, "How much water can this thing drop? It seems so small and compact."

I nodded. "It's got a 1,621-gallon tank capacity, sir, and because it's so maneuverable, can perform as many as one hundred and fifteen water drops a day, which adds up to over 182,000 gallons."

"Wow, that's impressive."

"Massive return on investment, sir. That's why it's called the First Responder and the fire bomber."

His eyebrows rose, the exact impression I wanted him to have. This aircraft cost a bundle but did so much more than it cost.

The people filed by and I forced my focus. These guys decided the bottom line, and if we were going to get more 515s, we needed their support.

In the last group of visitors on the walk-through, a handsome older man with salt and pepper black hair and a gaze that crackled with intelligence and interest stuck out his hand. "Mr. Murphy, I'm Chief Angelo Canali from Oroville station."

My heart leaped into my throat and my gut at the same time. Oh yeah, I recognized those dark eyes. I stuck out my hand. "Honored, sir."

"The honor's mine, son. You and your copilot literally saved my men's lives during the Sierra City fire. One of those men happened to be my son. I'm forever grateful."

"Glad we could help." I swallowed. "You got to see the First Responder in action that day." And I fell back into my spiel.

Canali's group moved down the tour and I finally ran out of people.

When I trudged down the stairway, Ty was standing there. "One more dog-and-pony done. People sure did like the baby, didn't they?"

"Yeah." We walked out of the hangar, and the warmth of sun on my face felt good. I arched my neck up to catch the rays as I walked.

"So you met Chief Canali?" He spoke softly.

I nodded.

"Looks just like his son. Dayum. But what they say about the alpha male factory over there sure ain't exaggeration." He chuckled, then glanced at me when I didn't. "How you holding up?"

After our maneuver that night at Tilly's, I'd told Ty things looked promising with Donny. Then after my gaff the next morning, I'd just texted him that I was wrong. Donny wasn't gay. No other information provided. That's all he knew and, despite us sharing a lot of secrets, I'd just as soon be light on the deets. Mostly because it was embarrassing.

"I'm okay. Just a little tired."

"Things all right at home?"

I plastered on a smile. "If you don't count my mam's new purple-and-green do." My grin warmed. "Actually, Gala's latest scan came back clean, so that's a huge relief."

He gave me a high five.

We got to the large open conference room that had been set up with refreshments for the guests and a low dais with chairs for me, Ty, Jed Johnson, and Chief Montgomery. We grabbed some iced tea, crammed a half sandwich into our mouths, and climbed onto the stage to answer questions for the next half an hour, during which my gaze constantly drifted to Chief Canali. Apparently, for my hungry eyes, any Canali would do in a storm.

When the Q and A was finally over, I gathered up my notepads to escape to my car and Gala's healthy lasagna. As I walked off the dais, a deep voice I immediately recognized called, "Pilot Murphy."

I turned and smiled, feeling oddly embarrassed to be talking to Donny's father when I'd been thinking about his son continuously for a week. "Oh, hello, Chief. Have another question?"

"Mr. Murphy—"

"Please call me Dell."

"With pleasure. And I'm Angie."

I nodded. As if I'd ever be that informal with him.

He said, "You may have heard that I've got three fire-fighter sons and assorted other relatives in Cal Fire. We live in a little town in the mountains named Resolute."

"The Canali clan is legendary, sir."

His face glowed with obvious pride. "So my crazy family gets together in big groups of a Sunday, and we like to invite special people to join us. Next Sunday, I've invited a few of our colleagues including your Chief Montgomery and your copilot to join us for a buffet lunch and some good conversation. Basketball could also be involved. I'm pretty sure the Warriors are playing." He chuckled as my heart slammed against my ribs. "We'd love for you to be there so all of us can thank you for what you did for Donny and my guys."

"Just doing my job, sir." I barely got the words out.

"I understand. But few have the flat-out skill to have maneuvered that challenging terrain to get those boys out safely and all of the Canalis want to thank you. Besides, I know you're new to the area and you'll get a chance to get to know some folks."

I swallowed hard. Damn. Half my brain, that could have been the small brain, longed to set eyes on Donny again, but my actual IQ screamed in warning.

Chief Canali saw my hesitation and added, "If next Sunday doesn't work, just say the word and we'll change the date. After all, this gathering is a lot about you."

Oh right. Say you're not available, Murphy, and he'll change the date on my chief and every other person he's invited! Fuck! "I'd be more than honored, Chief Canali."

"Angie." He grinned and took my hand.

I managed to smile back.

"Excellent. I'll be sending all the particulars to Chief Montgomery and he'll pass them to you and Ty. Look forward to having you with us." With that, he turned and walked back to a group that included Montgomery.

Ty walked up beside me looking shell-shocked. "Uh, did you know we somehow saved a Canali or two in that Sierra City shindig?"

I stared at the floor. "Yeah. I might have heard that."

"Jesus H. A whole afternoon hanging out with the brass. How uncomfortable can you get?"

I looked up at him but resisted saying he had no fucking idea.

# FIVE

## DONNY

"What's up with you? You seem a little off this week. You coming down with something?" Ma felt my forehead for fever as I tried to pour myself a cup of coffee.

I pulled away. "I'm not sick. I'm fine."

"Want me to make an appointment with Dr. Knox?"

I gave her a look. "Ma, I'm not sick. Why would I want to go see Dr. Knox? He giving away cotton candy or something?"

She made a face. "Men! It never hurts to get checked out."

"Yeah, it does. It's a waste of time. Not sick." I kissed her on the cheek to soften my words. "You worry too much, Ma."

"With a husband and five boys all determined to risk their lives every day, what's not to worry?" tsked Ma. "Want me to make you some eggs fresh? Those are cold."

"Nope. These are fine. Waste not, want not, like Nonna says."

As usual, Ma had made scrambled eggs, toast, and bacon for breakfast, and put out yogurt, cereal, and fruit. I'd made it over to the main house before she'd cleared it away. Pa and probably a half-dozen other family members had come and gone earlier, grazing the pickings down, but there was still enough left for a big plate.

I sat down to eat while Ma bustled around.

"You off shift today?" Ma asked.

"Yeah. Don't go in 'til tomorrow."

"A nice day off! You should rest. Mike went down to Sacramento. He and Shane are doing something today."

My ears perked up. "Oh yeah? Did he say when he'd be back?"

"He said not to wait for him at dinner. As if this family would ever politely wait for anything when food's involved." She chuckled.

Nice. My roomie was out for the whole day. Not that I minded sharing a house with Mike. We Canalis had a family compound in Resolute, with a bunch of separate houses and cabins my dad, brothers, and uncles had built. The little one-story ranch Mike and I shared was just a short walk away from the main house, where Ma and Pa lived, and where my sister Tessa had an apartment in the daylight basement. Having family around all the time was great, but today, I could use some peace and quiet.

It had been a week since I'd flown out of that Ione training class like a bat outta hell, and it was still a splinter in my chest that bugged me 24-7. I couldn't stop picking at it.

For instance, why hadn't I said something early on? When we were at the Waystation shooting the shit, it would have been so easy to say *Hey, I heard you're gay. So is my brother, Mike.* Or I could've commented on a hot chick in the room. Something. Anything. Only I'd *liked* the attention Dell was giving me. I'd liked it a lot.

I couldn't blame him for reaching the conclusion that he had. I was at least halfway responsible, jonesing after him like an eager puppy. But then, it shouldn't be a big deal anyway.

So what if he got the wrong idea and made a pass? It wasn't the end of the fucking world.

Except it felt like it.

It'd taken a lot of effort to smile and talk up the class to everyone at the station who wanted to hear about it—especially Chief Reiger who expected a full report. The class had been great, though, and I'd picked up enough of it to bullshit my way through. Still. It was hard to act like nothing had happened when I was so freaked out.

"You got any more training coming up?" Ma came in with a cup of coffee to sit down by me at the table.

"Nope. Just regular duty."

Ma looked disappointed. "At least when my sons are at Ione, I know they're safe. Did you hear about Uncle Ricky? His partner retired, so he's got a new one. He was over last night and told us all about it. The new partner's from narcotics and he's young. Ricky's not happy about it."

Uncle Ricky was my dad's brother, younger than him by fourteen whole years. Nonno and Nonna had had a big family too. Ricky was a detective for the Chico police. I remembered how happy he'd been when he'd gotten that promotion. The whole family had had a celebratory dinner. I'd been a senior in high school, and I'd bragged about it to my friends.

"It's good to shake things up now and then," I said. "Bet Uncle Ricky'll be tight with him before you know it."

"Yeah." Ma smiled. "That's what I told him. Ricky's a softie underneath. He'll take that boy under his wing."

"I doubt he's a *boy*, Ma, if he's a police detective."

She waved that away. "Tessa has to fly to Kansas City for some corporate retreat thing. That's next month. *Kansas City.* Who wants to go to Kansas City? They couldn't have a corporate retreat in the Bahamas?"

As Ma went on spilling the family tea, my mind wandered. And it went right back to Dell, like a boomerang.

If it had been some random guy who'd kissed me, like at a bar, maybe I could have laughed it off. But every time I tried to go down the *I'll just forget it and never see him again* route, I hit roadblocks. Dell was a star Cal Fire pilot and now I was ground liaison for my station. So we'd be working together at some point. And then there was the fact that I still admired the hell out of him. It had been exciting to be around him. Maybe if I hadn't reacted like such a tool, we could have forgotten the kiss and been friends. But now he probably thought I was immature and stupid. Maybe I was.

"What are you thinking about so hard?" Ma asked loudly.

I blinked at her. "Oh. Just work stuff."

"Something wrong at work?" She frowned.

"No, nothing's wrong, Ma. It's fine." I got up and carried my plate to the kitchen, rinsed it, and put it in the dishwasher.

Ma came in with her coffee cup. "You need anything from me today? I was gonna go shopping with Carlotta."

"Nah. Have fun. Thanks for breakfast."

"I love you, Donny!" Ma said abruptly as I left the kitchen. Man, she must really think something was wrong. Not that she didn't say *I love you* a lot, but this seemed like a Band-Aid thrown across the room.

"Love you, too, Ma. See you later."

As I walked back to my place, I thought about going for a run. But, no. I was in serious need of release of another kind, and I should use the privacy at home while I had it. Not that I didn't whack off when Mike was in the house. Hey, I had a lock on my bedroom door, earphones, and I could be quiet. Ish. But if he'd be out all day, I could let loose and take my time, be a little loud if I wanted to be. And man, I seriously needed that. I was wound tighter than a broken watch.

I put the chain on the front door just to make sure no family member barged in. I went into my bedroom, closed the blinds, and set my laptop on a little side table next to a comfy old chair in my room. I took off everything. I liked it that way —liked to have full access. Then I set a bottle of lube and an old towel I kept around for just this purpose on the table and slathered a palm-full of the lube on my dick, just to get ready. Not too much. That baby was cocked and loaded.

With a tingle in all the right places, I scrolled through the saved videos on my hard drive. They all had a similar theme. I definitely had a kink. Just thinking about it had me hard before I even cranked one up. Oh yeah, I needed this.

I propped one foot up on the seat and started to run fingers up and down my inner thighs and over my chest while the video started.

*"What are you doing in my apartment?"* demanded Construc-tion Guy. *He'd just kicked off his boots and taken off his tool belt after coming home when he saw the redheaded landlady trying to sneak past him. He stepped between her and the door, looking menacing.*

*"I was just… uh… checking your stove. Isn't your stove on the fritz?" She blinked coyly.* Ooh, she was so clearly lying.

*"Hell no." He took another step toward her. "You were sniffing around my stuff, weren't you? What, you get off on my dirty laun-dry? I see the way you look at me."*

*"No! No, I was just—"*

*Construction Guy wrapped his fingers up in Landlady's long ponytail. "Don't lie to me." His voice was sexy now but still commanding.*

*"I… I'm sorry. I have been watching you. I didn't mean any harm."*

*"Guess you'll have to make it up to me."*

*"Oh, yes. Let me make it up to you!"*

*He tugged on her ponytail and she went to her knees. She looked at the bulge in his pants. "I can take care of this." She petted it.*

Fuck yeah. Jesus, I was so hard and so horny, I couldn't resist a stroke. I wanted to make it last, but that wasn't gonna happen today. It felt good to be so turned on. I needed this.

*Zzzip.* Down went his fly and Construction Guy's dick sprang out, hot and big. A jolt of lust zapped through me. Damn. I'd watched this video before, but I always forgot how much he was packing. Landlady licked the tip, eyes raised, and that sent another wave of pleasure through me.

*"You're gonna take this." Construction Guy held the back of her head and fed his dick into her mouth—a little at a time, teasing.*

Oh fuck! I jerked my hands off myself and scrambled to pause the video. I'd about lost it right there, and I'd barely started. I leaned back in the chair, eyes closed. Deep breaths. I was gonna make this fucking last if it killed me.

I loved it when the guy was tough and demanding, but you could still tell, the way he touched the woman or whatever, that he was being gentle. I couldn't take real abuse toward women. No thank you. Ma hadn't raised that guy. It wasn't easy to find videos in that sweet spot—big, tough guys who knew what they wanted and were all commanding but weren't mean. Construction Guy was hot.

Wait.

I mean, it was hot watching him with that redheaded landlady. *She* was hot.

The way he fed her his dick. Dayum.

*Two times two is four. Four times four is eight, I mean sixteen. Eight times eight is sixteen. Sixteen times sixteen….*

Ugg. I wasn't a fucking mathematician. Think about spoiled milk instead. Or sewers.

I'd tried to be a tough guy like that with women when I got them in a bedroom. Tried to act like the macho guys did in the videos that turned me on so much. Only it never quite worked. Either the woman got huffy or she tried to out-aggro me. And even when they played along, *I* didn't feel right. Like my body knew I was faking it. And that idea was so disheartening, it was wilt city. Sometimes I had to close my eyes and imagine the videos I liked so I could get through it without embarrassing myself.

I *was* a tough guy. I don't know why I couldn't just be myself in the bedroom and have that work, like every other guy on the planet. It pissed me off.

One friend I'd talked to about it said maybe I watched too much porn. He said porn can be addictive and make regular real-life sex feel unsatisfying or something. He told me to go cold turkey for a few months.

But fuck it, watching porn was the only time I really got to feel totally turned on with no pressure and no expectations. It was the only way I got off that felt really good, like sex was supposed to feel.

Well, that train of thought was a boner-killer. I started the video again and stroked myself lightly as Landlady gave Construction Guy a blow job.

*Fuck yeah. That must feel so good.*

Construction Guy abruptly pulled away and gripped Landlady's arms, bringing her to her feet.

*"That's good, baby. I'm gonna fuck you so hard. But first, gimme a kiss."*

Construction Guy held her and kissed her real deep, owning her.

Like Dell had kissed me.

Dell. Fuck. He was the real deal, not a fake muscle dude roleplaying in a porn video. He was tough, and cocky, and all man. A real-life hero. But when I'd pushed him away, he'd backed right off. He'd never force me. He'd never force anyone. Why should he? Anyone would want Dell, and if they didn't, they could move the fuck to the back of the line. That was the kind of guy Dell was.

*But what if he* had *insisted? What if he'd taken control and guided me to my knees on that scree?*

I stopped that train of thought dead. *No.* But the feeling it sparked stayed frozen in my brain. I squeezed my eyes shut, trying to hang on to the electric thrill it sent through me, pumping faster. Being pushed gently but firmly to my knees. Oh fuck. Goddamn.

*"You're gonna take this."*

Dell's cocky, white-toothed smile, green-brown eyes boring into mine as he looked down at me, big hands firm but gentle, cupping the back of my neck, the kind of leader you'd never say no to because you just wanted to be theirs.

I came so hard, I cried out and curled up on the chair, jerking and shuddering. Jesus, it hadn't felt that amazing in ages. Sweet aftershocks rolled through me, one after another, making me shake and moan. Man. *Man.*

I finally came down enough to blink my eyes open. Construction Guy was pounding Landlady on the couch now, but I couldn't watch any more. I grabbed the towel to wipe off my hands and slammed the lid of my laptop closed.

I pulled on sweatpants and padded into the kitchen to get a glass of water. My limbs felt loose and heavy, and my heart was still beating fast.

Sipping water, I stared out the kitchen window at the little lawn that dropped off behind our house, and at the woods beyond.

I didn't want to think about what I'd just done—or what I'd thought about while doing it.

*I'm not gay.* I'd never been into gay guy stuff—like Shane with his decorating. Or shopping. Or whatever. I'd never been into gay *guys*. They made me uncomfortable. Though, I had to admit, Shane was real effeminate, and having him around had made me realize guys like that could be tough and smart-talking and brave. Shane was all those things. Hell, he'd won the Medal of Valor for the work he'd done helping Mike during the Crest Lake fire. And he was just a civie. I'd never won a fucking Medal of Valor. But still, Mike could have Shane and more power to him. Me? I'd never want to kiss a guy like Shane. Ever.

Therefore I wasn't gay.

End of.

*Dell's gay. And he's not like that.*

"Arg!" I punched the side of the fridge. Maybe pain would wake me the fuck up.

I *couldn't* be gay. It'd kill Pa, and I'd never do that to him. Anyway, I liked girls fine. Just fucking fine!

I had to stop thinking about Dell Murphy, that was all. Exorcise the guy from my head for good. Maybe I could do a reverse Tito and go to New York for a year or two, stay with some of the Brooklyn Canalis. Or, I dunno, join the foreign legion.

*Just stay away from him. Tell Reiger to assign someone else to be ground liaison. Start seeing a new woman. Maybe a decent one this time—that'd be a change.*

Shit. If I dated a nice girl, Ma would latch onto her in a heartbeat like she had Tony's wife, Viv, or Gabe's girlfriend, Anita, or even Shane. And then I'd be married before I knew what'd hit me. At least, dating the raunchy women I did, there was no danger of that happening.

*Would that be so bad though? Maybe you* need *to get married. That'd sure solve your Dell problem.*

Except, would it?

I didn't know what the fuck would solve my Dell problem except plenty of time and distance. One thing I did know for sure: I could never see Dell Murphy again.

# SIX

## DELL

"Jesus, where are you taking us?" Ty made the left onto the twisty mountain road that I'd just called out as our turn, but he frowned. "Are you sure this is right?"

I peered out the windshield of his racy little Fiat and nodded. "Yep. There was actually a small sign on my side that said Resolute with an arrow a couple minutes ago."

"Frigging Helm's Deep," he muttered.

I laughed. I'd spent my life awash in my mam's obsession with the Lord of the Rings—we'd spent whole days watching the series when I was a kid—and my brain never let go of the analogies. Ty had acquired his indoctrination over the last few years as Mam dragged him into marathon viewings of the series multiple times.

Ty grinned. "Don't you love the town name of Resolute for a family of firefighters? Sounds like a romance novel."

"Yeah." I forced myself not to frown. Associating anything romantic with the name Canali just made my gut tighten more than it already was. For a solid week, I'd been writing this event off as no big deal, and for every one of those seven days, my body wouldn't cooperate with my good intentions. I was editing a new training manual at work, and I noticed my belly felt like a drum full of bats trying to escape. In the middle of the night, I'd wake up with a raging boner, imagining fucking damned Donny Canali. I was going nuts, which was serious crap for a guy who felt fine flying what Ty described as *four inches above wildfires upside down.* Also a guy with a different man in every town and no regrets about any of them.

"Uh, Dell? Can I ask you a question, man?"

"Of course." I glanced at him like *who are you*? Ty asked me pretty much anything that popped into his head all the time.

"Are you nervous about this party?" He held up a hand. "No offense. I mean there's no reason why you should be nervous about going anywhere or meeting anyone. Come on. You're Dell Murphy. But you just seem kind of squirrely."

I sighed. Maybe it was time to come clean. "Truthfully, the morning I spent with Donny Canali at the end of the training didn't go exactly smoothly and we parted on edgy terms. I wasn't planning on seeing him again and certainly not in front of Chief Montgomery and the whole freaking Canali family."

"Jesus, what happened? Did you punch Donny out?"

"No. Close. I kissed him."

Ty stared at me for a second, then snapped his head toward the window.

I said, "Slow down. You're here. In Resolute, I mean."

"How can you tell?"

"Stop sign." I pointed.

He stomped on the brake and stared around. "Look at this place. I think you made it up in one of your tales. Like maybe a hobbit's going to walk out of that park."

Okay, I had to admit—Resolute was kind of quaint. Ahead of us was a town square, complete with a statue of some guy in the middle surrounded by trees and benches. Streets lined the square and situated on them were shops, like the Resolute General Store and the Resolute Café, all done in a folksy mountain theme. There were even barrels of goods standing on the sidewalk. "Yeah. It's the Shire, all right." I consulted my phone. "We go through town and out the other side for about a quarter mile."

"The town part might take thirty seconds." He moved slowly to the next stop sign and then was essentially through the downtown and into a section with pretty houses along residential streets.

"Keep going."

Ty nodded and pressed the accelerator. "Tell me about the kiss."

"He didn't like it. He got pissed and yelled he wasn't gay."

"Well shit, who could have predicted that? I mean the dude looked at you through the whole training like you were ice cream and he couldn't wait to have a sundae."

I gave him a quick glance. "You noticed that? Good. I thought I was losing my fucking mind."

"Nah, man. The whole time we were at Tilly's, he never took his eyes off of you. Honestly, I think that's why Janine ended up with me. She knew you're gay and I think she figured Canali was too."

"You're no second choice, my friend."

"Yeah, but I saw Canali. No illusions, man."

I laughed with him, but my brain was cheering from his confirmation. Not crazy. Not. "Regardless, he's got to be so self-deluded, he'll never get his head out of his ass."

"That means he's no good to anybody, male or female. What a freaking waste."

I raised a hand. "Slow down, it's around here some-where." I pointed to a partially concealed gravel driveway off the road, and he took it.

He glanced over as he maneuvered the winding lane. "So you're worried about how the dude's going to act around you?"

I nodded as my stomach flipped. I didn't mention I was worried about how I'd act around him.

About a quarter mile off the road, we came to a gravel parking area full of cars in front of a huge sprawling house framed by trees. Down a couple side pathways from this main structure, there were smaller buildings like cottages.

Ty and I slid out of his car and stared toward the house. Ty gave my shoulder a slap. "No worries, man. I got your back. Cal Fire's lucky to have you and so are the frigging Canalis."

I laughed at his ridiculous and flattering support and tried to settle into comfort I didn't quite feel.

The moment I knocked, the big wooden door flew open to reveal a medium-height woman, probably in her fifties, with curly dark shoulder-length hair and a brilliant smile. "Welcome to the Canalis. I'll bet you're the pilots, aren't you? I'm Lucille and we're so happy to have you in our home."

There was no way not to smile back. She was an embrace just standing there. "Thank you, ma'am. I'm Dell Murphy and this is my copilot, Ty Chan."

"Aren't you two handsome? I heard about the amazing thing you did for Brian, Jordy, and Donny. We'll always be grateful."

Chief Canali appeared beside her and slid an arm around her shoulders. "Right. We're so grateful, we're going to keep you standing outside all day while we thank you." He laughed. "Let them in, Lucy. Share the wealth."

Mrs. Canali laughed too. "Sorry. I'm just so delighted you're here."

She stepped back, and we followed the chief into a big room full of people. I recognized Chief Montgomery standing beside an attractive woman who I assumed was his wife. There were two other top dogs from McClellan, but most of the people had to be Canalis. Everywhere I looked was shiny black hair, dark eyes, square jaws, and cleft chins. Be still my foolish libido. The Canali women, who were equally attractive, congregated in a large kitchen, half open to the living room, separated by a huge island covered with bowls and plates and baskets of food.

But nowhere amidst the accumulation of masculine pulchritude did I see the most gorgeous one of all. Donny wasn't there. Even while my stupid heart dropped in disappointment, I took a small breath of relief.

Chief Canali led us around the room where people were talking in groups. A basketball game played with no sound on a big TV, and several men stood watching it. The chief said, "This is my oldest son, Gabe, my brother, Ricky, and my nephew, Tito."

Both Ty and I shook hands with them. Gabe was almost as tall as Donny, with heavier features, Ricky—*damn*—looked like someone had reincarnated Cary Grant at the age of thirty-five or forty, and Tito was a more refined, lighter-framed version of the Canali model with a cupid's bow mouth. He was obviously super shy. He never met my eyes.

After meeting a couple more Canalis including the chief's other son, Tony, who must have gotten his mom's welcoming personality, and his wife, Viv, whose fair hair stood out in the mass of brunets, we made it to the edge of the kitchen and met a blur of females including a cute daughter, an aunt, and a grandmother. And then there were two young guys.

I smiled and stuck out my hand as the chief said, "This is my youngest son, Mike, and, uh, his, uh, boyfriend, Shane."

*Finally.* "I'm happy to meet you both."

"You, too, Pilot Murphy. I've heard a lot about you." Mike's gaze was curious and friendly, and he shook my hand firmly. Second only to Donny, he won the Canali looks lottery, although the chief's brother Ricky was more up my alley.

Shane, a tall pretty twink in his early twenties with a mass of curly hair, stood out in this gaggle of Canali alpha males like a unicorn in a herd of wild mustangs. In fact, his pink T-shirt even featured a unicorn barfing rainbows emblazoned in gold to match his sneakers. He pressed his hands together. "You're the pilots who saved Donny, aren't you?"

"So we hear," said Ty with a smile.

I said, "We're the pilots that flew over the fire line in Sierra City and dropped water. Aka, our job." I added a smile. "And I'm really glad we helped your guys out."

Mike slapped my shoulder. "Well, we all sure appreciate it. There's only one Donny."

I nodded but didn't add that might be a good thing.

In contrast to Shane, Mike was very macho. Definitely a product of his family. But his sweet smiles and little touches to his boyfriend's back made my heart swell. Of course, Chief Canali did look a little red in the face.

The chief said, "I'll leave you two in Mike and Shane's hands. Boys, see that Dell and Ty get something to drink and some food, okay?"

"Thank you, Chief."

Chief Canali walked back to where Chief Montgomery stood.

Shane grinned. "Angelo figures I'll do a better job feeding you than any of the other guys." He leaned in. "It's the Queer Eye thing."

I snorted, and both Mike and Shane gave me a knowing smile, so they'd obviously heard I was gay too. A wave of affectionate comradery warmed me and helped loosen the band in my gut. It was heartening to see this couple in such a Cal Fire bastion.

Shane said, "What can I get you guys to drink?"

I asked for sparkling water and Ty requested beer. He offered to help, his gaze fixed on the pretty girl who'd been introduced as the chief's daughter, Tessa. Ty followed Shane into the kitchen.

As he walked away, I felt someone come up beside me and looked into the handsome face of the chief's brother, Ricky. He smiled. "I guess Shane beat me to the punch. I was going to get another drink and wanted to see if I could get you all anything."

Mike said, "Thanks, Uncle Ricky. I'm actually on hosting duty for Ma, so I'll leave you to get acquainted."

Shane came back with my sparkling water and rushed back to what appeared to be salad making. Ricky got a glass of red wine, and we strolled over to the food lineup to graze.

He said, "So you're the famous pilot."

I chuckled. "That seems to be the identifier I've acquired in the Canali family—as if Cal Fire only has one pilot."

"Hey, you helped save a Canali's life. We give our own medals." He had warm eyes and a dazzling smile.

"Are you a firefighter too?" I asked.

"Nope. I branched out. I'm a cop. Detective actually."

I scooped up some dip on a bunch of carrots and put them on a small plate. "Has anyone in the group considered becoming a violinist or a pastry chef?"

He barked a laugh. "Sounds like you've got our number. Public service, preferably as dangerous as possible, is the Canali way."

"Gotta admire that." I admired Ricky's cleft chin too.

"You wanna eat?" he asked me, a certain spark in his eyes. He waved at the table.

"Yes. Absolutely." I turned my attention to the food, but I was starting to think Mike wasn't the only *gay one* in the family. First Donny and now Uncle Ricky? Or maybe I was just totally misinterpreting the family charm.

I got a plate and scooped some meatballs onto it and added salad and lasagna. Ricky and I found seats near the hearth and continued chatting as we ate. He had interesting stories about the Chico police department, and it was a nice diversion from all my Donny obsessions of the last few weeks. Maybe this gathering wouldn't be so bad after all.

We'd just gone back to the island for another round, when the front door slammed and an all too familiar voice said, "Hey, Ma, sorry I'm late." Donny walked into the room, looked startled to see all the unfamiliar people, and then his gaze connected with me. A red flush traveled up his neck and turned his cheeks bright pink.

Ricky laughed. "Donny's been on California shift all week and we've barely seen him. Poor guy. Comes in expecting to put his feet up and have a big dinner and a game and finds out he's got to be a charming host."

Shit. That likely meant that not only didn't Donny know there was a party, but almost certainly he had no idea I'd be there. I braced for explosives.

Ricky raised a hand. "Hey, Donny."

California shift for firefighters was 24 hours on and 24 off for six days straight, followed by four days off. We didn't follow that schedule at McClellan, but the fire stations did. Donny had to be beat. Of course, he looked stupid gorgeous and the bright blush only added to it.

I inhaled slowly like I was practicing yoga. I'd been enjoying talking to Ricky and basking in the comfort of a pleasant male conversation, but one look at that fucking face and my heart pounded in my chest and cock did an Irish jig in my pants. What was his power? In a room full of handsome, he was all I could see. It went beyond his looks. Way past. There was something vulnerable in his eyes that got me. But I didn't really understand it. It wasn't like we'd had deep philosophical conversations late into the night sharing our hearts. We barely knew each other. But the sight of him, the sound of his voice made me vibrate like a fucking tuning fork.

I wanted to run out the door, and oh, I wanted to stay.

I forced myself to look away and scoop up more meatballs. Ricky said something and nudged my arm, which meant I could talk to him and try to ignore Donny. Good luck.

From the corner of my eye, I saw Chief Canali rush over and give his shocked-looking son a clap on the shoulder. "Hey, Donny, come say hi to Chief Montgomery from McClellan. And you already know Pilot Dell Murphy and his copilot Ty Chan, but I'm sure you'll be glad to welcome them to our home."

If I hadn't been so intimately involved, I'd have laughed. Obviously Chief Canali had noticed that Donny wasn't exactly responding with delight at seeing the gathered crowd and all kinds of subtle messages were being transmitted. The bottom line from Dad was *step up and be hospitable or I'll take you behind the woodshed.*

Yeah, I'd like to take Donny behind a woodshed.

I turned my back on Donny—let him stew in his own juice —and talked some more with Ricky. The big handsome detective had a fun, vaguely flirtatious way about him, but half my attention focused on where Donny was in the room. I knew the second he started toward us with his father.

Chief Canali said, "Murphy, you remember my son Donny."

I must have given myself away because for a second, Ricky got a funny expression, like he was sorry for me. Jesus, was I that transparent? But I turned with a smile. "Of course. One of our best students. Good to see you again, Canali."

Donny composed his expression, but it seemed fucking hard. He gave Ricky an angry glance, and then he said, "Good to see you too." For a second, he just stared awkwardly. Then he said, "I should say hi to Ty, but I don't see him."

Ricky said, "I think he's getting to know the Canalis by way of Tessa. They took their plates and went out back."

"Ah. Okay." Donny's smile wouldn't have paid for a carnival ride it was so phony. "I'll go say hello." Like someone set his tail on fire, Donny crossed the room and was out the double doors I assumed led to the backyard.

Shit. He was freaking out that I was there. I needed to bail before the hothead did something stupid. A quick glance at my watch showed Ty and I had been there over an hour. If I did some seed-planting, maybe we could get out of there. I murmured to Ricky, "Actually, Ty and I won't be able to stay much longer. I take care of my mam and sister and they have some plans for me later today." It was total chickenshit using my family as my excuse, but any coop in a storm.

"Oh, that's too bad. Lucille makes amazing desserts."

I grinned at my last bite of meatball. "If these are any indication, I'm sad already." Chief Montgomery was across the room and it wouldn't do to cut out without speaking to him and his wife, so I excused myself from Ricky, had a short conversation with Chiefs Montgomery and Canali and then headed for the back door. I stopped on the pretty outside deck, but didn't see Ty so I pulled out my phone to text him my sitrep.

*Time to go. Not sure Donny can maintain enough cool to make it much longer without a coronary.*

The bubbles bounced for a minute, and his text said, *Hanging with Tessa. Making my goodbyes. Meet at car. Agree on Donny. He stormed by like a Valkyrie riding into war. Yowza.*

Pocketing my phone, I looked around for an exit that would let me leave gracefully without running the gauntlet inside. There was a path leading off from the house that looked likely, and I followed it. It led back into the trees, but appeared it might come out near the parking lot.

I picked up my pace, trotted around a curve and wham! I slammed right into a body. As I staggered back, I blinked. Oh crap. Of course, who else would it be in this fucking fairy tale?

I started to say something funny, but Donny turned red in

the face. "What the fuck are you doing? Are you stalking me?"

I clenched my jaw and relaxed my fists. *Be a grownup here, Murphy.* "Don't flatter yourself. I was invited by Chief Canali and I knew my own chief would be in attendance so it wasn't something I could refuse."

He took a pugnacious step forward. "Oh right. You probably figured there were other Canalis like Uncle Ricky you could hit on, right? Well, I've got news for you, bucko. He doesn't like guys either!"

The veins on Donny's temples bulged and all my grownup resolutions flew out the window. Instead of doing the intelligent thing, like walking away, I took a step forward. "And I've got news for *you*. Ricky's not as straight as you think. And neither are you!"

Donny stared at me, breathing hard. We stood there for what felt like a solid minute in an electrically charged standoff. I thought he might punch me. My blood was up so high, I'd be more than happy to fight back. I wasn't backing down, not from Donny Canali.

Suddenly, he made an inarticulate noise and lunged at me, eyes desperate. His kiss hit the side of my mouth, awkward, almost frantic. Instinctively, I slid a hand behind his head and pulled so hard he fell against me. My mouth closed over his, hard.

Unlike the last time, when he'd been shocked and unsure before he got pissed, this time his anger flamed straight into passion. His tongue battled mine and his leg wrapped around my hip. Oh baby. No asking twice.

I yanked both hands around his butt cheeks and pulled. An erection so hard it cleared up any tiny particle of doubt I might have had rammed into my groin and sent shocks of fire straight into my cock. Still kissing so deep he should have choked, I staggered toward a tree I could use to prop us up.

When his back hit the trunk, he redefined nuts, trying to

climb me like the tree we were under and that was so fine with me. Stars flashed in front of my eyes every time our cocks pressed and rubbed. I wanted more. So much more.

I pulled back enough to moan, "Is there somewhere—"

"Dell? You here?" Ty's voice drifted toward us. Donny froze—giant gorgeous deer in headlights—then pushed me so hard I stumbled and fell on my ass in the dirt. With a strangled cry, Donny ran back along the path he'd arrived on like hellhounds were after him.

Yeah. Woof.

# SEVEN

## DONNY

I paced in the backyard of my little house where no one could see me. Back and forth. Back and forth. I was hyper jacked and couldn't calm down. Fuck!

Dell had kissed me. Again.

*Yeah, after you kissed him.*

This time, I couldn't deny the way I'd reacted. I'd never been that turned on, never felt overpowering lose-your-mind lust like that. Never even knew it was possible. When he'd kissed me and pushed me up against that tree, nothing mattered. Nothing except getting more and getting off. All the reasons why I shouldn't do it vanished. All I wanted was Dell —on top of me, over me, anyway I could get him. Jesus, I'd even risked someone in the family catching us—like Gabe. Or Pa.

"Fuck!" I screamed. I pounded a fist into my palm.

The sliding door at the back of the house opened and Mike poked his head out. Crap. I thought he was at the big house. I stopped pacing and tried to force a smile.

He looked at me like I might be crazy. "What's goin' on? What happened?"

"Nothing. Why?" I stuffed my hands into the front pockets of my jeans.

His expression grew wary. "Because you're acting like a crazy person?"

"Am not."

"Uh… yes, you are."

"No I'm not."

He rolled his eyes. "Okay. Fine. You always scream obscenities and hit yourself. My mistake."

"I didn't hit myself."

Mike made a sound of frustration. "You just punched…. You know what? Never mind. I came back to grab some stuff. Shane and I are heading to Sac. Oh. And Pa told me to tell you those two pilots are taking off. In case you wanted to say goodbye or, you know, act normal or anything."

I nodded vigorously. "Cool. Good to know."

He gave me one last *you're being weird* look and closed the door.

Dell was leaving. Without letting myself think about it, I went inside, grabbed my car keys, and ran to my truck. I fired it up and pulled onto the drive that led to the front of the compound. Pulling slowly around the side of the main house, I saw a red Fiat heading down the driveway. From the back, it looked like Ty was driving and Dell was in the passenger seat. I waited until they disappeared and then followed. The Fiat turned onto the country road we lived on. I gave it a few beats and crept out onto the road myself. Thank god there were a lot of blue pickups like mine around here.

I followed them through the little town of Resolute and then onto the freeway—heading south. I hung back, letting drivers pass me, but I kept my focus on that little red sportscar.

*What are you doing?* asked a voice in my head.

I ignored it. My blood was still pounding, my dick still hard in my pants. Lust, excitement, and nerves thrummed in my veins. I couldn't stop thinking about the way he kissed me—so firm and in control. The way he'd pushed me against that tree. The way his body had felt against mine. Damn.

*I'm not gay,* said the voice in my head.

Fine. Whatever. I didn't care and wasn't gonna think about that right now.

The Fiat took 80 heading east from Sacramento. An hour after we'd left the compound, the driver pulled off the freeway at an exit for a place called Florinda. I hung back as we drove down a strip mall boulevard and he turned onto a residential street. The car stopped at a little house and Dell got out. He leaned over to say something through the open door and laughed. Okay, so the Fiat was Ty's car. It fit him, all sleek and cool.

I was glad he was dropping Dell off. It was better if Dell was alone. I wouldn't let myself think about why. I parked a few houses down across the street.

As the Fiat pulled away, Dell trotted up the stairs to what must be an apartment above the garage. He went in and shut the door without so much as a glance in my direction.

I sat there, gripping the wheel tight. Now what? The whole drive here, I'd told myself I was just blowing off steam by following him. I was going to see where he went. That was all. Give myself a chance to calm down, get some air, and then I'd drive home.

But I wasn't any calmer. I was breathing like a bull—and my dick was still hard and aching. Every time I remembered what happened in the woods—the kiss, the way he shoved me against that tree, hot lust rushed over me like it had just happened.

I couldn't do this. I shouldn't do it. I hadn't done anything with Dell yet. Not really. There was still time to cut line and bail.

*Maybe you need to just get it out of your system.* A new voice in my head spoke up.

I froze. That was an interesting thought. Yeah. Maybe. In the past week, I'd had to face some things about myself. I had a kink I hadn't understood before. You could call it an Officer and Commander bent, maybe. I didn't want it. I wished to God I didn't have it. But I couldn't deny that it made sense out of a whole lot of shit in the past few years that had been frustrating me sexually.

I glanced at that little apartment above the garage then straight ahead again.

I'd never felt this way before, and maybe I never would again. There weren't many Dell Murphys out there, after all. He was one of a kind. Would it be so bad to just try it on for size, once? Just to know what it was like to feel that good during sex? Or maybe I'd end up hating it. That'd be even better. It'd be a relief, wouldn't it? Then I could fucking stop obsessing about Dell Murphy once and for all.

Just sitting there *thinking* about letting myself do it caused my skin to burn and my groin to tighten and throb. Fuck this. I wanted it. And Dell was gay. He'd come on to me. So it wasn't like I'd be hurting anybody. No one had to ever find out. I wasn't gay. I just had a Dell kink.

My hands were shaking, but I opened the door and stalked out—head down, hands in the pockets of my jeans as I crossed the street and climbed the stairs to Dell's apartment.

Dell opened the door when I knocked. He'd stripped off his shirt. Maybe he'd been about to take a shower. He frowned in confusion and glanced behind me, as if wondering if I was alone. "Donny?"

I didn't want to stand on the stoop. I felt exposed. I shouldered past him into the room.

Dell stared at me for a long moment, assessing, like maybe wondering if I'd come here to yell at him or what. Then he licked his lips and shut the door. "What do you need, baby?" he said in a low, sexy growl.

If he'd said anything else, I might have still gotten out of there without anything happening. But those words... fuck. My knees turned to water as all the blood rushed to my groin. I wobbled and Dell was there. He crowded against me, putting his hands on both my arms and walking me back until my shoulders hit the wall.

Damn, how did he do that? How did he seem so confident and in control while at the same time make me feel protected and safe? My head spun like I was on a Tilt-O-Whirl, and I grabbed his sides. His bare flesh seared my fingers.

"I don't know what I'm doing," I panted.

"That's okay, baby. I do."

*Just once*, the voice in my head whispered before I shut off my brain.

Dell's tongue was in my mouth, stroking and making lazy circles that made me want to die. Oh, fuck. It was so good. He paused long enough to rip the T-shirt over my head so our bare chests could rub together. I moaned. God! His chest was so big and strong against mine and the friction felt incredible. Every inch of my skin was alive, electric.

He ground his hips against me, a steel rod pushing against my dick. And, oh yeah, that was the spot. It shouldn't feel this good, but, god, it did. I was so turned on that every wave of pleasure was magnified. I grabbed his hips and rutted against him, sucking on the tongue in my mouth.

*Don't stop. Don't you fucking stop.*

But he did, pushing off the wall to break my hold on him. He stared at me. We were the same height, and in the fading daylight coming in from a kitchen window, his eyes had gone a deeper green and half-lidded. A pink sex flush washed the skin of his throat. I'd never thought I'd want a man to look at me like that, but I wanted Dell Murphy to. A thrill of pride struck me at making a man like him look at me like that.

I almost asked, *What do* you *want?* But I stopped myself. It was embarrassing to be so needy. And I didn't know what I'd do if he wanted something I couldn't do.

Dell reached out and popped the button on my jeans, lowered the zip, tugging slow, like he was unwrapping a gift. My dick sprang out, begging for his hand.

"You're so hot for me," Dell said, his voice low and thick.

I swallowed. I couldn't deny it.

I felt a moment of confusion though. I didn't know how to tell him what I wanted. I wasn't even sure myself. But I didn't want him to go to his knees. Not Dell. That felt all wrong. Should I go to mine? Was I ready for that? I didn't feel ready. I didn't know what the fuck I was doing, and I didn't want to embarrass myself. And what if he wanted to fuck me? I definitely wasn't ready for that.

But Dell didn't go to his knees. He pushed my jeans and boxers down far enough to clear the way. I flattened my hands against the wall and bit my lip, aching so badly. Dell unzipped his jeans and moved close. He wrapped one hand around us both and gently squeezed, sending a bolt of pleasure into my balls, then stroked us once. He gazed at where his fist wrapped around his dick and mine, the double package overflowing his grasp. That sex flush crawled higher up his neck as if he liked what he saw. I looked down too.

His dick was perfect, the bastard, just like the rest of him. It was as big as mine but shaped like a fucking porn model or something with a thick shaft and perfect plump head, rosy pink skin. I had to admit it was attractive, as dicks went. But when he rubbed us together, his head slick against that sensitive spot on mine, that was fucking amazing. I groaned, eyes rolling back in my head. Another wave of weakness had me slumping against the wall. He put his free hand on my shoulder and pinned me there.

Oh fuck, yeah. That. More of that.

"I've got you, baby," Dell said.

And, damn, that was hot. He was so strong. He was leading, and I was following, and there were no questions, no fear, only compliance. Only sensation. Only the look in his eyes and the feelings of his hands on my body doing whatever he wanted to me, doing it for both of us.

Fuck.

Pleasure shot around my balls and up my spine. I whimpered, then felt ashamed of whimpering, but when I looked at him, his intense, fixed gaze never wavered. No sign of victory or gloating. Just desire and certainty.

He stroked the two of us together. Since his fingers didn't fit all the way around, it made his touch both firm and teasing, making me ache for more and more and more. My hips arced toward him. He stroked us until my balls drew up, and then he stopped and squeezed both our heads in his palm in a light teasing pump that drove me wild.

"Dell," I gasped.

"Shhh," he said.

He stroked some more.

"Oh god."

"I'm right here." He gave me a slight grin, but it wobbled, and the sex flush on his throat was now bright red. Oh, yeah, he was close too.

He jacked us, played, and teased, and it was surreal. It was as if I'd been allowed into a private moment with Dell masturbating. Allowed to participate, allowed into his private game. And damn if he wasn't good at it. Teasing and edging, then stroking fast and hard, until I thought I'd lose my mind. Every time I got close, he backed us off until the sweet ache of the pleasure was almost more than I could take and still stand up against this fucking wall.

I peeled my hands away and put them on his bare shoulders. Jesus, he was strong.

"Kiss me," I said, with no thought in my head but getting more.

"Yeah? You about ready, baby?" he asked, voice trembling. I nodded hard. "Fuck yeah. But kiss me first."

He looked down at us one more time, as if he loved the sight, then came in close and put his mouth on mine. He kissed me deep, his hand between us, still jacking us. He stroked hard and fast and moans echoed in my throat. My whole body clenched, and I squeezed the hell out of his shoulders.

*Don't stop, don't stop, oh god, don't stop.*

Oh fuck.

I came hard, my vision blacking out. Dell jerked against me and moaned, his body bucking. He pulse-squeezed the two of us in his hands, drawing out my orgasm with the sudden lightening of friction. So fucking good. I shuddered and moaned until finally it was over.

Dell let go of our dicks, but not of me. With his clean hand around my back, he helped me over to the couch and lowered me onto it. Then he strode over to the little kitchen and rinsed his hands in the sink. Jesus, what a physique the guy had. With the jeans riding low on a well-formed ass, the exaggerated V of his upper torso was impressive.

How often did he work out? I should work out more. Yeah. I looked down and saw how dumb I looked with my dick lying there like a leftover noodle and my jeans halfway down my thighs. I mustered the energy to pull up my pants and button them.

I sighed, dazed and a little stunned. I wasn't gonna think about this. Not now. Only a coward has regrets. I came here of my own free will. I wanted this, and I took it, and it was amazing. And I wasn't gonna cry over spilt milk now.

Dell came over, wiping his hands on a towel. He looked like he was gonna hand it to me, but when he saw I was already buttoned up, he tossed it on a chair, then took a seat on the opposite end of the couch from me. He put his arm across the back and studied my face. "You okay?"

I shrugged, then nodded. "I'm not gonna freak out, if that's what you mean."

Dell gave a little smile. "Glad to hear it." Then he just looked at me, not talking.

His silence was unnerving. I had to fill it. "I told myself just once. Just to see."

Dell raised an eyebrow as if he doubted that.

"But…." I stopped. But what? I was about to say I wanted to see him again. But did I? Should I?

"But you're not gay," Dell said, as if finishing my thought. "Or bi."

"I'm not!" I said. That hadn't been what I was going to say, but it was the truth.

Dell's wry expression spoke volumes.

"I just… it's you. I dunno." I raked my fingers through my hair in frustration. "There's something about you. I really like you. Admire you. And… it's just… so hot. With you."

Dell gave a sad smile. "Well, to be perfectly honest, Canali, I could say the same. My head tells me to stay away, but you can see how good I am at listening."

I was relieved to hear that we shared this insanity. "So…." I wasn't sure where to go from here.

As usual, Dell had the answers. "Give me your phone."

I blinked and tried to remember where it was. It was still in the back pocket of my jeans. I took it out, punched in the passcode, and handed it to him.

Dell started to type. "I'm putting my cell number in here. Whether or not we do this again is entirely up to you. Understood? Unless I hear from you, I'm gonna pretend this never happened. Don't freak out if we see each other at work. I'm not gonna tell anyone. Is all that clear?"

He looked at me hard, still holding my phone as if it was hostage to my answer. I swallowed. "Clear."

"You're not gonna get weird if we happen to work together?"

I shook my head. No. I was over that. I hoped. "I'm the aviation liaison for my station. So I'm sure it'll come up."

"That's right. And you'll be one-hundred-percent professional."

I gave him what I hoped was a sexy smile. "Why wouldn't I be? It was good. Right? Fucking amazing. But we're not married."

"No, we're not married, Canali. It was just sex." He handed me back my phone.

I felt a huge relief in that moment. Okay. I could handle this. I had this weird-ass attraction to Dell, and we'd acted on it. And now it was done. Over. Finito. I could get back to my regularly scheduled life and no one would ever know.

I opened my mouth to tell Dell that I wouldn't call or text. But, looking at his face, I couldn't say it. Hell, he'd figure it out soon enough. There was no point in being all emo and talking about our feelings right now. "Cool," I said, putting my phone away.

Dell stood up, walked to my shirt, tossed it to me, and opened his front door. Time to eject, apparently.

I stood and pulled the shirt over my head. "Thanks. Uh. See you around."

"See you around," Dell said.

He closed the door the moment I stepped outside.

And fuck me that I already wanted more from him. How did he always make me feel that way?

I stuffed my hands in the pockets of my jeans and headed for my truck.

# EIGHT

## DELL

I stared out the window and watched his truck pull away from where it was parked across the street, then staggered to the couch and collapsed on it. Had I really just acted out that macho fable? *We're not married, Canali. It's just sex. See you around.* I chuckled as my eyes drifted closed. I believed that fairy story as much as I expected hobbits to crawl out from under the bed. We'd see about *one time.*

My very satisfied body quit thinking and I drifted off to sleep.

————

*Ow. Note to self. The couch makes a craptastic bed.*

I blinked my eyes open. Morning light shone through the windows as I adjusted my aching back. Still, I lay there staring at the ceiling like I'd landed in a bower of roses. Not like me. When the sky started to lighten, I was usually up, dressing and ready to boogie. Not today, sports fans. My back might hurt, but the same couldn't be said for my cock. Wow. What a rush.

Would I have guessed that big, powerful, macho fire-fighter Donny Canali was not only closet gay, but also a closet submissive? Holy fuck. Talk about my wet dream on a platter. Maybe I'd sensed it. Maybe that's why I couldn't resist the boy even though it made no sense. He embodied my dream come true.

I'd only seldom in my thirty-one years been able to resolve my complex fantasy—dominating an alpha. Such a concept defined oxymoron. Alphas led. Alphas took charge. Alphas topped. Not my dream alpha.

Donny was the first one I'd met since Bart. My lips turned up. Bart had been a mechanic when I'd flown choppers. Big, hairy, mean-looking. As apt to bite your head off as look at you. But oh man, he became a sweet, sweet man when I got him on his knees. He'd been fun, but Donny… Donny was so much better.

All Donny's little whimpers and moans when he'd been up against the wall danced through my brain like an erotic playlist and my cock bobbed his head around and said howdy. Down, boy. Yes, I needed to get up, but I didn't need my dick to take the lead.

I slid my legs over the side of the couch and planted my feet on the ground. I'd coaxed Gala into taking a quick drive around Sac State with me that morning just to get a feel for the place. I really wanted her to go back to school, but Mam fought me every step. Yes, Gala had been through hell and could have died, but she didn't. She was a survivor, and if I had anything to say about it, she'd stay one. That meant having a life. Hell, none of us knew when our number was up. We had to seize the day.

My text beeped and I grinned. Talk about seizing the day. Yeah baby.

I grabbed the phone off the coffee table where I'd

managed to set it sometime in last night's festivities—and frowned. The text screen didn't say Donny. It said Credit Card Alert. Fuck!

I wiped a hand over my hair since I could feel it sticking up like the Doc in Back to the Future. With a sigh, I tapped on the message. Shit. Mam was overdrawing the limit I'd set on her house credit card—again.

I dragged myself up, a lot less enthusiastic about the day, and headed for the shower. I hated to wash off the delicious smells I was exuding, but I might end up being followed by a pack of randy dogs.

After drying, I dressed for work, and using the chance to grab some breakfast as an excuse, I plodded down the stairs and across to the main house. Shit, I never enjoyed talking to Mam about money.

After she'd left my father, Mam supported the family on her own, kind of. With a cobbled together patchwork of jobs from retail clerk, to dog walking, to reading fortunes at a carnival for a few months, supplemented by borrowing from everyone she could get her wiles around, she'd managed to keep food on the table. She'd always acted as if there was plenty. In fact, she believed it. But even as a little kid, I'd known I had to bring money in. All through high school, I'd get calls from Mam's friends saying she was out of money and was trying to hock something or sell something. I'd grab some funds from my babysitting and lawnmowing savings and make sure the bills were paid. I was still doing it.

*Okay, get ready*. Who the fuck knew what I'd find when I stepped inside the kitchen? Mam was never boring.

I pushed down the lever on the door, and before it was even open, the smells hit me. Flowers, spices, and some caustic fumes that made my eyes water before I was even inside.

Holy shit. Chaos.

Mam stood in the middle of the kitchen wearing goggles,

rubber gloves to her elbows, and a rubber apron covering her entire front. She wielded a wooden spoon like an orchestra maestro. Behind her at the counter, Gala wore gloves and goggles, too, but had a dish towel tied around her neck and another one at her waist.

Every surface of the counters, stove, and cutting board were covered. At least four crock pots were plugged in and huge pots bubbled on the burners. Jars, boxes, and tubes spilled ingredients.

I coughed. "What the hell is that smell?"

Mam looked at me like I was crazy. "Lavender and orange. It's lovely!"

"I mean the fumes!" I waved a hand in front of my face as my eyes streamed.

Gala turned and gave me a sheepish look. "It's lye. Mam's making soap."

"Lye? Damn, you guys, that stuff's dangerous. Gala, get out of here. You shouldn't be inhaling the fumes. Go get dressed and we'll do our drive."

Mam planted her gloved hands on her narrow hips. Even after fifty-plus years of wild living, Mam stayed beautiful, her mane of purple, green and dirty blonde hair flying around her head and her wide, blue eyes flashing. "Rivendell Elrond Murphy, lye is not toxic."

"It is if it's swallowed and breathing it irritates the airway tissues. Gala doesn't need any assaults on her immune system. Besides, we have an appointment this morning. I took some time off for it. She needs to come with me."

Mam waved her arms wildly. "I need her help. I have seven batches going at once."

"Too bad. I told you I was taking her with me this morning. You shouldn't have planned on her assistance." I stared at her. Yes, despite her airy-fairy ways, she had a will of iron, but lady, heredity works. Irresistible force, meet immovable object.

Gala hovered in the background. She knew I sometimes gave in to Mam if I wasn't deeply invested or was in a big hurry. Sadly, her will didn't match Mam's and she battled a desire to simply stay home and let Mam baby her all the time.

I pointed to the hall that led to the bedroom. "Go." Gala went. Then I turned to Mam and pulled her out on the porch, away from the fumes. "Where's your credit card?"

She crossed her arms. "Don't know."

"Then how have you been using it night and day?"

She gave me a snippy glance. "I know all the numbers by heart."

"You have a limit on the card, Mam. A generous limit. You know they call me the moment you try to exceed it."

She ripped off her goggles, probably so I could see her full fury. "You want me to make money? Well, that's what I'm doing. I'm adding a new line to my Etsy store. Soap. And you can't make money on a new product without a substantial capital investment at start-up."

I wanted so badly to laugh. She'd likely copied those words from Elon Musk or someone similar. But instead, I matched her folded arms. "And have you done a competitive analysis?"

She raised her eyebrows but looked down.

I pressed. "How many Etsy stores offer soap?"

"A few."

"How much do they make selling soap?"

Her jaw muscle jumped. "Some make up to eighty thousand a year."

"How many?"

"Well, only one that I know of and they offer body products as well, but I plan to branch out into those."

I sighed softly. "Okay, offer soap, but no more capital investment. You need to see some ROI first."

For a second, she blinked. Then nodded. "Return on investment, right?"

"Yes. And then you can use your profits to help pay for Gala's tuition."

A look of actual pain crossed her face. I got it. Mam was lonely. Her flightiness meant it was hard for her to make and keep friends, plus I'd moved her away from the few she had in Oregon. Gala was her only entertainment and companion. But leaving them behind when I joined Cal Fire hadn't been an option, as I'd learned over the years.

When I'd graduated high school, the military had looked like a combination college fund, aviation training, and honestly, escape. A way to get far from the insanity of my life and still send money home. I wasn't even quite eighteen when I joined up. Thanks to the fact that my da had known how to fly and had taught me when he wasn't dead drunk, I walked into the military with a basic knowledge of aviation and a desire to learn so huge they couldn't keep me away from the aircraft. They taught me to fly helicopters first and then fixed wing. I loved it all. I might have stayed in after the ten years, except Gala got the cancer diagnosis. At that point, Mam's always tenuous grip on reality slipped even more. Bill paying also slipped. I found out she was digging a debt hole she might never get out of. Neither of them was making it on their own. That's when I left the military and became a family man.

Mam glanced up at me, maybe her mind traveling some of the same roads as mine. She smiled. "I'd like to help Gala."

I hugged her. "There's my girl."

Gala walked out on the back porch. "I turned off some of the crock pots, Mam. That way you can work on the batches one at a time and evaluate which process you like better."

"That's an excellent strategy, Gala." She nodded, but it was sad.

"We'll see you later, Mam." I led the way to my car, and Gala, now in jeans and a pretty sweater, walked beside me. Her charming looks always reminded me a little of Ty, though she was more traditionally beautiful, her curly black hair a halo around her head, but with my mam's light eyes.

When we got in the truck, I grinned at her. "Have you had breakfast? Because I'm starving."

She snorted. "No. The new enterprise was well underway by the time I hit the kitchen."

"Okay, breakfast sandwiches and lattes for us." I flipped on some music and started driving.

Gala glanced at me. "Not going to the drive-through?"

"Nope. Surprise." I flashed her a grin. It was only about a twenty-minute drive to the Sac State campus, and I made it in fifteen. When Gala saw the signs for the university, she started looking nervous, but she didn't say anything.

I parked and led her straight to the University Union building I'd scoped out a few days before. A Starbucks inside sent out tempting smells as we walked through the halls, packed with students coming and going.

Five minutes later, we both had food and lattes and had settled in at a table near the window. Gala took a bite of sandwich and said, "Lots of students."

"Yeah. It's a good-sized school."

"Really diverse."

I smiled. I figured that would matter to her. "Yep, it's like the third or fourth most diverse university in the state, and for California, that's saying something."

She nodded, but there was a glimmer of interest in her gaze.

I asked, "So do you still think you'd be interested in studying fashion design?"

She grimaced and half-laughed. "I dunno. It's not exactly practical."

"Hey, you're super talented. And I'm sure there are lots of different careers in the industry." I was guessing that was true. I made a mental note to do some research.

"Maybe." Gala looked doubtful as she picked at her sandwich. "Not sure it's a good idea."

I put my hand on hers and lowered my voice. "Come on, sweets, you beat it. You've been cancer-free for over two years. You're beautiful, smart, funny, kind… I hate to see you hiding away at home like a hermit."

"But recurrence is a bitch. You know that." She glanced at me and chewed her lip. "The last time I had to drop out of school, we lost a whole semester's tuition. What if that happens again?"

"Then I'll pay for it." I said firmly. "But it won't. You're doing all the right stuff. Come on, you've researched how not to have it come back until you could write your own book. In fact, you should." I grinned. "Practice. Preach. Right?"

She barked a laugh, took a long drink of her latte, and then grinned full of mischief and sass. "How's your love life?"

I snorted latte through my nose.

She laughed. "That good, huh?" As I blotted coffee off my jeans, she asked, "What happened to the dude you kissed? The one who isn't gay?"

I looked at that face, all innocence. "You turkey. How do you know me so well?"

"I don't know. You'd think we were related." She cocked her head. "Would that dude happen to be tall, dark, and handsome? Like so gorg that if he really is straight you should send him my way?"

I narrowed my eyes. "How do you know that?"

"Well, I just might have had trouble sleeping last night, and I might have decided to look out my window when I heard the sound of footsteps." She grinned with big eyes. "But I'm guessing, since I saw this dude leaving your place with a combination of shock and satisfaction all over his beautiful face and his clothes looking like they might have been, uh, euphemistically slept-in, I'm guessing you won't be sending him my way anytime soon."

Yep. I spit more latte.

An hour later, I'd shown Gala a little more of the campus while trying not to overwhelm her with expectations, dropped her at home, and driven to work. Good thing I got to wear coveralls today in the design lab, because my shirt boasted more than its share of the latte aftereffects, thanks to my saucy sister.

So she'd seen Donny.

The question was, would I see Donny? Was there any chance the boyo would stick to his resolution to take one taste from the Murphy fountain of lust and never repeat, or would he break under the pressure of his own erection? I didn't want to overplay my self-confidence. But if that boy hadn't been half-starved to death for what he'd gotten in my apartment, I'd eat my Cal Fire patch.

# NINE

## DONNY

I was lying on my bed, staring at the ceiling, when someone banged on my bedroom door. "Yo, Donny! Ma wants us over at the house." It was Mike.

"What for?" I wasn't in the mood.

"I dunno. Why don't you stop watching your videos and jerking off and go see for yourself?"

"I'm not jerking off!"

I heard the faint sound of Mike snorting in disbelief and then our front door opened and closed.

I honestly wasn't jerking off. I hadn't watched porn all week. My stash of videos just weren't doing it at the moment, since they couldn't compete with the video of Dell that played over and over in my head. I'd sure done my share of jerking off to that.

I sighed and flipped over, resting my chin on my hand. I hadn't felt very sociable this week either. Too much to think about. Or try not to think about. It'd been six days since I'd followed Dell home and had my mind blown. The day after, I'd felt like a million bucks, still warmed by a generous glow and confident it was only gonna be that once. I told myself it was the forbidden thrill of it all that made it so exciting.

But as the week went by, the glow faded into a gnawing hunger, restlessness, *horniness*. I'd had a dream a few nights ago where I was in this empty building with a million corridors. I was wandering around, trying to find the fire I was supposed to be putting out. And then that son-of-a-bitch popped up in that dream, cornered me in an empty closet, and ordered me to remove my clothes and jack off for him.

I'd woken up to find I'd creamed my sheets for the first time since middle school. Damn it, the dude was seriously fucking with my head.

I'd simply never had another sexual experience that had been that good. Or even close. I've never felt anything like that hot coursing lust. It was like I'd been getting a level-5 sex and thinking that was all there was, then I got slammed by a level 10. And sex, man. Sex was pretty fucking important to a guy. To me anyway.

I knew sex that good could be addictive, and that I should fight it now while I had the chance. But fighting it sucked.

The phone on my bedside table pinged with an upcoming text—once, twice, three times. I groaned. My family. I picked it up and looked at it.

Ma: *Come over! Big news. We're waiting.*

Tony: *Dude, where are you? Everyone's waiting.*

Mike: *D, come ON.*

I groaned and sat up, reaching for my shoes. If it was important, Ma had probably put out a spread. Maybe even tiramisu, my favorite. That got my ass moving.

When I entered the living room at the main house, everyone was there. Aunt Carlotta, Tito and Tessa, Nonna and Nonno, Tony, Viv, and the kids. It was unusual for a Saturday afternoon.

"So…" Gabe looked at his girlfriend, Anita. They stood in the middle of Ma and Pa's living room, holding hands.

Everyone was smiling at them, and the women were dabbing at their eyes. *Jesus, what's up?* "Dude, out with it," I said. "You guys having a kid or what?"

Anita gasped. "No, Donny. We're not having a kid. Sheesh."

"Donato, hush!" Ma waved a hand at me and then went back to smiling sappily at Gabe and Anita, her hands clasped over her chest.

"Show 'em, babe," Gabe said to Anita in a weirdly shy voice.

Anita's hand had been behind her. Now she brought it out and held it up with a grin, showing a ring. "We're engaged!"

Chaos ensued—a Canali mosh pit of hugging and congratulations and back slaps and the guys teasing Gabe.

"You folded, huh? I thought you said no way before thirty-five!" said Tony.

"Congrats! I never thought you'd be that smart, Gabe," said Mike.

"I'm so proud of you, son," said Pa, stepping forward to clasp Gabe's hand.

"Thanks, Pa." Gabe gave Pa a meaningful look.

Mike turned his face away at that and stepped back. I felt sorry for him. As if Pa was proud of Gabe but would never be of him because of the gay thing. Then my brain stuttered. *Him? What about me?*

Fuck! No way. I wasn't gay like Mike. No one in my family would ever know what I'd done with Dell, no more than they knew about my porn videos. Private was private. Just chill.

I gave Anita a hug and then Gabe and I exchanged back slaps. He looked at me a little funny. Normally I'd be the one teasing him the most, but my throat was tight and I wasn't in the mood to tease.

"I made a cake!" Ma announced.

That perked me up. "Yeah? What kind?"

"So you knew ahead of time and didn't tell me?" Pa asked.

"It was a surprise!" said Ma. "And, of course I knew. How else could I make cake?"

There was something wrong in that logic, but I didn't much care as Aunt Carlotta carried out a double-layer cake—chocolate with white icing. Fucking A. As we stood around eating cake and ice cream, Pa asked, "So when's the big day?"

Anita and Gabe looked at each other. "We're not sure," said Gabe.

"Lucille wants a summer wedding," said Anita.

"*This* summer?" Mike asked, surprised.

"Yeah, *this* summer," said Ma. "Why not? I'm sure we can get St. Michael's, and we'll have the reception here, in the meadow, so we don't have to wait on some fancy schmancy wedding hall. It's got such pretty views of the mountains! And Angelo and Gabe can put in some new rose bushes in just a weekend. Then all we need is to rent some chairs and tents in case it rains. And send out invites, of course."

"And a few other minor details," Anita said dryly, but she beamed.

"Can I go to the wedding?" asked Lucy, Tony's six-year-old cutie-pie.

"Honey, we'd love you to be in it!" Anita said. "As a flower girl. If you want."

Lucy looked shyly up at her mother, unsure.

"I'll talk to her about it," Viv promised. "Thank you for asking."

Nonna held up a hand and nodded sagely. "I predicted a summer wedding."

I'd never heard her say that, but none of us paid any attention to Nonna's predictions, which were almost always wrong.

"There's no use putting off 'til tomorrow what you can do

today," said Carlotta. "August looks very auspicious in the charts."

"Pshaw on your charts!" Ma waved a hand. "We're a good Catholic family."

"Well. There's something appealing about not spending a year working on it," agreed Anita.

I didn't say anything, but my gut twisted listening to the chatter. Just more proof about why I avoided nice girls like Anita. She was a dispatcher for the police station where Gabe worked. She was sweet, pretty, and came from a big family. If I ever brought someone like that home, Ma would have me standing in St. Michael's in front of the priest before I knew what'd hit me.

After we all finished cake, Mike and Tony wanted to go out and throw some ball. Gabe gave Anita a hopeful look, and she told him to go ahead. I snorted to myself. I'd never ask a woman's permission for jack. I went along too. Anything to get my mind off the rollercoaster.

We played a game of flag football in the meadow.

"Hey, look out for that tree!" I hollered to Mike as he went out for the ball, pointing to an oak at the edge of the field.

He flipped me the bird and caught the ball. I laughed. He'd run into that tree a few times.

We played for about an hour. When the game broke up, Gabe said, "Hey, Mike. Would you mind telling Anita I'll be a minute?"

Mike looked at Gabe, then Tony, then raised his eyebrows in understanding. "Oh. Right. I'll go do that." He ran off for the house.

Gabe and Tony walked up to me, faces serious.

"Uh-oh. What now?" I asked.

"We just want to talk," said Gabe.

"What? We can't talk to you, now?" said Tony.

I groaned. "You're ganging up on me. Never a good sign.

What, Mike didn't want to join in your scheme? What the hell is it this time?"

Tony shook his head. "You're Mike's roommate. He's not gonna get in your face about your shit."

"Like that's ever stopped him before." I crossed my arms tightly over my chest, then looked up at them. "So, what? What have you cooked up that's so dumb my baby brother won't be a part of it?"

Gabe cleared his throat. "So listen, Anita's sister, Beth, is going to be involved in the wedding."

I groaned.

"Just shut up and listen!" said Gabe. "She's twenty-three and just graduated from MIT with a degree in computer engineering. And she's a babe."

"Totally a babe," agreed Tony. "And nice."

I sensed an out immediately. "So what, she's going to MIT. Isn't that on the East Coast or something?"

"I just said she graduated. Didn't I say that?" Gabe asked Tony.

"You just said that," Tony agreed.

"So?" I said.

"So. She's moving back here to California. Got a good job in Sacramento."

"So?" I asked again, more desperately now.

"So I need a favor. You're gonna be my groomsman. Right?"

I nodded. I'd been a groomsman in Tony's wedding. It was pretty much a given.

"So. Beth's gonna be maid of honor. I thought you could work with her on wedding stuff. Maybe show her around the area."

"Easy peasy," said Tony. "Where's the harm in that?"

"Wait. I got a pic." Gabe started scrolling on his phone.

He showed me a photo of Anita and a woman who looked

very similar—long, light brown hair, brown eyes, pretty face, slender.

I held up my hands as if to ward them off. "Look. I'm sure Beth is nice, and I'm happy to do some wedding stuff with her, but just cool it with the matchmaker stuff, all right? You know she's not my type."

"That's what we wanted to talk to you about," said Tony.

I sighed. This was an old subject. "Okay. All right. So what is this? An intervention?"

"It's not an intervention," said Gabe.

"Maybe it's a tiny intervention," said Tony.

"Guys, come on! I get enough of this shit from Ma and Pa."

"Yeah, and you never listen," said Tony. "That's why we've gotta talk to you. I'm a family man now. Ace and Paul are doing great out on the road, both with steady girlfriends. Gabe's getting married. Even the baby of the family, Mike, is settled."

"Mike's not *settled*," Gabe complained, disgust in his voice. From the expression on his face, you'd think he'd just gotten a big lungful of raw sewage.

My stomach did a slow roll.

"He's got a serious boyfriend," Tony said to Gabe, irritated. "It's irrelevant whether or not you approve of Shane."

"It's not about Shane," Gabe raised his voice. "Shane's fine. But Mike's gonna come to his senses about this homo thing. You wait."

"Yeah, sure." Tony rolled his eyes and looked at me as if for backup.

I shook my head. "Mike's gay, Gabe. That's not gonna change."

"We'll see," Gabe said stubbornly.

"*Anyway*," Tony sighed. "The point is—"

"The point is," I interrupted, "now that Gabe's getting married, I'm the official whipping boy in the house. I get it.

Shit, couldn't you at least wait until he'd walked down the aisle to harass me?"

"We just want you to give Beth a chance. That's it," said Gabe. "This wedding is the perfect chance for you to spend time with her. Who knows? You might like having a girlfriend who doesn't have all her immediate family in the penitentiary."

"That was one chick," I shot back.

"Wasn't there another one whose father was in the slammer for robbing a bank?" asked Tony.

"Yes. But that wasn't her *whole family*, was it?"

Tony's little boy, Matty, ran over and threw himself against his father's legs, hugging him tight. He was five years old already and super cute with light brown hair and big brown eyes. One-hundred percent Canali. He beamed up at me. "Daddy! Unca Donny and Unca Gabe, I wanna play football too!"

Tony got a sappy smile and rubbed his son's head. "We're done playing, Munch. But maybe next time."

"Aw!" Matty pouted.

"We're gonna leave soon. Why don't you go ask your mom what time she wants to go and report back to me?"

Matty's eyes lit up at the idea of an important job to do. "Okay!" He ran back to the house.

"Are we done now?" I asked.

"You'll at least be open-minded about Beth, right?" Gabe pressed.

What would Gabe and Tony think of me if they knew what I'd done last Sunday night? The thought made me queasy and I felt my cheeks burn with shame.

"Aw, he's blushing!" said Tony. "I'm gonna take that for a yes!"

I opened my mouth to argue but closed it. Maybe it wasn't such a terrible idea. Maybe a nice, pretty girl was what I needed to get my mind off Dell. To get my shit straightened out. Maybe it really was the type of girl I'd been dating that was the problem. At the very least, it would make my family happy and distract them from what I was really doing.

*You're not going back there*, a voice in my head protested. But I already knew that was a lie.

"Okay," I said.

Gabe beamed. "Fantastic! Thanks, man." He patted my shoulder. "You'll love Beth, I swear." He held out a fist and we did a vertical bump.

"Hey, congrats again, man," I said. "Never thought I'd see the day."

"Honestly, me either," Gabe said, his own cheeks going pink.

My oldest brother, confirmed bachelor and player, was getting hitched. Times were changing. And what the hell was I doing? I had no idea.

———

I held out for two more days.

On Monday, Chief Reiger asked me when I'd be ready to give a thumbnail version of the aviation class to the rest of the station. I promised to do it the following week. After I left his office, I was practically giddy, heart thrumming, dick half hard in my pants. The idea had crept into my mind immediately that it'd be a good excuse to talk to Dell. After all, I might have some questions, right?

The sirens were quiet all day, so I set up my laptop in the lunchroom and reviewed the materials from class. I wrote down a list of questions. I could probably find the answers in the manual or online, but I didn't try.

I walked outside into the sunshine and leaned against the brick wall of the station. I took out my phone and stared at it. Shit. I was like an alcoholic just out of AA, staring at a bottle of fine whiskey on the dinner table.

I shouldn't, man. One and done. The more I gave in, the more complicated it would get.

*Yeah, but it's clearly not out of your system. Gotta get it out of your system, right? It might take a few times. A month. But so what, if it works? Can't have it haunting you forever.*

That was an excellent point. I shot off a text message to Dell.

*Pilot Murphy, sorry to bother you. My Chief wants me to do an aviation liaison training for my station and I need to check some details from the class. We could chat on the phone or get together if convenient. JLMK Firefighter Donny Canali.*

It only took a few minutes to get a reply.

*I'm free tonight if you wanna come by my place.*

He so knew my message had been horseshit. But so what? I was going to see Dell.

It was almost ten o'clock that night when I pulled up at his house. I'd gotten off shift just an hour before and then took a shower at the station. I hadn't even been sure I wouldn't cancel when I left the station and started driving. At least I told myself I wasn't sure. That didn't stop me from driving like a bat out of hell to Dell's place, horny as fuck.

Dell opened the door and leaned against the doorway. He was wearing low-riding Army sweatpants and a tight white Army T-shirt, like he just stepped off base. Damn, he practically glowed power. He held my eyes, an amused challenge glinting in his.

"Hey," I said. I pulled a piece of paper out of my jeans pockets and waved it like a flag of surrender. "I have questions."

"Do you now?" He stepped back. "Come in."

I stepped inside and heard the door close behind me. My mouth was suddenly dry. I licked my lips.

He plucked the paper from my hand and put it on the coffee table. "We'll get to that later."

*Fuck yeah.*

He studied my face as if waiting for me to say what I wanted. But I couldn't get myself to utter a word. I looked down at the floor.

"Okay," he said. "Bedroom."

Without waiting for me to reply, he put his hands on my shoulders and turned me, then steered me a few steps down a hall to a bedroom. The garage apartment was bigger than I thought, with a separate bedroom and bathroom, though they were small. Everything was plain but neat and organized. Orderly, like Dell himself. The light was low, as if he had a 30-watt bulb in the one lamp on the bedside table. A bottle of massage oil sat next to it.

He turned me around to face him.

My pulse pounded and nerves coiled along with arousal. I was alone with him again. I was really here. And, like before, the thought about what acts he might expect me to perform brought up doubts. Maybe I should have watched some gay porn this past week. I wasn't sure I was ready for some of the shit I figured gay guys got up to together. But I didn't know how to say that.

I raised my eyes to look at Dell. "You know I'm new to this, right?"

"Don't worry," he said. "I wouldn't be a very good pilot if I couldn't sense the proper way to fly the machine beneath me. Now take your clothes off."

I hurried to do it while he just stood there and watched. It wasn't that I was obeying him or anything, it's just that I was hard as a rock and anxious to get going. After ridding myself of the last article—my jeans, I stood there, my dick sticking straight out.

Dell looked me over appreciatively. "You are one fine man, Canali."

I wanted to cross my arms in shyness, but that was for wusses. I straightened my spine instead.

He smiled. "Lie down on the bed."

Yeah, lying down would be good. Last time he'd had to hold me up against that fucking wall, I got so turned on. I sat down and scooted back. At first I thought the bed was shaking, like one of those electric deals. Then I realized it was me.

Dell, his eyes fixed on me, ripped off his T-shirt and then pushed down his sweats. I was relieved to see he was rock-hard too. It wasn't just me.

"We're gonna talk," Dell said, reaching for the oil.

"What?"

"While we do this, we're gonna talk. Lie back, hands behind your head."

I did what he asked. Lying there like that, totally naked on his mattress, was weirdly erotic. My nipples tightened and raised up as if stretching toward him. My cock did the same. My skin jumped and tingled, craving touch. I had to clench my teeth hard to keep from begging. I had no idea what I was doing. But god, I wanted to keep doing it.

Dell held the bottle over me and poured a line of oil along my dick, from base to tip, and kept going, up my abs and chest. Then he put the bottle back on the nightstand.

"What's that for?" I asked.

"You'll see." He crawled onto the bed on his hands and knees, climbing over me. "Don't let the oil drip," he said as he nudged my thighs closed and put his knees outside mine. He lowered himself onto me.

Fuck, all that skin-on-skin contact had me arcing up and groaning. *Oh yeah.*

He rubbed his body back and forth against mine, first side to side, then in circles, spreading the oil between us, getting it all nice and slick. His hard rod played drumsticks with mine, rolling over and alongside. I lifted my hips to get more of that amazing friction.

"You like this?" Dell let his weight rest full on top of me and started a thrusting motion with his hips.

I nodded. "Feels good." Understatement of the year. It felt fucking amazing.

*I wouldn't be a very good pilot if I couldn't sense the proper way to fly the machine beneath me.* Those words echoed in my head and made me want to come. They made me feel safe—and seen. As if he'd always know what I needed, how to take care of me. Why was that so hot? Had anyone else ever really cared what I needed?

It was so… so Dell.

He watched my face as he thrust, tantalizingly slow. The intimacy was too much. I hooked my feet around his calves and closed my eyes. Fuck, the pleasure was so sweet—deep and aching and sharp all at the same time.

"Donny."

I pried my eyes open and looked at him. He was so fucking handsome. It was the first time I'd felt that in my gut, not just objectively. He was a stunning, sexy, powerful man. And he wanted me.

He lifted up onto his elbows, our lower bodies still pressed tight, so he could more easily study my face. He gazed into my eyes, and I didn't look away.

"I have some questions of my own."

"W-what? Now?"

His smile was sexy af. "Now. And you're gonna answer. Honestly."

"Uh… okay."

"You've never been with a guy before me?"

"No."

He circled his hips slowly. His dick sliding against mine. Oh, yeah.

"Ever done anal with a woman?"

I swallowed and nodded. "One girl. She liked it. We did it a few times."

"You penetrating her?"

"Well, yeah."

He shifted a little so that he was riding the muscle next to my hip bone and my dick was rubbing against his hip. It should not feel as good as it did. But there was a weird echo thing that happened as his dick rode on my body—it was like watching two screens in football, the live play and a replay, like I was imagining *his* pleasure as well as feeling my own, like I had two dicks, which would not at all suck.

"You like oral?" Dell asked, his voice getting shaky. "Like getting head?"

"Who doesn't?" I said, my own voice strangled. "Can I move my arms?"

I froze, blinking in surprise. Why had I asked him? I didn't need to ask another person if I could move.

"Yeah, baby. You can move them," Dell purred, making me absurdly happy. I removed them from behind my head and grasped his hips so I could pull him harder against me, give us both more friction.

"Like to have your balls sucked?" he asked.

"Fuck yeah."

"You like giving oral to a girl?"

"S-sometimes." Fuck. Right there.

"Think you'd ever want to try it with me? Maybe you could just lick the head."

Oh fuck, my balls clenched tight. I moaned.

Dell smiled. "You'd ever want my cock in your mouth? Maybe just suckle the head? I wouldn't give you much. I'd make you beg me for more."

Oh God! If he kept talking like that, I was gonna come. "Fuck! I'm close."

He stopped moving his hips and grabbed my hands, pulling them to the side. "Answer me. You can say no."

"Yes," I said at once. And I did. The way he said it, the feel of his hard dick against me... I could picture it suddenly. Licking, lapping. Suckling a little. Dell above me, looking down at me like I was so good—special. Like only I existed.

He'd never force me to take more than I could or make me feel uncomfortable. And suddenly, I wanted more than anything to lick it. I was so turned on. "Yes," I said again, louder. "If you want me to. I want to."

He smiled. "You are fucking beautiful, Canali."

He started moving again, thrusting hard.

"Will you… now? Aren't you—?"

"Right now, I'm happy where I am. I'm just reading the manual, babe."

*Oh. Oh God.* "Ah! Circle. Like that."

"Would you like it if I tied you up?" Dell asked.

I cried out and came.

# TEN

## DELL

A faint glimmer of early-morning light fell across my eyelids. My preferred alarm clock. I took a deep breath and started to stretch my arms—but I couldn't. Too much weight on my bicep. And, oh yeah. The rich, musky, slightly sharp smell of sex filled my nose and my memory.

*Oh fuck. I'm not alone.*

Very gradually, I turned my head. After all, this could be a trick of my mam's elves and any sudden moves might make it vanish. But no. A thick head of shining black hair nestled on my arm and against my chest. Mr. Donny I'm-Actually-Straight-and-No-One-Can-Ever-See-Me-With-You Canali had spent the night.

I couldn't help the little smile that crept across my lips, and I lowered them and pressed a soft kiss on his smooth forehead. No crease between his dark brows as he slept. The slumber of the innocent. I snorted. Nothing about last night fell into the innocent category.

"Umf." Donny snuffled against my chest a little east of my

nipple and the thing sprang to attention. Other members of the team joined in.

I snaked a hand under the covers and found a satisfying display of Canali morning wood all ready for a little hammering. And I had the nail to do it.

Moving carefully to my side so I didn't jostle Donny's head too much and startle him, I wrapped a hand around first his cock and then mine. When they were both firmly in hand, I gave a preliminary pump, watching Donny's face the whole time.

Those almost-black eyes flew open along with his mouth. "Holy shit!" The yell would have roused neighbors if any had been close, but fortunately, my garage apartment was set back from most of the surrounding houses.

His eyes widened wildly. "Wha—? Ohhhh." His eyelids fluttered closed, but his lips stayed parted wide enough to moan as the pace of my hand increased.

"You like it, baby? A little early-morning surprise? That cock of yours can't get enough."

"Not enough. Need, yeah, more. Shit, oh yeah. Yeah." His hips thrust so hard he nearly pulled his dick from my grasp and his head thrashed, breath rasping and gasping.

I was so entranced by his face, I wasn't ready for the shock of electricity that shot up my spine and into my balls, almost driving me over the edge. I gasped, increased pressure and speed until we were both bouncing on the bed in our desperate drive to completion and—

"Ooooohawwwwshiiiiiit." That was Donny.

Or maybe it was me.

Our bodies shook so hard we might have had a dread disease. Right. Dying of pleasure.

Sticky cum overflowed my hand and dripped down my forearm as we both collapsed flat on our backs, breath chugging from our lungs.

I chuckled. "Good morning."

For a second, he didn't answer, then said, "Uh… morning? So I slept over?" His voice was neutral. Could have been amused. Could have been freaked.

I turned on my side and rested my head on my hand. In an Irish brogue, I said, "Well, me boyo, perhaps the little people crept into yer bower at dawn and spirited you back to me bed so I could have me evil ways with ya. And I only had to promise them me pot o' gold and firstborn babe."

He chuckled shyly. "Glad I don't have duty today." He sighed, sat up with an *oof* and slid his legs off the side of the bed, revealing the crack of his gorgeous ass. "I'll likely have some explaining to do at my house, so I better get my show on the road, as my Nonna would say."

"Nonna?"

"Italian for grandmother. She's one of the hordes that live on our family compound. She and Nonno have a cottage near the main house." He smiled fondly. "They're the ones who started the family compound to begin with."

His obvious pride in his family made my chest warm and made me ache to pull him back under the covers. I'd have been interested in exploring the limits on the number of erections possible before breakfast, but unfortunately, I did have to work today.

He stood and stretched. "I'm gonna take a quick pee and wash-off and get on the road." He gave me a tight smile and then walked into the bathroom.

Damn. Canali was all *yes, yes, please give me more, sir* in bed, but the rest of him was complicated. I closed my eyes and drifted to give him a private minute and then went in to take my shower while he did what he had described as *wash off*. Yes, I'd have been happy to have company for my ablutions, but all he did was stick his head behind my shower curtain, waggle his brows lasciviously and say, "See ya."

"Yeah." I leaned over and gave him a short, wet kiss. A couple minutes later, I heard the door slam.

It took another ten minutes for me to finish shaving, dress, and grab my phone to check messages as I trotted over to the main house for my morning visit with Gala and Mam. Assuming Mam wasn't boiling toads to expand her Etsy store, there could be breakfast to be had.

I tapped as I always did, opened the door, and stared.

There sat Donny, grinning at me sheepishly from the breakfast table while Gala smiled victoriously beside him and Mam wielded a spatula at the stove from which wafted the smell of bacon.

Gala said in all innocence, "We told Donny we couldn't let him leave without a decent breakfast under his belt."

Donny said, "They were waiting for me at the bottom of the stairs."

Mam waved her spatula. "Of course. We weren't going to pass up a chance to meet such a *good friend* of Dell's." She gave me a smile that could have been as guileless as it appeared—in a pig's ass.

The muscle ticking in my jaw clued me into the riot of emotions galloping through me. While Donny sometimes talked about his family, and I'd been to his house, I seldom talked about mine except to Ty. My image was as a high-flying, daring pilot who happened to be gay and played the field, never settling down. I'd cultivated that impression and didn't do anything to change it, especially to guys who insisted *this is only sex*. Seeing Donny, the noncommittal, sitting at the breakfast table next to Gala gave me a feeling like a single-mother must experience when her child walked in from school early and met a casual date. Hell, I seldom introduced even my friends to my mam. She was just too eccentric. My whole family thing was hard to explain.

But here they all were. Jesus.

I gave Gala a glare, and she raised her brows in challenge but didn't stop grinning. Pulling out a chair, I said, "Can I get some of that decent breakfast?"

Mam said, "Of course." Plates clanked in a flurry of table setting.

Gala said, "Donny was just telling us that he's a firefighter and that you two became friends when he was in your class. How nice." She only emphasized the word *friends* with a tiny bit of irony.

Oh yeah, she was my evil step-sister.

She sipped from the cup in front of her and then said, "It was so nice of you to let him sleep on your couch when he had too much to drink and couldn't drive." Her lashes fluttered.

For a second, my gaze connected with Donny's before his dropped away. Of course he'd say that. Such a chickenshit. I sighed softly. But then he was an adorable chickenshit with the world's greatest ass. "Yep, that's me. Designated driver and couch provider to the overindulgers of the world."

Donny's small smile was half-embarrassed and half-grateful.

Mam put plates of eggs and bacon in front of me and Donny and then two more for herself and Gala. With the explanation for how Donny got there having been circulated and not questioned, he relaxed and got less awkward. While he might have suspected that Gala was skeptical since she wasn't being too subtle, my mam totally went with the story and launched into tales of occasions when she'd imbibed too much.

Donny chewed with enthusiasm that might have been real. Mam's cooking was always interesting. "This is really good, Mrs. Murphy."

"Just call me Titania, dear."

My mam's real name was Ann, but she'd adopted Titania years before in honor of the queen of the fairies and even used it on legal documents. I had no idea if she'd ever officially changed her name.

"Thank you, Titania. I must admit, I'm used to good food.

My ma, aunts, and grandmother are all whizzes in the kitchen. But this is very, uh, unusual. What's that spice?"

"Curry powder!" She waved her fork, her mane of hair flying as always. "I think it gives it an earthiness, plus sweetness and spice at the same time. Glad you like it."

Donny, bless him, nodded. "I'll have to tell my ma about it." With the compliments to the food exhausted, he turned to Gala. "So do you go to school?"

She looked down at her plate. "I used to. But I got sick and had to drop out."

"Damn. I hope you're okay." Donny frowned, and he sounded like he really meant it.

"She's doing great now," I said in an upbeat voice. "She's a fighter. Right, Gala? And she's incredibly talented. She was accepted to the San Francisco School of Art for fashion design before she got sick. You should see her sketches."

Donny raised his eyebrows. "Really? Man, I admire creativity. Do you wanna make dresses and stuff? Or, like, work for the movies? My sister Tessa sews, but just
clothes for her."

Gala glanced at me. "Um. Making costumes for films would be amazing. But everyone wants to do that." She shrugged.

"I don't think it's as competitive as acting," I said. "Anyway, not everyone has your talent." I looked at Donny. "That School of Art is super hard to get into. That tells you how good her portfolio is."

"Wow. I bet. I'd love to see that," Donny said.

It struck me that he was sincere. And that he was sitting here engaging with my sister, which was not something *just sex* guys did. But then, Donny came from a big family, so maybe he was used to being brotherly. In any event, this conversation was going down a weird rabbit hole. I was trying to nudge Gala back into living her life again, but Donny didn't need to be a part of that.

"Gala is certainly talented, but there's no hurry for her to do anything!" Mam said firmly. "She's still resting and getting back her health."

Yet another rabbit hole. But I didn't want to air our family's dirty laundry, so I changed the conversation. "Donny works for Cal Fire too. How long have you been with them, Donny?"

It worked. Mam and Gala peppered him with questions about the fire department until he'd eaten every bite of his breakfast. He was talkative, even charming. Fuck. His manner was all alpha male, but with Mam and Gala, his eyes were sweet. Donny Canali was not a bad guy. I felt a pang of disappointment that he was so firmly in the closet. It figured that I'd finally meet a guy I could really get into, one who was good with my family and even better in bed, and there was no possible future with him. Fuck.

At last, he stood. "Thank you so much for breakfast. I better get home so they don't worry about me too much. It was great to meet you both." He gave me a big, phony smile. "Thanks again for taking me in, Dell."

"My pleasure, I assure you." I didn't even wink.

Mam trailed Donny out to the porch as Gala and I stared at each other, holding in laughter.

She whispered, "Holy crap, Dell, the glimpse I got in the dark barely did him justice. He's gorgeous."

"Yeah."

"But like you said, really skittish. He's polished up that self-delusion like a new penny."

"Yep. Thanks for going along with his charade. It's one little step at a time with that one."

She shook her head. "Just don't get your hopes up. I don't want to see you get hurt."

I sighed as the door burst open and Mam came in grinning. "I've often said that the fact that my son's gay is the world's greatest boon to men and a loss to women." She waved her arm toward Donny's disappearing truck. "But that one being gay is a positive tragedy." She pressed her hands to her chest.

So much for Mam buying a word of Donny's ruse.

Oddly unsettled by the whole Donny-meets-family scene, I drove to work, surveyed the sitrep on current fires in California, and then Ty and I plunged into improvements to the flight line plan. About four, I was in my office reviewing emails when there was a tap on my cubicle wall. I looked up and almost gasped to see Chief Canali standing there. *Holy shit. Did he find out about me and Donny?*

Working hard not to look guilty, I stood. "Hey, Chief, nice surprise. What can I do for you?"

He looked pleasant enough so I relaxed. He said, "I had to be here for a meeting with Chief Montgomery and thought I'd see if you had time to grab a beer when you're done with work. I've got some questions I'd like to ask."

"Oh, uh sure. I'd be glad to answer them." I glanced at my watch. "Want to go now?"

"Excellent. Why don't you lead the way and I'll follow in my car? I'll need to get back to Resolute from there."

I figured what the hell and led the way to a small quiet bar not too far from the base but not jammed with coworkers. Once there, Chief Canali asked for a beer and an order of cheese fries for us to share. The waitress automatically brought me my sparkling water with a splash of cranberry.

When the fries arrived, he chuckled. "I'm breaking the rules here. Lucille doesn't like me eating fried food. But I figure a few won't hurt."

We both dug into the greasy, yummy fries and I waited, heart hammering a little, to find out what he wanted. He didn't seem angry. I told myself to chill. It was probably something work related. Around us, happy hour was getting underway, but even happy hour was a bit subdued at this place. Finally, the chief cleared his throat.

"This isn't about work; it's entirely personal. I'd like to ask you some questions, but of course there's no hard feelings if you don't want to answer. I've gotten the impression that you're a pretty straightforward, no-bullshit guy, so I thought I might be able to talk to you."

I cocked my head. This was interesting. "I'll try to answer if I can."

He stared at his fries with a frown. "I'm sure you've heard, hell everyone in Cal Fire has, that I have a son who came out as gay in December." He looked up at me tentatively.

I nodded, staying neutral. "Mike. I met him at your house. Seems like a nice young man."

He nodded and cleared his throat. "It turns out that he'd been tying himself in knots at the idea of telling the family and—" He shook his head. "—geez. He even contemplated suicide and tried, or at least didn't fight it when he fell through a fucking floor in a fire." He fully met my gaze for the first time. "He's doing a lot better now. He's got this, uh, boyfriend, seems happy and the psych evals are coming back good. They cleared him to go back to active duty, and he's thrilled about that. He's sure-as-shit dedicated to Cal Fire."

Oh god. I had no idea Mike had done that. It made me sick inside, but I nodded. "Glad to hear it. A lot of queer people consider suicide. Hell, a lot go through with it. The fact that he's been able to bounce back so fast shows he's got good support."

"Did you? Ever consider suicide?" He chewed his lip.

"No." I gave a soft snort. "My family had so many issues, my being gay was the least of them. It just never came up. One day, I was playing football, and the next, I was dating boys and no one cared." I sipped my drink. "I was lucky. It's damned hard to oppose your family. To go from being loved one day to being hated the next. No matter how strong and balanced you are, the message you get is that what you are is bad. That you're wrong somehow."

He stared at me with wide eyes. "My son's boyfriend, Shane, got thrown out by his family when he was sixteen."

"Sounds like they've both been through a hell of a lot." I didn't want to lay too much on him, but I couldn't entirely hold my tongue either. "Can you imagine that? Some fucking belief system's more important to you than your kid?" I shook my head. "I don't understand any parent who'd cut off a child just for being who they are."

He grimaced. "That's what my wife says. All the women in the family love Shane. Even Donny, who was the most, uh —well, he loves his brother and doesn't want to lose him."

I tried not to flinch. "Donny was the most what?"

Chief Canali blinked. "Well, he, Gabe, and I... we just don't get it. Homosexuality, I mean. No offense. I guess none of us were exactly tolerant in the past."

I didn't say a word.

"But Donny's been good with Mike. I guess he under-stands that Mike can't help it. Or so everyone keeps telling me. But, honestly, I'm still struggling."

I pushed that info about Donny away to think about later. Right now, Chief Canali was in front of me needing an atti-tude adjustment. But he was sitting here talking to me, actively looking to understand, so that was at least some-thing. I kept my voice even. "I'll be honest with you. Being described as *he can't help it* is not gonna make Mike feel accepted. It still says you think he's doing something bad, and he's too weak to straighten up and fly right."

Chief Canali's voice rose. "But the church says, hate the sin not the sinner."

I spread my hands and shrugged.

He flushed. "Oh hell. Yeah. Guess being called a sinner isn't great either. Lucille says it can't be a sin since God made him that way." He wiped a hand over his salt-and-pepper hair and exhaled sharply. "I mean, I try to understand. Mike's boyfriend, Shane—" He actually cringed when he said it. "—is a brave guy, I'll admit. He even won a Medal of Valor. But he's, you know, all rainbows and glitter and—he's just not like Mike and you and my other boys." Again, the pleading gaze, begging me to understand. "All I could think of when Mike told us was, what did I do wrong? I raised my boys to be men. Not—" He realized he was about to make a huge gaff and stopped. "It really helped me to meet you and see that other gay guys can be, well, like Mike."

The chief's attitude wasn't exactly new to me. But it made me angry and sad—for Mike and Shane and, yes, Donny too. I gave him a shark's smile. "Funny thing. It turns out we're everywhere."

He chuckled, missing my sarcasm. "I'm starting to get that."

"Gay men, just like straight men, come in all types. Even macho guys do—" I wanted to say, suck cock, but I resisted. "Date other guys."

"I guess so. I mean, look at your military record. But Mike dated girls in high school. What about that? Did you?"

Again, I shook my head. "No. I always knew my own mind. But I know a lot of gay men who did. Society tells boys they have to like girls. A lot of guys try desperately to make that true for them. Sometimes it is. Some people like multiple genders. But if society told boys they could like whoever they want, a lot fewer would make horrible mistakes in broken marriages, disappointed families, and half-lived lives." I leaned forward. "Honestly, sir. What fucking difference does it make? There was a time when procreation was survival, but that's long-since passed. Hell, we're doing the world a favor by adopting some of the children all those good Christians abandon."

He looked shocked.

"I'm sorry. I didn't mean to be snarky."

He let out a long breath. "No. It's okay. It's gotta be hard being gay. I mean that's one of the reasons why I didn't want Mike to be gay. Because I didn't want him to have a tough life and have to deal with a lot of harassment." He smiled wistfully. "He was always such a golden boy."

"He still is," I said firmly.

He looked up at me, surprised and maybe not entirely convinced. He shrugged and straightened his spine a little. "Well, until things change and life gets easier for guys like you and Mike, I've got to say I'm glad only one of the Canalis is gay. No offense." He smiled.

I choked on my sparkling cranberry.

# ELEVEN

## DONNY

"Okay, we've booked St. Michael's for the ceremony. And I told Father O'Brien I don't want any ad-libbing during the ceremony!" Ma said adamantly as she placed breakfast platters on the island for us to help ourselves. She gave Mike and Shane a quick glance. Father O'Brien hadn't been super supportive about Mike being gay, and she wasn't so thrilled with him these days.

It was Sunday morning, and I'd just gotten home from Dell's. I loaded pancakes, bacon, and eggs on my plate, using the opportunity of my outstretched arm setting down a platter to take a surreptitious sniff at myself. I'd washed up at his place, but I still was paranoid I smelled like sex.

*Mmm. Sex.* I took a big bite of pancake and looked out the sliding doors at the sunny lawn while my mind wandered away from the endless chatter about the wedding. That was all the fam talked about these days.

It'd been over two weeks since I'd caved and gone back to Dell's. I'd been going over there a lot. Like, four nights a week. Why shouldn't I? This was all to get it out of my system, right? So the more the better—to hurry up the process.

But damn, my dick was one hungry beast. It was Dell's fault. He was so fucking good at it. I loved the way he talked sexy. He played me like a goddamn flute. Reverse psychology or something. Like how he'd teased me about sucking him. He'd talked about it during sex a few times but wouldn't let me go there. Then, when I was getting irritated that he wouldn't let me try it, he got me on my knees and let me suck only the head, controlling me with a hand behind my neck, teasing me by tapping it against my chin, staring down at me with those sexy green eyes. Fucker. At this point, I was like Pavlov's damn dog. I saw him and I immediately wanted to go to my knees. It was so hot to have him in my mouth, him staring at me, totally focused on everything I did, everything I felt. Last night, we'd done sixty-nine, and he told me he was only going to give me as much as I gave him. And, fuck yeah, I gave him the works and got the best damn head of my life in return. How was I ever gonna get tired of that? It was like Ma's lasagna. Not gonna happen.

"Ma, what'd you put in Donny's pancakes?" Mike said loudly. "I want what he's having."

I blinked and looked at my little bro. He and Shane were across the table from me. "Shut up," I said, but I felt my cheeks burn. And, yup, I was hard at the breakfast table. I was an idiot. Thank god it was below the table where no one could see, and I was wearing sturdy jeans.

"Dude, get a room. By yourself. Guess we're going for a walk after breakfast, Shane." Mike teased.

"Shut it!" I said more forcefully. I threw a blueberry at him.

"Donato!" gasped Ma. "Blueberries stain! Stop that. Where *have* you been so many nights lately, hmmm? A new girl-friend?" She looked at me so hopefully.

I stuck with the only thing I'd been able to come up with lately to explain my absence. "I'm seeing someone."

"So mysterious." Tessa rolled her eyes. "You can just tell us, you know."

"Who?" Ma asked, and the glint in her eye told me she wouldn't be put off this time.

"Uh… it's… you know. Beth."

Ma gasped in delight and put down her fork. She clutched her hands in front of her chest. "Really? Oh, thank the blessed virgin! She's such a lovely girl."

Geez, why had I said that? Beth seemed like a safe choice, but now Ma would think we were serious. I'd seen Anita's sister, Beth, exactly twice. Once, when she'd come over to the house for a Sunday family dinner—and everyone had tried to push us together. The second time was supposed to be a lunch wedding planning deal except the only people there were me, Beth, Anita, and Gabe. So it was pretty obvious planning wasn't the main objective.

Beth was pretty and seemed nice. But she was so… *young*. Just out of college. And earnest. Now that I was used to how mature and confident Dell was, someone like Beth seemed like a child. She did nothing for me, honestly. But now that I'd lied, Ma might ask her about me staying over. Scratch that. Knowing Ma, she'd definitely grill her about it. And that would be bad.

I tried to backpedal. "And, uh, Darlene's back in town. So."

"Darlene?" Mike said in surprise. "Isn't she the one whose mother and grandmother are in a federal penitentiary near LA?"

"So?" I gave him a meaningful glare. *Have my back, bro. Come on!*

His brow cleared. "Oh, *Darlene*. Yeah. Cool. Um. Good for you."

"It is not good for him!" Tessa told Mike. "Donny, are you seriously saying you're seeing Beth *and* Darlene?"

"No, I—"

"Donato Alfonso Canali!" Ma scolded. "Beth is a nice girl! If she hears about this, you'll lose your chance with her. I taught you better than to be a two-timer. What would your father say?"

Just shoot me now.

"So!" Shane said brightly. "Fill me in on the wedding plans, Lucille. Have you guys picked out the bridesmaid dresses yet?"

"No!" Ma wailed. "Anita and I went to all the bridal shops in Sacramento last weekend, and she didn't find anything she liked. The colors are all hideous, according to her. Too bright. There was a lavender I liked, but she said it'd make the wedding look like an Easter Egg hunt. Do you think that about lavender, Shane?"

Phew. Ma was well and truly distracted. Mike gave me a look like I owed Shane now. But he'd been getting pretty free about staying over at our place since I was gone a lot. So I figured they still owed me.

"I can see her point," said Shane. "Lavender is very old-school. Something went by my timeline the other day that I thought looked nice." He put down his spoon and scrolled through his phone. His face lit up. "This."

He handed the phone across Mike to Ma. Ma took it and her jaw dropped open. "Oh, my. What is that? Sort of a peachy yellow?"

"It's called sunrise. It looks great with that ivory wedding dress. Isn't Anita's dress ivory?"

"Yes! You know, I think she'd love this. I really do. The longer I look at it, the more I adore it. You're so good with these things, Shane! Shall we ask Anita?"

Shane chewed his lip, frowning. "Let me check a few things first. The problem is, it's so new, it might be hard to find dresses this color. I don't want to get her all into it and then it's not available."

Shane took back his phone and tapped away on it, his brow furrowed in concentration, while Ma and Tessa talked excitedly about what flowers would work well with that color.

Weddings were so stupid, man. Like, fork-in-the-eye stupid. When I got married, if I ever did, I was gonna fucking elope. But at least they weren't talking about me anymore.

"Yeah," Shane announced with a sad shake of his head, putting down the phone. "You're not gonna find ready-made dresses in that shade. But there is some nice fabric available. Not much time left to find a seamstress though."

"Tessa sews!" Ma volunteered.

"You do?" Shane asked Tessa, surprised. "Why didn't I know that?"

Tessa shrugged. "I like to make clothes sometimes. But, Ma, making six bridesmaid dresses in, like, eight weeks in all my *spare time*? It's too much. I don't want to promise and then I'm totally stressed."

"Tessa! This is your brother's wedding," Ma said as if it was the Superbowl or something.

"I can help!" Shane said with a happy smile. "Okay, to be fair, I've never sewed. But I've always wanted to learn. And while I'm watching you and getting up to speed, I can help cut fabric or whatever else a newbie can do. And maybe I can actually be useful on the last few."

Tessa smiled. "That would be fun, Shane. I'd love to teach you."

Shane clapped his hands and wriggled. "Oh my god, this will be so much fun! And I'm off classes right now, so I can spend all kinds of time here." He glanced at me. "That is, if *Donato* is going to be staying out nights as much as he has been and doesn't mind."

"Whatever. I don't care," I mumbled. It used to bother me

when Shane spent the night, but I'd be a pretty fucking big hypocrite if I complained about it now.

"And if you're here, you can help with all the wedding details too!" Ma said with positive glee. "Oh, this is perfect! Donny, you can always sleep on the couch here if Shane and Mike need some alone time."

Now my own mother was kicking me out of my house for Shane. Great.

It was weird how much Tessa, and Ma, and even Carlotta and Nonna loved Shane. They didn't give a shit that he was gay and Mike's boyfriend. What would they think of Dell?

Hell, they'd *love* Dell. But Pa… Fuck, Pa.

It didn't matter. Because this thing with Dell was just that. A thing. No one in my family was ever gonna know.

"It'd be great if we knew one more person who had time and could sew," Tessa mused.

"Gala's great at sewing dresses." I said.

"Gala who?" Ma asked.

"Yeah, Gala who?" Tessa narrowed her eyes. "This isn't yet another girlfriend is it?"

"No! No, it's…" I swallowed, suddenly aware of the pit I'd dug in front of myself. "Um… she's, uh, the sister of Dell Murphy. You know Dell, Ma. That Cal Fire pilot that was here that one time."

"The hotshot gay pilot?" Mike sat forward, paying attention now. "You're friends with him?"

Whoo boy. You could say that again. I shrugged. "I had that training with him, and we've gone out for a beer a few times."

Mike looked intrigued. "Wow. Good for you. That guy's impressive."

"Mmm," I agreed. I took a sip of coffee, my heart pounding.

"But how do you know his sister?" Ma asked me, still suspicious.

"I'm not dating her, Ma, geez! I just happened to meet her. Never mind. Forget it."

Everyone stared at me. Fuck. They'd never forget it. I rolled my eyes. "Okay. So Gala hardly knows anyone in this area because they just moved. She really is good with dresses and shit, I guess. Was accepted at some fancy clothing design school, but then she got cancer and couldn't go."

"Oh, poor thing!" Ma was instantly teary-eyed. "Is she… is she going to be okay?"

"Yeah, Ma. She's in remission. She's doing good."

"Thank the Lord." Ma wiped her nose. "But still. Poor lamb. I bet Gala would like a new friend. Tessa, you and she would get along so well! You both like to sew."

Tessa sighed at Ma's pushiness, but she shrugged. "Well, if Gala wants to help with the dresses, I'm all for it. Sounds like she's a lot better than I am. Can you ask her, Donny?"

The pit in front of me grew a little bit wider. Why the hell had I mentioned Gala? Gala knew where I spent my nights. And yeah, I kept telling her I was just buddies with Dell, but she wasn't dumb, and I didn't want my family to know I was over there so much. Mike might put two and two together.

No, it was a seriously bad idea. I'd have to make up an excuse about why she couldn't come. Later.

"Um. I'll ask. She might be busy. I dunno. Gotta run. Thanks for breakfast, Ma." I shoved up and hustled from the house.

Jesus, this lying stuff *sucked*. And I sucked at it. I always got nervous and said stupid shit. Offering to bring Gala over! What had I been thinking?

I'd been thinking that Dell would like it, that's what. He wanted her to get out of the house more. And I wanted to please him. Like, I *really* wanted to please him, impress him. That shit was one thing in the bedroom, but I couldn't let it cross into real life. Nuh-uh. No way.

What the hell was I doing? I'd been right when I'd

worried that being with Dell might become addictive. I was hooked, and I didn't know how to quit. Now my fantasy life over there was starting to impinge on my real life *over here* in concrete ways. There were cracks, and it scared the shit out of me.

For the first time, I understood the despair Mike had felt before he'd come out. Not that I needed to come out or anything, but having to hide something like this could drive anyone mad.

# TWELVE

## DELL

I leaned against the wall and turned my face up to the sun. Waiting for Donny Canali was always a study in anticipation and uncertainty. Which Donny was going to show up? When I opened the door to my apartment and sex was guaranteed to be on the menu, Donny glowed. Positively vibrated with longing like an addict waiting for his fix. Other times, when he might get seen by others? Not so much. That's when the edgy, paranoid Canali showed up.

I sighed. Some days, I got sick of being Donny's personal cocaine. But then, I had a bit of a Canali habit myself, so mostly I was just happy to feed my addiction.

Footsteps clomped on the tarmac and I looked up.

You'd think, after inspecting his body with near microscopic attention, that he'd be unable to take my breath away. But damn. Donny walked toward me across the field and somebody should have been recording it in slow motion while love songs played by soaring violins enveloped us. He was just that damned gorgeous.

Of course, at the moment, that face was frowning and his

dark eyes shifted around, looking for predators. He gave a casual wave and said in a gruff voice, "Hey, Dell." Mr. Macho had arrived. Cute.

I smiled. "Hey."

He stuck out his hand and I took it, playing along with his bro display. The dude had the balls to give me a one-armed guy hug. "So what's up? You said you wanted to see me."

I'd texted him and said to meet me behind the northernmost hangar at McClellan. Since we generally met at my apartment and nowhere else, the invite had been unexpected, but I knew he was on his days off so he was free.

"I've got a surprise."

His expression got warier.

I lowered my voice and leaned in. "Besides, I needed to prove to myself that you actually do exist in daylight."

A smile tugged at his lips. He whispered, "Am I going to like this surprise?"

"I think so." I motioned with my head. "Come on."

Curiosity and suspicion warred on his face as we walked around the side of the hangar and got a look at the A-Star. He glanced at me when he saw the small helicopter, but when I kept walking in her direction, his steps slowed. "Uh, what's going on?"

"We're going for a ride."

"I-I thought you flew planes?"

"Sure do. But I think I mentioned I used to fly helicopters in the army. Cal Fire likes me to keep my license and certifications up so I can be flexible. They let me log hours on this old girl. She's actually the personal property of one of the instructors, but he rents her out to us for practice."

He still stood there. "That is so cool."

I grinned. "Never been in a helicopter?"

"No."

"Then consider this an opportunity to get used to it. You could be doing ground support after having one of these deliver you to a location now that you're the liaison. This particular craft isn't set up for water drops, but it's so small and maneuverable, it's great for reconnaissance." He walked forward a little warily as I opened the passenger side door. "Hop in."

He'd managed to strap himself into the front passenger seat and pull on his earphones by the time I slid into my position and opened the throttle.

As the rotors started to turn, I caught a glimpse of Donny's wide eyes. I'd love to have watched him, but even with all my experience, flying a helo needed an active brain. I increased the collective pitch and pressed the left pedal until I was light on the skids and lifting from the ground. As the cyclic became sensitive, I nudged us forward and we were flying.

Donny laughed into his headset. "Holy crap. This is awesome."

I grinned. Maybe he did trust me to fly as well as to fuck.

"Where are we going?" He leaned forward as if he couldn't already see enough in the one-eighty view.

"There are a few good places to put this puppy down in the Auburn rec area, I'm told. Then we can hike in a bit."

"I've only got on sneakers."

I gave him a quick smile. "I expect we'll mostly sit. Or lie down."

Oh yeah, that made him perk up. The boy was a sex machine. A gay sex-machine. I really wanted to ask him if he liked sex with women as much, but I couldn't figure out how to say it without making him defensive. This was one gift horse I didn't want to look in the mouth.

"Is it hard to fly this thing?"

I nodded. "In some ways. In a plane, once it's cruising, it's inclined to keep doing it and the pilot can relax. This beauty requires both hands and both feet to be active all the time."

Proving my point, I nudged the cyclic forward for a bit of extra speed.

"Oh, so distracting you isn't a good idea, right?" I wasn't looking at him, but his voice reeked mischief.

I chuckled. "Oh no. Distraction would be *very bad*."

"Got it." He slid his hand onto my thigh a fraction of an inch from my bulge and squeezed. "Doing something like this wouldn't be distracting, though, right?"

"Aw, hell no. Barely noticeable to a professional like me."

"And if we bumped in the air and my hand happened to slip." He demonstrated.

I gave a soft gasp as he closed a fist around my already more than half-mast cock through my jeans, but stuttered, "Nope. No problem at all."

He gazed at me and said, "So if I was to lean over and slip my lips—"

"Whoa." The helicopter lurched, although I'd mostly done it on purpose. Mostly. "We better save further testing of my professional mettle for the ground."

Donny nodded. He was holding onto his seat.

The day was breathtakingly clear—a perfect day for flying. It was only a few minutes to the Auburn rec area in the helicopter, so I took off north and followed the Sacramento river to the Feather that took us over wilder land. "I'll give you a little river tour while I log a few air miles, okay?"

Donny nodded madly since the noise of the rotors as we descended didn't exactly ease conversation, but he oohed and awed every time I went low and hovered over one of the wilderness areas.

Yeah, I was showing off. But it was fun watching his beautiful face behind the gear. Once he settled in, he was a natural. No fear, man. That was my baby.

Okay, not *my* baby, but a guy could dream.

After a little more exploring, I circled back until I was over the recreation area and found the remote spot I'd identified

on the map where I could land without danger or distur-
bance. I eased back on the cyclic and hovered over the flat
meadow next to one of the rushing streams the recreation
area offered. Grass and dust scattered from the wash of the
helicopter blades as we peered down. "Look good?" I asked.

"Great. How did you find it?" Donny raised his voice over
the noise.

"Some of the maintenance guys at McClellan told me
about the area and gave me a map. But it's even nicer than I
expected."

I lowered the cyclic and softened pressure on the left
pedal until I dropped the bird onto the ground and turned it
off. For a second, we just sat absorbing the sounds of rushing
water, birds, and no helicopter. Then I said, "Come on." I
climbed out of the pilot's chair, and then dug in the back
behind the passenger seats for the daypack I'd loaded earlier.

Donny gave me a look. "No fair. I left my lederhosen and
sleeping bag behind."

I grinned. "What I have is far more important, although
I'll admit the sleeping bag sounds good. But I've got lunch." I
waggled my eyebrows. Pulling the pack over my shoulders, I
pointed at the faint track I'd spotted going higher into the
trees. "Let's explore."

Staying within hearing distance of the water, we walked
for about thirty minutes into a more forested area. While it
was clear from the tracks cut into the dirt and brush that it
was an area frequented by hikers, we saw no one.

Donny said, "This is amazing. I'd expect more people here
in July."

"This spot is pretty remote. And it's a weekday."

"Our gain."

A few minutes later, we broke through a fairly dense stand
of trees into an area of dappled sunlight. I spread out my
arms. "This looks like a place favored by the fairies, me boyo.
Let's have lunch."

Choosing a spot where we had a nice tree to lean against, I pulled off the pack and took out a big cloth that Gala had pushed in at the last minute. "Grab an end."

We spread it beneath the tree and both plopped down. Donny glanced around and sighed. "Where I live is remote and quiet like this, but then—" He barked an affectionate laugh. "—I do live with my entire family within spitting distance, so this privacy's pretty sweet."

I sorted through the contents of the pack and started extracting containers. "Would you want to live on your own?"

He stared at the sky for a moment. "No. As much as I get tired of everyone being all up in everyone else's business, I wouldn't trade it." His smile warmed his whole face. "I want a life just like my folks, with a big family and all of them nearby." He shook his head. "Even when it's crazy-making. How about you?"

"Truthfully, I'm not that different. Despite having run all the way to Afghanistan to get distance from the craziness when I was eighteen, I actually like family around now. I don't mind being responsible for people. It's important to me to know everyone I care about is safe. Maybe having seen a good bit of combat makes that more important to me than most."

He looked over at me with a nearly naked face, no poses or pretense, and I caught my breath at the need, way deeper than the sex hunger he usually showed me. But it only lasted a couple seconds and was gone. So fast I wasn't sure it had ever been there.

"So, I take it you want kids," I said.

"Definitely. Two or three at least. You?"

"Yeah. Two or three sounds about right."

"And a place in the mountains—someplace where you can't see the neighbors but not too far in the boonies. I love cabins."

"On a lake'd be nice," I added.

"Hell yeah. Oh, and a dog. Gotta have a dog."

"Just one?" I grinned at him.

"To start," he said archly. "Butch, my imaginary dog, is possessive."

I laughed. "Got it. I'll see your Butch and raise you Fluffy."

"Cats and dogs living together. Sounds dangerous. Butch is gonna flatten Fluffy." Donny shook his head.

"Doubtful. Fluffy is a lion," I deadpanned.

He barked a laugh. "Sounds like you. Dell Murphy's always living on the edge."

"You know it. Hell, you live it, Fireman Canali."

He looked smug. "True. Gotta keep the adrenaline going in life. Keeps you young, right?"

We smiled at each other. Maybe it was lost on Canali, but I couldn't help noticing that our ideal futures sounded a hell of a lot alike. There was a tightening in my chest. Yeah. A lot alike except for the woman in his bed.

Maybe it wasn't lost on Canali after all, because he changed the subject, peering into the containers. "Um… Whatcha got?"

I took a deep breath, let it out, and smiled. "Hungry?"

"Always. Ask my ma."

I showed him loaded turkey sandwiches overflowing with cheese, tomatoes, and lettuce, a plate of deviled eggs, and a big container of sliced vegetables. Donny frowned at the veggies.

I said, "Hey. Give 'em a chance. I guarantee you'll love vegetables when you try them with my secret elixir." I extracted from the pack a sealed container of tahini dip I'd taught myself how to make after tasting it at a restaurant in Oregon. It had a tangy, rich flavor nobody could resist.

Donny wrinkled his adorable nose. "Nah. I'm not a veg lover. Except when Shane makes the salad, but no other time.

That stuff's for rabbits." He picked up his sandwich and took a huge bite. "Wow. This is good. Did you make it?"

"Yep. Me and Gala." I held out the container of dip, now uncovered. "It comes with a moneyback guarantee." I stretched out the word and waggled the container.

He eyed the dip suspiciously as he chewed. "Guarantee, huh? What do I get?"

"Hmm. How about a blow job?" He grinned, but I held up a hand. "You have to be honest. No cheating. You have to say if you like it. And you have to try one of each vegetable."

"That's a lot of rules."

I shrugged. "My blow job. My rules."

"Actually, I'm guaranteed to win, because nothing on earth can make me like cauliflower."

I just shrugged.

He shoved a small edge of turkey into his mouth as he stared at the carrots, celery, and cauliflower cut up in a divided plastic container as if they might attack. I smiled because he clearly wanted a blow job, but wasn't sure if he'd risk cauliflower to get it. The man must seriously hate vegetables.

He finished chewing turkey, wiped his hand on a paper napkin and then on his jeans. I wanted to laugh. Maybe he'd pull out his sword and cape next to face the mighty battle. Staring into the container of veggies fixedly, he carefully selected a carrot.

I snorted. "It's not an engagement ring. Just try it."

He scowled at me, but then sighed. "Okay. Carrots aren't too bad. If I hate it, I'm not eating the rest. I win, okay?"

"Okay. But you have to cover the whole carrot with my dip." You'd have thought we were negotiating world peace.

He dipped the carrot in the creamy sauce, glanced at me with a slightly disgusted expression, and then rolled it around until it was thoroughly covered. Practically cringing, he put the thing into his mouth and bit. Giving a quick glance at me, he chewed. And chewed. Just watching those lips move made me wish I was a carrot for a day. After he swallowed, he splayed his hands. "Okay, I'll admit that, with that stuff on it, a carrot isn't altogether repulsive."

I chose a piece of cauliflower and held it out to him.

He wrinkled his nose and actually sniffed. "Pucker your lips, baby, because you're gonna lose." He grabbed the vegetable, swirled it heavily in the dip, actually squinted his eyes, and took a tiny bite.

"No fair." I pushed the whole cauliflower into his mouth.

He sputtered, chewed in spite of himself—and stopped. Yeah, giant cute sheepish expression. He bared his teeth. "Okay, so it's actually not bad." Still chewing, he reached for the celery and slathered it in the dip. "Dayum. This sauce stuff is fucking good." He started to laugh and I joined in. Then he said, "So I guess I lose. Oh poor me. But you never said what you got if you won." His eyes sparkled.

I leaned back on my elbows. "That's true. I didn't."

His grin was half-shy and half-lascivious. "I think I need one more snack."

I grinned. "We've got eggs."

"Yeah, but I really do like that dip." He leaned over and methodically unzipped my fly. I was already more than half-hard, so he needed no help coaxing my dick from its hiding place. My heart slammed and cock jumped, but I kept leaning back, Mr. Casual. No problems.

Donny picked up the tahini dip, stroked a finger through what was left, got a huge dollop and then proceeded to apply it to my now totally erect cock. He said, "I figure if this stuff can make shit I hate taste good, how fabulous will it be on something I love?"

And with that, he started to lick it off.

I'd known exactly what he was going to do, but the sight of him licking my cock so energetically and saying it was something he loved, and maybe leftover response to his loving family and honest assessment of what he wanted, affected me oddly. Of course, my cock was a happy camper, but heat behind my eyes actually made me blink as I watched him trying so hard to please me. Where the fuck did all the sentiment come from? My Irish soul.

The sound of voices drifted to us over the breeze. Talk about enthusiasm dissolving in a hot second. Donny's head snapped up and he gaped, open-mouthed and with a tiny dollop of tahini dip still on his lip.

I'd flopped on my back, but now I pushed up on my elbows again, my stiff erection sticking up like a pole. It was rapidly getting the message that no one was about to salute, however. "The voices are pretty far away."

"Yeah. I dunno." He gazed anxiously back toward the trail that had led us there.

Paranoia one. Sense of adventure zero.

"Want to leave?"

He looked at me. "Yeah. Sorry. I promise to make it up to you."

I zipped up my pants, sat up, and started loading containers and trash into the pack. "No worries. I wasn't the one promised the blow job."

He was tense all the way down the hill, although he relaxed a little when we saw two women hikers sitting on a rock talking, nowhere near the site of our erotic picnic.

They waved at us. One woman said, "Is that your helicopter down there?"

I nodded. "Yep, or at least the one I borrowed for the day."

"Cool. It must be a rush to ride in it!"

Donny smiled. "Yeah. It's my first time in a helicopter. Total rush. You've got to give it a try."

We walked the rest of the way to the landing site and climbed in. Donny said, "I don't think they thought anything about us."

I tried not to sigh. "Why would they? Men hike together all the time, Donny."

"Yeah. Yeah, of course."

He didn't say much on the way back to the field, but he stared at the scenery with great interest and snuck glances at me as I worked the controls. I could tell he thought it was hot so I might have showed off a little. As we hovered for the landing, he put a hand on my arm and squeezed. "Thank you for going to so much trouble today. It was great and I loved every fucking minute."

"My pleasure."

"Great food, my first helicopter ride, and your sweet dick. Not a bad day." He flashed a grin and I had to return it. "I left you cold, though, man. How about I come over to yours and finish what we started? I still have to pay off that bet."

"Aw gee, if you insist, you can probably twist my arm," I said solemnly.

He snorted but still licked his lips. "Oh, I insist."

Another five minutes and we were landed and out of the helo. Charlie Hernandez came out of the hangar to check it over and give me my bill, but I had to watch Donny walk toward his truck across the tarmac.

Yeah those fucking violins were still playing.

# THIRTEEN

## DONNY

Ma and Pa's house was all lit up and there were a few extra cars parked in front. Carlotta and Uncle Ricky were there. I rolled quietly past in my truck. Hopefully, I could get my shower and get back on the road without running into anyone.

I really felt bad about giving Dell blue balls because of those women hikers. Jesus, they hadn't even been close. Good job acting like a wuss, Canali.

Aside from that, the day had been fantastic, and it wasn't over yet. I hoped anyway. Flying in a helicopter with Dell… holy shit, that'd been amazing. To watch him do what he did so confidently. Total control, man. It made me jones to take flying lessons so bad, but that was super expensive, and I'd never be as good as Dell no matter what. But man, it sure was something to go up with him.

*If you were dating Dell, like, for real, you could fly with him all sorts of places. Vacation up in Canada or fly over to the Grand Canyon or Zion in Utah.*

I shook my head, even though I was alone in my truck. *No*. This was just sex. And yeah, we'd been doing things besides sex. Having breakfast with his mom and Gala, both of whom I liked, spending the night, talking about work, sharing our day. Now we were taking day trips. But that's just because we got along so well. We were *friends*. That was it. Friends having incredible sex. But we weren't *boyfriends* or whatever. That was impossible.

My gut tightened and I started breathing too fast. My head got light. I pulled up in front of the house I shared with Mike and sat there for a minute, trying to calm my breath. I wasn't gonna think about that. I was just enjoying Dell's company. That was all. It wouldn't last forever. Sooner or later, I'd be back to dating women. Pa would never know.

I should ask Beth out. I had to anyway, to cover up the lies I'd told Ma and the others. I needed to do it soon.

But later. Right now, I had a bet to pay off.

By the time I finished my shower and got dressed, I'd managed to get rid of all the crap from my mind, and I was feeling warm and horny. I was going back to Dell's, and I couldn't wait. I had an idea. I took a trip across the lawn to the workshop in the garage of the main house. Pa and Gabe had a lot of stuff there for construction. I examined my options and picked up what I needed, then headed out. Luck truly was on my side—I didn't see anyone.

An hour later, I was standing on Dell's porch, hoping he'd be happy to see me.

When the door opened, Dell gave me a little smile. "Hi." He glanced at the plastic grocery bag in my hand, and I felt nervous and stupid.

His smile got bigger. "Did you bring me ice cream?"

"No." I laughed, but it sounded off. "The bet…."

"I told you, this was a one-way bet."

"No. No way. We bet and I'm not a cheat."

"Okay. So…come in." He stepped back, and I exhaled and walked past him. My own personal paradise.

His eyes had gotten that sparkly look I loved. "So what's in the bag?"

"I thought of something you might like. To make up for earlier. But we don't have to do it if you don't want. It's probably dumb."

Before I could ditch the bag, Dell took it from my hand. Jesus he was fast. Or I was slow tonight. He looked inside and a lascivious grin spread across his face. "Ooh, baby."

"We don't have to," I repeated.

Dell's eyes went all sharp and commanding, which always made my knees turn to fucking Jell-O. "Hell yeah, we do. Mr. Canali. Go into the bedroom, take off everything, and lie on the bed."

Part of me wanted to protest again. But screw that. He was offering. I was damn well gonna take.

"Yes, sir," I said. And I went.

I took my time taking off my clothes. Anticipation zinged through my veins, and I already felt heavy and weighted. Plus, I was stiff as Ma's ironing board. Not that now was the time to think about Ma.

I laid down on his bed. He must have been planning for sexy times because the lamp was set to the low-light setting and there was oil on the nightstand. *Mmm. Yeah.*

Dell came in wearing only snug black boxer briefs. Man, was the guy built. I instantly remembered watching him in control of that helicopter today. Seeing that gleaming physique now, so gorgeous, sent a wave of possessiveness and pride washing through me. So much pride I could burst. That I, Donny Canali, could deserve the attention of a man like him. Which was maybe really fucked up, but I felt it all the same.

That's when I noticed the rope in Dell's hand. He'd cut up

the shank of narrow white cotton rope I'd brought into four shorter lengths. I swallowed.

"Foot." Dell went to the post at the bottom right of the bed and tied the rope around it. The post was the old-fashioned type that had a ball on top, so it was perfect for this. I obediently moved my left foot as close to it as I could.

Dell made a loop with a slipknot and put it over my foot, tightening it around my ankle. "Okay?" he asked me in a quiet voice.

I could only nod. "You've done this before." I hated the stab of jealousy I felt. This was definitely a first for me, and I'd hoped it was for him too.

"Not like this. Not with you." Dell's eyes were serious and a little soft as he studied my face.

I wasn't sure what he meant exactly, but it made me feel better. He tied my other foot, then my wrists, taking his time, doing it right, making sure it didn't hurt. Dell did everything right.

I wanted to joke. Maybe something about how he couldn't have a heart attack and leave me tied up, like that one movie. Or how he had me at his mercy. But my throat was dry, my skin tingled everywhere, and my dick and balls throbbed. I was nervous, my brain scattered, but nothing about this felt like a joke.

When he was done, Dell stood at the foot of the bed and looked at me. His gaze crawled over me, from the top of my head, down to my toes, so heavy it was like a touch. I thought about how I must look—spread-eagle, my dick a ramrod on my stomach, my balls exposed. So vulnerable. And then I had to say something. "Getting good blackmail material?"

He shook his head. "Nope. Taking a mental picture of the sexiest thing I've ever seen in my life."

Prickling heat—part pride, part lust—rushed through me and I had to close my eyes. I didn't want him to see how much he affected me. Though I couldn't hide my raging hard-on—or the blush I probably was wearing.

I felt fingertips skim up my calf. I shivered. "No fair tickling," I gasped.

Dell just chuckled.

The fingertips continued up the inside of my thighs, ghosted over my balls, making them draw up, and then over my shaft. Dell's big hand splayed across my ribs. "You're mine to play with tied up like this, aren't you, Canali?"

I nodded.

"Say it."

I opened my eyes. "I'm yours to play with."

"I can do anything I like. Anything that gives me pleasure."

"Yes," I gritted out.

He took my dick between two fingers, tilting it up. He gave the head a broad flat lick. *Yes! Fuck, more of that.*

"Do you trust me?" He pulled back, his gaze intent on mine.

My dick was still in his hand, and I'd let him tie me up. So the answer was pretty obvious. But I paused and really thought about it. I thought about the way he'd saved my team's asses in that Sierra City fire, and he hadn't even known me then.

"Absolutely," I answered. "I trust you."

"You know I'd never let anything happen to you, right?"

"Absolutely," I repeated.

"I'd never let anyone hurt you or harass you. Give you a hard time."

I thought I knew what he was saying, what he was implying. But I didn't want to go there. "Sure."

His gaze was intent, his expression serious. "We fit each other. Do you know what I'm saying, Canali?"

I knew. He fit sexual fantasies I hadn't even understood I had. I hadn't known what I needed until Dell. Was he saying I fit him too? Was this what he needed? I felt a rush of that stupid pride again—hot and tingling. But it was also terrifying. Because if we really fit each other... This was supposed to be only a short-term thing. So what did that mean?

I didn't answer him, lowering my eyes instead. "Come on. I need you," I said, trying to urge him to move. And not just because I was dying to be touched.

The bed sank and he kneeled on it, then shifted over my body.

"Shhh. I'll take care of you." Dell rubbed my chest with a firm hand, lightly squeezed my pecs, nipples. "Relax. There's nothing you have to do. There's nothing you *can* do."

The words and his touch calmed me instantly. I relaxed back on the bed, my body going heavy again. "Yeah." Dell was in charge. I didn't have to do anything. I didn't even have to think.

"I can use you for my pleasure. And baby, it's gonna feel so good."

"Yes." I probably wouldn't agree to that with anyone else. But with Dell, I knew that, no matter what he said, he always made it good for me first.

Dell reached down to take my dick in his hand, stroking lightly, teasingly. "Have you ever played with your prostate?"

Huh? I knew that was down there somewhere, but I wasn't even sure exactly where. I shook my head, my hips automatically straining up to get more of his touch.

"It's like a warp speed button inside a guy. It takes sensation to level 10."

I was confused. Was he saying...? He wasn't saying he wanted to... do that. To me. I began to tense up. I wanted this to be good for him, but I wasn't sure I was ready for that.

Dell made a click with his tongue, like he was calming a horse. "Easy, boyo. I'm talking about me. I'm a fan of my *warp speed* button, but I don't get to play with it much. You could just lay there, at my mercy, and let me use this." He squeezed my dickhead firmly, then pulsed it lightly. "What do you say, Canali? Wanna fuck me?"

Between his words, the hot-commanding look on his face, and that pulsing hand, I almost came. "Stop! Stop. I'm —close."

He smirked slightly, removing his hand. "Is that a yes?"

"I… yeah. Okay."

My heart hammered as he got a condom out of the bedside table and rolled it down my shaft. He poured lube into his palm and climbed over me, up on his knees on either side of my hips. He reached behind himself, his gaze intent on my face.

I'd never even imagined fucking Dell. It didn't seem possible—or right. I figured if we ever went there, he'd want to fuck me. But this was Dell in charge, using me the way he wanted, and he was hot. So, so hot.

As usual with Dell, he was gonna talk his way through it —and ramp me up to the stratosphere in the process. "Gotta open yourself up to do this," he said. One hand worked behind himself, and with the other, he lightly stroked his dick. That rosy sex flush stained his neck and chest, his nipples were hard as diamonds, his six-pack and thigh muscles flexed. He wasn't so much giving me a show as he was confident enough to allow me into his private world. And, damn, it sure was a sight.

There was something about seeing Dell so aroused, so uninhibited that got me deep in the gut.

"You like doing that?" I asked doubtfully.

"I like it when it's done the way I want it," Dell said.

I had to smile at that, because it was Dell all over.

"You don't want to open yourself too much, though," he said. "It feels best when you get that slow burn." He straightened up so he was right over me. He held my dick and lowered himself down. He held me at the entrance, paused, then rubbed my dickhead around the slick. It was so soft and warm and slightly giving. I wanted badly to push. I gritted my teeth. Was this really happening?

"It feels so good, Canali," he breathed, eyes half-lidded. "You'll have to try it sometime. Let me tie you up like this, only with your knees to your chest. And I'll lick you and play with your ass until you're crying and begging me to fuck you."

I groaned. I could picture it exactly how he said it. And I knew, just like with the oral, that he'd drive me crazy with his words until I was gagging for it. Only Dell could get me dying for things I never thought I'd want to do. But he always made them so good.

"You can do it to me now," I said, totally turned on.

He smiled. "Oh, no, Canali. It's my turn. This bad boy's all mine." He sank down, half-inch by half-inch.

There was pressure—hot and slick and so tight on my dick. I groaned. Dell had a look of focused concentration and lust as he impaled himself on me until he rested on my hip bones. He rocked. "Yeah. Right there. Fuck, it feels amazing."

I bit my lip, fighting to hold myself back. I didn't want to come like a teen and ruin his fun, but holy shit, this was intense.

He watched my face. "If you're close, say the word. Understand?"

I nodded. "Close."

Dell stopped. He sat on my hips, panting. He leaned forward and rubbed my chest, soothing me while I ramped down from the point of no return. Dell squeezed me deep inside him. "Okay?"

"Yeah. Go."

He started to move, sliding me in and out, using his powerful thighs to lift and lower. He got a blissed-out expression. "Feels so good when you hit that spot. Sends shock waves everywhere. Builds a pressure like the one you get in your balls, but in a new place. Add in some friction on your dick and it's heaven." He reached out and gave himself a few fast strokes, grimacing at the pleasure. "Wish I could fuck you and suck you at the same time, Canali."

Oh God. He was gonna kill me. Between his words, the sight of him, and the exquisite friction, I could barely think. The rope was slack enough for me to brace my feet on the mattress, and I pounded up into him as best I could. Jesus. When he talked about fucking me, it actually sounded good, but it was hard to imagine anything feeling better than having my dick sheathed in Dell.

Fucking was always supposed to be the be-all-and-end-all thing that every guy wanted, but it had always disappointed me before. Like, I felt as if I was supposed to be super macho when I did it, in control. Or I felt like I was supposed to be all emotional—*making love*. And I felt neither of those things, so I was always faking it, one way or another. But with Dell, it was so real, honest. Just friction and pleasure and being let into Dell's private world, like a secret club. And having it happen to me while I was tied up, and could only move a little—God! It was the hottest thing I'd ever felt in my life.

Dell played with us both—taking us to the edge and backing off, surfing the pleasure like a giant wave. He'd stop and circle his hips lightly, keeping that tingling sensation but backing off the need to come, then start again. Finally, he leaned forward, one hand on the bed beside me and the other jacking his cock. He ordered me to pound up into him, holding firm for my assault.

His voice shook and he stared into my eyes. "Someday, Canali. Someday, I'm gonna fuck you so hard, you'll see stars. I'm gonna pound you until you come without being touched, just from the pressure I build inside you."

"Fuck yeah." I gasped, so close.

"And then you'll be mine."

My mind hiccuped at those words. I knew it was just sex talk, and I should agree. But I couldn't say anything to Dell I didn't mean. So I said, "I want you to fuck me hard. Fuck me, Dell."

At that he groaned. Come shot out of him, hitting my chest, my chin. My thighs locked as everything in me strained upward and into him as deep as I could get. He spasmed around me as he came, milking me, and the pleasure was so intense I really did see stars.

# FOURTEEN

## DELL

"Come on man, push. Push. Keep going. Little more."

I stood close by the weight bench, yelling encouragement, and spotting the 400 pounds of freaking weight Donny was pressing away from his chest. A couple other guys had stopped to watch, and they weren't the only ones interested. I was having trouble keeping my cock from coming up to observe, because man, Donny working out was something to see. Two-hundred pounds of glistening, sweating, gorgeous man, every muscle rippling under his golden skin. Shee-it, sports fans, this was a sight for the ages, and my baggy sweatpants weren't up to the task of containing the beast.

"Unh!" Donny hoisted the barbell to a straight-armed position, and I helped guide it back to the rack where it clanged into place. Donny took a huge breath, and a couple of observers applauded including one enthusiastic redhead who hopped up and down clapping her hands in front of her leotard-clad, curvy body accentuated by a weight belt.

"Good job." I grabbed his hand and helped haul him up to sitting. "New record."

He grinned at me as he wiped at the sweat running off his forehead. "You want to try next?"

I held up my palms. "Uncle." I'd made it to three-fifty on my last lift. "Let's face it, boyo. I'm just a pansy-assed pilot. If I want to get as strong as you, I'm gonna have to start hauling hoses and axes."

Our eyes met and suddenly sizzled. Donny murmured, "You're plenty strong enough." He didn't say "for me," but it was heavily implied.

"Oooh, are you guys firefighters?" The redhead stepped closer, her big blue eyes sparkling with interest.

I got to see the Donny charm machine in action. He did a quick glance around at the other people nearby, most of them guys since we were on the weight floor, and plastered on a smile as big as sunrise. "Yes. Yes, we are." He looked up at me. "Dell's actually a fire pilot."

"Oh my gosh." She beamed at me. "Thank you both for your service." She glanced at Donny's left hand and then across the long room. "Any chance we could buy you both a cup of coffee to show our appreciation for your hard work? My friend Bonnie's over there." She nodded toward a brunette pulling down a weight bar in the next machine bay, just as pretty but not as glamorous as the redhead. She flashed us a smile but kept pulling.

I smiled. "Thank you for the invitation, but I've got lots of plans for the day."

Donny nodded. "We rode together."

The lack of a definitive no seemed to encourage the young lady. "Maybe we could make it another time? We'd love to take you guys out for drinks. Maybe dancing?" Her smile crinkled her pretty eyes. "Since we all love workouts, you know." She laughed.

She was adorable and nervous, and I wanted to let her down easy. I flashed my best grin. "Well, sweet Colleen, I'd be taking your drinks under false pretenses since I'm as gay as a bag of Skittles, but I do thank you for the very charming effort."

Her mouth opened. "You're not."

"Oh yes."

"And—" Her head turned toward Donny whose expression had morphed into a brown-eyed deer in headlights.

"Uh, attached. Sorry."

"Well damn. Some days you can't win."

Pink was staining Donny's cheekbones, and he couldn't seem to figure out where to put his eyes.

The redhead looked at Donny. "Any chance I could borrow you for just a minute to spot me on the bench press? I mean you're so good and I need to know what I'm doing wrong." Right. No ring on Donny's finger meant there was still hope.

I glanced at him from behind the towel I was using to wipe my face. A veritable Chinese opera of emotions seemed to gallop behind his eyes before he said, "Uh, sure."

I wrapped my towel around my neck and tried not to let a hint of exasperation creep into my expression. "I'm hitting the steam room."

Donny looked at me desperately and then back at the girl.

I didn't want to watch. Turning, I walked to the men's locker room, pulled off my clothes, grabbed a towel, and slipped into the steam room. The jets were hissing when I opened the door, and the thick, white humidity filled every crevice so I couldn't even see the tile benches I knew were in front of me. Still, it felt empty. Feeling my way, I found a spot on the lowest bench, sat, and leaned on my knees. I loved the steam room. Like a cocoon. Hot like fire, but wet. So good.

I sighed and let the condensation drip off me. *Donny, Donny, Donny. What can I do with you, boyo?* I could tell he wasn't interested in the redhead, but it still tried my patience that he hadn't just said we were together. Every day I dug my way deeper into some kind of fool's fantasy, wanting things I couldn't have, seeing hope where there was none, and then being disappointed when reality didn't cooperate. I needed to wake up and smell the coffee as the saying went. I snorted. Right. The coffee offered by beautiful redheaded girls.

The door to the steam room flew open. "Dell? Are you here?"

"Uh, yeah. Here." But my stupid, gaslighted heart leaped.

Waving arms thrashed through the thick white and Donny emerged in front of me. His head turned for just a second, like he was looking to see who was here, but only a second, then he grabbed my shoulders, pulled me to my feet and kissed me. Freaking kissed me in the middle of the steam room. Then he nuzzled my ear. "Let's go home."

The cute redhead was never mentioned again.

―――――

## DONNY

When we got back to Dell's place from the gym, it was eleven. I paused after we got out of the Jeep. I should go home, but I needed to change back into my regular clothes. Showing up at Ma and Pa's in another guy's sweatpants and T-shirt would not be a great idea. Plus, after the whole girl-at-the-gym thing, I didn't want to turn around and leave. Fuck, I just didn't want to leave. Full stop.

Dell turned at the foot of the garage stairs. "You coming?"

"Yeah." I followed him up.

Once inside, Dell headed for the kitchen and grabbed a bottle of water. He tossed me one.

"Thanks. But, um, I should head out. It's Sunday. We have the usual Canali clan dinner and there's a big game on. Dodgers versus the Yankees."

"Oh, yeah, I planned to watch that. Well… have fun with the fam."

He said it all casual, but I didn't miss the way he didn't meet my eyes or the stiffening of his body. It sucked that I couldn't just invite him home with me. Especially considering the way his family had been so nice to me, feeding me so many mornings.

"You were gonna watch that game?" I asked, twisting the bottle in my hand. "I didn't know you liked baseball."

His smile was a little chilly. "There's a lot you don't know about me, Canali. Yeah, I played for years growing up. And I've got a soft spot for the Dodgers."

"Oh."

Shit. I felt guilty for leaving. I'd spent all day yesterday with him doing the helicopter ride, and then the epic sex last night, and the gym this morning. You'd think I'd be jonesing to go. Seems like I could never get enough Dell.

"I could hang out and we could watch the game here, if you want." I shrugged.

Dell took another long swig of water and studied me. "We could order pizza. Run out and get a six-pack, if you want beer."

I smiled. That sounded fun. And way more relaxing than going home and answering questions about where I'd been spending all my time. "Yeah, let's do it."

The warm smile I got in return made me feel a gush of pleasure.

Dell opened up all the apartment windows so it was bright and sunny inside. We ran out and got my favorite beer and pepperoni pizzas—turned out it was both our favs—then settled in for the pre-show. Sitting side by side on the couch, with both our bare feet on the coffee table, Dell was close enough for his arms to brush mine now and then. It felt… different. Like hanging out with a friend. Only Dell was a hell of a lot more than a friend. I was still in awe of him. And, even sitting on the couch, there was a little electric charge that never failed to spark in me when Dell was close by.

"God, it's a shame about Bauer." Dell waved his Gatorade at the TV. "Some of the reports say he'll probably never pitch for the Dodgers again after that sexual misconduct scandal."

"Right? Is he your favorite Dodgers pitcher?"

Dell shook his head. "I like Buehler and Urias. What teams do you root for?"

"The Giants. Mariners."

"I like the Mariners too. Oh! Turner's up to bat."

As we watched the game, we yelled at the screen and shouted jibes or prayers at the players. I thought about how it wasn't all that different from watching it at home with Pa and all my brothers. It was one of my favorite parts of the whole week—a chance to just chill and have some mindless entertainment, get excited or upset about the teams you liked, joke around with my bros. It was great with Dell too.

Which made me think about how Dell would fit right in with the Canali sports fans. Only that was never gonna happen. That idea kinda hurt. It was really stinking unfair—to him and to me.

The Dodgers were so far ahead by the seventh inning, it got a little boring. Dell's arm was across the back of the couch and I leaned against him. That spark Dell gave me flared up. I put a hand on his abs over his T-shirt. Fucking sexy abs. Who knew a six-pack could be so goddamn hot?

Dell put his hand over mine as if to stop me. He turned down the volume on the TV. "Good game, huh?"

"Yeah."

"Does your family always watch baseball together?"

I forced my mind out of the gutter and met his eyes. "We watch something every Sunday. It's kind of our thing. Basketball, baseball. Boxing or wrestling sometimes, if there's a big match. Football is the best though."

He nodded solemnly. "What was it like growing up in such a big family? I always wanted to ask."

He wanted to talk? Now? I pulled my hand away and

gave his question due consideration. "I guess it was pretty great. We played a lot of sports too—as a family. Touch football or soccer out in the field. Shooting hoops. Video games sometimes, but most of us prefer being outside. It was never lonely, that's for sure." I smiled at the memories. "Gabe was the oldest, so he was always a bossy fuck. Ace and Paul were next, they're twins, so they always had this special connection between them, you know? Sort of their own world. Now they're roadies for Beelzebub's Rib. They travel all over the world."

"Then you came next?" Dell played with my hair.

I shook my head. "Nope. Tony's next. He's, like, the family comedian and mediator. Always chill, everyone's best bud. *Then* me. Then Tessa and Mike."

Dell studied my face. "Sounds like you were the middle child in spades."

I chuckled. "Hell yeah. Tessa was the only girl, so she got tons of attention. And Mike was the baby, and always so damn cute, so he was spoiled rotten. I was the one who never quite… I dunno."

I couldn't say *fit in,* because of course I'd fit in, I was a Canali. Never had a special place in the family, maybe? It felt weird talking about this. Like I was whining or something.

"And the approval of your father, and your older brothers, meant a lot to you." It wasn't a question. Dell rubbed my temple with his thumb.

"Well… yeah. Sure it did. With that many kids, parental attention is kind of sparse on the ground. And Pa worked a lot. He was more like this distant hero. Larger than life. Maybe that's why so many of us became firefighters too."

Dell nodded. His gaze still locked on my face. "That makes sense."

"What does?" It suddenly occurred to me what he was thinking. I sat up straighter. "Wait. You're not implying that

I… that because I… have a certain preference in bed, that that's related to my father. Because that's just gross."

Dell chuckled. "Relax. I'm not saying you wanna have sex with your father. But it's possible that you like feeling… special. Singled out. Taken care of. Because maybe you craved that growing up and didn't get enough of it. Nothing wrong with that."

I couldn't deny it. But I felt all kinds of self-conscious. "You don't think I'm weird?"

"No, baby. It's not weird. No weirder than the way it gives me pleasure to take care of you. If you wanted to analyze it, you could say I didn't have enough control in my life growing up, and that's why I crave control now. But it doesn't really matter. What matters is that it works for us. Right?"

"Huh." I supposed that was fair. I relaxed back against his side. We hadn't talked about this, and I was curious now. "You know, I used to think I was addicted to porn. But I've hardly watched it since I met you. I think I watched that stuff because it was the only way I could get what I needed. Before you, I mean."

My cheeks burned. Yeah, that was TMI. I should shut up now.

"Oh, Donny." Dell's eyes sparked into fire and he kissed me.

You'd think, after the night before, I'd be sexed out, but no. We stayed on the couch, mostly dressed, kissing and rubbing and touching, the sounds of the baseball game in the background. My body felt heavy, exposed, as if the whole rope game had opened up a new level inside me. I wanted him, had to have this, but it also almost hurt because it was so raw. It felt flayed open in a way I'd never been before. As if there were no walls left between me and Dell.

One thing for sure—it beat the hell out of watching baseball at home.

I stayed the night again.

———

Dell and I went over to his mom's house to grab coffee in the morning. It'd become routine since his mom always had on a pot of strong java on, and we were both lazy when it came to shit like that. I'd pretty much quit pretending I was the world's biggest drunk who had to sleep on Dell's couch several times a week. Let them think what they wanted. As long as no one mentioned it.

Dell's mom and Gala were sitting at the table having breakfast. "Made enough for you two," Mam said, smiling at me and waving a hand at a platter of eggs and toaster waffles. "Come sit down."

"I have to leave for work soon," said Dell, pouring milk in his coffee. "Monday mornings. Gotta love 'em."

"I've got a half-hour or so," I said, happy to take a seat and help myself to the food. I piled up my plate.

"I met Tessa and Shane on Saturday," Gala said cheerfully. "They're both amazing. You're lucky to have such a nice family."

I froze in the middle of scooping eggs onto my plate. My face flushed hot then cold. A chill ran down my spine. "W-what?"

"Gala was gone all day. She seemed to really enjoy it too," Mam nodded happily.

Gala gave me a funny look. "Yeah. Tessa called two days ago and said they needed help with bridesmaid dresses for your brother's wedding. She said you told her I was good at that sort of thing. So I spent the day over there."

I glanced at Dell. He just looked confused.

Holy shit. Gala had gone over to the compound. Had she said anything? What had she told them? I'd been hoping my family would just forget I'd mentioned Gala. In fact, the whole thing had slipped my mind.

"How did they… how did Tessa get your number?" I tried to sound casual.

Gala took a sip of juice. "I think your father got Dell's home number from Cal Fire or something." She shrugged and looked at Dell, her eyes sparkling with animation. "Dell, it's so cool. They had this pattern that Anita had picked out— she's the bride. And it was okay but a bit stodgy, you know? So I suggested changing the neck and hemline and adding a cute little bustle on back, because Anita's dress is slightly Victorian. Tessa loved that. And Shane got the most gorgeous fabric. He's *hilarious*, by the way—" She grinned at me. "But we didn't want to waste the real fabric, 'cause it's expensive, so I quickly did a trial version with this gray cotton Tessa had. And it was so chic, Tessa wants to finish it and wear it for real! Like, just the mock-up. And Anita—"

Gala went on about the dresses, clearly in her element. The words rushed in my ears like the ocean. I sat there choking down eggs, which had turned to rubber.

Had Gala said anything about me and Dell?

Right now, at this moment, did my family know? Were they sitting around talking about me? Waiting for me to come home so they could confront me? The thought made me sick. And sure, Gala seemed completely happy, but she might not have picked up on any weirdness.

*Oh God.*

Dell put a hand on my arm. I looked up at his worried eyes. "You okay?"

No. I wasn't. Not at all.

Gala stopped talking. "What's wrong?" she asked. She looked between me and Dell, her smile fading. "Did I do something wrong? Was I not supposed to go over there?"

I tried not to show my panic. "No! I mean, it's great if you wanna help with the wedding. Thanks for that. But did, um…. Did you guys talk about me? While you were over there?"

Gala frowned. "Noooo. We talked about the dresses. Why?"

Thank God. But I still wasn't completely sure. "It's just… I don't want my family knowing my business. It's… private. You know?" Yeah, like where I was spending my nights. Or the fact that I'd become her brother's sex toy.

Gala looked between me and Dell, her brow furrowed. Then her expression cleared—and hardened. "Oh. I get it. No, Donny, I didn't mention Dell. We didn't talk about you at all."

Her words would be a lot more of a relief if she didn't sound so sad. Even… judgey? But Dell was her brother. And he was amazing. So I got that she might not like me hiding him. But I couldn't do anything else.

I stood up. I wasn't hungry anymore. "Thanks, Gala. Sorry. It's just… it's private. You know? And my family… big families talk. And. That's why I don't tell them private stuff. So I'm glad you're helping over there. If you could just… not mention me. Sorry. I gotta go. Bye, Mrs. Murphy. Bye, Dell!"

Dell's stoic face was unreadable as I waved a hasty goodbye and fled the house.

# FIFTEEN

## DELL

"Dell, are you okay?"

I scowled up at Ty from my position leaning over the engine compartment of our workhorse CL-415. "Yeah. Why?"

"Because that nut was tight about ten turns ago." He carefully removed the wrench from my hand and set it aside. "Let's leave maintenance to the crew, what do you say?" He took hold of my arm with a tentative grasp, like maybe I was a wild horse and I'd trample him. Then he led me out of the hangar and into the sunlight. "Take a few deep breaths." He grinned. "For all our sakes."

I stared at him for a second, the crease between my eyebrows so deep it was giving me a headache——and then I burst out laughing. "That bad, huh?"

"Worse. Jed begged me for an intervention on behalf of the entire maintenance crew." He flashed that snarky grin and led me over to a couple ratty metal chairs the guys kept outside for coffee and cigarette breaks. We both flopped down and he said, "You want to tell your troubles to Auntie Ty?"

I let out a long breath and wiped a hand over my hair. "I'm just suffering from whiplash."

"Canali?"

I nodded.

"I was in the hangar a few weeks ago when he arrived for your helicopter ride. Looked like he was about to be attacked by wolves he was so edgy."

"Yeah." I turned my face up to the sun and closed my eyes. "But when we're alone, damn, the man is sweet. Seriously sweet."

Ty was quiet for a minute, but I could feel the weight of his stare. I opened my eyes. "What?"

"You really like this dude? I mean like more than anybody I've ever seen you with." It was only half a question.

Did I? I grimaced since it was hard to admit. "Yeah. Maybe so."

"Despite his fear of wolves?" He flashed the grin again and I barked a laugh.

"It seems like an army of orcs can't keep me away from Donny Canali."

Ty chuckled since he'd endured many an evening of my mam regaling him with stories from the Lord of the Rings.

I sighed. Or at least the orcs couldn't keep Donny out of my bed. Damn, I'd been so disgusted when he'd practically run out of my mam's house that one morning when we'd learned that Gala was working with Tessa on those bridesmaid dresses, I'd been ready to call him and tell him to stick it where the sun didn't shine as the old saying went. But then I remembered where he'd *been* sticking it and I couldn't get my damned fingers to push the phone keys. It wasn't just the sex. I could find a dozen men who'd let me ride their cock until the hobbits occupied Sacramento. No, it wasn't the sex itself, but what? The heart above the cock. The deep need covered by the thick layer of macho bullshit. The incredible vulnerability hiding behind the armor.

Ty said, "If I was a gay man, I might explore those complex emotions flickering across your face." He grinned. "But TMI is TMI. So I'll just say, you're a man who gets what he wants, Dell. Be sure you're clear on what that is."

His words were still sinking in when my phone buzzed in my pocket. I glanced at the screen and said, "Gala." I clicked it on. "Hey, dear heart. What's up?"

"Could I impose on you for a ride? Tessa picked me up this morning, but it's so far for her. I hate for her to have to drive me back home again today. I thought maybe you could swing by from McClellan."

"Whoa. Wait. Start over. Where are you?" I frowned at the phone.

"I'm at the Canalis in Resolute. Sorry. I should have started there. I'm having so much fun! But can you pick me up later?"

Maintaining distance from anything Canali seemed like a high priority. But on the other hand, I'd wanted Gala to get out of the house and that's exactly what she'd been doing, spending all kinds of time with Tessa for the past few weeks. She was getting excited about fashion design again and making new friends—all things she desperately needed. Donny was on his 24-hour shift, so at least I wouldn't drive up to the Canalis and have Donny running out the back door screaming.

"It's not exactly a *swing by*, but sure. I'll get you. It'll take me an hour and a bit to get cleaned up and drive there. I'll text you so you can meet me out front."

"Perfect." She lowered her voice. "Tessa insists she can drive me home, so I want to make it seem like you stopping by to get me is no big deal."

"Okay, sweets, I'll be your no-big-deal man. See you soon." I clicked off.

Ty said, "I heard a bit of that. Gala sounds excited."

"Yeah. Apparently, Donny's sister is making dresses for

their brother's wedding, and Donny mentioned to her that Gala can design and sew. Now she's their chief designer." I shook my head.

Ty's eyes widened. "Why would he do that? I mean, isn't that inviting the wolves in?"

"I was as shocked as you. I think maybe it happened by accident. Like he blurted it out?" I shrugged. "Anyway, somehow the Canalis tracked down Gala and she's over there having the time of her life designing bridal clothes."

"Well, dayum, that's good, right?" He grinned. Ty knew just how good it was.

"It is. She wants me to come get her, so I need to get changed." I pointed to my coveralls. "It's a drive to Resolute, as you may remember."

"Oh yeah." He slapped my shoulder. "So into the valley of death ride the six hundred?"

"My, aren't we the literary one today."

"You're not the only one who can spin a yarn." He laughed and I headed for my locker.

Unfortunately, he had a point.

An hour later, I was passing that ridiculous and charming Resolute General Store. How would Mam survive in a tiny town like this? Probably take over the community, organize everything in her wacko way, and start soup kitchens for squirrels. Who knew? Small towns had a high tolerance for eccentricity, if storybooks could be believed. She might fit right in.

I maneuvered to the other side of the square and stopped to send a text. *Be there in five. Meet you out front.*

I pressed the accelerator. Despite my uneasiness at being in Canali Central, I was looking forward to the ride home with Gala. I wanted to hear all about her designs and creativity. It felt great to have her involved in a project again. If Donny had gotten her into this by accident, it was a happy one.

I pulled off of the main road onto the long gravel drive that led to the Canali compound. A shiver ran up my back. My last time here had been the day of the infamous kiss that pushed all Donny's buttons. And mine. If I'd meant to show him that he couldn't resist me, I'd been caught in my own trap.

The big house came into view, the lights shining in the windows against the growing twilight. As I turned into the parking lot, Gala stood at the end of the walkway, waving at me. I pulled up in front of her and clicked unlock on the doors.

As she walked toward my car, the front door opened and Tessa came bounding out. She ran to Gala, gave her a hug, and then made a motion to me to open the window.

I replaced the frown that wanted to pop up with a smile. I said, "Hi. Sounds like you two are having a good old time with your dress designing."

Tessa hugged Gala with one arm. "We are! Your sister's a genius. We couldn't have done this without her. Hey, Ma really wants Gala to stay for dinner, and we'd love to have you join us. Do you have time to stay? Please say yes! Gala's practically part of the family. That makes you one too, right?" She chortled.

Gala gave me a wide-eyed stare. I had the impression that she was pretty clear that Donny's and my relationship went way beyond complicated, and that he didn't want his family to get a whiff of it. At the same time, this was an important new aspect of her life and I wanted to encourage it. She said, almost shyly, "Whatever Lucille's making smells really, really good. And you could see some of my designs." Her eyes pleaded with me.

That did it. My sister would always be my weakness. And, hell, I knew Donny was going to be at the station all night, so it didn't have to be weird. "Love to. Thank you. Where shall I park?"

A couple minutes later, with a lovely escort on each arm, we walked into the house. Like the last time, the food smelled incredible. It was a Saturday, and the men hung out in front of the TV watching baseball while the women, plus Shane and Mike, scurried around the kitchen. There just weren't as many people as there'd been the day of the party.

Mrs. Canali and Chief Canali converged on me from opposite directions. The chief said, "Dell, great to see you. We're certainly enjoying getting to know Gala."

I shook his hand. "She's also enjoying it immensely, sir."

Mrs. Canali threw her arms around me. "It's like having a new daughter in the house. She's so talented! You must be very proud of her."

I smiled. "I am, ma'am. You can't imagine how much."

Gala hugged my arm and gave me a big smile.

Chief Canali waved at the couch. "Come join us for a little baseball. Dinner will be ready, uh—"

Mrs. Canali gave him a look like *gotcha*. "In about twenty minutes or so. I'm so happy you and Gala can join us."

"Our treat." I looked toward the TV. "I'd love to watch the game, but first I want to see some of Gala's designs."

Tessa punched the air. "Yay for gay brothers!" I snorted and Chief Canali swallowed hard.

"Tessa, behave yourself," Ma tsked. But she was smiling.

Tessa yelled, "Shane, come on. Dell wants to see the wedding designs."

Gala never let go of my arm as we trooped down a set of stairs to a large open studio in the daylight basement. It looked like a corner of the space might qualify as a bedroom, but mostly it was consumed with drawings pinned to cork-board walls, a huge work table where fabric was laid out, and three dress forms, two of which wore matching peachy yellow dresses that appeared to be different sizes and the third one had a gray dress of the same style I liked even better. Thread, paper, and cloth bits littered the floor.

Tessa rushed over to the dress forms and made a sweeping gesture. "Ta-da! These are Gala's designs. Aren't they great?"

Gala shook her head. "I just altered an existing pattern. That's easier than designing from scratch."

Shane had gone to the other side of the dress forms. "Not true. She changed them dramatically. Aren't these wonderful? Don't you love the neckline?" He spun the form around so I could see where the dresses gathered and kind of flounced out in the back. "And this bustle is to die for. Seriously, these dresses are so different than the pattern. These are modern and original. The pattern was really passe."

I grinned. Shane was cute. It'd be fun for me and Donny to double-date with him and Mike and get to see Shane in action in Lavender Heights and—fuck. I'd certainly drifted off into Neverland. An odd pain stabbed under my pec.

I blinked to get my mind back in gear and went over to examine the dresses close-up. While I was no fashion expert, I appreciated good design in a plane or a dress. "These are gorgeous, Gala. I'll bet the bridesmaids will love them." I grinned.

"You really like them, Dell?" Gala worried her lip.

I nodded. "Of course. Mrs. Canali is right. You're crazy talented." I gave her a quick hug and kiss on the forehead. It made my heart soar to see her so alive and happy. I'd worried I'd never see that Gala again.

We went back upstairs where people were gathering around the table. I noticed Uncle Ricky wasn't there, which was a damned shame since I'd enjoyed talking to him last time. The oldest brother, Gabe, sat down next to me, but his fiancé, the one all the dress designing was for, had to work. Tony and his wife, Viv, sat across from me, along with the shy cousin Tito, the one with the cupid bow lips almost too pretty to be real. The aunt, Carlotta, and the grandmother they called Nonna sat at the end of the table close to Mrs. Canali and closest to the kitchen. Mike sat beside Shane. Snuggled might be a better description since they looked at each other, grinned, and gave each other little nudges pretty often. The grandfather slept in his recliner.

As roast chicken, manicotti, salad, and other goodies got passed and we dug in—it tasted even better than it smelled—Viv said to Gala, "Do you go to design school, Gala?"

Gala gave me a quick glance. "Uh, not currently. I dropped out a few years ago over some health issues." She smiled genuinely. "But I must admit, working with Tessa is inspiring me to get back into it."

Tessa clapped her hands together. "Yes! Where will you go?"

Gala looked a little scared, but more inspired by all the enthusiasm around her. I didn't say a word, just kept eating. She swallowed some water and then said, "Well, Sac State doesn't have an actual school of design. Theirs is Fashion Merchandising, but there are a few design classes. I was, uh, thinking I could take those and see how I like it."

Shane raised a glass of water. "Yes to that. We'd be fellow Hornets, and I could introduce you to my friends. They'd adore you."

Gala grinned. "That would be fun. It'd be nice to know someone."

Mrs. Canali asked, "But it sounds like you might have to go somewhere else to get all the design, right?"

Gala gave me another of those glances that said *don't go holding me to this.* "I figured I'd go as far as I could around here and then, maybe uh, try to get back into CCA in San Francisco."

Shane nodded. "Wow, that's an amazing school. And we could all come and hang out with you. It's only an hour and a half."

Gala blinked hard and every cell in my heart glowed. Oh

yeah. Donny Canali's accidental invitation just became my secret weapon. I wanted to stand up and cheer.

I'd just taken my last bite of roast chicken, when Gabe said, "So, Murphy, I understand that's quite a plane you fly."

I grinned. My other girl, besides my sister. "Yep, the CL-515 fire bomber, designed specifically for firefighting. She can take off and land places other planes just can't access and carry a literal boatload of water. Maneuverable as all get-out. She's a joy to fly."

Chief Canali looked up from the end of the table. "But you also fly helicopters, is that true?"

"Yes, sir, I flew helicopters in the military. Cal Fire encourages me to keep up my license in case they need an extra helo pilot."

Mike waved an arm. "Yeah, I heard Donny got to go up with you. Is that true?"

For a second I was too stunned to say anything.

Mike went on, not realizing I'd been turned to stone. "One of our crew was over at McClellan for some kind of maintenance thing a few weeks ago and said he saw Donny getting in your helicopter. Damn. Uh, I mean darn." He glanced at his mother. "If you ever need another guinea pig, count me in. I'd love a chance to go up."

"Ooh, me too!" said Tessa.

"Isn't that dangerous?" Ma asked worriedly.

"Not at all, ma'am," I managed to slather a casual smile on my face. "Yeah, Donny mentioned, when he took the fire liaison class with me, that he'd never been in a helo. I was going up, so I invited him along. But there may be a chance for more firefighters to fly with delivery of fire teams into burn areas. Of course, that would more likely be in one of the fixed wing craft. The only reason we took the helo was because I'm recertifying." I sipped my water and tried to assume the look I got from Chief Canali wasn't suspicious.

"Well, you guys can have it." Carlotta shuddered. "I don't even like commercial flights."

"Unless it's to an astrology convention," Mrs. Canali teased, smiling at her sister.

"Well, when it's worth it, it's worth it," agreed Carlotta.

"I'd love to take Giuseppe back to Italy one more time," said Nonna sadly. "But the flight is so long. I don't think it's going to happen."

"I want to go to Italy, too, Nonna," said Tessa.

"And we *want* you to go to Italy." Mike grinned. "So I can take the basement apartment."

Tessa stuck out her tongue at him.

The family banter went on. They were funny and clearly very close, the whole clan. Gala and I shared a look, both of us smiling. Gala was right. The Canalis were a nice family. It was easy to see where Donny had gotten his family values.

Sadly, I also understood where he got the fear and self-doubt. Mike was at the table with his boyfriend, and on the surface, everyone accepted them. But I could feel the tension in Chief Canali, and beside me, Gabe, the oldest brother, practically vibrated from holding himself in check. Shit, Mike and Shane had to be so brave to just ignore the crap and accept the love.

But that wasn't Donny. He was used to the support and admiration of his father and Gabe, and he needed it. Craved it. Hell, he'd probably gotten the most attention and acceptance from echoing his father's ideas. Being his dad's man. Even if that meant going against his own heart and soul. Damn, poor Donny.

I drew in a long slow breath. I shouldn't be in the middle of this. But somehow, I was. It didn't feel right, being here under false pretenses, lying to Chief Canali and the rest of the family. Not to mention risking my heart in a drama that played out beyond my control. I needed to let Donny be

Donny, no matter how that ended up, but fuck, I was so far gone.

When everyone had finished eating, Mrs. Canali stood and grabbed plates and I sprang up to help. When I got to the big kitchen with my arms full of dirty dishes, she waved her hand. "No need for you to do that, Dell. But thank you."

"Not a problem. Thank you for a delicious meal."

"You're welcome any time." She started squirting whipped cream on slices of pie already arranged on small plates. "You can take these in for me though."

I smiled, grateful for the distraction. "Yes, ma'am."

When I delivered what looked like chocolate cream pie to Gabe, he said, "Man, Donny's gonna be sad he missed this. It's one of his favorites." I tried to get back to the kitchen without imagining chocolate cream spread on my dick.

A few minutes later, I was forcing myself not to lick my fork, the pie was so delicious, and Mrs. Canali tapped her water glass. "I just wanted to extend the thanks of our whole family to Gala for all her creative work. We're so happy to get to know you and want you and Dell to be sure to put August 13 on your calendars so you can attend the wedding you've worked so hard to make beautiful."

Gabe nodded at Gala. "Yeah. Anita told me to make sure you were invited to the wedding. She really hopes you'll come and so do I." I'd seldom seen Gabe smile, but this one seemed genuine.

Gala's whole face brightened. "I'd love to come." She hopped in her chair a little. "I'm dying to see how the dresses look walking down the aisle." She smiled. "And the people, too, of course."

"And you'll come, too, Dell. Yes?" Lucille gazed at me. "And your mother, of course. Gala's told us it's the three of you."

What the hell could I say? "Of course, ma'am. I'd be honored."

Twenty minutes later, as our car cleared the Canali drive-way, Gala grabbed my arm. "What do you think Donny will say when he finds out we're coming to his brother's wedding?"

Yeah, that was the million-dollar question.

"I don't know, sweets. I don't know."

# SIXTEEN

## DONNY

I pulled into the parking lot of St. Michael's in Oroville and stopped my truck. I checked my watch.

"We've got ten minutes to spare." Mike opened up the passenger door and got out, then looked back at me. "Dude, you coming?"

"I'll be there in a minute."

He shrugged, closed the door, and jogged to the church.

I just wanted quiet for two seconds to catch my breath. My hair was still damp from the shower I'd raced through, and the new rust-colored button-down shirt Ma had bought me and put on my bed—*thanks, Ma*—itched a little. I ran my finger around the collar and opened another button.

The wedding had come up like a speeding semi-truck filled with flowers. I couldn't believe it was time for the rehearsal already. But then, the whole summer had flown by. I'd been spending so much time with Dell. Then for the past eight days, two different wildfires had kept me, Mike, Tony, and Pa working around the clock, and I was in a tailspin. What genius thought a wedding in August in a family full of firefighters was a good idea? Though, to be honest, our busy season used to start in September. Now, it was more like June or July.

I hadn't had time to go to Dell's for over a week, and I was beyond grumpy about it. Worse, I worried about him. I'd seen his plane a few times, though he'd never directly worked with my station. I knew he'd been air support at the Knoll's Canyon fire, and he'd been working as much as me. It wasn't that I worried he'd crash. He was fucking good at what he did. But shit happened, and there was a gnawing pain in the pit of my stomach that wouldn't relent until I knew he was done and safe. I felt the same when anyone in my family was working a fire and I wasn't there. Only it was worse with Dell because it just dog piled on top of the anxiety I already felt about him all the time.

Like what the fuck was I gonna do about him? Him and me. *Us.* There was definitely an *us.* I could tell Dell was getting used to the idea. It was in the things he said some-times, in bed and out, nudging me toward a future he wanted. I wasn't stupid. Maybe I liked being nudged with his talk when it came to sex, trying new things. But when it came to promises and white picket fences and shit—it just freaked me out.

Meanwhile, fuck me very much, I hadn't had time to take Beth out on a real date thanks to my extra work hours. Now my whole family would be at the rehearsal dinner tonight badgering her about our dating life. Because that's what my family did. I'd sent her a text yesterday asking her to go out with me after the rehearsal dinner, which was waaaay too little too late, but I had to hope it all didn't hit the fan.

I plastered on my cocky smile as I walked into the church. The rehearsal was only for the wedding party, so Ma was over at the restaurant prepping for the rehearsal dinner with Aunt Carlotta. There were a dozen people standing in the foyer of the church, including Pa. He gave me the hairy eyeball as I strolled in.

"Donny! Where you been?" he barked.

"Mike said we had ten minutes," I mumbled.

"Sorry," Pa said. "Just anxious. Hey, Mike, Donny, and Tony have been working hard the past week or so." He said the last bit for everyone else's benefit, slapping me on the back. He gave me a proud look. That look from Pa never failed to make my heart blow up like a balloon.

"Just doin' my job," I said. "But it's been a rough week."

"Damned heroes." Ace stepped up and gave me a one-armed man hug, then Paul. I hated that I'd hardly had time to see them since they'd arrived a few days ago from Tokyo. They were roadies for a famous rock band and were hardly ever home.

"Hey, so glad you guys are here," I said.

"Wouldn't miss it," said Ace.

"Had to see the Gabe-man tie the knot," agreed Paul with a teasing smile.

I turned to Gabe. "Hey, big bro. How badly are you sweating?"

Gabe chuckled, but his face was pale. "Nah, I'm good."

"Yeah, you look it," said Mike. "You look like that time you barfed on the water rollercoaster at Six Flags. Ma never did salvage those shoes."

Gabe punched Mike lightly in the ribs. "Shut up."

I turned to Anita. Beth was next to her, and she turned away quickly as if she'd been watching me.

"Hey, Anita." I kissed her cheek.

"Donny. Glad you're here. We're still waiting on Father O'Brien."

I nodded and smiled, glad I wasn't the one holding everything up. I turned to Beth.

She looked pretty in a short, sleeveless green dress that left nothing on her slender body to the imagination. She was very petite with small boobs and no extra body weight at all. Her light brown hair was long and shiny and fell around her shoulders. I felt a pang looking at her. It wasn't attraction so much as guilt and sadness that I *didn't* feel attraction. Because, come on. She was cute.

She saw me looking at her and gave me a big smile. Yeah, now was a good opportunity, with everyone standing around, to put on a little show.

I stepped close to her, slid an arm around her tiny waist whispered in her ear. "We still going out tonight?"

She beamed and leaned into me. "If you want. Where are we going?"

"Maybe out for a drink?"

"Sounds fun. We could go dancing. Do you dance?"

Hell to the no, I didn't. And wouldn't. Well, except for the obligatory rocking from side-to-side at the wedding, which Ma had informed me I *would* do. But I could change Beth's mind later. For the benefit of the people watching us, I laughed and nuzzled her cheek before stepping away.

I looked up to find everyone watching me with such… *hope* and approval in their eyes. Tony even gave me a goddamn thumbs-up.

"Glad to see you've upped your game while we were gone, little bro," said Ace.

My stomach lurched. I had to struggle to keep the smile on my face.

Why was everyone so invested in me dating a *nice girl*? Why couldn't they just leave me the fuck alone to do what I wanted to do? But with a family like mine, that was never gonna happen. I loved them, but, man, talk about a double-edged sword.

"All right! It looks like everyone's here." Father O'Brien came in rubbing his hands together. He glanced twice at Mike, then away again, his happy expression going a little strained. I knew from Ma that Father O'Brien wasn't exactly onboard with the whole embracing-the-gay thing. But if he said anything, I swear he'd be shitting his collar out in a few days' time.

"We're all here," Anita confirmed, face shining.

"Wonderful. Perfect. Groom and groomsmen, follow me. I'll show you to the room where you'll be dressing and waiting before the ceremony. The rest of the wedding party, please wait here until I return."

Father O'Brien waved his arms like he was a cop directing traffic. I trooped along with Gabe, Tony, Mike, Ace, Paul, and Gabe's friend from work, Axel. There were six of us groomsmen with Tony being the best man.

As we filed down wood-paneled corridors, Tony slung an arm around my shoulder. "So. You're hot and heavy with Beth, huh?"

I shrugged nonchalantly. "Maybe. I don't kiss and tell."

"Good for you, bro. Good for you." He patted my head. "But you'd better not hurt her, or Anita will kill you."

"Yeah, yeah," I said.

Damn. He had a point. If I didn't want to ruin my relations with my new in-laws indefinitely, I'd have to tread carefully with Beth. Maybe take her out a couple of times but keep my distance, so I didn't really hurt her when we broke up after the wedding. Maybe I should even act like a jerk, so she'd dump me.

The idea of being an asshole to her didn't sit well though. Fuck, this lying shit was complicated.

Why was I even doing this? Oh yeah, because I'd used Beth as an excuse about why I'd been staying out nights. And because the more I was off doing something I knew Pa would hate, the guiltier I felt, and the more I wanted to pretend I was really being the good son.

I suddenly couldn't breathe. I stopped in the hallway and gasped for air.

"What's wrong?" Tony asked, looking concerned. "You get hurt at work?"

I shook my head. "Nah. I'm good."

Up ahead, Father O'Brien opened a door. "In here, Gentlemen."

I shook off Tony's grip on my arm and hurried to catch up.

The rehearsal went about how I expected. There were a few directions I had to remember and lots of standing around. As a groomsman, I didn't have to do a thing except show people to seats and then follow the guy in front of me out to the nave when it was time. After that, I only had to stand there and not pick my nose or otherwise make a fool of myself. Beth was maid of honor, so she was escorted by Tony. I escorted a friend of Anita's named Jeanette. She was nice and had those invisible braces on her teeth.

The rehearsal dinner was at a fancy Japanese restaurant, and I sat next to Beth. I worried she'd ask me basic information that would make it obvious to anyone listening that we hardly knew each other. So I started talking about my week at work. She wanted to hear all about the recent fires, and I went into a lot of detail. I found myself telling her all about the CL-515, Dell's plane, and stuff I'd learned about how fire aviation worked. It passed the time and she seemed really interested, her brown eyes focused on my face.

Ma was in her element. She looked great in a new blue silky dress, and she went around the big table talking to everyone. Shane was at the dinner, and Tony's wife, Viv, so it was very couple-y. By the end of the meal, I had my arm around the back of Beth's chair and Beth's hand was on my thigh. I drank a couple of beers, but made myself stop when Pa frowned at me.

Yeah, right. I was driving. Best not to kill myself and the maid of honor the day before the wedding.

After dinner, it took forever for everyone to hug and say goodbye, and to make sure Mike could get a ride home with

Ma and Pa since Shane had to go back to school. But at last I was alone in my truck with Beth. I started the engine and pulled out of the restaurant parking lot, heading for downtown Oroville.

"So where do you wanna go?" she asked brightly. "If you're up for dancing, I know a good spot."

I sighed. "I'm pretty whipped after this week. Do you mind if we just go out for a drink?"

"Oh of course! Sorry, I wasn't thinking." She put a hand on my shoulder. "You must be dead on your feet."

"I am." I hoped that'd give me an excuse to make this a short night.

"Do you know a place?" Beth asked. "Or do you need me to look something up on the phone."

"Nah, I know Oroville. I'm good."

Beth trailed her hand down my arm and rested it on my forearm. I could have taken her hand. I had an automatic transmission. But I kept both hands on the wheel like I had no idea how to drive.

We stopped at a quiet little bar and got a booth. We ordered drinks, and I asked Beth about her degree and kept her talking. She told me all kinds of detail about her classes. She had to be really smart because they sounded crazy technical. I heard all about the college she'd gone too, MIT, and her hopes for getting a good job in Sacramento.

The waitress came by.

"Another round?" Beth asked expectantly, looking between me and the waitress. Her Margarita glass and my beer were both empty.

I shook my head. "I'd love to, but I really need to get some sleep."

Beth's face crumpled into a pitying look. "Yeah, of course. Poor boy." She patted my hand and looked at the waitress. "This big lug is with Cal Fire. They've been working nonstop the past few weeks with all the wildfires."

The waitress's tired face lit up. "Really? Thank you so much for what you do. My brother's ranch was saved last year thanks to Cal Fire. I was terrified about his horses being trapped and burned and all, but they were fine. You guys are true superheroes as far as I'm concerned."

"Right?" Beth smiled at me, caressing my hand. "Such heroes! My sister's marrying into a whole family of fire-fighters."

"Lucky her," said the waitress, putting our tab on the table and offering me another grateful smile before leaving.

"Yeah, lucky her," Beth said quietly, smiling at me. "And lucky me for being here with you."

I squeezed her hand. "Wish I could live up to my reputation tonight."

She laughed. "Oh, no! You don't want to do that. I'm hoping to be the *exception* to your reputation!" She slid out of the booth.

I drove Beth back to her parents' house. It was a good thirty-minute drive from the bar in Oroville, but at least it was headed in the right direction—south. When I pulled into her driveway, the house was dark. She made no move to open the passenger door.

I had to kiss her. At the very least. Today had been fine—no one had asked Beth any probing questions about our relationship, probably because she was sitting right next to me. But I doubted I'd be so lucky at the wedding. I should kiss her and ask her out again.

I sat there feeling the weight of her eyes on me in the dark. "Well…." she said, moving for the door handle.

"Hey, Beth." I grabbed her hand. "Sorry I've been quiet tonight."

"No worries! I know your job's intense. I imagine anyone you go out with has to be patient, you know? I understand that. The important work you do… saving lives, saving trees… You're a good guy, Donny Canali."

I was so *not* a good guy. But I smiled. "Thanks. So, uh, this weekend is the wedding, but maybe we could do something next weekend. Go to a movie or something?"

"I'd love that." She leaned toward me in the dark and this was it. All I could think of was Dell as her lips pressed to mine. Dell's confidence, the way he possessed me with a single touch. It felt so wrong to be thinking of Dell. It felt so wrong, period. I pressed my lips to hers for several weird moments before I pulled back.

"It was fun hanging out with you," I said. "Good night."

She laughed breezily. "Such a gentleman. I had fun too. Good night, Donny." She opened the door and hopped out.

I waited until she got safely inside, then headed for the freeway. I paused only briefly at the freeway entrance. Fuck it. I turned onto the southbound ramp.

It was after eleven when I got to Dell's place. I thought I saw a flash of relief cross his face when he opened the door, but it vanished as he stepped back to let me in. "I thought you had rehearsal dinner tonight."

"I did. But it's ended early. So."

I tossed my keys on his coffee table and plopped down on his couch. And suddenly I was as tired as I'd pretended to be with Beth. Dell locked the door.

"Want a beer?" he asked.

I nodded. He went into the kitchenette and came back with a cold beer and a sparkling water. I took a big slug of the brew as he sat down next to me on the couch and propped his feet up next to mine on the coffee table. His big warm shoulder pressed against me.

"Busy week," he said.

"Too fucking busy," I agreed bitterly. I didn't want to resent the wedding activities for Gabe. I mean, this was his big show. And everyone was so happy—Ma and Pa, Gabe and Anita, Anita's family. And it was great having Ace and

Paul home. But I sort of did resent it anyway—especially the whole Beth thing.

Dell cleared his throat. "Hey, I need to tell you something. You know Gala's been working with Tessa on the wedding dresses?"

"Yeah?"

"Well, Gala's been spending a lot of time over at your mom and dad's house 'cause Tessa lives there too. I went to pick her up one time, and your mom invited me to stay for dinner. I didn't know how to refuse. Then she invited Gala, me, and Mam to the wedding."

I stared at him. Visions of planes colliding and trains derailing spooled through my head. Right. A disaster waiting to happen.

"Donny?"

"Hmmm?" I blinked at him.

He frowned. "Look, Gala really wants me to see the dresses in the ceremony. It's important to her. And you know I've been encouraging her to get back into design. But if you really don't want me to be there, I'll just drop Gala off. And… I don't know… come back to get her later."

Sure, he said that. But his voice had gone hard and his posture stiff. I knew I was displeasing him. A lot. I hated that.

"Well…" I had no idea how to finish that sentence.

How could I tell Dell, a guy I'd been screwing for almost three months, that I didn't want him around my family, *at all*, when I had breakfast with his every morning when I stayed here? How did I tell proud and confident Dell that I was ashamed of him, ashamed of myself for being with him? And how the fuck did I tell him that I was supposed to be dating the maid of honor?

"Fine," Dell snapped. "I'll tell your mom and Anita I can't make it." He got up and stalked into the kitchenette, tossed his mostly full seltzer in the sink where I heard it gurgle down the drain.

Fuck. I'd never seen angry Dell before. A few flashes of pissed, but never full-on angry. I hated it. And it was my own stupid fault for getting Gala involved with the dresses.

"No!" I said. "It's fine. You can come to the wedding. It's just… I'll be really busy. I'm in the wedding party. And I'll have to sit at the head table at the reception, and… I'll just be busy. So, you know, I won't be able to hang out with you."

Dell leaned against the kitchen counter and crossed his arms over his big chest, his eyes still cold. "Yeah, I know that, Donny. I'm not expecting you to give me the first dance or declare your undying love."

"Okay. So there's no problem then." I forced a smile. Fuck, this was such a big problem.

Dell studied me for a moment longer, then sighed and rubbed his face. "Look—"

He paused so long, staring off into space, that I started to dread his next words. Any conversation with someone you were dating that started off with *look* never ended well. Not that I was exactly dating him.

Was he going to break up with me? Tell me to fuck off? A bitter taste flooded my mouth and my head spun. No, not yet. I wasn't ready for this to end yet.

I stood up. "Come on. Let's just chill, okay? Come to bed."

He glanced at me, frowning. "No. I don't think so. You're welcome to spend the night. It's a long drive, and it's late. But we're not doing that."

"Doing what?"

"Having you be all sweet and vulnerable and adoring in bed, and then the minute you're out of here, I don't exist for you."

I glared. "What? We took that helicopter trip, didn't we? And… and we've worked together."

"No." He held up a hand. "I'm not gonna argue. I know there's a lot of family stress around this wedding, so I'm giving you a pass. But when that's over, we need to talk about what we're doing. Because the truth is, Donny," He shook his head. "I've got two people in my life already that I have to *adult* for. I really don't need another one. You need to figure out your own shit."

His words hit my chest like a wrecking ball. That wasn't fair. I'd done so much to spend time with him—lied to my family, snuck around. He had no idea how I'd complicated my life for him.

"I just wanted to have this! To feel this good. For once in my goddamn life," I said, my eyes hot and my chest aching. I had no idea what I was even saying. I grabbed the keys from the coffee table and walked to the door. When I turned to look at him, he was still leaning on the counter, arms crossed, expression inscrutable.

"You can have this, Donny," he said quietly. "All you have to do is find the balls to reach out and take it."

I laughed bitterly. "Find the balls, huh? That's so easy for you to say." I shook my head, feeling sick. I had to get out of there. But I still wanted him so goddamn bad I thought I could die from it. "You know what? We're both dead on our feet after this week. And, like you said, this wedding shit is stressful. So let's just pretend I never came over tonight. Okay?"

I looked at him pleadingly and he finally nodded.

I turned slowly and opened the door, hoping every second that he'd stop me, that he'd pull me into his arms and make me forget everything for a while.

But he didn't. I found myself back at my truck. I got in and headed home. The cracks were getting bigger—not just in my real life but now even in this fantasy world.

Why couldn't everything just fucking stay the same?

# SEVENTEEN

## DELL

"Honey, are you okay? You seem kind of quiet." Mam leaned over from the back seat and peered at me as I drove, then gave Gala's arm a pat. "Oh, baby, I'm so excited to see your creations. Tell me about that color again."

I wanted to point out to my mam that I was quiet because she hadn't let anyone get a word into her nonstop monologue that had been going on since we left home for our trip to the church in Oroville. But no way I'd squelch her enthusiasm. Today might be about getting married and partying to the Canalis, but for me, it was all about Gala and my mam. Gala was almost bouncing in her seat she was so excited about seeing her dresses walk down the aisle. And for my mam, who didn't have a circle of friends in California yet, this was a big social occasion. I wanted her to have fun and, if that meant her talking for twelve hours straight, that was okay with me.

Plus, she was right. I was quiet. While I wouldn't miss Gala and Mam's day for anything, I'd happily miss all the rest. The confrontation last night with Donny haunted me.

Yes, it was time to fish or cut bait in our relationship as the saying went, but damn. I had a fucking lot of bait at stake in this fishing contest. I'd been all Mr. Cool *I've already got two people to adult for* the last time we'd seen each other, but the fact was I didn't want to lose Donny. I was well and truly hooked. I loved what we did in bed and, on those rare occasions where we hung out, watching baseball, cooking a meal in my apartment, or having a picnic in the damned mountains, I felt at home. Like I'd come home. I'd passed the hookup stage with him a long time ago. I couldn't lose Donny without a big fucking hole in my heart.

We were so perfect together. Why couldn't he see that?

Gala pointed. "That's it. St. Michael's. Tessa said there's parking in the back, and that I can go in the side entrance."

I nodded, glancing at the imposing structure, shining in the morning light. Very Catholic, which of course was my Irish religious heritage, too, but long-since abandoned. You didn't grow up the gay son of a drunk trying to help your mother and sister stay alive and do much clinging to faith. Mam used to go to church sometimes and take me with her. She loved all the beautiful statues, flowers, and elaborate costumes. But for little Rivendell, one sermon on the evils of *the sin that dare not speak its name* when I was about ten had queered the church for me, literally.

I pulled into the back lot that still boasted quite a few available spaces. It was early. The wedding didn't start for just over an hour.

As I parked, Gala barreled out of the passenger seat, hauling a couple tote bags full of stuff. Mam followed her. Gala leaned down and said, "Come inside, Dell, and turn right. Wait in the hall. I'll check that everyone's dressed and then give you a wave."

"No worries. I can stay in the hall. I don't want to invade the temple of the goddesses."

"No, I need your opinions and good eye."

I grinned. "Happy to lend them." She slammed the door and she and Mam hurried away, but my grin didn't fade. I was betting Gala wanted to show off her expertise to me a little and that did my heart good. So much of the last few years had been about Gala's fear and worry. The cancer diagnosis, surgery, and chemo had been so traumatic for her. It seemed like it had crushed her will to live. I was damned grateful to see this side emerging again, the bright, creative, happy Gala of her childhood. I really did owe the Canalis a debt of gratitude, whether Donny had done it all by accident or not.

A few minutes later, I sat on the hard bench in the polished granite hall surrounded by the smell of new flowers and old incense. The door on the opposite side of the hall opened and Gala leaned out, smile as big as the Cheshire Cat. I followed her into chaos. A dressing room at a drag show couldn't have been wilder. Every bridesmaid appeared to be there, along with miscellaneous mothers and friends. No bride. She must be dressing somewhere else.

Clothing draped on every surface, cosmetics littered the tables where large lighted mirrors had been set up and about a dozen people, most of whose pronouns were likely *she* and *her*, scurried around the room.

"Tiffany, I can't get this sash tied. Can you do it?"

"Is this too much eye shadow?"

"God, Anne, don't eat *that* in your dress!"

Gala laughed at my expression, which must look a bit like Frodo arriving at Mount Doom.

Gala raised her voice. "Hey, all, this is my brother, Dell, who I told you about."

A couple women raised their eyebrows, and I got a leer or two.

Gala said, "Don't hit on him. He's gay. And he's here to render the Y chromosome opinion." She grinned at me and pointed to a chair against the wall. Someone pulled Gala to one of the tables, so I sat down and settled in to look as invisible as a six-foot-three-inch man could in a sea of chiffon and tulle. Of course, the fact that I knew what the fabrics were probably gave me a hall pass.

Gala raced around the big room adjusting hems, adding necklaces, and touching up makeup. She never once looked uncertain or apologetic. Mam trailed after her, doing her bidding, but she seemed to mostly contribute compliments to the ladies.

After about half an hour, an officious woman bustled in and waved her arms. "Bridesmaids, we need you to line up. This is your ten-minute warning."

That elicited a few shrieks as a couple of women hurried into the bathroom for a last-minute pee and Gala started parading each of the attendants by me. "So what do you think?"

I grinned. "First off, I think you're amazing. The dress looks wonderful on everyone." That was no joke. Five women who ranged from tiny and plump to tall and athletic all looked like the dress had been picked out just for them.

The tallest woman said, "Aren't they great? I honestly will wear this again. Jeez, my boyfriend's going to have to think of places to take me."

The last person Gala showed off to me was a pretty, petite woman with light brown hair and a lovely smile. "This is Beth, Anita's sister and maid of honor. Beth, this is my brother, Dell."

"Hi, Beth." The gown she wore had a similar pattern on top to the bridesmaid's dresses, but hers was longer and the gathering in the back became a short train. "I love that version of the dress."

Beth smiled. "I know. Isn't it spectacular?" She did a half-turn to show off the back.

Gala grinned. "With a figure like Beth's, it's easy."

Beth gave a demurring shake of the head, then studied my face. "You must be the pilot I've heard so much about."

"I'm a Cal Fire pilot, yes."

"All of the Canalis talk about you." Her expression was pleasant, but her gaze was assessing. "Especially Donny."

There was something in her tone that grated—like she was close to Donny. For one wild and crazy minute, I was tempted to say, *That's because he's my boyfriend and we fuck several nights a week.* Instead, I performed my trained-seal job. "He's my ground liaison for the Gridley station, so he's had the most contact with our crew at McClellan."

The door opened and Tessa peered into the room. "Gala, can I get you to help me arrange Anita's gown for the procession? And Beth, you're needed." She smiled at me. "Dell, you and your mom can go get seated and save a place for Gala, okay? Probably best to go around the church and come in the front. It's a madhouse between here and the narthex."

"Sure thing." I gave Tessa a smile. "Good luck today."

She gave a nervous exhale, but her eyes shone. "Thanks. It's exciting!"

I escorted Mam out the side door of the church. "Hey, Mam, you look great." The medium blue dress she wore showed off her fair hair and rosy skin.

"Gala designed it for me. Isn't it wonderful? She really is talented." I'd never point out that was the talent Mam had been squelching with her overprotection, but hell, letting go was hard.

My gut started clenching about halfway to the entrance, where a line of mostly dark-haired Canali relatives moved slowly up the steps and into the church. We fell in behind them.

The exotic-looking woman I remembered as the aunt, Carlotta, hurried up the stairs beside us wearing bright purple with feathers in her hair. "Oh hello, Dell. So glad you could come. This must be your mother." She clasped Mam's hand. "I'm Carlotta Canali, aunt to the groom. I must say, this event simply wouldn't have been as splendid without your wonderful daughter, Gala. We're so grateful."

Mam looked pleased. "Isn't she amazing? Blessed by the fairies, that one."

"Oh I so agree. When is her birthday?"

"My baby's a Pisces."

"Well of course, the most creative of us all." She glanced toward the entrance door where Lucille Canali was waving. "I better hurry. See you after the ceremony."

"What a lovely woman." Mam smiled. She might have found a kindred spirit.

Inside, the cute cousin with the pretty mouth, Tito, greeted us with a shy smile. "Bride or groom?"

My mother said, "Groom's side, please."

As he led us to a pew packed with obvious Canali relatives and their various spouses, I saw Donny hurrying back to the entrance for his next guest. Holy shit, in a dark suit and peach tie the man ought to be fucking illegal. That half-disappointment and half-relief feeling crept into my stomach. Luck of the groomsman draw that Donny wasn't seating us.

It was a little intimidating seeing how large a clan the Canalis really were. I'd known it was a big family, but there had to be several hundred here, all clearly related. Donny had mentioned that there were relatives coming from the East Coast for the wedding too. The men were all tough guys, from the littlest to the oldest, and the women all pretty and groomed to the max with big hair and makeup. There was an attitude of intense camaraderie between them. I loved family, but still, it was hard to imagine what it would be like to be part of such a large clan—or to try to breach the walls as a significant other. Especially one that didn't fit and wasn't welcome. Though I saw Shane a few rows ahead, dressed in a nice blue suit and sitting with an older man since Mike was in the wedding party. He'd managed it somehow. God, the guy had some balls.

I fanned myself, suddenly overheated.

"What's wrong?" Mam asked.

I shook my head. "Nothing."

Gala slid in beside me a few minutes later. Seconds after that, Chief Canali led his wife, Lucille, down the aisle to the front row. The chief held his back stiff and proud, and Lucille was beaming and radiant in a peach dress. A middle-aged lady I assumed was Anita's mom was led in by a young man. Then the music started. A flower girl—Tony's daughter—marched down the aisle to a chorus of awwws, followed by his son carrying a pillow with the rings. Tony's wife, Viv, knelt at the end of the aisle, anxiously egging the boy on against the obvious distractions represented by the people he knew and the ribbons decorating the flowers at each pew that were just begging to be pulled and unraveled by a five-year-old. He made it to the end without incident and the bridesmaids started down the aisle. Gala grabbed my hand and squeezed as she stared at her handiwork.

I squeezed back and whispered, "They look wonderful."

Truthfully, I only gave them a fast glance because I couldn't pry my eyes away from Donny, who'd filed in with the groom and groomsmen and now stood at the front of the church. Fuck he was devastating in that suit. And seeing him like this—dressed immaculately in the front of a church—did something to my gut that I didn't want to think about too hard. I couldn't be that stupid. Gala nudged my arm and pointed to the aisle where the pretty maid of honor, Beth, was passing in her dress with the train. I nodded my appreciation, but my heart was beating so hard you'd think I was flying into combat.

Finally, the bride made her procession on the arm of her father. Gala pressed a hand to her mouth and fanned her face against tears. So did Mam, despite her bad track record with the glorious institution of marriage. Hell, even I blinked a bit harder than normal. Fucking weddings, man. I tried not to stare at Donny, but the couple times I did, he was staring right back. *Yeah, you idiot. Get it. We're as much a couple as the two tying the knot.*

The ceremony was solemn and quietly joyous. It went by fast or maybe I was just lost in thought. Pretty soon the newly married duo walked back up the aisle and everyone applauded. There were lots of hoots and whistles from the assembled Canalis.

I would have liked to suggest we just go home, but no way I'd wreck Gala and Mam's fun day. So forty minutes later, we pulled into the gravel parking space in front of the Canalis' home with a gazillion other cars and followed the crowds around the house to the backyard.

The big space I remembered so well had been transformed. A couple of bars were set up under the trees. What had been a patio now served as a dance floor and a trio of young guys plus a girl, at least one a likely Canali, strummed away on guitars and a base, as the girl sang softly into a microphone. Probability of the music getting louder later? One hundred percent.

Round tables had been set up all across the yard with a rectangular table occupying the place of honor at the apex of the group and a large circular table on either side of the head table. At the moment, all three tables of honor were empty. Farther back, food was being laid out on a long, long buffet.

Another Canali-ish looking boy came up to us with a tray. "Would you like one? Those are champagne and that's ginger ale."

"Thank you." I handed champagne to Mam and Gala and took ginger ale for myself.

A waving hand caught my attention. I looked over at one of the tables where a guy I knew from my training sessions at McClellan was sitting. I guided Mam and Gala over to them.

The firefighter, Randy Millhouse, stuck out his hand. "Good to see you, Pilot Murphy."

I grinned. "And you. This is my mother, Titania, and my sister, Gala."

Randy smiled. "Hi. And this here is Brian and his wife, Katie. Brian works at the Gridley station. You saved his life back at the Sierra City fire and he hasn't stopped talking about it since."

Brian's eyes were wide with a familiar starstruck look. "Honored to meet you, Pilot Murphy. And you, ladies."

Katie said, "We're forever grateful. Truly."

I shook my head. "Laying down water is my job. And just call me Dell."

Brian leaned over and pulled at the chair closest to him. "Please, sit and join us. Uh, unless you're expected at another table."

I shook my head and we all sat. "Thank you. Actually, we don't know the family that well outside of work. Well, except for my brilliant sister who helped design the bridesmaid's dresses."

Katie pressed her hands together. "Oh my gosh, they're gorgeous. Did you really design them?" And the conversation was off and running.

Halfway through my ginger ale and a description of the CL-515, the musicians gave as big a fanfare as they could manage with no horns and the bridal party started marching in from the house, the groomsmen escorting the bridesmaids first.

My gaze clung to Donny as he walked the woman he'd escorted down the aisle to one of the side tables where a man came up and joined her. Must be her husband. Donny sat at the table as well and seemed to work hard at not looking in my direction. He smiled and applauded as the other attendants came in, but to me, he appeared tense and nervous. Was he really bothered that I was here? It wasn't like I'd be interacting with his family much or demanding his time. But no, he had plenty besides me to occupy his mind today.

When Tony, the best man, brought in the maid of honor, Beth, he walked her to an open seat next to Donny. Donny rose and pulled out the chair. Beth flashed a smile at him that would have warmed metal. When they were seated, she leaned in to whisper something in his ear, her hand on his shoulder.

My gut clenched and I felt more than saw Mam glance at me. But I took a conscious breath. Fuck it. I wasn't going to get tweaked about a flirtatious woman. Donny was gorgeous. Of course, he got that kind of attention. Still, relaxing the tension that had crept through my body wasn't happening. I'd thought today might be awkward, but this was downright uncomfortable.

The bride and groom walked in to big cheers and took their place at the head table where the Chief and Mrs. Canali already sat with Donny's grandmother and grandfather. The bride's parents sat on the other side.

Tony Canali stood up and delivered a toast I barely heard, and then the bride and groom walked to the dance floor and started dancing. Next came the bride's parents and the chief and his wife, and then Tony, dancing with his wife.

My fists clenched as Donny stood and extended his hand to Beth. She held onto him all the way to the dance floor and then melted against him in a slow dance, staring adoringly into his eyes. I couldn't watch this. Just couldn't.

Through the ceremonial dance, I chatted determinedly with Brian and Randy about their station and then the food service was announced. Like a freaking, smiling robot, I led Gala and Mam to the buffet, got food, and brought it back to our table, trying to ignore snatches of conversation I heard drifting from the head tables. I thought I was hiding my turmoil well until Gala gripped my arm and stared at me with dripping compassion. Fuck. I smiled at her and went back to my food, even though I didn't want it and couldn't even taste it. Anything to keep from looking at Donny and Beth.

My brain kept repeating that this had been a monumental mistake coming here. I should have dropped off Gala and Mam and kept driving. No wonder Donny hadn't been too keen on the idea of me at the wedding. And yeah, I'd known he wasn't exactly going to sit on my lap or hang out with me. But this… this felt bad. Way worse than I'd anticipated. Maybe it was the juxtaposition of the wedding, and the vows, and all the happy couples, and then being utterly ghosted by the man who shared my bed. I can't lie. It hurt.

After a while, waiters circulated through the tables to pick up dishes. One of the musicians said, "While the cake is set up, feel free to stretch your legs and dance."

Mam actually clapped her hands. "Oh good, cake!"

Brian and Katie went to dance and immediately, Carlotta came and filled the chair next to Mam. "I'm so looking forward to getting to know you better. Tell me more about Gala's rising sign."

As the two women put their heads together in mutual astrology, Gala looked at me and whispered, "I think we can go soon."

"Yeah." My voice was gruff. "But let Mam have fun for a few minutes more."

She nodded and smiled, totally getting it. I made the mistake of glancing at the dance floor and saw Beth pulling Donny out for another dance. He took her in his arms like it was second nature. Gabe and Anita were dancing nearby and they moved closer to Donny and Beth. Gabe said something and they all laughed.

It had never been clearer to me that this was Donny's world—and there was no place for me in it.

Gala must have seen me flinch, because she said, "I think Donny's just hanging out with Beth for the wedding."

I tried to shrug and turned back to Randy. I didn't want to ignore Gala, but damn.

Mrs. Canali's voice came from over my shoulder. "I'm so delighted to meet you, Mrs. Murphy. All of my firefighters are big admirers of your son. And we're all madly in love with Gala. I'm so happy you were able to come to the wedding."

Mam replied, "Thanks so much for inviting me. You'll have to give me some of your recipes. This food is delicious."

"Oh, I'd be happy to."

Just as I was about to turn and say hello, Mrs. Canali said, "Before you go, I hope you can meet some of my children. Especially Donny. My goodness, Dell saved my boy's life in the Sierra City fire."

The train was coming, like it had materialized out of thin air, and there was no way to prevent the smash-up. I started turning, but it was slow motion. "Mam, I—"

My mother's voice rang out. "Oh, I know Donny very well. Half the week, he's at my breakfast table."

Images of tangled wreckage filled my mind.

I reached out to grab Mam. Plant a hand over her mouth if I had to.

Mrs. Canali looked confused. "He is?"

"Yes, but I keep wondering, who's that girl he's dancing with?"

Turned to stone. I couldn't stop the answer from coming, because I had to hear it too. My life depended on it.

Mrs. Canali beamed. "Oh that's Beth. Donny's girlfriend."

My hand on my mother's shoulder froze, but not as much as my heart.

And Mam's irate voice rose just as the music stopped. "Girlfriend? Where does Donny get time for a girlfriend when he spends at least three nights a week in bed with Dell?"

# EIGHTEEN

## DONNY

The words reverberated around the garden *in bed with Dell, in bed with Dell, in bed with Dell.*

My first thought was that my paranoia and anxiety had conjured up that voice. It had to be my guilty conscience talking. It couldn't possibly be real. I'd been freaking out since this morning, worried about Dell being at the wedding and having to keep up appearances with Beth. I'd told myself I'd just smile, smile, smile and be distantly polite to both of them. But Beth had torpedoed that plan—sitting next to me at the table and hanging all over me, dragging me out to slow dance. She was in the wedding party, so I couldn't exactly avoid her.

So those words were exactly the sort of nightmare my frazzled brain *would* invent. But the shocked look on the faces of everyone staring at me put that option off the table. Someone had actually spoken those words out loud. And everyone had heard them.

The song was over, but my arms were still loosely around Beth. They were frozen as she stepped back, her eyes wide, glancing from me to somewhere to my left, which I knew was where Dell was. I'd known exactly where Dell was this entire day—like he had a beacon on or something.

Beth looked shocked for a moment, but then her eyes narrowed. She hissed. "You could have just *told* me. Asshole." She stormed away.

Oh. Fuck.

I turned to look at Dell, still hoping this was all a mistake or that maybe he'd laugh it off or something. But all I saw was his back as he led his mother from the garden, heading around the house. He was leaving—leaving me here alone with this. *He was leaving me, period.*

Then I saw Mike's face. He was at the drinks table with Shane—shocked, angry. And beyond him, Ma talking rapidly with her hands to Pa, who looked confused.

I was still frozen there, arms around empty air, when Gabe crowded into me and hissed in my ear. "Tell me that's a lie, Donny. Or I swear to God—"

"Fuck off." I pushed him out of the way, turned, and ran.

Somehow, I made it to my house. Mike had fucking locked the front door—probably because there were so many people around for the wedding.

I didn't have my keys, so I had to go around to the side, rip the screen out of my bedroom window, which I'd left cracked open, and crawl in through there. Something tore on the rented suit pants, but I didn't care.

I fell onto my knees on the bedroom floor and curled up, head in my hands. *This can't be happening. This can't be happening.*

My family knew. They knew about me and Dell. Hell, everyone at the wedding knew, which included some big brass from Cal Fire, a few guys from my station, and every fucking relative I had.

And, if that wasn't bad enough, I'd been caught lying my

ass off and making a fool of myself with Beth. Anita would be so pissed.

And to top it all off, Dell had walked away. *You need to get your shit straight.* I'd already been on thin ice with him, and I'd really fucked up today—ignoring him and letting Beth act like we were a couple. And I needed Dell right now. I needed him to tell me to be strong, to show me how to navigate this with some fucking dignity. But I'd been such a jerkwad that he'd walked away. And I deserved it.

My mind went to Pa, my usual rock. *Pa.* Oh God, Pa knew.

My stomach lurched. I stumbled to my bathroom and deposited a round of wedding food and beer into the bowl.

"Donny?" Out in my bedroom, someone banged on the door. It was Mike.

I flushed the toilet, got to my feet, and rinsed out my mouth in the sink. My reflection stared back at me. I was still decked out in a blue suit jacket, white shirt, and fucking peach tie, my hair still perfect from the way I'd styled it this morning. Donny Canali—macho firefighter stud. What a joke.

"Donny." Mike's reflection joined mine in the mirror. He'd apparently barged right in and was standing in my bedroom, an angry frown on his face. But when he saw me, his expression softened. "Hey. You okay?"

I barked a laugh. "Fuck no. *Okay* might as well be fucking China, that's how far from it I am."

He stepped into the doorway, sniffed, and got a grossed-out look. "Did you puke?"

"What do you think, Sherlock?" I pushed past him, sat on my bed, and dropped my face into my hands. I wanted to tell him it was my own private puke in my own private room and he could leave, but I really needed my baby bro.

I felt Mike sit on the bed next to me. "I gotta hand it to you, bro. You sure shocked the hell out of everyone. I've heard there's always gotta be one disaster at a wedding. So, you know, congrats for providing that."

"What did *you* look pissed for?" I asked, because he sure had looked pissed in the garden. And if anyone should be on my side, it was Mike.

He stiffened next to me. "Well, it's pretty rank that you never said a word to me. Not even when I was going through all that shit, when I came out."

I dropped my hands to stare at him. "I didn't know then! It wasn't until Dell that… Fuck."

Mike looked intrigued. "Seriously? What happened?"

I sighed and looked down at my feet. Well hell. I was still wearing polished black dress shoes. With a grunt of disgust, I kicked them off. "He kissed me."

Mike barked a laugh. "What? Dell just up and kissed you? Guess he's not just a daredevil in the air, huh?"

The words shot a spark of pain through me as images of him flying filled my head. *Dell. Oh, Dell.* I squeezed my eyes tight and clamped my fingers over them. My chest felt like it'd been filled with hot, toxic gas.

"Aw, Donny." Mike slung an arm around my shoulders. "It's gonna be okay."

I shook my head. No to the *hell nope* on that score.

Mike rubbed my back. "I guess the big mystery about where you've been spending so much time is solved. The idea that you were with Beth never quite felt right."

I didn't say anything, just tried to swallow down the heat in my throat.

"So why were you all over Beth today? With Dell here? That must have killed him. I mean, did you guys agree to that beforehand or what? Wait. Have you actually been dating Beth too? Did he know?"

I shook my head, finally under control enough to drop my hands. "I only went out with her once and nothing happened. I was just… I told everyone I was seeing Beth when I stayed out nights. And I didn't *want* Dell to come to the wedding. He did because of Gala."

Mike blinked at me, a furrow on his brow. He started to speak, stopped, started again. "You didn't want him here? That's pretty cold."

"Look, this isn't some big love affair like you and Shane! It was just supposed to be a temporary thing. No one was ever supposed to know."

I expected Mike to understand, but he just frowned harder. "It's been a few months at least."

"So?"

"So that's a pretty shitty way to treat Dell. I don't know him well, but I know he's gorgeous, and out, and fucking accomplished. He deserves better than that, just like Shane deserved better than me denying my feelings for him to the fam."

"Dell isn't my *boyfriend*," I said hotly, though the words felt like a huge stupid lie. "It's just sex."

Mike studied my face. He shook his head. "Sorry. I call b.s. You've hardly ever dated anyone for this long. I think you do care about Dell. But I think your head is so far up your ass, you can't even admit it to yourself."

The heat returned to my eyes and I rubbed at them in frustration. "I don't know what the fuck I feel."

Mike stood up. "Just level with the family. That's it. You don't *have* to hide this, Donny. They survived me coming out. Just be honest with everyone, apologize to Dell, and maybe you can see where it goes with him."

"I can't do that!" I shouted, looking up at him. "It would kill Pa, and you know it! *Especially* after you. It's like he finally… he finally…." I couldn't finish that sentence.

Mike's lips pressed tight. "He finally paid attention to you once he decided to write me off?"

I shook my head to deny it. 'Cause that was pretty crappy for Mike. But he wasn't wrong.

Mike thought about it, eyes distant. "It'll be rough on Pa," he admitted. "But you can't live for him, Donny. Believe me. I tried. I tried to please everyone for a long time. But in the end, I had to face the fact that it wasn't possible. You can make Pa happy or you can be true to yourself—and to Dell." He sighed and stood, then gave me a sad look. "But I guess you're the only one who can figure out your priorities."

Mike left the room.

I laid on my bed and stared at nothing. Gradually, the light faded and night fell. I thought about texting Dell and apologizing. God, I wanted to do it so bad— but I didn't. Every time I tried, my fingers froze. What would I say? I'm sorry. I want to come back? And then what? Have sex every night of my life and tell no one ever? Yeah right. Dell was so over that. But damn, that sounded good to me. I'd never had anything, anyone in my life that came close to Dell. Not just in bed. Everywhere. I loved talking to him, laughing with him, sleeping beside him.

Shit! I sat up. *Quit. Stop this crap.*

I had to end this obsession with Dell. Look where it had brought me. I'd told myself—hell, I'd told *Mike*—it was temporary. It was time to cut the rope. Hell, Dell had probably already cut it for me, so I should just let him go.

Pain stabbed my gut, and I fell back on the bed again.

Mike was right. Dell deserved a hell of a lot better than my sorry ass. The thought made me want to puke again. How could a pretender like me ever be good enough for somebody as strong as Dell?

Vaguely, I heard the music in the distance and then, faintly, the sounds of car doors slamming and engines starting. It got darker. And still I lay on my bed in that fancy suit.

My eyes drifted closed. *Just forget.*

The beeping of my phone shocked me out of a terrible nightmare, flailing through a huge fire, my skin burning, looking for Dell. Always looking for Dell.

I swallowed hard and glanced at the phone. Text from Ma. *Family meeting. Come over right now.*

I could get up and drive away. Avoid it all. I'd rather poke my eyes out than have this conversation. Because I knew what I had to do.

A dull dark settled over me.

But this was my life—my job, my brothers and sister, my ma—and Pa. Some piece of my heart remembered I loved those things.

There was no avoiding it.

I got up and changed into a pair of old jeans and a T-shirt. I brushed my teeth and took a few aspirin for a throbbing headache. I couldn't look at myself in the mirror. Eyes down, gut clenched so tight it ached, I left the house and walked to Ma and Pa's. When I let myself in the back door, everyone was seated in the living room. Gabe and Anita must have left, and I was grateful for that. I knew Gabe would be pissed. But Ma and Pa were there, Mike, Ace, Paul, Tessa, Tony, and Nonna.

I stood at the low partition that separated the living room from the dining room, hands stuffed in my pockets. My face was hot and my hands ice cold. I had a vague memory of being called on the carpet by Ma and Pa when I was little— maybe six—after I'd broken one of the headlights out of Pa's truck. If only it were that simple this time.

"Donny, honey, we need to talk about what happened today," Ma said anxiously.

I glanced up at her. Her face was lined with worry, and she twisted her hands in her lap.

"Hope I didn't ruin the wedding," I said flatly.

"You didn't ruin anything," said Ace. "We cut the cake and threw rice as they drove off and all that jazz."

"Yeah, don't sweat it," said Paul.

I nodded. That was good.

"So you've been seeing Dell—*like that*—behind our backs?" Pa's voice. Angry.

"Angie, let the boy speak," said Ma.

I dared a glance at Pa. His face was set in stone. Worse, behind the coldness I caught a glimpse of absolute heartbreak in his eyes. I looked down again quickly. That hurt so badly, I wanted to collapse to the floor—wanted to disappear through it.

"What's going on, Donny," Tony asked. "What was all that stuff with Beth?"

"It's okay, Donny." That was Mike. "Just talk to us."

"It's not okay if he was leading Beth on," Tessa snapped. "But go on, Donny. Explain."

Their words were like flies buzzing in my ears compared to that look in Pa's eyes. I'd tried to think of something to say in the past few hours—from outright denial to declaring Dell was my boyfriend as if I didn't give a shit. But now, facing Pa, there was only one thing I could say.

I swallowed hard and looked up at him. "I have been… spending time with Dell. I guess I… I just figured it was private. My business. But I like women. I wasn't lying all these years or anything."

"That's called being bisexual, Dell," Ma explained in a patient voice. "And it's okay if that's how you feel, honey."

Ace snorted and looked at Paul with a raised eyebrow. "Progress comes to Resolute."

"Right? Finally," said Tessa. Her gaze on me was curious now.

I swallowed hard and shook my head. "I'm not..." I started to lie, but I couldn't to Ma's face. I couldn't deny that I was bi any longer, not to myself, but they didn't need to hear me admit it.. "I've only ever been with Dell that way. And I'm not gonna see him anymore." I looked at my father. "I prom-ise, Pa."

I was lying to Ma. Dell had been the ultimate fantasy I

didn't know I had. But I'd liked being with him, with a man —a lot. I couldn't delude myself that I was straight any longer. I was bisexual. But I *could* date women, and I would. I always had. Anything to get that look out of Pa's eyes.

"What about Beth?" Ma asked, still wringing her hands. "Sounds like you were dating her under false pretenses, and she's such a nice girl. I don't understand what you were thinking, Donato."

"I only went out with Beth a couple of times." Right, if you included the times we'd met with Gabe and Anita. "It was never serious. Like I said, I figured my private life was private. I never meant for the thing with Dell to be made public, and I'm sorry. So there's nothing else to talk about."

Mike shook his head in disgust, like he was disappointed in me. And that stung. But, as he'd said, I couldn't please everyone.

Tony grimaced. "Geez. I mean, objectively, Dell's pretty impressive. And good-looking. I guess if you had to fool around with—"

"Tony, shut it," Pa barked.

Tony shut up, biting his lip.

Pa stared at me and I stared back. That horrible look in his eyes was gone, thank God. But he still looked pissed. "You're not going to see Dell again?" he asked me. "You telling me the truth? I want your word on that."

"Yes, Pa. I won't see him again."

"I sure as hell hope not."

"Angie, we should listen, not tell," said Ma.

"He's my son, too, Lucille," Pa said firmly. He stood up. "I think we've said and *listened* to all that needs to be said about this subject. The family meeting is over. And I don't want to hear this mentioned ever again." He left the room.

Ace and Paul came over to me, and Ace slung an arm around my shoulder. "Man, that sucked. Good luck getting any privacy around here." He shuddered.

"Yeah," agreed Paul. "You ever decide you wanna get out of Canali central for a while, you can come hang with us. We'll be in Tokyo most of the fall."

"Thanks," I said. I really did miss them. But I couldn't imagine living their life, being on the road all the time. And I'd never leave Cal Fire.

"We were gonna go out to hear some live music in Sac. Wanna come with?" Ace asked.

I shook my head.

Ma was next. She hugged me tight, one of her patented mom hugs. "I love you so much, Donny. I just want you to be happy."

"Thanks, Ma." I started to lose it again and swallowed down the huge lump in my throat.

Finally, there was Mike. He stood in front of me and studied my face. He shook his head sadly. "Guess you made your choice. I hope you don't regret it, Donny."

"I won't," I said.

And that was a lie too. Because I already did.

# NINETEEN

## DELL

"Is it true? Did it really happen? I mean, it must have, right? Because who'd make this shit up?"

I rotated in my desk chair—the spot where I'd been hiding out all morning since my talk with Chief Montgomery— and looked up at Ty. I gave him the loud sigh his question so richly deserved and waved toward the door of the office. No way I was answering him in here. Too many ears.

I stalked down the hall and out the building entrance with Ty on my heels. The sun hit me like a frying pan. Man, California summer heat was so different from Oregon. Hotter. Dryer. And reflection from all the buildings didn't help.

I got to the shade of the maintenance building and sat in one of our old familiar chairs.

Ty took the other and said, "So what the hell happened?"

"I found out why Donny was so reluctant to have me come to the wedding." I blew out a breath and stared across the tarmac. "Donny was there with a girl he's been dating. Sister of the bride." I shrugged my tense shoulders. "My mam saw the obvious disconnect between Donny showing up for breakfast at her house three or four mornings a week and Mrs. Canali's claim that the girl in question was Donny's girl-friend." I glanced up over at him with a tight grin. "Let's say, Mam remarked on it at the top of her voice. Explicitly."

"Holy shit."

"Yep. But that's my mam. Subtle as the proverbial brick."

"Yeah and also protective of her son."

That's why Ty and I were such good friends outside of work. He really got it. My mam might be eccentric, but she loved her kids and we never doubted that. I wiped a hand over my hair. "Let's just say it was a clusterfuck all the way around. Donny was outed in the middle of his brother's wedding, which I'm sure he really appreciates." I rolled my eyes. "And I... well, I got what I deserved for being such an idiot. Do me a favor. If I ever so much as glance at a guy who's straight or closeted again, kick my ass. Hard."

Ty smirked. "As if I could. Have you talked to Donny?"

I shook my head.

"What do you think he told his family?"

"No idea."

"But you don't think he's wrapped himself in the rainbow flag."

I barked a bitter little laugh. "Ah, that would be a no."

"So what happens next?"

Damn, it was hard to catch my breath. "Nothing. He goes his way and I go mine."

Ty gazed at me, all his snarky humor erased. "I'm really sorry, Dell."

He didn't say anything else, but the deep sincerity and compassion in those few words made me blink hard against sudden heat in my eyes. Yeah, he got how much it hurt. "Thank you."

The sound of a door slamming made me look up. "Well, fuck me very much." Walking across the tarmac like some avenging fire angel came Chief Canali.

Ty whispered, "Shit. Sorry, dude, but this wingman is out." He disappeared into the maintenance hangar like he'd never been beside me.

I stood and took a few steps forward, holding the smallest hope that Canali had come for a reasonable conversation. His scowl and waving arms squelched that idea.

He stopped a few feet away and snarled, "I trusted you. I invited you into my home, even though I knew—I trusted you based on your record, and this is the thanks I get? You seduced my son."

"Sir, that's not what happened."

"Right. I'll bet. I can't believe—"

I held up my hand. "Stop. Just stop. What you believe isn't true—"

"I don't have to listen to you." He stalked a few paces away and then turned to pace back.

"No, sir, you don't. But you came all the way here for a reason. You could have yelled at me on the phone."

He took another step forward, pugnaciously. "I can't believe there's any excuse for your behavior."

I shrugged. "Perhaps you'd like to hear what happened?" I didn't add because that was obviously what he'd come for.

He crossed his arms tightly. "Go ahead. But I don't promise to stay."

"Want to sit down?" I motioned at the chairs.

He shook his head. Okay then.

I took a breath. "I met Donny when he took my fire aviation class."

"Right! When you were his *teacher*." He spoke the word like he'd said priest.

I shook my head. "I was his instructor for two days. I'm not Donny's commanding officer, nor do I outrank him. We're not even at the same station. A personal relationship between us is in no way against regulations. Chief Montgomery has assured me of that." Canali's brows descended and he glared at me, so I went on. "I'd heard that one of the Canali fire-fighters from Gridley was gay, and I mistakenly thought it was Donny."

Chief Canali's face paled and he seemed to lose a little steam, but his mouth was pressed tight.

"Maybe Donny was impressed by me or grateful because of that rescue at the Sierra City fire. I misread that admiration as his being interested in me, and I made it clear I was interested in return. When he told me he was straight, I immediately backed off. Even if I was inclined to go after straight guys, which I'm not, my time in the military would have taught me it's a fast ticket to a broken nose."

Chief Canali didn't respond. Just continued to glare at me.

"But later, Donny—" I took a breath. "—came to see me. He expressed interest in continuing our relationship."

"How do you know he didn't just want to be friends?" the chief demanded.

I gave him a steady stare. "There wasn't much room to misinterpret, sir."

The chief stared at me wide-eyed. His jaw worked. "You could have refused him. You must have known he was confused."

A spark of anger lit me up. "He didn't seem all that confused," I shot out.

Chief Canali's face did something complicated. I sensed the fight had gone out of him.

I wiped a hand over my face and reminded myself that the chief was struggling. I softened my tone. "Yes, I could have refused him. But I wanted to be with him as much as he wanted to be with me. That's why my mother so inappropriately blurted out what she did at the wedding. She knows I care about Donny a great deal, and when Mrs. Canali described the young woman Donny was dancing with as his girlfriend… it was not a good moment for me. My mam was just protecting me."

He seemed to think about that, his expression going from confused to bleak to even a trace of sympathy. "If you honestly care about him, you should have damned well left him alone."

"Perhaps, sir. But Donny told me what happened with Mike. So perhaps you can understand that living a lie in order to please other people is soul-killing."

He threw out his arms. "Donny isn't like Mike. Donny's explained to us that it was just a… a thing, and that he still likes women. He's promised not to see you again."

I sucked in air. It honestly wasn't a surprise, but it hurt like fuck. "Sir, Donny loves and admires you a great deal. I felt that way about my own father, but Donny… it's especially true for him. He acts tough, but he's got such a soft heart. And a deep need for your approval. I expect he'd do or say anything to make you proud, even if, in doing so, he hurt himself. I can only ask you to consider whether you really want to force him to make that choice." I looked the chief straight in the eye.

A saw a flicker of doubt cross his face, but then his jaw set. "Donny's straight, so there's no problem. He doesn't need this. You."

I held my palms out. "Believe what you want, sir. We're done. I offered my resignation to Chief Montgomery this morning." Chief Canali looked shocked, but I went on, "But he asked me to stay, and I value my job with Cal Fire very much, so I will." I sighed. "Nevertheless, I won't initiate contact with Donny. It seems like he's made his choice, and I wish him the very best, no matter how sad that makes me. I wish you the best, too, sir. I honestly do." Suddenly, every hour I hadn't slept landed on my shoulders like lead weights. "I appreciate you trying to understand. I hope you'll excuse me."

He frowned but gave a jerk of his head, and I walked

across the field to my office. Hell, it was quitting time somewhere. I was going home.

Forty minutes later, I pulled into my driveway and
climbed out. I didn't even go upstairs to my apartment to
decompress. Once I made it there, I'd be done for the night.
But I hadn't spoken to Mam and Gala that morning since I'd
wanted to get in early at work to catch Montgomery. Of
course, Gala, Mam, and I had talked in the car the night
before on the way home from Resolute, but most of that had
been about reassuring Mam that she hadn't screwed up my
life. No. I'd done that with no help from her.

I grabbed the two boxes of pizza from the back seat and
then tapped on the door of Mam and Gala's house.

When I walked in, they'd both turned in their chairs and
were staring at the door. Had they been discussing me? Oh
yes they had. I held up the boxes. "Let's make a salad and
have some pizza. Whaddy'a say?"

Mam looked at me meltingly. "Oh, honey—"

Gala pressed her hand to Mam's arm and shook her head.
"We'd love some pizza, bro. I'll get the lettuce."

An hour later, I sat with my hands on my belly full of
pizza and salad. We'd laughed a lot while assembling it and
even thrown an olive or two at each other. It felt good. Like
family. And there was nothing I needed more right then.
Maybe I could plaster over the hole that'd been ripped in my
heart with their love and concern. Hell, I could try.

Gala grabbed the plates and scraped the excess crusts into
the trash. "Feel like talking now, Dell? Or would you rather
sleep?"

I stretched. I wanted to sleep, but I needed to include
them. "I'd like to talk a bit. Mostly I wanted to apologize to
you guys for getting you involved with the Canalis and then
making it tough to associate with them, so—"

"Wait." Gala plopped into the chair next to me. "Wait,
wait, wait. Did you somehow think that her father's weird

attitudes have any influence on Tessa?" She grinned. "Not a chance. She'll be hanging out here with me, and I'll still be going there too. She has a separate entrance so I don't even have to see anyone else in the family if I don't want to. In fact, we're talking about creating an online business together."

I stared at my gorgeous sister. "You're amazing."

"I know." She hugged me. "And the reason I know is because of you."

In a couple seconds, I was going to be wiping my eyes. Saved by Mam.

Mam sat back in her chair. "And by the way, I'm having lunch with Carlotta on Thursday. She said she admires my bluntness." She didn't exactly polish her nails on her lapel, but it was implied.

Gala settled a hand on my arm. "You're the one with the Canali problem. Want to share what's going on?"

I hadn't really planned to tell them much, but my mouth opened and words fell out. "I went to my chief to be sure I hadn't crossed any lines in regulations by seeing Donny, and I guess I didn't. I offered to resign—"

"You what?" Mam came half out of her chair. "They should be so lucky as to have you."

I grinned. "Fortunately, they agree with you."

"Damned straight," she huffed and sat back down.

"Chief Montgomery really put a lot of feeling into asking me to stay."

Gala chuckled. "I love begging."

I didn't correct her, because she was close. Montgomery was shocked when I offered to resign, and I think would have started flying rainbow flags for me if I'd asked. I sobered. "Then I had a confrontation with Chief Canali."

"Where?" Gala frowned.

Mam snorted. "That man might be handsome, but he seriously needs an enema to get rid of that stick up his ass."

"He came to McClellan to ream me out. I explained my

side and—" I sighed. "—told him I wouldn't initiate contact with Donny."

"That's a bunch of bull pucky," Mam growled. "That boy loves you and his heart's breaking because his father's making him choose between you and him. It's total crap."

Any time I thought my mam was an airhead, she came up with stuff like that. "Thanks, Mam. Sadly, he's already promised his family he wouldn't see me anymore. So I guess that's that."

"Oh, honey." She clutched my arm and Gala wrapped an arm around my shoulders.

"I'm really sorry, bro."

A heavy, dark feeling settled in my chest. No matter how many times I told myself I should have known better, that didn't make it hurt any less. I kept seeing Donny in my mind's eye. The bedroom scenes were nice, but the one that haunted me the most was Donny, laughing and looking at me with such admiration, in that helicopter. The two of us, flying into the sun.

"So am I, dear. So am I."

# TWENTY

## DONNY

"Come on," said Pa. "Put on some real clothes and let's go. We're going bowling."

I blinked at him. I couldn't remember the last time he'd bothered to walk over to my house and knock on the door instead of just texting me or asking Ma or Mike to get me.

"What for?" I asked. "I just got off shift. I'm tired."

"It's Friday night, two-for-one at Busta Lanes, and I wanna bowl. Uncle Ricky's gonna meet us there. You love bowling with me and Uncle Ricky, so let's go." Pa had that set look on his face that said there'd be no arguing with him.

"Okay fine. Can I just meet you there? I need a shower."

"Yes. But be there in thirty," Pa warned.

I shut the door and stripped as I walked toward my bathroom. Fuck, I so did not want to go out tonight, not even with Pa and Uncle Ricky. I didn't want to do anything except get drunk, watch a little TV, and fall asleep.

It'd been almost three weeks since Gabe and Anita left for their honeymoon and the rest of family moved out of the chaos of wedding planning back to our normal everyday chaos.

I'd dreaded going back to work that first time after the wedding. But, weirdly, nothing happened. My station-mate, Brian, who'd been at the wedding, thought the whole gay rumor was a joke, that I was too much of a ladies man to take it seriously. He just wanted to hear all about Beth. And if the Cal Fire big brass who'd been there had thought otherwise, they respected Pa enough to keep it quiet.

So everything was fine. Everything except for one thing—me.

I didn't understand it. I'd dated dozens and dozens of chicks, and it had never been hard to let go. Even the rare couple of times the chick dumped me, I'd bounced back within a day. So maybe I'd been ignorant thinking that this thing with Dell would be like that. I'd figured it would end someday—*had* to end someday. And I'd get over it, kick the habit. Like giving up cigarettes.

But I wasn't getting over it. Instead of getting easier every day, it got worse. My chest ached and my insides cramped up tighter and tighter, my mood got more and more irritable. Even my appetite—*my* appetite—went downhill until it wasn't even worth going over to Ma and Pa's for dinner. Not even for the tiramisu Ma made to tempt me. I couldn't even get back into my old porn habit. Every video felt like a pathetic imitation of Dell. My dick was as sullen as my stomach.

It *sucked ass.*

Mike was no help. He just gave me looks that were half pity, half ticked-off and telling me he was there if I wanted to talk.

I didn't want to talk. What I wanted was a fucking case of amnesia.

I hurried through my shower because Pa was waiting. I threw on some jeans, a T-shirt, and a hoodie, and drove over to Busta Lanes, Resolute's only family entertainment venue. It had ten bowling lanes, a little arcade section of old games like Pac-Man and pinball, and a small café. Me and Mike had spent a lot of time there growing up.

Pa and Uncle Ricky had gotten a lane. Uncle Ricky was testing bowling balls and Pa was putting on his shoes when I walked up.

"Hey." I stuffed my hands in the pockets of my hoodie.

"Donny!" Uncle Ricky put down the ball he'd been holding and came over to give me a back-slapping hug. "Glad you could make it. Off-shift, huh?"

"Yeah. Nice to see you too. Guess murderers must be thin on the ground these days if you've got spare time."

"Knock on wood." Uncle Ricky rapped his knuckles on my head.

That made me smile even as I dodged away. He used to do that when I was a little kid.

"We got chips." Pa waved a bag of Bar-be-que flavored chips he'd gotten from the café. "And beer."

"Great. Thanks, Pa." I picked up my beer and took a long pull. The tap beer at Busta Lanes wasn't great, and it was served in plastic cups, but it was so familiar it made me feel a little better. Something inside me eased, and suddenly bowling didn't sound half bad. "So, you two old guys ready to have your asses kicked?"

"You can try, son. You can try," teased Uncle Ricky.

"Big talker!" Pa said a little too loudly. "You're forgetting, Rick, that it was me who taught you how to keep your ball out of the gutter." He turned to me. "You shoulda seen him, Donny. For a couple of years, every single ball he threw— every one—went right into the gutter. He'd bowl zero the whole game!"

"What can I say? I curve to the right," said Uncle Ricky cheekily. "But I outgrew it—in bowling at least."

For the first time in days, I laughed. It was fun seeing Pa

and Uncle Ricky rib each other. Uncle Ricky was fourteen years younger than Pa, sort of in between his generation and ours. But they were still close. Besides being a detective, Ricky was—according to popular wisdom—the most handsome of all the Canalis with that deep dimple in his square chin.

I picked up a ball and tested the weight. "Well, I was born a natural. So watch and learn."

We played three games. I won the first and was having a good time. It was nice being with Pa and Uncle Ricky. For the first time since the wedding, I didn't wanna crawl out of my own skin.

But then, in the middle of our second game, a new party moved into the lane next to ours. It was an older couple and their son. He was in camo uniform. Military.

And, like that, it all came back. *Dell.*

Uncle Ricky was up so I sat heavily onto the plastic bench seat at our lane, went to chug the rest of my second beer only to find it was mostly gone, and put my face in my hands.

"What's the matter with you?" Pa sounded irritated.

I forced myself to lower my hands. "Nothing." My gaze drifted over to the young guy in uniform. Had Dell's uniform been like that one? I didn't know enough to recognize what branch that guy was in. Dell had been Army. I'd seen some photos in his apartment of him at his helicopter. He'd looked like a god.

"Donny! You're up," Pa barked.

I got up and bowled. I got a gutter ball. "Oh, damn," I said. But I didn't really care.

Pa and Uncle Ricky tied on the second game. Pa won the third.

"Congratulations," said Ricky after Pa did a victory V, "but I'm still the young, good-looking one."

Pa waggled his eyebrows. "Maybe. But I'm still the guy who won Lucille over all comers."

"No argument there. You were a legend, brother. How about we grab a burger next door?"

I wanted to go home, but Pa had been watching me all night with this sort of fixed expression, like I'd better damn well have a good time. So I kept trying. We walked next door to Pat's Tavern. It wasn't crowded, and we got a small table. It was cold from the AC, so I put up my hood. I wished I could disappear under it.

"Three burger baskets," Pa ordered, when the waitress came up.

"Two," I said. "I'm not hungry."

Pa glared at me. "Whaddya mean, you're not hungry? You're always hungry."

"Two," I told the waitress stubbornly. "And I'll take a shot of Jack with my beer."

She left to put in our order. Pa tapped the table with his thumb. "What the hell is the matter with you?" he blurted. "I brought you out tonight to cheer you up. We were having a good time!"

I looked up at Uncle Ricky. He was watching us, expressionless.

"I am having a good time," I lied.

"You've been walking around for three weeks like someone shot your dog. Even Reiger talked to me about it."

My station chief had talked to my dad about me? "What? Why would Reiger do that? What'd he say?"

Pa waved a hand. "It doesn't matter. I saw him at a meeting, and he mentioned he was concerned. And you're drinking way too much, Donny."

"Who told you that? Mike?" I was getting pissed.

"I have eyes, Donato."

"I've hardly even been over at your house!" I exclaimed. No way Pa had *seen* my drinking.

"The trash is overflowing with all your empties!" Pa shot back.

Oh. Right. Fuck recycling, man.

"Your mother's been chewing my ear off. Swears you're in love, but that's ridiculous. You said it was no big deal. This… this thing with Dell. You said you weren't…" Pa looked around and lowered his voice, "*gay*."

Something broke inside me and a dark tide spilled out. "What the fuck do you want from me?" I shouted. "You don't want me to see him, so I told you I won't! You wanted me to come out tonight, so I came. Sorry I can't be the perfect son you want me to be!"

I never would be. That much was finally clear. Something Mike said about Pa finally paying attention to me when he fell in love with Shane washed over me. What happens when you finally get the thing you always wanted only to realize it's not worth the cost?

"Whoa, whoa, whoa!" Uncle Ricky held up his hands, his voice low. "Keep it down, you two."

Pa's face was red, and I realized people were looking at us. I wiped my mouth with my hand. "Sorry. I should just go."

I stood up, but Uncle Ricky grabbed my sleeve. He jabbed a finger at my chair. "Donny, sit down."

I sat. The waitress brought our drinks. But after what Pa had said about my drinking, the shot and mug of beer looked like a frosty-glassed recrimination. I kept my hands stuffed in my pockets.

"Okay, first of all, Ang," said Uncle Ricky in a low and firm tone, "it doesn't work that way. Donny can't just say he's not gay and it's all fine."

"What do you know about it?" Pa snapped, which was weird. I'd never seen him snap at Uncle Ricky before. "You weren't there. Donny told us—"

"I know because I'm gay," Uncle Ricky said in angry exasperation. His gaze shifted around the room, and he looked slightly disgusted, though with himself or me or Pa wasn't clear.

Pa and I stared at him. What?

Pa glowered. "Why would you say something like that? You are not."

Uncle Ricky turned his beer mug around on the tabletop, an uncomfortable grimace on his face. "You know I like to keep my private life private. Hell, my sex life and my family, exist in alternate universes as far as I'm concerned. But—" He raked a hand through his thick jet-black hair. "It's true. I sleep with men. Always have."

Pa scoffed. "Bullshit. I don't believe it."

Uncle Ricky raised his eyebrows. "I think I'd know, brother. I don't recall seeing you in my bedroom. Thank God."

"Holy hell," I muttered. Uncle Ricky was pure cop, kind of old-school. He was gay?

"But…" Pa's face was red now. "I never saw any signs…."

"You know my best friend through high school, Paulie?"

"Yeah. So?"

Uncle Ricky smirked. "Well, all those times he stayed over with me in the tree house, we weren't playing with GI Joes."

Pa looked aghast and somewhat horrified. "But… if that's true, how come we never knew?"

Uncle Ricky shrugged. "It's none of your business. I don't wanna know what you get up to in the bedroom, do I?"

Pa rubbed his head like it hurt. "Jesus Christ. What's happening? I don't know a goddamn thing anymore."

Uncle Ricky sat forward, voice lowered and face intent. "Look, the only reason I told you now was to make you see that it doesn't matter. I'm the same guy I always was. So is Mike. So is Donny." He looked at me with sympathy in his eyes.

And I realized Uncle Ricky had come out to Pa like this,

now, for me—to support me. And that made my chest feel so tight I thought I might choke.

Also—Uncle Ricky was gay?!

Though it sort of explained some things now that I thought about it. It was like one of those weird pictures where you keep seeing a lady sitting at a mirror, but once your vision shifts, and you see the skull instead, you can't unsee it. Uncle Ricky never brought women around. Never. Whenever anyone asked him, he always said he liked his freedom. We'd always assumed he played the field, being so good-looking. Or worked too many hours. We'd never actually seen him with a single female. Whoa. Trippy.

Uncle Ricky went on. "Men aren't just one thing, Ang. They don't just like one thing sex-wise. Not even tough guys."

"But this isn't just about what goes on in the bedroom, is it?" Pa said bitterly. "It's the way the world views us."

"That's their problem." Uncle Ricky shrugged. "I mean, I'm a hypocrite, I know, because I haven't exactly waved the rainbow flag at work. But you know me, I'm a private guy. At the end of the day, if other people wanna be prejudiced and ignorant, that's their affair. Doesn't affect how I feel about myself—or how I feel about Mike or Donny."

"But Donny said he's not like that!" Pa looked at me. His eyes were desperate. "Right? You said you like women. Hell, you've dated lots of women. You said this thing with Dell was more like a one-off. Why wouldn't you go back to dating women if you could? I don't get it."

I took a big gulp of beer, unable to resist it any longer. "I like women fine. It's just…." Yeah, it wasn't the bits and bobs that were the problem. It was the fact that I'd never met a woman who could make me feel the things Dell made me feel. And maybe there were women out there who could act tough, try to dominate me or whatever. But it wouldn't be the same. Because they wouldn't be Dell. But no way was I ever explaining my kink to Pa or anyone else. "Look, you just don't understand, and you never will."

Uncle Ricky shrugged. "Ang, it doesn't matter. Whatever Donny is, just let him be it." He leaned forward. "As for what other people think, it's like this. Let's say a hurricane was coming, and it was supposed to go right over the Resolute compound."

"We don't get hurricanes in California," said Pa impatiently.

"Well, these days, who the fuck knows. As I was saying, there's a hurricane coming. Now you've got two choices. You can stand outside and shake your fist at the sky and yell about how you don't want a hurricane or you can batten down the hatches and do whatever it takes to bring your family safely through it. Which of those is more productive, and which is a total fucking waste of time and mental anguish?"

Pa shook his head angrily. He took out his wallet and threw two twenties on the table. "I'm done trying to understand any of this. I'll see you both at the compound later." He stood up.

I couldn't stand seeing him that angry and despondent. "Pa, I made you a promise, and I meant it."

He waved me off and stalked out. Uncle Ricky watched him go, his face sad. Then he looked at me. "You shouldn't go making promises you can't keep, Donny. Believe me, it's not worth it."

And that pissed me off too. "Yeah, better not to say anything, right? Ever? Do you know what Mike went through? And you never said a word."

Uncle Ricky clenched his jaw. "I'm here now."

I had no idea what to say to that. My head was full of Dell and Pa, of regrets and a kind of terror that I'd never be all right, never be good enough for anyone. And Uncle Ricky had come out to Pa tonight, and I appreciated that. But also

—*Uncle Ricky was gay!?*—I wished he'd done it years ago. Maybe if we'd grown up in a world with *that* Uncle Ricky, none of this would be so fucking hard.

"Thank you for that," I said, now just tired. "I'll see ya."

I left just as a confused-looking waitress brought over two burger baskets.

I couldn't stand the idea of going home. I found myself driving. And then I found myself pulling off at the exit to Dell's place. I pulled up across the street from his house, like I'd done the first time I'd followed him home. I parked and turned off my lights.

It wasn't even so much the promise I'd made to Pa that kept me from knocking on the door. It was the fact that Dell would probably give me the coldest look to have ever been looked coldly at another human being, and then slam the door in my face. So I just sat there and imagined going in and remembered what it had been like when I *could* go in— arriving all happy and excited to see Dell and anticipating… what? I'd been fooling myself that it was *just sex*. Hell, even hanging out and watching TV with him was great, or making microwave burritos or his patented cheese omelet. When Dell was in the room, it was like nothing else existed. Being with him was a total release from everything. From myself. He led and I followed and it all just worked.

There was no escaping myself now. Still, being parked there was better than being anywhere else. Just being this close to Dell made me feel more human—loosened the knots in my gut. Knowing he was in there, imagining him in his big bed with the beige comforter, warm and sleepy. It helped.

I thought about what Uncle Ricky had said. Was I gonna spend years of my life fighting something deeply rooted inside me only to be miserable and ultimately fail? But Uncle Ricky was one end of the spectrum. He'd hidden his sex life from everyone.

On the other side of the spectrum was Mike—Mike and

Shane. They were totally open about who they were. It was fitting that they'd won the Medal of Valor award together before they even started dating. Because talk about standing up to pressure. Of course, I had his back at the station and so did Chief Reiger. Still, it took balls, man, even if I knew he'd struggled a lot before he'd finally confessed all to the fam.

And then there was Dell. He'd been out in the military. He was just so goddamn perfect, so good at everything, so confident and cocky, that people had to respect him, no matter how grudgingly.

I wasn't as perfect as Dell. I wasn't as brave as Mike. And I couldn't just hide my sex life like Uncle Ricky. That horse had left the barn. So where did that leave me? Apparently it left me sitting in my fucking truck all night watching my ex-lover's house like a pathetic loser.

I was awakened by a loud knocking. I jerked my head up. Someone was standing outside. In the bright daylight. Shit. I'd fallen asleep.

Gala stood at the driver's window holding a mug and staring at me. She didn't look amused.

Sheepishly, I rolled down the window. "Um… hey."

She thrust the mug through the window. "Coffee to go. You're welcome. And, by the way, you're gonna ruin your back sleeping in your truck. I don't think Cal Fire would appreciate that."

I took the cup. "Thanks. I…." I looked toward the driveway of their house. Dell's Jeep was gone. I checked my watch. It was 7 a.m. "Dell left already?"

"Sure did. Hence, his missing vehicle."

"Did he… did he see me sitting here when he left this morning?"

Gala raised an eyebrow. "Seeing as how my brother isn't blind, what do you think?"

I took a sip of the coffee. It was great, as usual. "Did he say anything about me? Being here? Or in general?"

Gala rolled her eyes. "No. He was in a hurry to get to work. There's some big fire going on. But oh, here's a crazy idea, why don't you just talk to him?"

My shoulders slumped. "He probably hates me."

"He doesn't hate you. Just talk to him. But don't keep fucking him around, Donny. Believe it or not, my big brother has a tender heart, and you've already caused it a lot of damage. I mean it." Gala gave me a threatening scowl before walking back to the house.

I grabbed my phone from the passenger seat. Shit. I had a bunch of texts including several alerts from Cal Fire.

***Butte County fire. These units called in: Oroville, Stirling City, Gridley, Lorna Rica….***

"Oh fuck." I threw the truck into gear.

# TWENTY-ONE

## DELL

I leaned in and pressed my lips against the hot fuselage. "Do your thing, baby."

For just a second, I rested my forehead against the plane. What a night. Donny Canali sat outside my place in his pickup truck for a big chunk of the night, while I, idiot that I was, paced inside like some caged fucking lion trying to decide whether to go out and eat him. What was he doing there? I wanted to talk to him, hold him so bad I hurt, but no way I wanted to be the one who pushed him. Forced him into something else he'd deny. Fuck.

I'd still been pacing when my phone alert went off. Five minutes later, I was driving past Donny's truck toward my plane at a zillion mph with him sleeping inside, and all I wanted was to feel his lips for a second. A lifetime.

Now here I stood on the tarmac. The weather agreed with my mood and that horrific hot, dry wind that always meant fire in the west swirled around me. I shuddered, uneasy. I had a bad feeling—real bad. But fuck. I hadn't felt like myself in three weeks, so what did I know?

I climbed into the cockpit where Ty was already going through the checklist. "Hey. Everything okay?"

He gave me a nod but didn't look up as his fingers clicked through the switches and dials of the flight deck. My girl was a fancy schmancy dame. Nothing but the best visualization equipment and heads-up displays. Of course, considering how many millions she cost, every one of those dials should have been gold-plated. Ty asked, "Is this really a big enough deal to haul out the fire bomber?" He frowned. "Especially in this wind?"

I automatically ran through my preflight steps. "Yeah. It's not a big fire yet, but that whole area's a giant tinderbox, too hard to defend if it gets out of control. It could head to Oroville. They want to hammer it into submission before it spreads too far."

"And we're the official hammer." Despite his snark, he looked worried. "So, Montgomery's willing to risk her?" He didn't add *and us*.

I gave one hard nod. "It's borderline with this wind, but if we get in and out fast, we should be okay. They're figuring we can put the fire down before ground crews can access it." I looked up at him. His blue eyes peered out from inside his helmet.

"Let's get the baby in the air."

My girl only needed a small amount of runway space to taxi and takeoff, but since we had plenty of room here at McClellan, I stretched her out and let her get used to the crosswinds. Yeah, her and me both.

A couple of random gusts hit us hard as we pulled up the landing gear and Ty glanced over at me uneasily. Right. If it was this bad taking off, how would the wind affect the fire and vice versa?

"You're clear, Fire Bomber," tower control reported. We had an informal tower protocol at McClellan. "How is it, Murphy?"

"The winds are pretty random, but we'll be good if it doesn't get a lot worse. Fire update?"

"About ten acres are involved, all remote. Go save the trees, guys."

With a full belly of water and fire retardant, the plane was heavy and we remained relatively stable as we made our way north, a plume of dark smoke our beacon on the horizon.

Ty covered his mic. "Hey, how you doing, man? We haven't talked much since fire season got serious."

Yeah, the last few weeks had been the worst so far, with us joining formations of tankers to dump water on blazes from the ocean to Idaho. Ty and I had staggered to our respective beds for a couple hours of exhausted sleep between emergencies. At least I'd barely had time to think about anything but fire.

"I'm okay. Mam and Gala have been hugging me tight in the few minutes we see each other every couple of days. Everything else is a smoke-filled blur."

"I've got to admit, you look tired and that never happens."

"Yeah." I didn't mention that not closing my eyes the night before hadn't helped.

He grinned. "You ready to get back on the horse? I actually made it to Tilly's two nights ago and a guy even I have to admit was cute came and hit on me. I told him his gaydar had failed him, but I bet you'd like him. Macho but pretty, you know?"

All I could see was Donny's face in his truck, troubled even in his sleep. "No. I think I'm out of the rodeo for a while."

"Yeah." He gave a soft sigh. "That last bronc threw you bad, pardner." He gave my arm a squeeze just as the bomber dropped a hundred feet in a powerful wind eddy leaving our stomachs behind. "Whoa. We better not drop that far when we're two-hundred feet above the fire or we're barbecue, baby."

I gave him a reassuring chuckle, but it didn't dissipate the tension in my gut.

The smoke that had been part of the scenery started to swirl around the plane, and we clicked into our respirators, making conversation harder. Just as well, because that so-called little fire we'd headed out to knock down looked more than nasty. Flames surged into treetops and ate up the brush below, encouraged by what looked like a forest of dead trees down there and the nasty Santa Ana winds. On the com, I said, "McClellan, be advised the wind has kicked up and the fire with it. But there's a river not too far from what looks like the center of the blaze. I'm dropping this load and will go in for a refill as often as the wind'll let me. Over."

"Roger that, Fire Bomber."

I gave Ty a hand signal pointing toward a hot spot and he nodded. I dropped altitude gradually until the gusts subdued, then banked hard over the fire, flying as low as we could get without singing my baby's tail. We dropped over sixteen hundred gallons of water and fire retardant directly onto the flames. You could practically hear it sizzle.

While getting shot at in the desert had been one kind of weird rush, I had to admit the rage of fire made every one of my nerves tingle, my gut clench, and my teeth with it. The battle was oddly personal. Mere mortals against the fire monster. Mythic. I pulled up out of the direct path of the flames, but not far because the river was nearby and we were going to go sit on it for a few seconds.

I circled my super-maneuverable baby until we were lined up with the water. Despite California's dry summers, this river was wide and fast and the current looked as pissed at all the wind as we were, splashing up in waves and whitecaps.

I dropped my girl down until her belly touched the $H_2O$, and the siphons refilled my tank in twelve seconds flat.

Nothing could beat my baby. She could do one hundred and fifteen water drops in a day. Yeah, well, not on this day. Way too much like the weather in hell. But usually.

With another belly full, we circled back to the fire, waited for our opening, dropped down, gave it a kick in its flame-ridden ass, and then ran for our lives.

For an hour, two, we repeated the pattern—fill, circle, drop, go back for more— until even through the equipment, smoke seemed to seep into my lungs, my blood, and my attitude. The wind got angrier and so did the fire, despite all our efforts. But we'd become Avengers, the only measly super-hero between the beast and destruction.

Ty called for backup. I vaguely heard, "Things are getting worse fast. Send the tankers. This is difficult terrain for fighting on foot."

I just kept circling. Fill, circle, drop. My girl's engines droning in my ears.

The com echoed in my smoke-laden head. "Fire Bomber, conditions are deteriorating. Good effort, but it's time to return to base."

"Roger that, McClellan. Uh… we're in position for refill, but we'll make this our last run."

"Roger, Fire Bomber. McClellan out."

I sucked a breath, blinked against my glazed eyes, and only then realized how badly the plane was shaking and bouncing—like the bronc Ty said threw me. Still, my girl settled over the river and sucked in water like a princess sipping champagne despite battling real current. With a full tank, I took off again from the water. Were the flames closer?

I banked toward the fire.

A sound like a freight train filled the plane as a huge tree beside us went up in flames like a piece of nylon hit by a blowtorch. Shit, my baby got burned. The force of the flame and the wind driving it slammed into the 515, and I pulled up hard. Ty glanced at me, tense and wide-eyed.

Fuck. We were low over the flaming treetops in dense choking smoke and more and more trees went up around us. That was one thing about fire aviation. You had to fly so low, there was no forgiveness for much of anything.

I said, "Ty, I'm flying us out over the river to get away from flames."

Ty spoke calmly into the radio, but I could feel the tension ratcheting off him. "McClellan, we've taken some fire damage and the wind is increasing. We're following the river until we can find a more comfortable elevation. Over."

"Roger that, Fire Bomber. You guys be careful. McClellan out."

Rock and hard place, baby. I needed to increase elevation to avoid the blaze, but I couldn't go much higher without getting walloped by the wind. If I could find a track low over the water, we'd be good at least for a while.

I dropped us lower, the river raging below us. Our enemy, the wind, had taken up a hard cross blast, and my poor burned baby struggled to stay aligned with the flow of water. Only a few dozen feet off the wet, the crosswind shifted and sent us skimming back and forth over the river like a water spider.

Holy shit. I saw it coming, like a scene from a movie, but nothing to be done. A burning tree the size of a skyscraper succumbed to the wind and fell, fell, fell straight at us. I pulled up but too late.

The first noise that hit us was a sickening *womp* that ripped through me like a heart attack. We'd lost an engine. Then with a terrible crunch, the branches and huge limbs slammed into the side of the aircraft, pushing us into the river and hard against the far bank.

Much worse, it fell on Ty's side.

"Ty!" I unstrapped as water rushed in, but we were propped against land. We weren't going to drown at least. But that was assuming Ty was going to do anything ever again. I screamed into the com, "Mayday! Fire Bomber down and I have an injured copilot."

"Location, Fire Bomber?"

I rattled off some coordinates from the control panel.

What I didn't add to our location was *Up Shit Creek…*

But I should have.

———

## DONNY

It took me almost ninety minutes to reach the command post. It was in a big field with tall brown grass surrounded by sparse trees. I tasted smoke in the air and the view was hazy, but the fire wasn't real close. I felt guilty for being late, but there were lots of other engines and vehicles arriving with me. They were calling out the troops for this one. I found command central. Pa, Chief Reiger, Chief Montgomery, and a half dozen other officers stood around a large portable table and white board that had been set up in the grass. Maps were taped to the board and teams were listed to one side. Pa was speaking into a radio when I walked up. He gave me a stiff nod and I gave him one back. We'd left things in a weird place last night, but we were both firefighters and we'd damn well do our jobs.

Reiger saw me. "Hey, Donny. Thanks for getting here. Gridley station's over there—" He pointed. "Still waiting on our marching orders. We'll probably be going in soon, so hang tight."

"Sure thing, Chief."

Before I went over to the cluster of guys from my station, I took a look at the map. Little flame decals denoted the exact location of the fire. It would be a hike in—the roads weren't close. And it was dense and bigger than I'd thought. Maybe a hundred acres. Shit. The Santa Ana winds buffeted my back, hot whispers of danger, as if a dragon was standing behind me. Air support wouldn't be flying in this, surely. Maybe Dell had done some runs earlier and was already down? I looked around but had no idea who to ask, so I went to find my engine and get into my gear.

Mike was standing with the Gridley station. He gave me a funny look as I walked up. "Where were you last night? We got the alert this morning, and I went to wake you up, but you weren't there."

"I went out bowling."

He lowered his voice. "All night? Where'd you go after that?" From the hopeful look in his eyes, I figured he wanted to hear I'd been with Dell.

I shook my head. "We can talk later. We've got a fire to deal with. Have you heard anything about air support?"

Mike frowned. "No. It's pretty windy for that. Is Dell flying?"

"I think he *was*. Earlier."

Fuck. He had to be on the ground by now, right? I went to the engine and put on my gear—fire pants and jacket, helmet, SCBA mask, boots, tool belt. I was already sweating in the stuff, and I hadn't done anything yet.

Back out with the crew, I traded some jibes with Brian, Rachel, and Jordy. Everyone was tensed and ready for action. Sometimes the hardest part of the fire was waiting for your assignment—just knowing that beast was out there getting bigger every minute, and that none of us would be going home until this was over. But at least I'd made it in time. I hated to think about how long I'd have slept if Gala hadn't woken me.

Reiger walked over to us. "Okay, listen up. You guys are moving northeast to Forest Service Road 731. You'll be setting up a fire break there. It's gonna be a long one, so take your time and do it right. Give it everything you've got. This whole area has a shit-ton of dead trees. We can't let this thing grow out of control and move toward Oroville."

He turned toward Jordy, our station's comm guy. "I'll send you the coordinates."

Jordy nodded. "Yessir."

I blurted, "What about air support, Chief? You need me on the horn?"

He shook his head. "Nope. Air support was just called off. Conditions are shit for flying."

"Goddamn it!" A loud curse came from over at the command area a few feet away. People gathered by the comms looked upset. Whatever it was, it wasn't good.

Chief Reiger glanced over and then turned back to us. "Okay, you guys get moving. Take both engines. I'll be on the horn with Jordy." He turned to go back to command.

My station mates headed for the trucks, but I stood stock still. I scanned faces for Pa. He was near the radio. His mouth was set in a grim line, and when his eyes met mine, they were bleak. My heart fell to my shoes, and I hurried toward him.

"Donny! Where you goin'?" Mike called out, right on my heels.

I reached Pa, but he wouldn't meet my eyes. That's when I knew it was bad.

"What happened?" I demanded. "Who is it?" It could be anyone—Tony or one of our cousins in Cal Fire. Or—

"Canali, get to your engine!" Chief Reiger barked. I ignored him.

Mike tugged on my arm. "C'mon, Donny."

"Pa, what is it?" I said, louder.

He straightened his spine and looked me in the eye. He started to speak, hesitated, his face full of regret. "Pilot Murphy's plane went down."

The words hit me like a blow. The world tilted sideways, then spun away as cold dread and horror washed through me. "No."

Pa held up his hands. "Donny, he's okay. He survived the crash. We've had radio contact. But his copilot's injured. Broken leg, probably more. And… and they can't get the plane back in the air."

"He can't get out?" My voice was a whisper.

"They went down in a river. That plane's not going anywhere." This was Chief Montgomery, head of Cal Fire's air support. I was surprised he'd even acknowledge me, he outranked me by so much. But then I remembered he'd been at the wedding, and he was giving me a pitying look now. He knew. He knew about me and Dell.

"We need to mount a rescue operation, ASAP," he continued. "The fire's moving fast. I want paramedics to go along with the firefighters."

"I'm going," I said firmly.

"Me too," said Mike. His hand on my arm had shifted and now he was holding me up rather than trying to pull me away.

There was a tap on my shoulder. I turned my head and saw Reiger. He didn't look pleased. "You two have your assignment." He pointed toward the Gridley engines. "We'll take care of this."

"Please," I said, in as much of a begging tone as I'd ever used in my life. "Please, I need to be with the rescue team." I looked at Pa for help.

He was still my father—the man I'd always admired most in the world. He had to support me now. Oh god please. I knew he wouldn't. Not for Dell. But I couldn't stop hoping. Begging. "Please, Pa."

Pa raised a hand to stop my words and looked at Reiger, his face pale. "If you can see your way clear to sending Donny with the rescue mission, I'll give you one of my best guys to work with Gridley. I think… I'm not sure Donny will be much good to you if he doesn't get to go."

I almost cried in relief. Pa's voice held compassion, regret. Like maybe he understood after all.

Reiger looked at Pa, then me. He sighed. "Fine. Donny, you're with the rescue party."

I clenched my fists. "Great. Let's go."

"And me, Chief," Mike said.

Pa shook his head. "No, Mike, This is gonna be risky. I don't need two of my sons out there."

Mike lifted his chin. "Dell's family. I want to go."

Pa sighed and wiped his face. "It's up to you," he said to Reiger.

Reiger ground his teeth. "Christ. Donny, Mike—you're with the rescue team. Angie, give me two guys for the fire break. And let's damn well move it."

It only took about ten minutes for the rescue team to be assembled—four regular firefighters and two who were certified paramedics—but it was still way too long. The comm in the plane must be damaged because all they got was static. Dell's personal radio was working only sporadically—the range was too great and we didn't have repeaters set up yet— but we had his GPS coordinates from the transponder on his gear. His plane had gone down in a river. *In a fucking river. Oh shit.*

They were inside the boundaries of the fire. It took everything I had to stand still and listen and not do something stupid.

Dell had to be all right. If he died in this fire feeling like I'd betrayed him... I didn't know how I could live with myself. Hell, living the rest of my days without Dell didn't sound like a viable plan either.

# TWENTY-TWO

## DELL

I gently unhooked Ty from his seat harness. "Hey, man, can you hear me?" He wasn't responding. The leg that had gotten crunched had a ripped pantleg, a gash, and stuck out at a funny angle. Almost certainly broken.

And to make our happy day fucking complete, the com was down. I'd gotten one call through, but now it was just static.

I pulled an emergency blanket out of the pack and wrapped it around Ty. As I rooted for first aid supplies, he moaned.

I wiped a hand over his head, ignoring the sound of wind and crackle of trees outside our space. "Hey, man. How are you feeling?"

His eyelids fluttered. "What the hell happened?"

"No big. A tree fell on you."

"Jesus, you sure it wasn't two trees?" He tried to move and I gently pressed him down.

"Your leg's broken and you could have a concussion. Stay put. They know where we went down. Hell, our girl has dual

GPS. They'll be sending help soon." It would have to be on foot given this wind, but I'd save that information for later. Plus, I had no idea why the radio wouldn't work since this plane could likely provide communication to a city, but there you have it. The luck of the Irish in reverse. And to add to that flaming luck, this body of raging water was too big and too swift to cross with a broken leg or carrying another person.

"Where are we?"

"On the side of the river. After the tree scrunched us, it politely pushed us out of the water, so at least we didn't drown." I glanced uneasily through the window. Unfortunately, we also weren't far enough into the river for it to protect us from the fire if—make that when—it got too close.

Ty said, "I seem to recall there's a wildfire out there."

"We're okay for now. Hell, I expect Legolas to come out of the trees any minute and save our ass."

Ty chuckled, but it sounded painful. "Shit, Legolas. I may be straight, but even I'd make an exception for him."

"You and everybody else, boyo." We both laughed, and it would have felt good if the wind hadn't chosen that moment to hammer the side of the plane—in the direction the fire was moving.

Ty's words slurred a little. "Who was that boo-beautiful lady elf?"

"Galadriel. That's who Gala's named for."

"Oh yeah. She can come rescoo me." His eyes drifted closed.

My heart slammed. If he had a concussion, he probably shouldn't sleep, but for general healing, sleep was the great doctor. Fuck, at this moment, Ty out of pain was a good thing. Let him sleep.

I pulled my cell phone from my pocket, but, of course, no bars. We were in the middle of nowhere and trees almost never made cell phone calls. I shoved it back in and took another look toward the blaze. Bad news, baby. Only a few rows of trees back, I got glimpses of red.

I spoke into the com. "McClellan, this is Fire Bomber. I've got no idea if you can hear me, because I can't hear you, but I have to leave the plane with Ty. The fire's getting too close and I can't take him into the river. Too dangerous." I pulled on my SCBA mask that had the built-in radio for short-range communications and fastened Ty's on him, grabbed the emergency pack with food and water in case it took Legolas a long time to get to us, and slid out of my side of the plane into a foot of water, surprisingly cold for August.

Shee-it. Smoke, heat. Even the gear didn't keep it out completely. I patted the fuselage, now scraped, burned, and battered, but she'd fly again if the fire didn't get to her first. "Take care, baby. I hate to leave you behind."

I hauled the pack to dry land and then went back for Ty. As carefully as I could, I pulled him across to the pilot seat and then out of the plane. He moaned and cried out, every yell stabbing through me. Once I could get him somewhere safe, I could look for a splint that would keep down some of the pain.

"What's happening?" He sounded freaked.

"Sorry, man, but I've got to pick you up. The fire's getting too close. Hang in there."

"I-I can walk if you help."

That theory lasted about three hopping steps, and I gave him kudos for the try, but no way—too painful and too slow. With a heave, he went over my shoulder. "Hey, man, they don't call this fireman's carry for nothing."

Bless his handsome heart, he tried to laugh.

Even though he was tall, Ty was slender, and that was a damned good thing because I was a trained pilot but not a lifelong firefighter. I hadn't hauled huge packs and hoses for fun like Donny. With the combined weight of the emergency gear and my copilot, I definitely knew I was carrying something. But I moved down the riverbank away from the heat and smoke, putting one foot in front of the other and trying not to feel the weight. Hell, I should be good at that. I'd spent three weeks trying not to feel anything.

———

## DONNY

"We're gonna have to go in on foot. The closest we can get you is here." Montgomery tapped the map. "At the end of this fire road. From there, you're gonna have to blaze a trail for about a mile to get to his position. Anticipate rough terrain and over a thousand-foot elevation gain. They've had to leave the plane, so Murphy's on foot carrying Chan. Rough duty."

Blaze trail? Hell, right now I felt like I could rip the forest apart with my bare hands.

"The main thing is just getting them out of there as fast as possible," Montgomery continued. "That fire's on the move and they're in trouble."

We took one of the smaller engines around to the fire road. The drive took thirty minutes, the last two miles on a deeply rutted dirt road. The driver kept a steady but glacial pace. I wanted to scream at him to go faster.

Mike was next to me on a jump seat. He leaned in. "He's gonna be okay, Donny. You and me, we're Canalis. We'll get him out of there. I promise."

I shook my head. We both knew the danger was very real. Not only from fire but smoke alone, not to mention the injuries from the crash. Poor Ty could die of shock if his leg was badly broken. And Dell had radio'd that he was okay, but he'd been in a fucking plane crash. He could be more injured than he realized.

Finally Alex, who was doing comms for the team, pointed. "There. We'll be going in there."

We'd reached the end of the fire road. Larry, the driver, pulled the engine over. I was out of my seat the moment he hit the brakes.

The smoke was thick here. We had to be close to the blaze. There was a ditch we had to hop over and then—unbroken forest. There were so many dead pine trees here, the landscape was checkered green and brown. It looked like beetle damage and probably drought, a forest of kindling just waiting for a spark.

"Donny, Mike—you guys take point," Alex said. "Paramedics in the back. Larry, you help them carry the stretchers."

I put on my SCBA mask and took out my axe. Mike did too. We'd worked fire breaks together before and we operated as a smooth unit. Mike went first, 'cause he had the best eyes, picking out the path of least resistance, whacking through the small stuff. I followed with my axe, doing the heavier cutting where it was needed and stomping brush down with my boots. We made good progress. Larry and Alex were behind me and the Cal Fire paramedics—a woman with a long brown braid in back and a chubby redheaded guy—walked stoically in the rear.

My arms got tired, but I kept swinging the axe. I was picturing us coming back this way with a stretcher, and we needed room. I just prayed it would only be *one* stretcher. Hopefully Dell would be walking.

"Their coordinates have stopped moving." Alex's voice came over my headset.

We were nearly at the top of a rise, and Mike paused to catch a breath and wait for the paramedics, who'd fallen behind. I propped my axe against a tree, breathing hard. "What does that mean?"

Alex shrugged. "It just means they've stopped. They're still at least a half mile ahead."

"Can't you radio them?" Mike asked.

"They probably have their SCBA radio, so we'll have to get close to make contact. But I'll try again."

I held my breath as Alex got out the comms radio and tried it. It had a lot more power and range than our SCBA helmets but was still limited, especially in such rough terrain. "Attention, Pilots Murphy and Chan. Looking for Pilots Murphy and Chan. This is your rescue party. We're enroute. Do you read? Over."

I listened hard, praying to hear Dell's voice. But he didn't respond.

"We read you," came a voice. It was Chief Montgomery's back at command central. "No contact yet? Over."

"No, but it looks like we're about a half mile out from intercept. We'll keep moving. Over."

"Good luck. Out."

Alex looked at my face and shook his head. "Just because the pilots don't respond doesn't mean anything."

I didn't bother to reply, just turned and started swinging my axe again.

―――――

## DELL

One foot in front of the other had become a way of life. Every time I thought I'd gone far enough, I'd look back and see that the smoke and flames seemed to be following me. I kept plodding until I couldn't. And I was pretty sure Ty couldn't. He tried to hold back his moans of pain, but I could tell he was in agony. I was worried he'd go into shock.

I picked out a spot in a small clearing not too close to highly-flammable underbrush and slid the pack to the dirt. I went to my knees and set Ty on the ground as gently as could be managed. Grabbing a canteen, I held it to his lips. He opened his eyes.

"I dreamed I was traveling through the desert on the back of a camel."

The idiot could still make me laugh. "Close."

He slurped some water, then glanced around. "Where are we?"

"No clue except that we're north of the fire." I stood. "I'm gonna find something to make a splint. It'll keep you from bending and jostling your leg. Meanwhile, here's a protein bar to tide you over."

Twenty minutes later, Ty looked like something out of *Swiss Family Robinson* with his leg stretched out and splinted to a tree branch by about a mile of stretchy gauze stuff from the plane's first aid pack. It was a hot mess. Yeah, in my case, pilot one, medic nothing. Of course, after the crash, maybe I was pilot nothing too. I knew I'd done the best I could in the weather, but ditching one of the only CL-515 fire bombers in existence would not get me a freaking medal. Shit, Montgomery might be begging me to leave, not the other way around.

Ty ate two more bars, drank water, and now lay on his metallic blanket on the ground, his eyelids heavy. "Hey, Dell."

"Yeah."

"Looks like Legolas isn't coming." A second later, a soft snore drifted from his lips.

I dropped my head to my knees. How was it possible for life to get so fucked up so fast? First I'd gotten my heart stomped on, and now I'd crashed my plane and my best friend was seriously injured. The fire was getting closer, the smoke was thick in my lungs despite my mask, and I couldn't move Ty any farther.

We could actually die here, and my tired brain kept returning to Donny.

Why had he been sleeping outside my house that morning? Jesus, it seemed like a year ago. But it didn't matter. I knew a year from now, five years, if I survived this, I'd still be asking why? How could I have been so stupid as to get tangled up with Donny Canali? And how could I let him go?

I reached for some water, but somehow it was too far away and my arm too heavy. I knew I had to stay alert to save Ty. Keep him away from the fire for as long as I could. But all I could smell was smoke and all I could hear was the wind and my heart beating in my ears saying, *Donny, Donny, Donny.*

Sometime? A month later? A minute later? A voice squawked in my ear. "Fire Bomber, come in."

"What?"

"Fire Bomber? Is that you, Murphy?"

The voice was in my head. No. In my helmet. Shit, that meant they were close enough to hear on the short-range comm. Fuck me.

"This is Fire Bomber! Pilot Murphy here." Come on. Give me good news.

There was a sound of scuffling and squeaking and a voice saying, "Give it to me. Damn it. Give it to me."

Then a sound I thought I might never hear again filled my head. And my heart. "Dell, god, Dell. Are you okay? Are you hurt?"

"D-Donny?"

"Yes, babe, it's me. Oh god, are you all right?"

"I'm okay. Smoke's bad. Ty's hurt, and he's sleeping right now. Or unconscious. We need to get him to a hospital. Over."

"We will. We've got your GPS coordinates, and we're coming in on foot. Two paramedics are with us. How close is the fire? Over."

"Too damn close. Over."

"Damn, babe. We'll get there soon. Just hang in there, okay? Please. Over."

I wanted to scream *what should I hang in there for*, but hell, half of Cal Fire could be on this fucking com. Donny didn't want any more bad publicity than he already had from me. Still— "D-did you call me babe?"

"Yes, Dell. I'm coming to get you because I fucking need you. I'm gonna get you and Ty out of here, and then I'm going to prove that to you. Do you hear me?"

I smiled. "Roger that."

"See you soon. Out."

I let out a sigh, dropped my head back to my knees, and actually smiled. Legolas had come to my rescue.

———

## DONNY

Everyone on the rescue team kept glancing at me curiously, except the paramedics who didn't know me so probably thought little about my declaration via comm. I just kept moving—toward Dell. It seemed to take forever to make that last half mile, with Alex keeping us on track in the middle of nowhere. I could tell we were getting within spitting distance of the fire. Every firefighter who battles wildfires knows the signs—the slow-roasting heat, the sounds fire makes as it consumes, the texture and color of the smoke. I could tell the others in the group were getting spooked, but no one mentioned backing down. Everyone in Cal Fire was badass. As for me, a hundred percent of my focus was on finding Dell. And then—

"Stop!" Alex called out. "They should be right here." He looked between the GPS device in his hand and the surrounding woods.

The smoke was thick with ash particles, and I couldn't see much. I pulled off my mask and shouted. "Dell! Dell!" Shit, I could barely catch my breath, so I strapped it back on.

"Here!" The cry was faint, but it was enough to give me a direction.

I headed to the right, calling out again. "Dell!"

I went past a cluster of birch trees and saw them. There was a small clearing, no more than eight feet across, with an old giant of a downed tree providing a log bench. Ty was propped up against the tree, his leg out and splinted, eyes closed, probably unconscious. Dell was standing next to him, turned toward me. I couldn't see his expression thanks to his mask, but his broad shoulders stiffened when he saw me. He took a step forward. "Donny?"

I ripped off my mask because I needed him to see my face. I dropped it and my axe and strode toward him, reaching out for him. And then he was in my arms. It was awkward thanks to my heavy coat and pants and his mask, and something hard poked my chest, but it was the best moment of my life. I held him so hard.

"Dell. Oh God. I about died when I heard your plane went down." I kissed his neck.

He pulled back enough to look at me. He shoved his mask to the top of his head as if to see me better, and there he was. His face was dirty, exhausted, and pale from worry. A small cut with dried blood stained his forehead. His eyes, as he studied me, were relieved but also wary. At that moment, he held my fate in his hands. The whole rescue mission, I hadn't allowed myself to think what would happen if Dell wanted nothing more to do with me.

"I'm so sorry," I blurted. "I'm sorry about the wedding. I'm sorry I've been such an idiot. It never was just sex, was it?"

Dell's face softened into an expression that was warm and slightly confused. He glanced over my shoulder. "We're not alone."

"I don't care."

I heard a throat clear. "Everyone's coming up," Mike said, again, as if to warn me.

"Pilot Murphy?" Alex's voice. "Glad we found you guys. The paramedics are right behind—oh, here they are. Good."

The two paramedics moved to Ty and dropped down beside him.

Dell gave me a serious look. "Thanks for coming for us. We'll talk later, Donny."

He started to pull away, but I had to show him. "No wait." I gripped his arm, and when he looked at me, I kissed him on the lips, hard.

When I pulled back, he blinked at me, face gone pink. "Holy hell, Canali."

I had to admit, it was sort of nice seeing Dell surprised for once. I smiled. "Just wanted to get that out of my system. Now let's hightail it out of here."

# TWENTY-THREE

## DELL

The walk out of the fire zone was all about pain, worry, and wondering.

I didn't want to admit it, but my lungs burned with every breath, and each leg had to weigh a hundred pounds by itself. Adrenaline crash will do that to you. I dragged myself along the narrow track through the undergrowth, following Ty's stretcher, and couldn't even hold his hand or give him moral support. Not that he would notice, since he was unconscious. I'd volunteered to be a stretcher carrier, but the rescue team told me my carrying duties were done for the day. Mike and Donny got assigned both ends of the stretcher since they were the strongest. Thank you, Canalis.

Sweet Jesus, had Donny really kissed me in front of the whole fucking rescue team? Must have, because even though their masks hid most of the evidence, the heads of the other firefighters kept turning toward me, like who the hell are you to get Donny Canali to do something like that? Who the hell indeed?

Why had he done it? I wanted to barge up to the front of

our plodding line and yell at him. *Why?* Did he think about it or do it in the spur of the moment?

Much more important—did he mean it? Or was it a dramatic gesture he'd take back the minute he caught sight of his father? Not that most guys would jeopardize their careers for a gesture, but hell. Donny had managed to convince his family that he wasn't gay after he'd been fucking a guy for months! That was wizardry, man.

A gloved hand touched my arm and I looked over at Alex, the comm guy, who'd been following me on the whole slog. "How you holding up, Murphy?"

"Okay. I'll be glad to get Ty in a damned ambulance."

"It'll only be a few more minutes. We're almost back to the truck." His radio squawked and he turned away.

The conversation on the radio got more active and we all sped up as the sound of engines drifted to us over the woosh of the wind. Around the next bend, my knees threatened to buckle when I saw the ambulance, big as you please, parked in a clearing, and two more paramedics poised to run toward us.

I pushed past Mike and came up beside Ty on the stretcher, pulling up my SCBA and grasping his limp hand. "Hang in there, boyo. You're gonna be fine. Help's here."

I got a slight squeeze back and almost cried from relief. Fear and worry thrummed through me. If Ty didn't make it, I'd never forgive myself.

The paramedics rushed forward with oxygen for Ty and motioned Donny and Mike to bring the stretcher to the ambulance. They slid Ty inside.

I pushed forward. "I'm Ty's copilot. I need to go with him."

The female paramedic looked at me quizzically. "You're the pilot? Damn, man, of course you're going. Get in. We need to get you on oxygen too."

"I'm okay," I insisted. But I had to admit, a little fresh air would taste mighty fine.

She stepped back to let me in, but I turned to look for Donny. He stood a few yards behind me, his ear pressed to the radio, gesturing madly, his glance flashing to me every couple seconds. I smiled and he returned it, but clearly the conversation was intense. Mike stood closer, smiling at me from a dirty face.

I raised a hand. "Thank you so much for coming to get us."

"Donny was going in regardless. Gotta have my big bro's back. And yours."

I looked back at Donny still talking away. He met my gaze, his expression tense, and held up a finger to me. Just the sight of him was better than a warm shower and a cold drink of water.

"We have to go," said the paramedic.

"When he gets off the comm," I told Mike, "tell him I said —" Hell, where to begin? "—tell him I said, Thanks and I'll talk to him soon."

With a wave to the rest of the team, I turned and climbed in the ambulance.

The ride felt interminable. Ty was hooked to IVs and wore an oxygen mask. I'd rejected the offer of an immune drip but drank in every breath of the oxygen that poured from my respirator, so not much conversation happened.

I drifted and thought. All the sentences in my mind started with why? Why did he come? Why did he call me babe over the radio? Why did he kiss me in front of the rescue team? I should be thinking about what I'd do and where I'd go if Cal Fire dumped me for crashing their gazillion-dollar plane. My poor baby. But my mind just wanted to think about my other baby. Donny. If he really was my baby anymore.

A montage of the Dell and Donny show played on the screen of my brain. Tossing popcorn at each other in front of the TV, Donny's radiant face as he gazed out the windscreen of the helo, Donny staring at me adoringly in fire liaison class. And, of course, Donny on his knees, vibrating with need when I took control.

Damn. The images lined up beside the angry, paranoid, embarrassed, dismissing glares of the other Donny. Donny holding Beth at the wedding, ignoring me. And then denying me to Chief Canali.

Oh shit, I was one confused puppy.

The female paramedic, Gloria, unhooked my mask and said, "We're almost at the hospital. They'll take Ty in for X-rays and tests right away, and they'll want to see you too."

I shook my head and pointed to the oxygen mask. "That was literally a breath of fresh air. I feel like a new man." Just to prove it, I flashed a grin. I didn't mention I felt like a new man who'd been kicked by a horse.

"Still, they need to do a few tests to prove your *good as new* status." She grinned back.

A weak voice said, "Don't give that guy anymore of my oxygen. He'll use it all up. Damned bogart."

I sprang forward and grabbed Ty's hand. "Hey, boyo. How you feeling?"

"Like I got stomped by orcs."

Gloria chuckled. "Good thing you had your very own knight in shining armor to save you."

Ty snorted mildly. "He's no Aragorn. Definitely Gimli." He coughed.

Gloria slapped the mask back on him. "You guys are hilarious, but let's save the ribbing for later."

I clasped Ty's hand tighter. "Hang in there, boyo."

The ambulance careened into the emergency entrance of a hospital, the doors opened, and they pulled out Ty's stretcher so fast I barely had time to let go of his hand. A male nurse reached up to help me down, but I jumped to the asphalt of the parking lot. The nurse gave me a frown, which forced me not to grimace with the pain in my legs that my stupid jump had just caused. He pushed a wheelchair at me.

I shook my head. "Nope. Thanks anyway."

Another frown, but he must have decided not to piss off the patients. Especially the really big ones. He said, "Come with me."

"I want to go with Ty."

"You won't be able to see him for a while. Meanwhile, come with me."

I sighed and started after him—then stopped.

Standing in front of me was literally a sight for sore eyes. Donny gazed at me, his expression worried and—hopeful?

I put up a finger toward the nurse. "Hang on a second." I hurried to Donny and took his arm. "What the hell are you doing here? Aren't you supposed to be fighting fires?"

He shook his head. "I got permission to come with you and Ty so I can send back status and be sure you have whatever you need."

"That must have been some kind of fucking special dispensation." I raised an eyebrow.

He smiled shyly. "Yeah. It was called the *get rid of the pain in the ass* dispensation." He paused. "Pa knew I wasn't any good to anyone until I was sure you were really okay."

I had to take a breath at that. Chief Canali had approved it? "Why did—"

The nurse's voice cut in. "Mr. Murphy. We have a doctor standing by. We need to get you inside."

Donny said, "Go on. I'll be right here."

I followed the nurse inside, glancing over my shoulder twice. Donny was talking to a paramedic who pointed at the hospital.

Over the next hour, I was pretty sure that the poor overworked staff were writing new essays on the definition of uncooperative. I didn't really intend to be a pill exactly, but I had two focuses. Foci? Finding out about Ty's condition and getting out of the fucking exam room to talk to Donny.

Finally, after they determined I'd inhaled too much smoke, had some lacerations, none of which required stitches, and was suffering from exhaustion—duh—they finally released me from their tender mercies.

I grabbed a nurse, and for the twentieth time, I asked, "Who can tell me how Ty Chan is doing?"

She managed not to look irritated. "I've been assured that someone will find you and give you a status report soon. You can sit in the waiting room." She pointed the way.

When I got there, a guy who looked very doctory stood talking to Donny Canali. Talk about the two perfect birds with one stone.

Donny looked up and waggled his hand toward me. "Dell, this is Dr. Hernandez. He was just telling me—"

I interrupted. "How's Ty?"

The doctor, who had a mask draped under his chin and wore scrubs, said, "Ty's doing way better than he has any right to expect considering the situation."

I nodded. "He's a tough bird."

"He's also a lucky one, and I'm told part of that luck was having you as a pilot. Good job. How are you feeling?"

I waved off his concern. "I'm fine. But what does that mean that Ty's lucky? How is he really?"

"He'll be going into surgery in a few minutes. It's a complicated break and we need to do some repairs before we can cast the leg. Fortunately, he didn't suffer a severe concussion so we can anesthetize him." He put his hand on my arm. "You won't be able to see him for several hours. You could go home and get some sleep."

I shook my head vehemently. "No. I want to be here when he wakes up."

"Well, in that case, you have several hours to wait. So get

food and maybe a catnap." He looked at Donny. "Your friend seems prepared to help."

Donny's expression was sympathetic and intent, completely focused on me, on what I needed at that moment. And maybe it was the idea that I had someone else to lean on, but some of the fight went out of me. I turned back to the doctor. "Okay. Thanks. The hospital has my number. Can someone call or text if Ty wakes up sooner than expected?"

"You bet." The doctor walked away. I stepped to the nearest plastic chair and slumped into it.

Donny sat in the chair next to me. "Ty's gonna be okay."

I nodded. "He was telling jokes in the ambulance." I blinked hard.

"That's good." He wiped his hands on his jeans. "What would you say about going to my place for some coffee? You look like you could use it. It's way closer than your house. It'll be quiet since Mike is working the fire, and you can rest." He took a breath. "Or we can talk for a while."

Talk. Damn. The questions lined up like planes for takeoff. "Sounds good."

As it turned out, if I'd planned to talk on the drive to the Canali compound, I batted zero. The minute the motion of the truck and a little background music hit my nervous system, I was so asleep it's a wonder Donny didn't have to leave me there all night. But the minute his truck stopped, my eyes opened.

I blinked around at the sight of his place, the dense trees, and the main house across the lawn. "Whoa, boyo. I've got some memories about this place."

He sighed. "Yeah. I'm sorry so many of them are bad."

I didn't bother to argue. The wedding was still fresh in my mind.

I'd never been inside his place, which turned out to be a cute single-story house suffering from some single-guy messiness. But it wasn't too bad. Donny gathered up a couple extra napkins and beer bottles from the coffee table and took them with him as he hurried to what I assumed was the kitchen. He called, "Make yourself at home. Lie on the couch if you want. More sleep would be good. I'll make coffee and something to snack on, okay?" He gave a little laugh and it sounded nervous.

"Thanks." Now that we were here, I echoed the nervous part. I sat on the couch, not tired at all. The last three weeks had been all about getting used to the idea of not having Donny in my life ever. No matter how much I told myself that I'd get over it, nothing pulled the ten-inch blade out of my heart. Fuck, I'd been a sad, pathetic, melodramatic bastard. The only thing that had saved me was fire season—well, and Mam and Gala, but mostly work. All that distraction had kept me from bleeding out.

And now here I sat and today's fire had done the opposite. It had brought a Donny I didn't recognize, all sweet and lovey-dovey in public no less, to my rescue.

I ricocheted back and forth between touched, hopeful, and totally pissed-off.

Donny walked in balancing two mugs of coffee. Before I knew it, I was on my feet with words pouring out of my mouth. "What the fuck is all this, Canali? Why are you suddenly acting like you give a damn after three weeks without a word?"

He stopped, mouth open, coffee mugs poised precariously, and stared at me. Right. What happened to his cool and calm Dell Murphy?

# TWENTY-FOUR

## DONNY

Holy shit. This was what a pissed-off Dell Murphy looked like. Scary. And man was I not prepared. I'd been operating on pure gut instinct ever since I left Uncle Ricky at the restaurant last night. Spending the night parked in front of Dell's place, the rescue, the declaration, the kiss. Fuck, I wasn't even sure where it all came from, but it was such a relief not to fight my heart anymore. I hadn't thought much about how Dell would react. No, not true. I knew I deserved the worst, but I'd hoped for the best. Yeah, hearts and flowers. But Dell looked ready to sock me.

I stammered, "I-I always gave a damn. I just did what I had to do today." Carefully, I set the mugs on the table before I dropped them and then stared at the man I—fuck, just say it Canali. The man I loved. "I *had* to go after you today. And I had to stay with you." I'd always stay with him. If he'd let me.

Dell's anger deflated like a popped balloon, and he flopped back to sitting.

He threaded fingers through his thick hair. "Look, I love

that you rescued me, and I especially love that you kissed me in front of a Cal Fire team and called me babe on a radio frequency that could be heard by the entire organization. Jesus, Donny." He gave a half smile and my heart leaped. But then he frowned. "But I'm so pissed!" He waved his hands in the air. "That fucking wedding! And then I don't hear a word for three weeks. Do you know how that felt?"

I dropped to my knees. "Yeah, I do. 'Cause to me it felt like having my guts ripped out. I'm so, so sorry."

He held up a hand. "Stop."

I stopped, shut up, and tried to swallow.

"Nobody knows better than me that big crises prompt big emotions and big statements. That was my da's life, Donny. Not mine. No one lies like a drunk, to themselves and everyone else. I'm done with that. I'll never hear it again." His voice got singsong. "*Oh I'm sorry, Dell, I'll never do it again. Please believe me. Trust me.* Fuck, no! Promises mean jack. All I believe is what you do. You're sweetness and light in the bedroom, but damn. Outside in the real world, you've acted like I don't exist. I can't do that anymore, Donny."

Oh God. I knew I deserved that. "It won't be like that, Dell. I swear. I tried to show you today. Even with Pa—he… I told him I had to go after you, and he made Reiger assign me to the rescue team. I'm not gonna hide how I feel—not from Pa or anyone else."

That quieted him.

"I didn't plan to call you babe or kiss you or that other stuff. I just had to do it, do what was real for me." I took a shaky breath. "And I didn't care what happened as long as you were okay and I had the chance to tell you what you mean to me." He was blinking hard against shiny eyes and I almost screamed in hope. Knee-walking like an idiot around the table, I dropped my head in his lap. "I'm so sorry. I know I fucked up. I never meant to be an asshole. I was just… just trying to burn the candle at both ends. See you and please my family too. I didn't understand what you meant to me, because I've never had anything like this. But I know now. And, fuck, I'm so sorry." A tight band squeezed my chest. I'd suspect a heart attack if I was older. I clung to his leg like a fool, but it was Dell. I'd happily be a fool for Dell.

He cupped the back of my head with his big warm hand. "Christ, Donny. You realize you came out to the entirety of Cal Fire today on that radio?"

I gave a desperate little laugh. "Yeah, I did. Ma says I'm in love, and maybe I am, because these past few weeks without you have been the worst of my entire life. And when I thought you might die, and I'd never…" Hot tears burned my eyes. In a choked voice, I whispered, "Please tell me it's not too late, that I'm not such a fuck-up that you hate me now."

"Donny."

I looked up and saw his eyelashes were damp and his eyes held so much emotion I gasped.

He leaned down and kissed me. His hands slid to my jaw and neck, holding me firmly in place. His mouth was hot, as if he had a fever, and he kissed me deeply, demanding. In an instant, my body surrendered to him, turning to putty as heat rushed to my dick. In seconds, I was throbbing.

"God, I missed you," Dell groaned, as he released my mouth to attack my neck. He sucked and bit, and all I could do was cling to his arms. "I'd wake up at night reaching for you. It killed me thinking we'd never be together again."

I thought I'd burst with relief at those words. "Jesus, Dell. Need you."

Abruptly he let go of me and stood up. He stared down at me, eyes blazing like some kind a god—a very horny god given the huge bulge in his pants. "Get naked and get into bed. Now."

A thrill of happiness and lust shot down my spine, and I scrambled to obey. God, yes. There was my Dell. This was what I needed. *Desperately*. I hurried to my bedroom, tearing my shirt over my head and pushing my jeans down my thighs. I kicked everything off and crawled onto the bed. It was unmade but not too grungy. Me, I smelled like smoke and sweat, but I didn't care. I wanted Dell like this, both of us just out of the field, still smelling of fire. Because we were made of smoke and fire, Dell and me.

He came into the room, not in any particular hurry. I lay on the bed, watching him remove his clothes with slow intensity, his eyes locked on me, as if he were a big cat stalking me. I had to grab my dick in my hand and squeeze it to hold back my excitement.

"Don't touch," Dell ordered. "That's mine."

Oh hell yeah, it was. Now and forever. I let go and put my hands behind my head to avoid the temptation. I was trembling as if it was cold in the room, but there was nothing but heat.

Naked and erect AF, Dell stood and looked me over, head to toe.

I squirmed. "I got stuff. In case you ever— It's in the nightstand."

Dell moved to the nightstand and opened the drawer. I heard the bottle of lube roll around.

He looked at me, eyes narrowed.

"I want it," I blurted. "You made me want it. And then we never did it. And I've been thinking about it. Is that okay?"

Dell's Adam's apple bobbed as he swallowed hard. "You're not asking for this as some sort of punishment, are you?"

I blinked. "Hell no! Nothing with you could be punishment. I just want *you*. I want…."

I didn't know how to explain it. I wanted him to cover me and invade me and possess me. I needed to know I was worthy of him, that he still wanted me. I just needed *him*.

Dell took the lube and a few condoms from the drawer and tossed them on the bed. "Turn over."

He was using that hardass voice, like maybe he was still a touch angry with me. But it gave me chills, and I was happy to do anything he asked. I turned onto my stomach and stretched out my arms. My dick was so hard and aching it took everything I had not to grind into the mattress.

The bed shifted under Dell's weight. He nudged my legs apart, then knelt between them. My heart rate rocketed, and my skin wanted to leap off my body it was so sensitive.

"Lift your hips."

I did, though it wasn't easy with my legs parted. He reached between my legs for my dick and pulled it so it was pointing straight down toward my feet on the mattress, then pushed my hips down again. He petted the top of the shaft and head lightly as he opened up the bottle of lube with his other hand.

Oh. Oh fuck. I could picture what he saw—me, spread open and dick down so he had a close-up view of it all, asshole, balls, and dickhead arranged like a buffet. I buried my face in the comforter and groaned. I hadn't come in three weeks, and now this? I wasn't gonna last ten seconds.

"Fuck. I'm gonna fly apart," I warned him.

"Shh. I've got you."

A cold, slick finger nudged against me and he pushed. I couldn't hold back a gasp. I'd never done anything down there and the sensation was a lot. It didn't hurt, just felt weird. I tensed up and he rubbed my back. "Relax."

I made my muscles let go and moved my hands under my head so I could bury my face and still breathe. He continued, adding more lube and fucking me with that finger. The sensation made me half uneasy and half ready to come. I chanted in my brain that this was Dell. I wanted this. I'd wanted this for a while. The sensation might be unfamiliar, but I had to go there if I wanted to take this step.

And then I felt him shift and his tongue swept over my

dickhead as he moved his finger inside me and *shit*. A wave of prickling heat coursed through me and I cried out.

Dell removed his finger and mouth—*hell no*—and slapped my ass lightly. "Get up on all fours."

I did—anything to get more of that. He nudged my legs wider, smeared more lube around my hole and in me, then bent down. He pulled my dick back and put the head in his mouth, suckling, as he pushed what felt like more—two fingers maybe—slowly inside me.

I dropped my head and squeezed my eyes shut, panting. *Oh fuck.* The combination of the sweet teasing pleasure of his hot mouth, tugging and releasing my dickhead in a rhythm, and the blunt invasion of my body, was good. Really fucking good. The pressure and slight burn kept me grounded and the tug of his mouth made me wanna beg for more.

I spread my legs wider, lowering my shoulders to the bed, pushing my ass at him.

He made a pleased sound and tickled my cock slit with his tongue while fucking me with those fingers. In. Out. Thrusting. Rubbing on something inside me which sparked up my spine. And suddenly I got it. I got how fucking could feel so good on the other end of things, being invaded, filled up with Dell—*taken* by Dell. Just the thought made me so hard it hurt.

"Fuck me," I gasped. "Not your fingers. Come on."

He released my cock and it flopped down, heavy, to point at the bed. "I can make you come like this."

"No! No, please. I want you to fuck me. Wanna feel that."

"I should make you wait," he growled.

And I knew Dell could and probably would. He loved to torture me that way. But it was the last thing I wanted. "Please. I thought I'd lost you, and I just… I need this. Please, Dell." I was begging, my voice all needy, but I meant every word.

"All right. Shh." He pulled his fingers out of me and

rubbed my back again with his other hand. I heard him open the condom.

I tensed on the bed, unable to bear the anticipation, and maybe a trickle of fear crept in too. But God, my body was so ready for this. I felt like I could shatter into pieces.

His hand held my hip firm as his dick, blunt, pressed at the entrance. He inhaled, loud, and then he pressed forward.

It was a lot. It was big. I moved back up onto all fours because it eased the pinch a bit. I looked down at my hands, fingers spread on the bed. A few hours ago, they'd been wielding an axe. Now they shook for Dell.

"Take deep breaths. Relax your muscles," Dell instructed.

I did, my head going swimmy from hyperventilation, the feeling of invasion, of pressure, growing inside me in a way that was both scary and exhilarating. An adrenaline junkie thrill spread warm through my body, adding to the arousal and emotional upheaval, and I was suddenly flying. I moaned and pressed back, wanting the burn.

"There's my boy," Dell rumbled, fond and possessive, and I wanted to purr.

*Your boy. Your boy.*

"Baby," Dell gasped as his thighs touched the back of mine, his balls whispering against my skin as he bottomed out. He ground in place, as if trying to go deeper. I pressed back, needing him to. "Fuck, you feel so good, Canali. Damn."

The wavering pleasure in his voice nearly undid me. Dell over and inside me and needing me. Fuck yeah.

He pulled out a little, pushed in. As in everything, Dell was a master at giving me just enough to make me beg for more. He fucked me slow, grinding more often than thrusting, one of his hands on my hip while the other reached under me and lightly teased my dick. It was so good. I opened wider, dropped my shoulders back to the mattress, pressed into him, wanting more—more of his hand, rougher fucking. I had been dancing on the edge for what felt like forever, and I wanted it hard and I wanted it now.

"Please, Dell. Faster."

"Grab the headboard." He sounded pained.

I rose up enough to grab onto the headboard with both hands.

"Brace us," Dell ordered. Then he fucked me in earnest—hard and fast thrusts interspersed with slow ones, working himself inside me, moaning out his pleasure. This new position changed the angle of his thrusts in a good way and pressure built up inside me as he battered me, until I thought I might explode. It sparked and tightened like an impending orgasm, but different. Hell, just the noises he made were enough to make me blow.

I was caught between holding still for his thrusts and wriggling to get more. He panted, "Keep one hand on the headboard and stroke yourself with the other."

Oh God. I touched my dick and it was so hard and so sensitive it leaped in my hands, sending a shock wave through me. Pleasure licked at my balls and wrapped them tight, and suddenly, I couldn't hold back. "I'm coming," I gasped.

"Yeah, baby. Come while I'm fucking you."

*Fucking you.* Those words, in Dell's gritty voice, shot down to my dick and exploded through me with my orgasm—bright blasts of ecstasy that wracked my whole body. I heard Dell shout and hold my hips tight, pressing in as far as he could go. He pulsed inside and that sent another wave reeling through me—shivery, blinding delight.

We collapsed onto the mattress and laid there panting, letting our heart rates slow. I turned to face Dell and cuddled against him. Yes, cuddled. I still wanted to touch him, couldn't get enough.

He combed fingers through my hair and looked down at me with a little smile.

"What?" I asked.

He shook his head. "You okay?"

"Hell yeah."

"So what did you think of your first time bottoming?"

I considered it. "It actually takes some balls to do it. Like, it feels a little dangerous. And you know me. I love danger."

He chuckled. "I can see that."

I pondered some more. "I think I've just gotten schooled on respecting guys like Shane, Mike's boyfriend."

"You sure he's the bottom?" Dell asked me, voice amused.

Huh. Crap, I really didn't wanna think about Mike and… that. "I know I brought it up, but maybe we could not talk about my brother's sex life."

"Okay." Dell raised his arm to put it behind my head and paused, sniffing. "Jesus. We both need showers. And I need to get back to the hospital." He swung out of bed, went to his jeans on the floor, and dug out his phone.

"Did the nurse text you?"

He checked the screen and shook his head. "No. But I'd feel a lot better if I was there." He smiled. "Well, not better exactly, but I gotta be there for Ty."

"I know. I'll make you a sandwich while you take a shower. Then I'll take mine."

He nodded.

We took turns doing a fast wash-off in the shower, despite my fantasies of a leisurely game of drop-the-soap.

As we walked toward the door with coffees to-go and sandwiches in hand, he stopped me. "There's still more to say. Lots more. But for now—" He gently kissed my lips.

I nodded and tried not to let my nerves show. Lots more to say? Even after the amazing revelations of the last hours, hearing, *We need to talk* was still a scary damned thing.

# TWENTY-FIVE

## DELL

I stared out the doors of the hospital where Donny's truck had driven away. He'd gotten a text to check-in with his Gridley team, so he'd dropped me off with the promise to come back for me. Which was good since I didn't have my Jeep here.

I settled down in one of the uncomfortable chairs in the waiting room and opened my sandwich and my coffee. The nurse had just come out to tell me that Ty was in recovery but it would be hours before he'd be awake. She raised her brows like, *the doctor told you to go home*, but I needed to be here. Once Mam and Gala got their hands on me, it would be tough to get away. I'd called them and told them I was fine. They didn't believe me, but until I got Gala her own car, they had no wheels. Mam had once had a license but let it lapse. She said California freeways intimidated her.

When the last bite of sandwich got washed down, I settled back to think.

Damn, what a ride. Donny's sweetness. Donny's submission. Donny's ass. They all did it for me down to the ground.

But Donny out and proud? The last couple hours had been earth-moving, but the future remained to be seen. We'd been great at sex since the moment our lips met the first time. Could we be good at commitment?

I closed my eyes.

—————

"Mr. Murphy. Mr. Murphy, you can go in now."

My eyes flew open and I blinked. The horrendous pain in my neck plus the daylight flooding the waiting room signaled it must be morning. "Sorry. Hope I wasn't snoring too badly."

She grinned. "Just a little. I let you sleep until Chief Montgomery left. I figured you needed it."

The chief had been there? I wish I'd had a chance to talk to him. I managed to get myself on my feet, stretched, and followed the nurse down the hall.

The nurse said, "I didn't tell him you're here, so it's a surprise."

I pushed the door open and stuck my head in the crack. "Hey! Look who's awake."

Ty laughed. "And look whose rumpled clothes says he slept in a chair all night."

I walked in and clasped Ty's arm to reassure myself he was alive and reasonably well, despite the beeps of the instruments he was connected to. "We're going to have to put you on a diet, son. Man, you are a load."

He gave a gasp of faux outrage. "I resent that. I'm a mere waif of a thing and should be barely a strain for a veritable orc like you." Despite being a little pale, with his leg in a huge cast, his dark eyes sparkled and my heart thumped with relief. He was alive and on track for a full recovery, according to the docs.

I pantomimed my clean and jerk. "I guess that means I'll

be pumping more iron in the near future, in prep for my next fireman's carry."

Ty's face sobered a little. "How about we just don't dump any more planes?"

I nodded as I sighed. "Yeah. I'm really sorry about that, man." I settled into the chair by the bed, still holding his hand.

"Sorry? Fuck! You saved my damned life. How many pilots could have landed that plane without turning it into a fireball? And then you got us out of that hellhole and carried me halfway to Canada without collapsing?"

I gave him a sideways glance. "I guess we could argue that a really smart pilot would have gotten us the fuck out of there *before* a tree fell on us. Or never flown into the hellhole to begin with."

"Fuck that!" He half sat up, and I pushed him back down. "We were ordered into that fire. No way you could have known."

"I had a bad feeling."

"Yeah, well, that and fifty bucks will buy you a hamburger in San Francisco. Come on, Dell. When Chief Montgomery came in, he said the same thing. In fact, he said they've got that fire under control thanks to our early intervention."

I rested my forehead against the side of his bed. "That's good news." But I knew that any other time I would have trusted my gut more. I would have quit that fire sooner, gotten out while the getting was good. I'd been too self-involved and not trusted my instincts. Still, I was glad that was just my own personal evaluation. I liked my job and wanted to keep it. I looked up. "I hate that I dumped our girl in the drink."

"Yeah, well like me, she'll recover. Montgomery said they're hauling her out today, now that the winds have died down. He said they may even be able to fly her out." He grinned. "So, I hear it was a pretty, uh, *eye-opening* rescue. Sorry I missed it."

I snorted. "Who told you that?"

"The Chief —in so many words. I'm good at reading between the lines. Sounds like the radio communiques were epic." He chuckled.

My chest got warm and probably my cheeks were a little pink, "Yeah well, it's easy to make declarations in the middle of a crisis. We'll see where we go from here." Although, man, where we'd gone so far had been mighty fine. We needed to talk, but with that boy around, I forgot to use my words.

"You and Canali?"

I nodded.

"Where is Mr. Mack-on-you-in-front-of-the-entire-rescue-team?"

I laughed at Ty's teasing. "It was a simple kiss, hardly macking." Yeah, but it had shocked the hell out of me. "And Donny really wanted to be here when you woke up, but he had to go back to his station for debrief."

"No, he wanted to be here *with you* when I woke up."

"Semantics."

As if somebody said *cue the firefighter*, voices sounded from the hall. A nurse said, "No, sir, I need to check with Mr. Chan and the doctor before you can—"

The door burst open, and Donny stepped in with a nurse clinging to him like a barnacle.

He smiled bashfully when he saw me. "Hi."

Ty laughed. "It's okay, Linda." Yes, Ty had already charmed the nurses. "He's one of the people who rescued us."

She frowned but nodded and closed the door partway as she left Donny behind.

Donny stood there and never took his eyes off my face. I knew, because I couldn't look away from him.

Ty laughed. "Hi, Donny, good to see you too."

Donny blinked and looked at Ty, "Oh hi, Ty. How are you feeling?"

"Like a tree fell on me, but hell, that's better than the two I swore attacked me earlier."

Donny nodded. "Good. That's really good, man." His gaze drifted back to me.

Ty glanced between Donny and me. "Uh, I'd leave you two alone, but that's going to be tricky since I'm in a hospital bed. Why don't you go talk and let me get some more shut-eye? Everyone keeps telling me I need it after surgery."

I could tell he was exhausted, though he'd never admit it. Jesus, he wasn't the only one. I said, "Good plan. I'll, uh, come back in a little while."

Ty settled into his pillow. "Nah. My mom's flying in from LA in an hour or so and you'll never get close to the bedside."

I gripped his arm. "But you'll come home with me and let me and Mam and Gala take care of you."

He made a face. "Great as that sounds, I think my mom is warming up the oven to make chicken soup and corn bread for the duration. Man, she hasn't been able to catch me standing still in years." He looked up at me with those lustrous eyes. "Thank you, Dell. I appreciate—everything. And I'll tell mom that I have an alternative to Mama Chan's home cooking in case she needs to get home."

I snorted. "You kidding? I may be coming to your place. Mam Murphy's creative culinary experiences aren't quite as nurturing, as you well know." We clasped hands and then I turned and let my eyes feast on the big guy watching me so longingly.

Yep. The question of the day. Donny had found me. Now what did he plan to do with me?

When we got into the hall, Donny glanced around at the nurses and orderlies moving fast up and down the corridors. His chest expanded as he took a breath, and then he turned, pulled me closer, and kissed me, softly this time. True, it wasn't the epic kiss he'd laid on me during the rescue, or the passion we'd shared when he'd taken me to his place, but it was damn sweet. And it was also in public again. Big points. Huge.

I rewarded him for his bravery with a smile and got one back. "Shouldn't you be fighting a fire?"

He shook his head. "No. They released our station. They've got the blaze backed off in no small part thanks to you and Ty, and I get my four days off."

"Maybe you could take me to get my Jeep?" I paused, trying to think. "Shit. I'm not even sure where it is."

"McClellan."

"Oh right." I shook my head, still kind of fuzzy from my weird night. "I parked it before I crashed a plane." I gave a little chuckle.

And just like that, I got swept up in Donny's arms again. Damn, it felt good.

"Oh, babe, that was so scary. I knew you could handle that plane better than anybody, but shit happens."

"Trees happen."

"We'll get your Jeep later. Right now, I'm going to drive you home. It's the only way I can avoid getting one more call from Gala threatening my life." He shook his head. "Damn, your mom is a force of nature. She's talked to every doctor in the hospital including the hemorrhoid specialists, making sure you're okay."

I laughed. "That's because she knows I can be an asshole."

He snorted.

I said, "I talked to her earlier, but I probably wasn't making a ton of sense."

"Yeah." With one arm still tight around me, he guided me toward the exit. "The doctors told your chief you're not hurt, but you need lots of rest. I figure the chances of that happening are zero without an intervention. Consider me the intervener. We'll get you tucked into bed, and then Gala can go with me to get your Jeep."

That sounded like a great plan. And it was nice to have someone offering to take care of me—that hardly ever happened.

We got to his truck, and he held the door for me, then tried to help me in. I kind of wanted to laugh, he was so sincere. But as he leaned over me in the passenger seat, he said, "I told the chief I'd see you went home and went to bed. I didn't tell him what you'd be doing there." He chuckled as he closed the door, and I took a big breath.

I watched that gorgeous man striding around the truck and had to force myself to be strong. We really did need to finish our talk, much as I'd like to repeat our earlier reunion.

I must have drifted off for a few minutes, because the distance to my house seemed to evaporate, and as we pulled in front, a shriek came from Mam's back door and she came running out with Gala behind her. Just as I hopped out of the truck, she hurled herself into my arms and I caught her, staggering back against the passenger seat. She chanted, "Oh my god, oh my god. We've been so worried."

"Whoa."

She stopped wriggling and placed her hands on my chest. "Oh, honey, I'm sorry. Are you sore?"

"I'm fine, Mam."

"I knew you would be! If you'd been dead or badly hurt, I'd feel it. But we heard about the crash on the news and tried to call someone. It was so hard to get through and you didn't answer your phone, and—"

Gala pulled her back gently. "Give him a little space, Mam. Let's get him inside and feed him soup or something."

Donny spoke up. "Ma'am, the doctor said he should go to bed right away. Maybe we should get him up to his place while I'm here, and—"

I held up my hands, palms forward. "Uh, guys, I carried

Ty for over a mile *after* the plane crash. I think I can get up the stairs to my apartment."

Mam smiled up at me as she slid an arm around my waist. "Of course, you can, honey." And with that, my hundred and thirty-pound, five-feet-five-inch mother proceeded to guide her six-feet-three-inch, two-hundred-pound son up the stairs. I didn't even laugh.

An hour of unique vegetable soup, pillow-fluffing, and hand-holding later, Gala managed to drag Mam to the door with the promise that Donny would come and get them if I needed anything.

Still, from the bedroom, I heard Mam say, "Donny, do you still have a girlfriend? Because if so, I expect you to leave now. Is that clear?"

"No, ma'am, I never did. My mother misunderstood."

"I'm sure you played a key part in that misunderstanding."

"Uh... Yeah. I'm afraid I did."

"And you've changed that?"

"I'm honestly working on it."

Gala said, "Mam, I think the boys need to talk."

"All right. Stay and talk. But I hope my son doesn't let you off too easily. You don't deserve it." The door opened. "And don't you dare tire him out." The door slammed.

I barked a laugh. Neither Gala nor I had ever doubted that Mam was on our side.

Donny walked in with a big grin, but it was sheepish. "Man, let's hear it for mama bears."

I nodded. "Don't mess with her cubs."

He sat on the edge of the bed, leaned in, and kissed me.

The sheer pleasure of those lips on mine rolled through me like a wave. Donny wriggled closer until the weight of his chest rested on me and his tongue plundered deeper.

My brain tiptoed toward surrender, and then, a trickle of recall slipped in. Right. I thought I'd never kiss Donny again, not so much because a fire nearly consumed me, but because the asshole came to his brother's wedding with a woman he claimed was his girlfriend and had never bothered to explain. "Hold it." My eyes flipped open. "We need to talk."

Donny's breathing came fast and his eyes were hazy with desire, but he sat up straight. "Right. I'm ready."

Since I didn't feel like getting up and putting my jeans back on, I pointed at the end of the bed. "But since my resolve is weak, you sit down there."

He grinned, but I'd used my officer voice and he moved.

I wiped a hand over my face. "When we started this adventure, I was fine with it being on the down-low. I enjoyed the sex as much as you did, but I'm past that." I barked a laugh. "Uh no. That came out wrong. I love having sex with you. It's just that I want more." I took a breath. "I care about you, Donny. Too much, in fact."

He leaned forward, like he could push his sincerity across the bed. "I care about you too."

"I need for you to understand. I want it all, Donny. More sex, more kisses, more pizza in front of a football game. But if we continue, it'll be me as your boyfriend, and not just behind closed doors. I'm your guy or nothing. That's just the way it's gotta be."

Our eyes met and held. Then Donny nodded. "I want that too. I feel like I already came out, because, like you say, everyone at incident command heard me on that radio. But I know I still have a lot of people to talk to."

I nodded. "I know it's not easy. Maybe we should just… hold off until you work it out."

He shook his head adamantly. "No way. I haven't thought about anything else since I left you last night. I know what I need to do, and I'm going to do it, Dell. Show you with my actions. With my family, my station, and—" He took a big breath. "—with my pa. I mean, he knows, but I need to say the words. And I will, right away. I mean, not this minute, but as soon as I go home. Okay?"

I leaned forward and put a hand on his arm. "I'm looking forward to it from the bottom of my heart." I was not even a little bit kidding.

He wiped a hand over his face. "It's been horrible without you. *I've* been horrible." He gave a wry smile. "I don't think anyone in my life is gonna be shocked to know I've been carrying a major torch."

"Same. The whole fucking world is pretty much over me mooning around."

He smiled shyly. "They are?"

"Oh yeah." I pressed my hands to my chest. "I've been bleeding from my so-sensitive Irish heart all over everyone."

He snorted.

I sighed and leaned back against my pillows. "So we'll just take it one day at a time. Right? There's still work to do."

"Yeah."

I yawned. "At the moment, I think you're gonna have to do your assigned job and tuck me in because, I hate to admit it, but I'm done. Last night in that chair about killed me. I've got to get some real sleep." I grinned. "Feel free to tuck in beside me."

The last thing I remembered as my eyes closed was the sound of his boots hitting the floor and his warm body next to mine. Not damned bad.

————

When my eyelids fluttered open, I was vaguely aware of sunlight outside the window, but it was low in the sky. I could barely see it because I was staring into two dark eyes about five inches away.

Donny smiled. "You look like a little kid when you sleep, all cute and snuffly."

I smiled back. "Nonsense. I'm sure I'm a very dignified and formidable sleeper. The veritable alpha male of slumber."

He laughed, leaned in, and kissed my lips gently. "We have an invitation to a late lunch/early dinner, should you ever wake up."

I stretched. "Oh, I don't know. I might just like to stay here and gaze at you, boyo."

"I can't guarantee you won't get a knock on the door in midgaze, but I'm game." He searched my face with so much affection it took my breath away.

At that moment, my body rebelled and gave the loudest stomach growl outside of a Saturday morning cartoon. I laughed. "My belly makes a liar of me."

Fifteen minutes later, washed and well-kissed, we walked to my mam's kitchen door.

Donny knocked lightly, opened the door, and let me walk in. Mam was at the stove, no doubt being creative, and Gala was setting the table. Mam rushed over and hugged me. "How do you feel, honey?"

"Still tired, but more hungry."

"Good. I made pork chops, mashed potatoes, and a big salad. Gala said you needed something simple and nourishing." She brandished her spoon.

"Sounds wonderful." And it did. I winked at Gala. Pork chops were one of Mam's less *speculative* dishes, and we both liked them.

I was just about to sit at the table when I looked back at Donny who was still standing kind of awkwardly at the door.

Mam noticed him too. "What's the matter, honey? Aren't you hungry?"

"No, ma'am. I mean, yes, ma'am, I'm very hungry, but, uh, I wanted to introduce myself to you."

Mam looked confused, but Gala seemed to catch on. "Go ahead. Do it." She smiled.

I gazed at Donny who shifted feet, then stood ramrod

straight. "How do you do, ladies. My name is Donato Canali. People call me Donny. I'm a firefighter with Cal Fire. While I'm currently a rank-and-file firefighter, I want you to know that I have excellent prospects for the future. I've been selected for a number of supervisory assignments and hope to make Lieutenant in no more than two years. I'm a member of a big family and deeply appreciate Dell's commitment to his family." He cleared his throat, stared at his boots for a second, and then said, "I've been seeing Dell for a number of months and have become very serious about our relationship, which I assure you is *entirely exclusive*." He glanced pointedly at Mam. "I'm honored to call him my boyfriend. I just wanted you to know."

My mam said, "Good for you, honey. Good for you."

Gala looked moony-eyed the way she did watching *Pride and Prejudice*.

And I gazed at Donato Canali, blinking hard against the heat. It wasn't the same as coming out to his family or his fire station, although he'd taken steps in declaring himself to both groups. But this? This moment had to be about the cutest damned thing I'd ever seen.

I jumped to my feet, wrapped him in my arms and kissed him. "Thanks, *boyfriend*." I grinned. "Want to sign on for a long tour of duty?"

He gave me a sexy smile. "Sir, yes, sir."

Mam said, "It's about damned time. Now come eat."

# TWENTY-SIX

## DONNY

I didn't want to leave Dell. If I could have stayed there at his apartment watching over him for a week, I would have. But he was right—I still had work to do. And I didn't exactly look forward to it, so I just wanted to get it over with.

I left the Murphy residence after our late lunch of pork-chops. It took me a minute to think what day it was. It was a Sunday, so there should be lots of family around. I texted Mike as soon as I got in my truck.

*Hey. I wanna call a family meeting. Can you let everyone know? I'll be there in 60.*

Mike answered immediately. *What for? Where've you been? You disappeared after we got Dell and Ty out. I think some of the guys at the station heard something, cause they looked at me funny when I joined them, but I don't know if they believed it. What's going on?*

I rolled my eyes. Leave it to Mike to turn a text into a novel. But his comment about the guys at the station made my stomach do a slow roll. When I'd gone back to the fire yesterday, I'd been assigned to work with another crew at the command post, so I hadn't seen my team yet. That was next on the list though. For now…

Me: *So many questions. Hence the need for family mtg.*

Mike: *Ok. Ok. I'll rally the troops. You hungry?*

That made me smile. We Canalis were all about food.

Me: *Just ate.*

I tossed the phone on the passenger seat and started to drive. I turned on music, loud, and tried not to worry too much on the way home. This had to be done. It had to be done for Dell. I wasn't gonna leave him hanging ever again. Even thinking about how I'd treated him at the wedding made me burn with shame.

I should have been there with him, not Beth. And that was the bottom line. But that was my future. I needed to clean up my past.

Pa's truck and Tony and Viv's car were in the driveway when I got there. The fire must really be minimal now if all of us were home. That was good news.

I took a deep breath. Yeah, focus on the good news. There was the conquered fire. And there was the fact that Dell wanted me back. With a firm nod to myself, I went inside.

They were all waiting for me in the living room—Mike, Ma, Pa, Tony, Viv, Tessa, Nonna, and Nonno. I'd never been so glad in my life that Gabe was still on his honeymoon. He and Pa would be the hardest.

"I made cookies." Ma stood up from the couch and picked up a platter from the coffee table. She gave me an encouraging smile. "Peanut butter."

That was my favorite. Ma was the greatest. And, hell, there's always room for cookies.

"Thanks, Ma." I crossed to her and took a cookie. Impulsively, I gave her a kiss on the cheek too.

"Well, someone's feeling better," Tony remarked dryly.

"Shut up," I said lightly.

"Gee, wonder where you've been this afternoon?" Mike

teased with a raised eyebrow. "Does this mean grumpy bear is gone? Please, God, let it mean that."

"Don't take the lord's name in vain," scolded Ma.

"What? I'm serious. That was a sincere prayer."

"Please, God, let this meeting get to the point," said Tessa with an eyeroll, but she gave me a look that said she and I were in on the joke. "I wanna hear what Donny has to say."

"I want to hear too," Nonna said. "I predict he's won the lottery! Or possibly found a suitcase full of money. It's definitely a windfall of some sort."

Well, hell. She wasn't wrong.

"Sit down, Donato. Here, sit by me." Ma plopped down on the couch practically on top of Mike, so he had to scoot over.

I sat next to her and dared a glance at Pa. He was sitting in his recliner, and he'd apparently just gotten home, because he was still in his Cal Fire T-shirt and work pants. His face was grimy and tired, and it was the first time he looked really old to me. His expression was grim.

I looked down at my hands. I got a strong stab of that old feeling—that I loved Pa so much and wanted him to notice me, be proud of me. Only now it brought sadness with it. Because I knew that ship had sailed. Like Mike said, I couldn't make both Dell and Pa happy. And Dell had won. No, I had won.

"Eat your cookie." Ma nudged my arm.

I took a bite. It was good but kind of stuck in my throat because my mouth was so dry.

"Mike, get your brother a soda," said Ma.

"Me?" Mike squeaked.

"Didn't I say *Mike*?" she countered.

Mike grinned. "Yeah. But you usually call me at least four of my brother's names before you get to *Mike*, so a name doesn't mean much."

She glared at him, and Mike went to the kitchen, glancing

back as he walked. He came back, handed me a cold seltzer—
Ma had started stocking that since it was Shane's drink of
choice. He smirked at me and went to sit down. I opened the
seltzer and took a big gulp.

"Not to get off topic or anything," said Viv. She was sitting
next to Tony on the other couch. "But would you mind if I
take some of the leftover turkey for the kids' lunches this
week, Ma?"

"No, take it!" Ma turned to me. "Don't worry, Donny. I
put some aside for you." And back to Viv. "Also, I made a
casserole we didn't eat today. Take it with. Add a salad and
garlic bread, and you'll have a nice ready-made dinner this
week."

"What kind of casserole?" asked Tony.

"Guys, can we not get distracted with food at this precise
moment?" Mike asked loudly. "Donny asked for a meeting.
Let's hear what he has to say." He gave me an encouraging
look and a nod.

"Yeah, Donny, spit it out," said Tony, which earned him an
elbow in the ribs from Viv.

And then everyone was staring at me again. I quickly
swallowed the rest of the cookie, took a drink, and then a
deep breath. It didn't help. My body was rigid as a tree.

Ma took my hand in hers. "Go ahead, Donato. We're all
here for you."

I looked at the cookie platter rather than at their faces. "So.
What I wanted to tell everyone is… well, Dell and I got back
together. And that's what I want. To be with him. He's really
great and… he's my boyfriend now."

Heat crept up from my stomach to the top of my head,
and I knew my face was flaming. The room was very quiet. I
looked up to see a mix of love, surprise, and resignation. The
last from Pa. He took a sip of beer and looked out the
window.

"Well damn," said Tessa. "It's really not fair that two of

my brothers now have gorgeous boyfriends and I don't. Ma, tell them it's not fair."

"I knew it!" Nonna exclaimed. "Didn't I say that Donny would get married, not to worry? And I said she'd be unusually tall, didn't I say she'd be tall?" She tapped her temple with a knowing look.

Ma sniffed and dabbed at her eyes. "I told Angie this would happen. I'm your mother. I know when my son has lost his heart." She gave me a pitying look and then a hug. "It'll be okay, Donato. I know this won't be easy, but we're here for you."

She made it sound like I had cancer or something. And, while I got her concern, I didn't feel that way at all. "Don't worry, Ma. Dell has been out for a long time. And I have Mike. I have some pretty good shoulders to lean on if I need it."

"And you have us," Ma said firmly. She looked at my father. "Right, Angie? Donny has us. We're family."

I finally looked at Pa. He didn't look angry—just sad. He shook his head. "I've been taught a lesson in humility lately. Turns out there's a lot I don't know about this stuff. And I also learned I can't change my children. Donny, you do what you need to do to be happy. And if you get any shit at work, you come to me, you hear?"

"Thanks, Pa," I said, my chest heavy. Maybe I wasn't Pa's new favorite anymore. But it was better than I hoped for.

"So… is this for real?" Tony asked, looking confused. "I mean, Mike, I get… but Donny?"

Mike gaped at him. "What's that supposed to mean?"

Tony held up a hand. "No offense. It's just that Donny always the one with the biggest mouth when it came to gay people."

"He also said he supported me one-hundred percent when I came out," Mike said defensively. "So, Donny, you'd better believe I have your back—with the family and at work. I love you, bro."

"I'm not saying I have an issue with it." Tony held up his hands. "I mean, it's a shock but whatever, man."

"Look at it this way," said Viv. "Donny's actually dating someone who has a great job, military medals, and a whole lot of personal ethics."

Tony made a *you-have-a-point* face.

"Dell's amazing," Mike agreed enthusiastically. "For f—er, crap's sake, he was a military pilot. And bonus: he doesn't have twenty piercings in his face. I'd call that a win."

Tony smiled. "So all it took for you to date someone decent, Donny, is that it was a guy? Cool."

"There's some deep psychology in there somewhere," Tessa piped in. "But I'll let Donny and Dell figure it out. I think it's great. I love Gala, and she talks about Dell like he hung the moon. He takes care of his mom and sister, and that's good enough for me."

"He does?!" Ma exclaimed. "I love him already. Donny, you have to bring him for dinner soon. What do they like to eat? What's his last name? I forget."

"Murphy," said Mike. "Pilot Dell Murphy." He gave me a bemused look like who'd have ever guessed that would be the name of my sweetheart? But the name warmed me.

Hell yeah, Pilot Dell Murphy was all mine.

Ma frowned. "That's not Italian. What do they eat at their house, Donny? I want to make something he'll like."

And of course—the conversation moved back to food.

————

"Guess this is my last big hurdle," I said nervously as Mike and I got into my truck to drive to the station three days later. We were going back in for a twenty-four hour shift, and it would be the first time I'd faced my crew since I'd come out on the radio during Dell's rescue. Mike thought most of them hadn't believed it then, or didn't hear it. But, either way, I figured it'd be best to just pull the Band-Aid off and announce it.

Mike gave me a look. "Uh… hate to be the bearer of bad news, but it's definitely not your last hurdle. There'll be hurdles from here on out, bro. Sometimes when you least expect it. You'll always be meeting people who don't know you're gay."

"Last *big* hurdle, I said. Don't bust my chops. I'm nervous enough."

Mike rolled his eyes. "Okay, fine. This is the last time you'll ever have a care in the world about dating a man. Lucky you."

I grumbled but didn't argue. I was glad Mike was by my side. This was gonna suck. But it'd suck less with my brother there.

When we got to the station, I heard Chief Reiger was in his office, so I went in to speak to him first.

"Well, that explains why you called Pilot Murphy *babe* on the horn," Reiger said. He leaned forward and looked at me sternly. "You know our policy is LGBTQ friendly. I don't have an issue with it, though I'm not sure you should remain our station's air liaison since you're, er, personally involved with Pilot Murphy. I'll have to speak to admin about it. But as for the rest, you don't have to do this—make a formal announcement to everyone in the station. It's nobody's business but yours."

I squirmed uncomfortably. "I know. But I plan to be open about Dell, and I'd rather get it over with at once, if that's okay with you."

Reiger set his mouth in a grim line and studied me. "How's Angie with this news?"

"Pa's been good about it, considering."

"Well, the Canalis certainly don't do anything in half

measures. Okay. When we have our debriefing, I'll give you five."

We always had debriefings at the start of a new shift where Chief went over the fire map and status of various blazes in the state. My palms were sweaty and I could hardly sit still while Reiger went through the data. And then he said, "Before we break up, Donny has something he wants to say."

Shit. Mike gave me a nod of support, and I stood up. I made myself lift my chin. "Like Chief told me, this doesn't really deserve an announcement or anything, but I figured there'd be rumors so... The thing is, well, I'm dating Pilot Murphy. So, yeah, I guess that makes me bisexual. In case anyone gives a shit. Anyway, that's all I have to say."

I sat down heavily in my chair. There was silence in the room.

"Okay, ladies and gentlemen. Back to work." Reiger picked up his folder and left the meeting room.

Brian came up to me first, and he was laughing. "Holy shit! That rumor at the wedding was true? What the hell, man? What about all the chicks you've dated?"

"What part of *bisexual* confuses you, Bri?" Mike asked testily.

"The part where Donny's only ever dated women, Mike," Brian snapped back.

"I didn't know until Dell. Anyway, it's nobody's business." I tried to sound more casual than I felt.

Rebecca came up and gave me a hug. "Way to go, Canali. Except you broke my heart."

I laughed. She was just yanking my chain. "I bet your husband would be interested to hear that."

She grinned. "Seriously, I've got your back—you and Mike both."

"Thanks, Rebecca."

"Yeah, thanks." Mike gave her a fist bump.

"So much for the great, legendary Hot Cannolis," Jordy sneered, pushing past us.

"Maybe they're all queer," said Dwayne, an older guy who I knew was conservative.

I started to go after them, but Mike grabbed my arm and shook his head. And he was right. There'd always be assholes out there. I should know. I'd been one of them. But at the end of the day, talk was cheap. If they got in my face though—or Mike's, or Dell's—then they'd have a serious problem with me.

Brian's expression softened. "Ignore them. So Dell Murphy, huh? He's good-looking, I guess. If you like movie-star types. He makes you happy?"

"Happier than I ever thought I could be with another person," I said honestly.

"Daw," said Mike. "I have to tell Shane about this. He's gonna freak. I never knew you had it in you to be romantic, bro. Like, seriously. I thought you'd never have a real relationship. Who knew all it took was a pair of green eyes and a hot airman?"

Yeah, I hadn't seen Dell coming. And he'd changed everything. It would take a long time for the dust to settle. But at least now I could maybe be the boyfriend he deserved.

# EPILOGUE

## DELL

"Look! It's Carlotta!" Mam waved over my shoulder from the back seat.

My Jeep tires had just crunched on the gravel of the Resolute compound's parking area and I was already engulfed in Canalis—Canali women specifically.

It had been two weeks since the plane crash. Donny and I had spent every night together when he wasn't at the station doing a 24-hour shift or we weren't both out on a fire. Often we were only in the bed for sleeping, since in early September, California was just one big match waiting to be struck and we were both exhausted. This Sunday however, had miraculously worked out, and it looked like all the Canalis were here to pass judgment on Donny's shocking choice of a partner. Pulling up in front of this house gave me seriously mixed feelings, a ton of them bad.

Lucille Canali, Carlotta, Tessa, Donny's grandmother, and his sister-in-law, Viv, all gathered at the porch steps as I pulled into my spot. They crowded the Jeep when I turned off the ignition.

Mam and Gala were out their doors before I'd unfastened my seat belt. Gala and Tessa hopped up and down like they hadn't seen each other for months as opposed to days, while Mam got hugged in welcome by all the other ladies.

By the time I was out of the driver's seat, the women were halfway to the house.

But I felt welcomed just fine because Donny stepped out from behind an SUV and, before I could even smile, I was wrapped in his arms with his mouth on mine. When we finally parted lips, he grinned. "I persuaded my ma that we had to make your mom and sister feel *really* welcome. I figured this was my best chance to get you alone for a minute."

I pressed my lips to his again and let my tongue slip into warm and secret places. I'd happily stay right there for the rest of the night, just drifting and dreaming in Donny's arms, but that's not what this dinner was about.

He loosely linked his arms around my waist. I loved being able to stare directly into his dark eyes and feel the strength and power of his body so close to mine. Not many men could stand toe-to-toe beside me without looking small. Not my baby.

"You ready for this?" he asked.

"I want your family to like me, but bottom line?" I touched his cheek. "You're the one that matters to me. It's you that's important."

"I know." He nodded, but all those complicated emotions flowing across his face spoke loudly. Donny cared for me, yes. Hell, he'd come out to be with me and that was huge in his life. But his family had always been the measure of his heart and to have me and not them would never be enough, no matter how hard he tried.

So the truth was, tonight and every night I spent with the Canalis was important to the man I loved, and that made it enormously important to me. *No pressure, Murphy.* I took his hand. "Let's go see the family."

When we walked into the delicious-smelling house, it felt like a hundred pairs of dark eyes stared at me. Probably more like fifteen or twenty. All the men sat in front of the TV except for Mike and Shane. According to what seemed to be Canali rules, the women were all in the open kitchen, including Mam and Gala. Mam looked like she was in her element, waving a spoon in the air. Gala was leaning against the wall talking to Tessa, perfectly happy, so I turned my attention to the Canali men. Of course, I recognized the chief, and the elderly man who I knew was his father who slept in a chair. The friendly brother—Tony, maybe—stood and smiled. The brother who'd gotten married, Gabe, barely looked at me, but the cousin with the bow-shaped lips managed a shy grin. I didn't see Uncle Ricky, the Cary Grant look-alike, but the fewer the better for this first dinner. I assessed the most likely areas for enemy flack—the chief, even though Donny said he'd been better lately, and Gabe, who wasn't taking this new development at all well. Donny hadn't told me a lot, but it was clear Gabe was a homophobe who'd been pissed to have a second brother come out. Well, if he gave Donny shit today, I was ready for it.

I smiled politely and nodded at them all. "Hey, guys."

Mrs. Canali hurried over to me and Donny. "Dell, we're so glad you're here," she said loudly. When she got close, she dropped her volume. "We promised Donny we'd give you two a few minutes alone." She winked and took my arm. "Let me introduce you to everyone again."

The elderly Mrs. Canali walked over from the kitchen archway and patted my chest, which she barely came up to. "I'm Angie's mother. Call me Nonna. Didn't I tell you all that Donny would get himself a gorgeous spouse?"

Donny's cheeks turned pink. "Come on, Nonna. Dell's my boyfriend. We're not married."

She giggled and tapped her temple. "You will be. I have the sight."

Lucille sounded exasperated. "Please, Nonna. We don't believe in that nonsense. We're a good Catholic family."

Nonna huffed at Lucille, but then flashed me a wicked grin one last time as she walked away.

I couldn't help it. I laughed, even if I was getting harnessed for matrimony. Damn, what would that be like? I'd never even thought about it. My time with Donny had been such a tightrope-walk, I hadn't felt on sure enough footing to even consider it. But the idea ignited something inside me and I pushed it into a private corner of my heart to consider later.

Lucille guided me to the group of men where she did her reintroductions. The oldest brother, Gabe, stared stonily at the television and got a glare from Lucille, but the friendly brother, who did turn out to be named Tony, waved a hand at one of the couches. "Sit with us, Dell."

His mother gave him an approving nod and released my arm. "Yes, make yourself at home. Donny, get Dell something to drink, and there are snacks on the coffee table." She hurried back toward the kitchen.

"Wanna sparkling water?" Donny asked, obviously a little nervous but putting on a brave face.

"Absolutely. Thanks."

He went to get it and I scooted into an empty spot on the sofa near Tony. I glanced at the TV. They'd lowered the sound, but I recognized the game and smiled. "Damn, it's good to have football back. The Dodgers were fun to watch this year, but there's nothing like football. Do you think the Bucs will be a factor once Brady's gone?"

Chief Canali, who'd given me a nod but no other reaction when I walked over, gazed at me levelly. Then he smiled. It wasn't big and welcoming like Tony's, but it did make it to his eyes. "I heard there's a chance he might play another season. But I like Russell Wilson."

I nodded. "Yeah, he's strong. He can chuck it deep. If the Bucs can get him away from the Seahawks."

"What do you think about Garoppolo as an option?" asked Tony.

"I like Watson," said Tito, munching on a chip.

Donny came back and handed me a bottle of sparkling water. He sat next to me on the sofa and joined in while we chatted back and forth about quarterbacks.

Gabe watched us. He didn't say anything, but he appeared—surprised? And I could be wrong, but he didn't seem too pleased with the way the chief was engaging with me.

Beside me on the couch, Donny gradually relaxed and got more animated. Apparently, I'd lucked into starting the one conversation that could make me the most welcome in the House of Canali.

I'd really have liked to go into the kitchen, say hi to Mike and Shane and see if I could help, but I didn't. I stayed glued to the game, downed some chips, and cheered in appropriate places. Being one of the guys was important in the Canali household and I could do that as well as the next guy. Hell, I'd been in the military. If they wanted alpha male, I could damn well out-alpha them all. Actually, considering I was gay, I guess I sort of gave new meaning to the term *man's* man.

The game ended and Lucille called us to dinner. Clearly the thing that surpassed football in priority in the Canali household was food. It only took a few seconds to remember why. The huge dining room table with chairs and a long bench allowing people to squeeze in tightly must have been yelling uncle under the weight of all the food. There was roast beef with potatoes and carrots around it, plus an additional dish of mashed potatoes and gravy, a large platter of lasagna, green beans and peas in separate bowls and, a huge salad that, oddly, everyone seemed anxious to get heaped on their salad plates.

Donny chuckled. "That's a Shane salad and it's so good, we all fight over eating green stuff."

Even though Lucille had indicated that Donny and I should sit in chairs near her, Donny pulled me over to the long bench that occupied one side of the table. I found out why real fast, because our thighs pressed together from hip to knee. How to have a boner bigger than the cucumber used in the magic salad!

We might have focused more on teasing each other under the table if the food hadn't been so damned good. As it was, we needed two hands to eat.

Everyone was making polite conversation about the weather and how were things at the station and wasn't the food good. Not Mam. She smiled at Gabe. "So didn't you just get back from your honeymoon? Where's your wife?"

He blinked. "She's at work, Mrs. Murphy. She's a police dispatcher and is on duty a lot of nights."

Mam raised her eyebrows. "And you're a cop, right?"

"Uh, yes, ma'am, but I'm transferring into the IT department next week."

"You got that job?" Shane asked, eyebrows raised. "Congrats!"

Gabe smiled at him. "Yeah. I get to stay in my station and everything. Thanks for your help with that."

"Shane helped Gabe with his resume," Lucille informed me. She beamed at Shane. "He's so talented at things like that. If you ever need a resume, Dell or Gala, you simply must get Shane to help you."

"Be warned," said Tessa. "Once Ma identifies your skill set, you'll be doing that for the family forever."

Shane waved his hand. "I'm also the napkin-swan guy. And Tessa fetches hemorrhoid medication."

"I did that once!" Tessa apparently kicked Shane under the table because he jumped a little, then grinned at her. "It's more like Gala and I will be making bridesmaid dresses for the family forever," Tessa said.

Gala smiled. "That's okay with me."

"Well, if you need a plane flown or water dumped, I'm your man," I said.

Donny grinned. "You never know when you might have to drop a bunch of water on a Hot Cannoli."

All the men grinned.

Mam looked intently at Gabe again. "IT? Like computers?" She always was one to never let go of a bone.

"That's right." Gabe actually smiled. "It's fun."

"That's a good job. Can you work from home?"

"Yes, sometimes."

"Good, so you can share child care. Let me tell you, working and taking care of kids isn't easy when it's just you." She shook her head, took a bite of mashed potatoes, and said almost to herself, "Men just have no clue how hard women work." Then she glanced up at Gabe again. "Bet your new job increases the chance that you'll have kids soon."

He chuckled self-consciously. "Well, it's definitely in the plan. But not soon."

"Famous last words," said Tito with a smile.

"I repeat, not soon." Gabe knocked on the table.

Mam went back to eating, then said, "I hope your wife's sister wasn't too upset about Donny loving Dell instead of her." She waved her fork. "But come on, she would have been disappointed sooner or later. Clearly, Donny needs Dell." She shrugged and robustly cut into another hunk of roast beef.

I took a breath and glanced at Donny. This was why I'd been leery about bringing Mam today. She had zero filter. But, hell, if we were all to be one big family, they'd have to get used to her sooner or later. At least Donny didn't seem freaked.

Tessa clamped a hand on Mam's arm. "Mrs. Murphy, I love you."

"I love you, too, dear. And call me Titania."

"You're not wrong," Lucille agreed matter-of-factly. "Now that I see Donny and Dell together, it's as plain as the nose on my face."

I was relieved that Mam's bluntness was taken in stride in this big noisy family. Hell, she fit right in.

I asked Tessa about the plans she and Gala were discussing for an online business. Tessa had really pulled Gala out of her hermitdom, and I was grateful.

Tessa smiled at Gala. "We've been brainstorming names and looking at Etsy policies and other potential platforms."

"I checked out business licenses online." Gala nodded. "Man, those forms are hard. You'd think you were signing away your firstborn or something."

"Ask Tito," Lucille said. "He's the one who's good at all that online form stuff. He always helps me renew our car tags."

Nonna snorted. "Speaking of firstborns, I wish you'd all get a little busier having them. Gabe, Tessa, the burden's on you now. Now that two of my grandsons are out of the baby game." She waved a hand toward Mike and then Donny.

Mike shook his head vehemently. "Not true, Nonna. Lots of gay couples have kids. You can adopt or use a surrogate. Shane and I want to eventually, but come on. Shane's not even done with school yet."

"And you haven't proposed, Light-of-my-life," Shane said breezily. "There's that."

Mike reddened. "Yeah. I mean… if, uh, Shane agrees to marry me and, uh, you know, stuff like that."

Tony snorted. "Nice save, bro."

"So you two are discussing marriage?" Viv leaned over anxiously.

Mike winced and waved a hand. "Can we move on from

this conversation please? I was just saying it's possible." But he gave Shane a grin and got one back.

Nonna pointed a fork at Donny. "In that case, Donny and Dell, don't take too long with this courtship business. Donny's not getting any younger."

Donny squealed, "I'm twenty-five!"

"That may be. But Dell's sperm is aging, so get on the stick," Mam said.

I barked a laugh and had to clap a hand over my mouth to keep from sharing peas, then managed to swallow before my laughter poured out of me like water. Part of it was pure relief that this dinner was going so well, but damn, Mam was funny. For a second, Donny just looked at me in surprise, and then he started to laugh too. After all the months of uncertainty and fear, it felt so good I just couldn't stop.

Tessa and Gala joined in, then Shane and Mike, Tony and Nonna, Mam and all the women.

The chief and Gabe managed to look befuddled until the elderly gentleman, Nonno, who, after a few bites of food, had been sitting at the table dozing, went "Ha. Aging sperm. Good one." And then he was off, laughing away.

It was too much even for Chief Canali and Gabe. It was a wonder the table didn't collapse from so many people holding onto it for support.

As we were all drying our eyes, Lucille said, "Phew. I think we all needed that."

"To family," Chief Canali said abruptly. He raised his glass.

Everyone raised theirs. "To family!"

I shared a look with Gala and both our eyes were damp. It had always been just the three of us. But maybe it didn't have to be that way anymore.

"Cannolis will be served in the living room!" Lucille announced.

Minutes later, we all sat around by the fireplace, with the

TV off, eating delicious cold Italian dessert. Chief Canali looked over at me and cleared his throat. "Dell, I wanted to tell you how much your honesty and candor have meant to me. I may not always have liked what you had to say, but it helped me get to a place I had to be if I was ever going to be happy again. And more important, to support my son's happiness. I, for one, am glad to have you around." He glanced over at Mike and Shane on the sofa. "That goes for you, too, Shane." He swallowed as his voice got gruff. "And if I've ever missed telling you how much I appreciate you, Viv, I apologize. You've transformed my son's life and meant so much to our family. Our family's been blessed with our new additions."

Viv and Shane wiped tears from their cheeks.

I looked at Donny who glowed. He took my hand and was blinking hard. I valued the chief's acceptance, but I valued my baby's happiness much more. I said, "Thank you, Chief. I look forward to many more football games together."

"And fantasy football," said Tony. "We have high stakes."

"Yeah, mowing the lawn," Gabe grumbled. But he was joining in the conversation so I took that for a win.

After dishes had been returned to the kitchen and, wonder of wonders, most of the guys helped—Mam strikes again—Donny and I walked out into the rapidly cooling evening. California could get hot as blazes, but the lack of humidity meant the temperature dropped fast at night.

As we walked hand in hand down the path, Donny said, "I wish we could stay here tonight for a change, but Shane's sleeping over and I think two gay couples yelling in ecstasy in one house may be more than the Canali compound is up for."

"Happy to take you home, baby."

He sighed happily and held my hand tighter. Suddenly, he stopped walking. "Do you know where we are?"

I smiled. "We're standing on the spot where you kissed me for the first time."

"No."

I looked around. "It's not?"

"Well, that's not all it is. This right here is the spot where my life changed. Where I stopped kidding myself. Where I knew that nothing would ever be the same because I was falling in love with Dell Murphy."

I cocked my head. "Are you really in love, baby?"

He nodded. "Yeah. I mean, it's such an unfamiliar condition you could argue I've got no basis for knowing, but—" He shook his head. "Actually, that's the reason I know it's love. Because I've never felt anything like it before."

"Jesus, man, what turned you into a poet?"

"Hanging out with an Irishman."

I sighed. "I love you, too, baby. And I have to say I know for the same reasons. No one ever came close." I chuckled. "But I must beg to argue. It was on this spot that you realized that you wanted me in your pants. Love might have been a wee bit later."

He put his arms around my neck and kissed me gently. "It was a process."

I kissed him back, deeper and hotter until his leg traveled up my hip to bring our cocks closer.

I pulled back and laughed. "Oh yes, I remember. It was a process that began with you climbing me like a tree."

He gave me that deep, dark, lascivious Canali gaze. "Right." He squeezed me tight. "Come on, babe. Let's go home so we can make crazy love all night."

I laughed and it sounded young and carefree. "Make that forever and you've got a deal."

# BURNING FOR MORE?

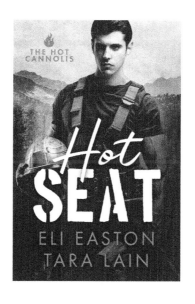

# HOT SEAT

## THE HOT CANNOLIS, BOOK ONE
## AVAILABLE NOW

*Wait. Can a Canali be gay?*

Hero firefighter, youngest of six macho Italian brothers and—
in love with Shane Bower, who never met a unicorn T-shirt he
didn't love? How does that even work?

When Mike Canali meets Shane Bower, his attraction to the
guy is off the charts. But then his huge family and intense job
full of rules and expectations intrude and he never calls.

Until they both get a medal—
    and his mom falls in love with Shane at the ceremony—
    and all of a sudden Shane's all over his life, whether Mike
likes it or not.

The butch Canali family face-to-face with sparkly Shane
Bower? This is a wildfire of its own.

.  .  .

Shane worked damned hard to be who he is—fantastic, femme and in-your-face. He won't compromise that, even to have the super-hot man of his dreams. But can he really ask Mike to give up his family and future just to have his fabulous self? Especially when he's falling in love with the Canali family too?

HOT SEAT is a hot firefighter, big crazy family, coming out, opposites attract, forced proximity, romantic comedy—with all the feels.

Check out HOT SEAT on Amazon

# FIREMAN'S CARRY, BY ELI EASTON

## FREE PREQUEL

**In the midst of a California wildfire, two opposites find that their only hope for survival is each other.**

This was Shane's worst nightmare—a wildfire that threatened the California mountain town where his grandfather lived. He had to get Pops out of there. Thank God for the young firefighter they assigned to him at the barricade. With the handsome but oh-so-butch Mike Canali along for the rescue mission, everything would be okay. Or at least that's what Shane kept telling his inner drama queen. This wasn't the time to panic!

Mike had been on the job with Cal Fire for only two weeks, but he came from a big Italian family full of firefighters, so he recognized serious trouble when he landed in it along with the flamboyant gay guy named Shane, and Shane's crotchety grandfather. Trapped, with no way to escape, Mike had to come up with a plan to save their lives—and the lives of all the other drivers stuck on the road.

. . .

One day can change the course of a life—especially when that day involves surviving an inferno. Even two opposites can find they're stronger together. When the superficial is burned away, what's left is what's real—true bravery, the true self, and, maybe, true love.

———

FIREMAN'S CARRY is available free as part of the Your Book Boyfriend's Boyfriend giveaway on Prolific Works.
bit.ly / YBBBGroupGiveaway

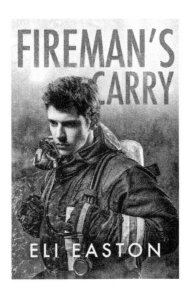

# ABOUT THE AUTHOR - ELI EASTON

As always, I very much appreciate my readers posting recommendations for my books on social media and reviewing on Amazon and Goodreads. Thank you! Your reviews truly make a difference in drawing other readers and that helps me continue writing full time.

It is awesome to hear from you and to know that I made someone smile or sigh. Feel free to email me: eli@elieaston.com.

You can also visit my website: www.elieaston.com. I have first chapters up for all my books and some free stories too. And you can sign up for my newsletter to get a monthly email about new releases and sales.

https://www.subscribepage.com/ElisNewsletterSignup

My Facebook group is a place to chat about Eli stories and get opportunity to read ARCs, excerpts from works-in-progress, and other goodies.

https://www.facebook.com/groups/164054884188096/

Follow me on Amazon to be alerted of my new books.

https://www.amazon.com/author/elieaston

I can promise you there will always be happy ending and that love is love.

> Eli Easton
> Olympic Peninsula, Washington, USA

———

ELI EASTON has been at various times and under different names a preacher's daughter, a computer programmer, a game designer, the author of paranormal mysteries, an organic farmer, and a profound sleeper. She has been writing m/m romance since 2013. As an avid reader of romance, she is tickled pink when an author manages to combine literary merit, vast stores of humor, melting hotness, and eye-dabbing sweetness into one story. She promises to strive to achieve most of that most of the time. She currently lives on Puget Sound with her husband, dogs, and lots of very large trees.

Her website is http://www.elieaston.com

You can e-mail her at eli@elieaston.com

twitter.com/EliEaston
goodreads.com/elieaston
bookbub.com/authors/eli-easton
amazon.com/author/Elieaston

# BOOKS BY ELI EASTON

**Stand Alone Titles**

Before I Wake

Boy Shattered

Falling Down

Five Dares

Heaven Can't Wait

The Lion and the Crow

Puzzle Me This

Robby Riverton: Mail Order Bride

Snowblind

Superhero

**Collections:**

Gothika: Tales of Love & The Supernatural

**Christmas Books:**

Angels Sing (Daddy Dearest #2)

Blame it on the Mistletoe

Christmas Angel

Desperately Seeking Santa

Merry Christmas, Mr. Miggles

Midwinter Night's Dream

Unwrapping Hank

The Best Gift

**Nerds Vs Jocks**

Schooling the Jock

Coaching the Nerd

Head to Head

Betting on his BF

**The Hot Cannollis**

Hot Seat

Hot Wings

**Sex in Seattle Series:**

The Trouble With Tony (Sex in Seattle #1)

The Enlightenment of Daniel (Sex in Seattle #2)

The Mating of Michael (Sex in Seattle #3)

The Redemption of River (Sex in Seattle #4)

**Men of Lancaster County Series:**

A Second Harvest (Men of Lancaster County #1)

Tender Mercies (Men of Lancaster County #2)

**Howl at the Moon Series:**

How to Howl at the Moon (Howl at the Moon #1)

How to Walk like a Man (Howl at the Moon #2)

How to Wish Upon a Star (Howl at the Moon #3)

How to Save a Life (Howl at the Moon #4)

How to Run with the Wolves (Howl at the Moon #5)

**Clyde's Corner Series:**

A Prairie Dog's Love Song

The Stolen Suitor

One Trick Pony

**Daddy Dearest Series:**

Family Camp (Daddy Dearest #1)

Angels Sing (Daddy Dearest #2)

**Ever After, New York Series:**

Billy & The Beast

https://www.example.com

# MEET TARA LAIN

Tara Lain believes in happy ever afters - and magic. Same thing. In fact, she says, she doesn't believe, she knows. Tara shares this passion in her stories that star her unique, charismatic heroes and adventurous heroines. Quarterbacks and cops, werewolves and witches, blue collar or billionaires, Tara's characters, readers say, love deeply, resolve seemingly insurmountable differences, and ultimately live their lives authentically. After many years living in southern California, Tara, her soulmate honey and her soulmate dog decided they wanted less cars and more trees, prompting a move to Ashland, Oregon where Tara's creating new stories and loving living in a small town with big culture. Tara loves animals of all kinds, diversity, open minds, coconut crunch ice cream from Zoeys, and her readers. She also loves to hear from you.

———

**Come visit my website for a FREE download of my Sample Book. https://taralain.com/**

If you like to stay up to date on books in general and mine in particular, come join my Reader Group, HEA, Magic, and Beautiful Boys

https://www.facebook.com/
groups/TaraLainsHEAMagicAndBeautifulBoys/

Subscribe to my Newsletter and get a drawing for fun prizes in every issue -- https://bit.ly/TaraLainNews

Follow me on Amazon for all the new releases, and on Bookbub for specials and to see the books that I love.

Of course, you'll find me on Facebook, Twitter, Pinterest, and Instagram

facebook.com/taralain

twitter.com/taralain

instagram.com/taralainauthor

bookbub.com/authors/tara-lain

amazon.com/author/tara-lain

goodreads.com/goodreadscomtara_lain

# BOOKS BY TARA LAIN
## AVAILABLE IN KINDLE UNLIMTED

Lord of a Thousand Steps

Fool of Main Beach

## LOVE YOU SO

Love You So Hard

Love You So Madly

Love You So Special

Love You So Sweetly

## THE MIDDLEMARK MYSTERIES

The Case of the Sexy Shakespearean

The Case of the Voracious Vintner

## PENNYMAKER TALES SERIES

Sinders and Ash

Driven Snow

Beauty, Inc

Never

## THE ALOYSIUS TALES SERIES

Spell Cat

Brush with Catastrophe

Cataclysmic Shift

## EVER AFTER, NEW YORK STORIES

Better Red

Holding Hans

## FUZZY LOVE

Passions of a Papillon

Prancing of a Papillon

Perils of a Papillon

Fairy Shop

Taylor Maid

Rome and Jules

Hearts and Flour

The Fairy Dance

———

Audiobooks by Tara Lain available at Audible, Amazon, and Audiobooks.com

Printed in Great Britain
by Amazon